Micah studied Hope. Something was bothering her, but she'd been adamant it wasn't finances. Had he upset her by walking so near?

Though he warned himself to move away, he hadn't been able to resist the temptation. And each time his hand brushed hers, he fought the urge to entwine his fingers with hers.

She'd taken his hand several times, and the memory of her gentle touch set his blood racing. His body still held the imprint of her hug that morning. But each time, she'd only meant to comfort. If she had any idea of what her kindness had stirred in him, would she keep her distance?

Yet her eyes told a different story. Or had he only imagined what he'd dreamed of seeing? Right here, right now, the softness of her gaze invited him to . . .

To what?

He lost his train of thought as she leaned nearer, and her shoulder rubbed his biceps. If she tilted her head the slightest bit, her *kapp* would graze his chin. He resisted the urge to tip his head in her direction, but his mind conjured up fantasies of touching his lips to the glossy brown hair peeking out from the front of her prayer covering . . .

BOOK YOUR PLACE ON OUR WEBSITE AND MAKE THE READING CONNECTION!

We've created a customized website just for our very special readers, where you can get the inside scoop on everything that's going on with Zebra, Pinnacle and Kensington books.

When you come online, you'll have the exciting opportunity to:

• View covers of upcoming books
• Read sample chapters
• Learn about our future publishing schedule
  (listed by publication month and author)
• Find out when your favorite authors will be visiting
  a city near you
• Search for and order backlist books from our
  online catalog
• Check out author bios and background information
• Send e-mail to your favorite authors
• Meet the Kensington staff online
• Join us in weekly chats with authors, readers and
  other guests
• Get writing guidelines
• AND MUCH MORE!

Visit our website at
http://www.kensingtonbooks.com

His Unexpected Amish Twins

RACHEL J. GOOD

ZEBRA BOOKS
KENSINGTON PUBLISHING CORP.
www.kensingtonbooks.com

ZEBRA BOOKS are published by

Kensington Publishing Corp.
119 West 40th Street
New York, NY 10018

All Kensington titles, imprints, and distributed lines are available at special quantity discounts for bulk purchases for sales promotion, premiums, fund-raising, educational, or institutional use.

Special book excerpts or customized printings can also be created to fit specific needs. For details, write or phone the office of the Kensington Sales Manager: Attn.: Sales Department. Kensington Publishing Corp., 119 West 40th Street, New York, NY 10018. Phone: 1-800-221-2647.

Zebra and the Z logo Reg. U.S. Pat. & TM Off.
BOUQUET Reg. U.S. Pat. & TM Off.

First Printing: March 2020
ISBN-13: 978-1-4201-5042-1
ISBN-10: 1-4201-5042-1

ISBN-13: 978-1-4201-5043-8 (eBook)
ISBN-10: 1-4201-5043-X (eBook)

10 9 8 7 6 5 4 3 2 1

Printed in the United States of America

Chapter One

Not again! Hope Graber planted her elbows on the scarred maple table, lowered her head into her hands, and rubbed her damp forehead. She could barely breathe in the sweltering summer air. Squeezing her eyes shut, she prayed that when she opened them, she'd find she'd misread the letter spread on the kitchen table.

She eased her eyelids open but kept her gaze slightly unfocused. Maybe it would lessen the shock.

Please, please, be wrong.

But the blurry numbers on the sheet before her sharpened. *Impossible*. The bank must have made a mistake.

Unless . . .

Stomach churning, Hope stood on shaky legs and headed toward the staircase. "*Daed*," she called.

No answer. Had he known the bank statement would arrive today?

She snatched up the paper and marched upstairs. The scorching heat increased with each step, and so did her temper. When she reached the landing, faint snores issued from *Daed*'s bedroom. Very odd.

First of all, he never slept during the day, except when he was ill. And second, his usual breathing pattern at night consisted of a buzzing chain saw that rattled the windowpanes followed by a series of shrill train whistles.

One hand on the doorknob to her father's room, Hope hesitated. The Bible said to honor your parents, and she always tried hard to treat *Daed* as God commanded. But what about in this situation? Would it be disrespectful to accuse *Daed* of faking?

She needed answers and she needed them now. With a quick snap, she opened the door and barged into the room. "*Daed*, do you know anything about this?"

The gentle snores persisted.

"You don't fool me," Hope said. "We need to talk about this bank statement." She rattled the offending paper to get his attention.

Avoiding her eyes, he groaned and maneuvered his bulk to a sitting position. "I wasn't expecting that so soon."

Really? Then why had he been pretending to sleep? Her father never stretched out on a bed fully clothed in mid-afternoon.

Hope pinched her lips together to control the flow of accusations gathering in her throat. He was her father. The man who'd loved and cared for her as a child. The man who'd always enjoyed jokes and hearty laughter. The man who'd taught her to follow her faith and led by example. The man who'd worked hard to build a thriving horse-boarding business. The man who'd tenderly cared for *Mamm* during her last days.

Flashes of that man still flickered through this unkempt, sweat-stained, bleary-eyed stranger, his rotund chest straining his suspenders, the fabric of his shirt stretched taut over his burgeoning belly. Perhaps she'd been wrong to take charge of the farm. She hadn't meant for him to stop working completely.

Usually, children gave their fathers the money they

earned until they turned twenty-one, but just before she turned nineteen, she and *Daed* sat down with the bishop and church elders to discuss their financial situation and *Daed*'s problem. He'd confessed to them, but the church leaders had suggested he not handle money for the next year or two.

Rather than accusing *Daed* or reminding him of the past, Hope held out the bank statement. "Unless the bank's made a huge error, a large sum of money is missing from the savings account. Should I call them to see if that's the case?"

Daed hung his head. "No, *dochder.*" His grave words were barely audible.

"Please tell me you still have the money," Hope pleaded, praying her dreams and plans hadn't just disappeared.

"I–I can't do that," he mumbled.

Nooo. Hope bit her lip. Taking a deep breath to keep her voice calm and measured, she emphasized each word. "That money was to pay the therapist who's coming tomorrow and to pay for start-up costs."

She'd placed ads, bought the signs, purchased therapy equipment . . . All those bills needed to be paid. She'd offered free horse therapy sessions over the next few weeks to introduce people to the farm's services, so she'd have no income.

Her father's voice wobbled as much as his double chins. "I'm so sorry."

"But how did you—?" *Daed* had barely been out of the house this month. No way could he have gone somewhere to gamble.

"Art stopped by two weeks ago. He was heading to Penn National. I told him I couldn't go, but I was sure one of the horses would be a winner. You were having lunch at

Priscilla's, so . . ." *Daed* hung his head, muffling the rest of the sentence. "Art drove me to the bank."

Their *Englisch* neighbor Art had been the one who'd introduced *Daed* to gambling. He and *Daed* had gone to the horse races in Grantville, where *Daed*, with his knowledge of horses, had had great success.

Art had been thrilled. So had *Daed*, although he'd kept it a secret from the family. He'd invested the money in the business, and he'd expanded the barn so they could board even more horses. Maybe no one would have discovered *Daed*'s secret life if Art hadn't convinced *Daed* to try other forms of gambling.

Daed's luck hadn't held, and he'd lost all of the profit he'd made and more. Instead of quitting, *Daed* took even greater risks. Especially once *Mamm* got sick. He wanted money to cover her hospital bills. Instead, he'd ended up deeply in debt. But he'd covered it up, and no one suspected.

Hope worried about him as he grew haggard and depressed. To help, she decided to surprise him by taking over the accounting. Only she ended up being the one who was surprised. And shocked, scared, and sick.

When she'd confronted him, he'd confessed and agreed to meet with the church leaders. He admitted he had an addiction. The bishop's solution had been for Hope to take over their finances.

After that decision, Hope ended up in charge of the horse-boarding business. She was the one who informed all the owners she couldn't board their horses anymore. She didn't tell them why, only that the business was closing.

They'd been left with three gentle, older horses of their own and their buggy horse. With her friend Priscilla's advice and support, Hope planned to start a new business, another horse-related job that fit her better. Priscilla's autistic younger brother had served as the inspiration. The sign had been ordered and would be installed next week: "Graber's Horse Therapy: Hope for Children."

That dream had sustained Hope as she worked long overtime hours at the restaurant. She'd paid back every boarder, caught up on bills, kept them out of bankruptcy, and saved every extra penny each week for more than two years.

Finally, she'd saved enough to pay a licensed therapist, start her own certification course, and place ads in a few local newspapers that were still in circulation. She'd also sent a letter to the *Die Botschaft*, describing her start-up services, not that she expected many Amish customers. Most of the children who came would most likely be *Englisch*. Eventually, she hoped to convince some of the parents of special-needs children who went to the Amish schoolhouse how beneficial therapy could be.

Now her nest egg for the business had disappeared. They had barely enough to pay this month's bills. Her eyes stung. What would she do?

She had to get away, do some thinking. The broiling August heat seared her as she fled to the barn. Being around horses always soothed her, but not this time. As she strode past the stalls, questions crowded her mind. How would she pay for the horses' daily upkeep? Would she have to sell off the few horses she'd kept? Close down her business before opening day?

She wanted to talk to someone, but she'd spent so much time covering for *Daed* and hiding the truth. From the outside, they might appear to be a normal father and daughter, but their *g'may*, with the exception of the three leaders, had no idea what lay beneath the surface.

Who could she trust? Would sharing her concerns about *Daed* be a betrayal?

Her best friend, Priscilla, always provided a listening ear and sound advice, and she could be trusted to keep a secret. Several years ago, Hope had told Priscilla about their financial difficulties, but she'd never confided the reason. Priscilla's father, though, had been one of the church leaders who met with *Daed*, so Priscilla might already know or suspect.

Though Hope was reluctant to expose her family's shame, she had to discuss this problem. Perhaps she and Priscilla could come up with a solution.

Hope trudged out to the barn to hook up the buggy, and soon Biscuit was clomping along the country roads while Hope cooked inside the buggy's interior. After she arrived at the Ebersols', she wiped the beads of sweat dripping from her brow and peeled her damp dress from her skin.

When she tapped at the back door, Priscilla's cheery "Come in" greeted Hope through the screen. She slid off her shoes in the mudroom beside the kitchen and padded through the doorway to find Priscilla ladling jam into jars. The battery-powered fan on the kitchen table did little to dispel the heat in the steamy kitchen.

"Almost done," Priscilla said. "What's the matter?" With her usual sensitivity, Priscilla had picked up on Hope's distress.

"Let me help you finish the jam first." Hope followed behind her friend, inhaling the sweet scent of warm raspberry as she wiped jar rims and screwed on lids.

When all the glass jars gleamed in neat rows, Priscilla poured them each a cup of lemonade, and Hope sank into a chair at the kitchen table and spilled her problems.

Priscilla sat silent for a minute, then she leaned closer to Hope. "I have an idea. *Daed*'s been setting aside the money I've been earning on the jam. I don't need it for anything right now, and I'll be making money teaching in the fall. Why don't I lend you that money?"

Hope shook her head. "I couldn't take anything from you."

Leaning forward, Priscilla fixed Hope with an intent gaze. "Would you accept it if I promise it isn't charity? I'd like you to pay me back when you can, but take your time. And I can even charge you extra if that makes you feel better."

"I don't know." Priscilla's offer sounded like an answer to Hope's prayers, but taking money from a friend didn't feel right.

Priscilla rose from the table and returned with a pad and pen. After she did a little figuring, she slid a paper across the table. "Here's what I'll give you, and this is when you can pay me back."

Hope glanced at the numbers and gasped. "How could you possibly have that much?"

"I've been working nonstop this summer, and I get a small percentage from each person I train for the jam business. It adds up."

"I don't have to pay anything for six months? And no extra?" Hope shook her head. She couldn't accept these terms.

"In the end, I'll get about the same amount as leaving it in the bank. Meanwhile, it will benefit you and all the children who need therapy, including Asher."

"But we already agreed he'd be coming for free." Hope refused to charge Priscilla's family for her brother's therapy. She'd never have this business if it weren't for Priscilla and Asher.

"Exactly. You want to do kind things for me, so let me do something in return." Priscilla rose from the table. "The boys and *Daed* will be back from the hardware store soon.

I need to start supper, but if you come back tomorrow, I'm sure *Daed* will go with you to the bank to make the transfer."

Supper? Hope should be home making a meal for *Daed*. Dazed and overwhelmed, she headed for the door. "*Danke*." She still didn't feel right about taking Priscilla's money, but right now she had little choice. And the children's needs had to come before her pride. Once the business became profitable, though, she'd pay Priscilla back at a much higher interest rate.

Clucking to get Biscuit moving at a faster clip, Hope hurried her horse along the winding roads, her heart a little lighter. They swung around a curve, and Hope sucked in a breath. Yanking on the reins, she swerved onto the shoulder and dragged Biscuit to a stop. At the sight ahead, bile rose in her throat.

An overturned buggy. A car with a smashed windshield. Its front end crumpled. Facing the wrong direction, one wheel stuck in a ditch.

No! Hope pulled her buggy to the side of the road and tied Biscuit to the nearby speed limit sign. Then, whispering prayers, she raced toward the accident.

A car screeched to a halt on the opposite shoulder, and a man jumped out, carrying a cell phone. He jabbed at it, then yelled into it as he sprinted across the street. He reached the buggy before she did.

Among the grasses alongside the road, a flash of blue stood out, and Hope halted. A small girl lay sprawled on the ground, her eyes closed. She must have been thrown from the buggy. Hope's insides churned. Was she hurt? Dead?

The *Englischer* would help the occupants of the buggy. Someone needed to stay with the child.

Hope knelt beside the girl, whose chest was rising and falling. Thank God, she was alive. As a farm girl, Hope had assisted the vet with animal emergencies, so the sight of blood shouldn't shock her. But it did. The young girl looked so fragile, so innocent. Hope longed to gather the child in her arms and hold her close, but the little girl's arm was bent at an odd angle.

A gash on her forehead bled profusely. Hope had to stop the bleeding somehow. She needed cloth. Her apron. Swiftly, she unpinned her half-apron, folded a section of it into a compress with the clean underside facing out. She applied pressure to staunch the flow. With the opposite corner of her apron, Hope gently wiped the girl's eye and cheek.

Cars screeched to halt near the buggy, and people rushed to help. People called out questions or shouted out directions in the background chaos behind Hope. A woman offered to do CPR for the buggy occupants, but then screamed and stumbled away. A deep voice ordered everyone back from the buggy. One man held up traffic so vehicles coming the other way could inch around the accident scene.

Hope tried to block out the pandemonium to concentrate on the child, but the noise and confusion surrounding her filled her ears and her mind. Her breathing tight and rapid, she stayed beside the little girl and prayed the ambulance would hurry.

"Is she all right?" a woman asked. "It's a bad scene over there. I don't think they've noticed her over here."

Hope raised her eyes to meet the woman's. "How are the people in the buggy?"

"I couldn't get close enough to see, but it looks terrible. They're keeping everyone away."

That didn't sound good.

"Do you need help?" The *Englischer* gestured toward the little girl.

"She's bleeding, but she's breathing." Definitely a

blessing, given how far the child had been thrown. "Her arm, though . . ." Hope nodded toward the injured arm.

The woman grimaced. "She's unconscious?"

"*Jah*, I mean yes."

Just then the small girl whimpered, and her eyes fluttered open. "*Mamm?*"

"She can't come right now." Hope scooted over to block the smashed buggy from the child's view. "I'll stay with you."

"Want . . . *Mamm*."

Hope reached for the small hand. "I wish she could be here with you, but she isn't able to come."

"It . . . hurts."

"I know. Someone will be here soon to help."

In the distance, an ambulance siren screamed. The girl shivered as it drew nearer and then pulled past them to stop close to the crash. Police cars arrived to set up flares and direct traffic. A fire truck pulled in front of the accident scene. All around them, lights pulsed blue and red, and sirens shrieked.

The small girl cringed at the flashing lights and ear-splitting racket.

EMTs spent several minutes at the car and buggy before one came to check on them, her face grim. The EMT did a quick assessment. "Let's get you to the hospital," she said to the little girl.

Then she glanced over at Hope. "We'll be transporting the boy too. I think it would be best to keep them together."

"Jabin?" The small girl's voice shook.

"Is that your brother?" the EMT asked softly. At the girl's barely audible "yes," the EMT said, "Can you tell me your name?"

"Chloe . . . Miller."

"All right, Chloe. We're going to put Jabin in first, then take you."

"I . . . want . . . *Mamm*," she wailed.

The EMT gazed at her with compassion. "We can only fit the two of you into the ambulance. I'm so sorry."

Hope stayed beside Chloe, holding her hand until she was on the litter.

Before they wheeled her away, the little girl clutched Hope's hand. "Don't . . . go."

How could Hope leave this little one whose parents couldn't take care of her? She glanced at the EMT, who nodded, and Hope climbed into the back of the ambulance to accompany two young children she didn't know to the hospital in place of their parents.

Chapter Two

Ring! Ring!

Micah Miller jerked awake. Who would be calling at this hour? Rubbing sleep from his eyes, he stumbled out of bed and across the room, stubbing his toe hard on the dresser leg as he passed. He bit back a yelp and hopped a few steps on one foot.

"*Sohn?*" *Daed* called out.

"I'll get it," Micah assured him.

The ringing ended, then began again. Now that his eyes were accustomed to the dark, Micah hurried downstairs despite his throbbing toe. He opened the door to the kitchen, where the receiver from the black box kept dinging. Suddenly, it stopped. Blessed peace reigned.

But not for long. Whoever had called would leave a message. You didn't phone this late at night unless it was an emergency.

Brrinngg. The phone started up again, and Micah snatched up the receiver.

"I apologize for calling after nine." The woman's voice on the other end didn't sound familiar. "My name's Hope Graber, and I'm calling about Anna . . ."

Anna? Micah's sleep-fogged brain struggled to place the name. Two older ladies in their church district were named

Anna, one toddler, and . . . *Wait! Not Anna his sister-in-law.* "Anna from Lancaster?"

"Yes, Ben and Anna . . ." The line went silent except for a strangled sob. "I'm so sorry—"

"They what? Is something wrong?"

"Didn't the police get through?"

"Police? *Neh.*" Had those been the calls he'd missed? "Has something happened to them?"

"A buggy accident," she choked out.

Micah shook his head, as if that could dislodge what she'd said. Buggy accidents were often horrific. "Are they all right?" He hoped she'd say they were. But if they hadn't been hurt, they'd be calling themselves. Of course, they'd have waited until the morning. And she'd mentioned the *police*.

Her stifled sob prepared him for bad news, but not for the full impact of her barely intelligible, stark statement. "They were killed instantly."

Each word dropped like a heavy boulder, crushing his heart. The kitchen swam around him, and Micah slumped into the nearest chair. It couldn't be. Not his older brother Ben, the brother Micah had always tried to outdo but never succeeded. And Ben's lovely, sweet wife, Anna.

"I'm so sorry," the woman whispered, her voice thick with tears. "Everyone who stopped by to check on the children said Ben and Anna are, *were* . . . the sweetest couple. So in love."

"Yes, they—" His air passages closed completely. He couldn't say they *are*, but the word *were* stayed stuck in the back of his throat, creating a barrier, blocking the flow of his sentence.

A picture flashed through his mind of Anna, cuddling the twins on her lap when he'd visited last month. Ben stood behind her, smiling down at her and the children.

A pang of envy had shot through Micah at his brother's perfect family.

If Micah had known his brother only had a few weeks to live, he'd never have begrudged Ben his happiness. Now, when it was too late to tell Ben, Micah realized how much he loved his brother, despite their childhood rivalry. He should have put aside his petty jealousy and appreciated their time together.

"Are you still there?" the soft voice drew Micah back to the receiver in his hand.

He had to speak, to ask what had happened to the twins. He forced out his question, the simple phrase pain-filled and raw. "The twins?"

"They have some injuries. Chloe had surgery for her broken arm and needed stitches in her forehead. They're keeping her in the hospital for observation because of head trauma. Jabin has two broken ribs and a partially collapsed lung."

Micah sucked in a breath. "So . . . they're alive."

"Covered in scrapes and bruises, but, yes, they're"—her voice shook—"alive."

She sounded so close to tears, Micah wanted to reach out to comfort her.

After drawing in an audible breath, she said, "I'm here at the hospital with them now."

"Thank you. I'll get there as soon as I can." Micah set the receiver on the counter, but instead of moving, he sagged back in the chair and tried to put his world back together. Except none of the pieces fit.

"Micah?" *Daed* called from the head of the stairs.

A faint light shone from that direction. *Daed* must be carrying the battery-powered lantern. *Mamm*'s deep, hacking cough filled the air.

"I–I'll be right up." How would he break this news to his

parents? *Mamm* and *Daed* had always favored their older son. Micah had been only a shadow who followed Ben's every move and tried to imitate him, but Micah could never measure up to the skills of a brother who was five years older. Whatever Micah tried, Ben had always accomplished it before him. In school, on the playground, and in farm chores, Ben had always known more, done more, excelled more.

And now Ben was gone.

"Is everything all right?" *Daed* started down the stairs.

Micah scraped back his chair and rose. "I'm coming." Now he'd be the older brother, the responsible one, the one who carried all the weight on his shoulders.

Climbing the stairs was like swimming upstream through thick sludge, lifting each foot became a chore. *Daed* stared down at him, his face grave, but he waited until Micah reached the landing before speaking.

"What is it? What's happened?"

Micah motioned toward his parents' bedroom. "I'll tell you both." He wasn't sure he could get it out the first time. Once he did, he'd never be able to repeat it.

After they reached the room, *Daed* turned to him. "What's wrong, *Sohn*?"

Micah took a deep breath to steady his nerves, but the overpowering odor of the onion *Mamm* had strung about her neck inside a cotton mesh bag stung his nose and eyes. He blinked to clear his vision.

"There's been an accident." Micah took a deep breath and, pushing the words past too-tight vocal cords, he repeated what the woman had told him.

Daed sank heavily onto the bed, his head bowed. He reached out and grasped *Mamm*'s hand. She hadn't said anything, only stared at Micah. No, not *at* him, but *through* him, her eyes glazed.

"I'm so sorry," Micah said. "I wish—"

Waving a hand to cut him off, *Daed* responded in slow, measured tones, "It's God's will. 'Thy will be done, in Earth as it is in heaven.'" Yet, even as he recited the verse, the huskiness and trembling in his voice revealed his uncertainty. And the bleakness in his eyes reflected his questions.

The agony of missing Ben still seared Micah's spirit, but the familiar prayer offered some comfort, some support.

"'The Lord giveth, and the Lord taketh away,'" *Daed* repeated, his words shaky. "'Blessed be the name of the Lord.'"

Daed seemed to be trying to remind himself and them that Ben's passing was God's will, and Micah believed it, but right now, his heart ached too much to calmly accept the loss of Ben and Anna.

He wanted to smack his fist into his palm, to demand an answer. To lift his head and shout at the ceiling, *Why? Why? Why?* And rail because the Lord hadn't given him a chance to make amends with Ben, to confess his resentment, to ask for forgiveness.

For the first time, *Mamm* spoke. "I should go to Lancaster. The children are my responsibility." Coughs racked her body.

"You're not well enough for that," *Daed* insisted. "And you can't take a chance of giving the twins pneumonia. Especially not when they're recovering." He lowered his head into his hands.

"I'm going." Micah made sure his tone was firm. He didn't want *Daed* to argue with him. "I told the person who called I'd come to the hospital." Maybe in this way, he could atone for long-held grudges.

"I see." *Daed* stared off into the distance. "That might be best."

All three of Micah's younger sisters were married and had young children. *Daed* couldn't leave his business. He'd miss Micah's help with the harnesses, but it wasn't as great a loss as it had been when Ben refused to move to New York State with the family nine years ago. His brother had chosen to remain in Lancaster to court Anna.

If Ben had come with them instead, would he be alive right now?

Micah shook his head. He shouldn't entertain such thoughts. "I'll call one of the *Englisch* drivers."

"I wish I could go with you." *Daed* glanced over at *Mamm*. "But I'd better stay here."

"*Jah, Mamm* needs you." Although if Micah had a choice, he'd prefer to let *Daed* handle things.

When his father pursed his lips and looked doubtful, Micah said with more confidence than he felt, "Don't worry. I can take care of it."

"We'll . . . be . . . praying," *Mamm* wheezed out.

"*Danke*." He'd need all the prayers he could get. The whole world had just crashed around him. Ben had been the measuring stick Micah used to judge everything he did. He'd always ask himself: *Did I do this as well as Ben?* The answer was always no. Micah had never come close to matching his brother's accomplishments, but he tried again and again. Now the central pin he'd revolved his life around had disappeared, leaving him adrift.

Numbness set in as he trudged downstairs to the kitchen. He forced himself to keep moving, to put one foot in front of the other, to do what needed to be done.

The receiver still lay on the table. *Pick it up, dial*, he repeated to himself. If he concentrated on what he needed to do, maybe he could hold back the waves of grief and guilt threatening to wash over him.

Lifting the phone, Micah stared off into space. *Who should I call?* He disliked phoning people at this time of night, but he needed to get to Lancaster right away. Several drivers answered with the TV blaring in the background. At least he hadn't wakened them. After calling four drivers, he found one who could make the five-hour trip to Lancaster that night. The others all had appointments for the next day.

Then Micah rushed upstairs to pack a bag. *Daed* came and stood in the bedroom doorway. His slumped shoulders and bowed head made him appear much older than fifty-five. Rather than his usual ruddy cheeks, his complexion almost matched the strands of gray threaded through his hair.

Despite *Daed*'s feeble appearance, he gripped Micah's shoulder with his normal strength. "God be with you, *Sohn*."

Mamm called from the bedroom, "Bring the children"— a spate of coughing interrupted her words—"home as soon as possible."

Micah winced at the raspy breaths that followed her request. Then he met *Daed*'s eyes. "Will you both be coming for the funeral?"

With a quick glance down the hall to where *Mamm* lay in bed, *Daed* shook his head. "I don't think— Your *mamm* will expect to go, but I doubt the doctor will let her make the trip. He wants her in the hospital, but she's determined to stay here."

Micah couldn't blame her for that. He tamped down the terror snaking through him at being in a hospital. He knew it all too well. The strangeness. The loneliness. The scariness of being surrounded by strangers. Were Chloe and Jabin frightened?

"If I can find someone to stay with her, I'll be there." *Daed* pinched the bridge of his nose and looked down.

"Your *mamm*'ll put up a fight until I remind her she could make others ill. That'd be the only thing that will keep her away."

"Yes, she should stay here," Micah agreed.

Then he went downstairs to wait for the driver. And to prepare himself for the future. A future without his older brother.

Numb inside, Hope paced the hospital room, trying to keep herself awake. Confined spaces made her claustrophobic. She longed to be in the open air with her horses, but she needed to stay here in case the twins woke. If they did, she had no idea how she'd explain about their parents. Would either of them remember the accident?

She prayed the trauma had blocked any memories. Rounding the bed, she strode down the narrow aisle between the two beds, pivoted, and headed back the way she'd come. Then she circled the other bed. Her aimless wandering did little to stop the walls from closing in around her. With each step, the room seemed to grow smaller and to suck out more air until her chest constricted so tightly, she could barely breathe.

Hope forced herself to concentrate on the children rather than her own distress. Chloe lay so pale and still, the bandage on her forehead made a huge white slash across her ashen skin. The accident had drained her cheeks of a normal rosy tint.

Hope had requested that the twins be allowed to room together. It went against hospital protocol, but she'd convinced the staff that, with the trauma they'd been through, the two of them would need each other more than ever. And Chloe might only be here one or two nights.

Shoes squeaked on the floor just outside the door, and

Hope prayed it would be the twins' *onkel*. Her spirits drooped when a nurse bustled in.

"Just here to check their vitals," she whispered. Her cheerful smile seemed at odds with the pall that had settled over the room, and over Hope's thoughts. "Have either of them woken?"

"Not yet." Hope dreaded being here when they did. Once her business got off the ground, she'd have to deal with children who had many different emotional and physical challenges every day, but telling two sweet, innocent children their parents . . .

"Are you OK, honey?" The nurse studied Hope as she held her fingers on Jabin's pulse.

"It's hard." Hope had been through an emotional day, and her concerns about *Daed* and gambling still hadn't been addressed. Tomorrow she'd end up deeply in debt— even if it was to her best friend—to start a business that would bring in no income for at least several weeks. But all that paled beside this nightmare. Two seven-year-olds had become orphans.

"It's a tragedy for sure," the nurse whispered. "Poor little ones."

Hope couldn't even imagine how the children would face the future. They'd been taught to trust God in all situations, but would losing your parents at such a young age shake your faith? How would they deal with the pain and loss? Would the family members who were coming for them treat the children well, make them a beloved part of their family? Would Jabin and Chloe adjust to their new life?

She'd known these two children only a few hours, yet she felt fiercely protective toward them. Almost as if they were her own.

A sharp pain pierced her heart. Children she'd never have.

The closest she'd come to mothering would be spending time with the little ones who came to the farm. And the therapist who was helping her in the business had warned her against getting emotionally involved with any children who came for sessions.

Startled, Hope glanced up as the nurse eased the door shut. She'd been so lost in thought, she hadn't even noticed when the nurse finished checking the twins.

Hope glanced at her watch. Almost four in the morning. When would the twins' relatives get here?

"How much longer?" Micah asked as they wound their way along another dark, narrow country lane that snaked in and out of the woods. Swollen creeks had flooded their usual route, and they'd been following a circuitous detour on back roads for the past forty minutes.

The driver, Kurt Lehman, glanced at the GPS on his dashboard. "Looks like we'll get there a little after four thirty."

Only a half hour to go. Micah had often made this trip with his family, yet never before had it seemed so long. Every minute it took was another minute away from Chloe and Jabin.

He hoped they weren't awake and alone. Hospitals could be scary for children, more so at night. And especially when they didn't have their parents. Did they know what had happened? Had anyone told them? If so, they needed someone there to comfort them if they woke in the night.

Micah tried not to *rutsch* in his seat because he didn't want to distract Kurt from concentrating on the hairpin curves. He'd suggested several times that Micah try to sleep, but the bumpy roads combined with worry for the twins had kept him awake. And each time he closed his eyes, pictures of Ben floated past. Micah would regret his lack of rest in the morning, when he had to care for the children.

After they finally returned to the highway and the car picked up speed, he breathed a sigh of relief. At least about getting to their destination. He tried to calm his prickling nerves the closer they came to the hospital.

Even the word "hospital" made him shrink back in the seat as the past haunted him. He often woke in the night, shaking and gasping for breath, after a recurring nightmare. Except that horror had once been a reality.

The start of those awful months after he turned five remained vague. Only a few details stood out. His fascination with the horse's twitching tail. His father's shouted, "Nooo!" Then a gray fog closed in, obscuring everything until he drifted awake in a strange room.

Clanking metallic sounds. Beeps and blips. Sharp, pungent odors like the ammonia *Mamm* used to clean floors. Bright, blinding lights hurt his eyes.

At the swish of a lady's skirt, he croaked out, "*Mamm . . .*" He waited for her cool hand to settle on his aching forehead.

Instead, a soft voice responded, "It's all right."

He turned toward the sound. A lady with blond hair dressed in blue stood beside him. *An angel? Was this heaven?*

He barely registered her words when she explained he was in the hospital. He was trapped in a prison—a bed with bars. One that glided through the room and into a hall. He might have been floating except for the bumping and rattling.

Daed was waiting for Micah in the room, but his father didn't stay long. A nurse came to call *Daed* to the phone.

When he returned, he apologized for leaving. "I wish I could stay longer, but the Hasselbachers called to say *Mamm* needs me right away."

The Hasselbachers were their *Englisch* neighbors, and Micah's parents sometimes used their phone for emergency calls. That was twenty-three years ago, before some of their community sneaked black boxes into their barn or cell phones into their homes.

When *Daed* returned the next day, he brought news from home that explained why he'd cut his visit short. "You have a new baby sister. *Mamm* needs to stay home with her."

Another sister? Weren't two of them enough? Micah wanted to fuss for *Mamm* and ask those questions, but the deep frown lines between *Daed*'s eyes stopped him. His *daed* looked ready to scold . . . or cry.

If *Daed* cried, Micah would too. He wanted to be brave, so he held in his tears, as well as his fears.

But after *Daed* left, Micah shivered at the strange shadows dancing on the walls. And at all the odd noises, even at night. Sirens screamed outside his window, startling him awake. Small lights glowed in the room, and faint light seeped in under the door, so unnatural at night. Nights should be dark. Except in this mixed-up *Englisch* world.

When *Mamm* could travel, *Daed* loaded up the buggy, and all his siblings came along. Those visits were rare because *Daed* had a business to run. Micah had stayed for ten days and endured physical therapy. The worst of the ordeal was waking up at night alone and in unfamiliar surroundings.

He didn't want Chloe and Jabin to face that. But unlike Micah's *mamm*, who'd stayed missing during most of his hospital visit, their *mamm* and *daed* would be gone forever.

Chapter Three

Outside the car window, familiar landmarks and road signs took shape through the blackness surrounding them. As they drew closer, the ache in the back of Micah's throat increased until he could barely swallow.

Kurt flicked on his turn signal. "We're here."

Micah had needed no announcement. The minute they'd entered the parking lot, all the old feelings washed over him. If he were younger, he would have hunched over with gut pain. Instead, he forced himself upright, rigid against the seat. The last thing he wanted was for Kurt to suspect his cowardice.

The building looked almost the same as when he'd been trapped in a room here years ago. Kurt pulled up to the entrance, and Micah fumbled with the door handle while he struggled to control the panic rising inside.

For a few moments, he concentrated on counting out Kurt's pay and saying goodbye. As he drove away, Micah fought the urge to wave the driver back. Only the twins' needs overcame his reluctance to enter the place where he'd spent his loneliest childhood hours. Until those scary weeks, he'd never been away from his family. Neither had Chloe and Jabin. Until now . . .

After a quick intake of breath for courage, Micah

straightened his shoulders, pushed the door open, and strode into the lobby. The whole place had been updated, but once he rode the elevator to the pediatric ward and stepped out, the odors hadn't changed. Soggy cafeteria food. Disinfectant. His stomach roiled. If only he could flee. Yet he was as trapped as he had been as a child. This time he was the adult, and though he had the freedom to leave, he had no choice but to stay.

The staff at the nurses' station no longer wore blue scrubs. Instead, they had animals and comical characters scattered across their tunics. As soon as he mentioned the twins, he didn't even need to give their names.

"Two doors down on the left. And you are—?"

"Their uncle, Micah Miller." He glanced away from the pity in the woman's eyes, but he suspected she'd nudged the nearest nurse and pointed him out as he hurried down the hall.

Micah eased open the door so he wouldn't wake the twins if they were sleeping. He entered the room and stopped. For a second, he mistook the woman beside the bed for that long-ago nurse-angel. But this woman shone brighter. The dim light over the bed cast faint highlights on her light brown hair, giving her a sparkle. But an angel wouldn't dress in Plain clothes. And a nurse wouldn't be sitting in a chair, rubbing her eyes.

Eyes that widened the minute she spotted him. She jumped to her feet and rushed across the room. "I'm so sorry. For almost falling asleep." She paused before adding in a gentle voice, "And for your loss."

Even with sleep-blurred eyes, Micah's brain registered her pretty face filled with sympathy. He wished for that comfort, that caring. But he had no time to think of himself or of her appeal. Chloe and Jabin needed him.

Even in the dimness, a flush suffused her cheeks. "I don't

want you to think I haven't been paying attention. I only sat down for a minute. But I stayed awake the whole time in case . . ." She gestured toward the beds. "I didn't want to leave them alone."

She cared enough to stay until the wee hours of the morning? "I appreciate that." More than she'd ever know. "You're a friend"—he choked up, but forced words past the block in his throat—"of–of Anna's?"

"No, no. I don't—I mean, I *didn't*—know her. Or Ben." The light in her eyes dimmed, and she squeezed them shut for a second. "I, um, came upon the scene of the accident."

She was a stranger? His dazed mind scrambled to make sense of her kindness. Most people would have remained at the scene until— His mind refused to picture the buggy. Or the ambulance. "You stayed all this time?" He was in-credulous.

She avoided his gaze. "Chloe had been thrown from the buggy. I—well, someone else, an *Englischer*, rushed over to help the rest of the family." Pinching her lips together, she stayed silent for a few moments, then continued, "I stayed with Chloe. When the ambulance came, she was ter-rified. I couldn't let a small girl ride to the hospital alone."

Every cell in Micah's body recalled that terror. That iso-lation. That feeling of abandonment. He never wanted Chloe or Jabin to experience that fear.

"When I found out what had happened to their parents, someone needed to be here. At least until you arrived."

"*Danke.* That was thoughtful of you. Most people would have gone home after they'd reached us."

Her eyes glistened with tears. "But they had no one to be with them. How could I possibly leave? What if they woke and didn't know where they were or what had hap-pened?"

If only Micah had had an angel as beautiful and kind as

this one to keep him company during his lonely nights in the hospital. "I can't tell you how much I appreciate what you've done, um—" He paused, trying to remember if she'd said her name.

"Hope," she supplied.

Micah blinked. At first, he mistook the word for advice. Then his tired brain realized she'd said her name. What a perfect name! She'd given him more than kindness; she'd given him hope.

Hope lowered her eyes. The gratitude shining in Micah's eyes made her uncomfortable. She hadn't done anything special. Anyone would have done the same.

Now that he'd arrived, she could leave, but something inside compelled her to stay. He might need rest after traveling through the night. The tired lines on his face and grief in his eyes as he studied the twins urged her to help.

"I could watch them a little longer if you need some sleep," she said, and immediately regretted it. She needed to be awake for her eight o'clock meeting with Logan. They had a lot of planning to do before the business officially opened.

"*Neh*. I'm grateful for all you've done, but you need your rest."

She hoped he hadn't said that because she looked haggard. Inwardly, she scolded herself. What difference did it make? She had no interest in courting. With starting the business and coping with *Daed*'s problems, she had no time or energy left for relationships.

Hope had to admit, though, despite the weariness in his face, Micah gave the word "handsome" a whole new meaning. His clean-shaven jaw held a slight hint of a shadow, highlighting his masculinity. When he sat in the chair beside

Chloe's bed, he removed his hat and set it in his lap, making Hope wish she could cup his face to relieve his pain.

"I don't want to hold you up," he said.

Although he'd given her permission to go, the questions lingering in his eyes belied his words. In her therapy training, Hope had learned that talking about a tragedy could be an important step in healing.

"Before I go, did you want to know anything more? About the accident, I mean. I don't know how much the children will remember. They might wonder what happened."

Micah's lips pinched into a tight, straight line, but he nodded.

Hope recounted what she'd seen. "It wasn't your family's fault. I know that for sure."

She had no idea how the accident happened, only that the car had been on the wrong side of the road. Tomorrow's— no, today's—newspapers might have more details. And pictures. She had no desire to see them; those images had been burned into her memory.

Micah's Adam's apple bobbed up and down several times before he spoke. "*Danke* for telling me. And for waiting with Chloe and Jabin."

"Did you have a chance to speak to any of the nurses?" she asked.

"No, I wanted to get here as quickly as I could. I worried about them being by themselves, waking up in an unfamiliar room." He shot her a thankful smile that did little to remove the lines of grief incised around his eyes and mouth. "I wish I'd known you were here. I would have been less stressed on the drive."

"I'm sorry."

"For what?" Micah tilted his head to one side, and surprise flickered briefly across his features.

"I should have told you I'd be here with them, so you wouldn't worry." Why hadn't she offered that reassurance? Because she'd been so preoccupied with *Daed*'s gambling and then the suddenness of the accident. Two totally different shocks so close together had addled her brain.

"It's not your fault. I should have trusted God." Micah leaned forward and gripped the rail on Chloe's bed, his face a mask of pain. "*Mamm* always says if you're scared or worrying, it shows you're not trusting."

Despite his words of faith, his face remained tightly pinched as he stared off into the distance.

"Are you all right?" As soon as she said it, Hope caught herself. Of course he wasn't all right. His niece and nephew were lying in hospital beds, and he'd just lost two family members.

"It just doesn't seem real," Micah said. "I keep expecting Ben and Anna to walk through the door. Or that I'll wake up and find it's all been a dream."

The only thing that seemed real—more than real—was the old terror that gripped him over being in the darkened hospital room.

"It's not unusual for your mind to deny it at first."

Micah only wished his mind would deny his childhood memories too, or at least erase them. He pushed away the past. Right now, the twins were all that mattered.

"*Mamm*," Chloe moaned.

She didn't open her eyes. Maybe she was crying in her sleep. Micah dreaded having to tell her the news.

With a groan, she moved restlessly on the bed. He bit his

lip as he leaned over the bed, unsure whether to respond. He didn't want to startle her awake and then have to deliver the news, but he couldn't leave her cries unanswered. He reached out to hold Chloe's hand, but Hope brushed past him.

"Let me," she whispered as she took Chloe's hand. "She may think it's her *mamm*. Perhaps it will calm her nightmares and let her sleep."

Although he appreciated Hope's thoughtfulness, he should be the one comforting his niece. Chloe clutched Hope's hand convulsively. Micah worried his niece was crushing Hope's fingers, but after a few minutes, Chloe quieted. Hope had been right.

Once Chloe remained still, Hope withdrew her hand and shook it in the air. "She has quite a grip," she said with a smile.

"She's always been the livelier of the two." Would her parents' death temper her spunk?

"That may help her adjust," Hope suggested.

Micah hoped so. Although he had no idea how any child adjusted to being an orphan.

Hope stepped back from the bed, and Micah not only missed her connection with Chloe but also her comforting presence.

Chloe whimpered again, and they both turned toward the bed. Her eyelids fluttered.

Micah eyed her warily. Then he took a deep breath to quiet the tension twisting his stomach.

"*Mamm?*" Chloe blinked several times. Only this time, her eyes remained open. "Micah?" Her gaze roamed the room. "Where are we?"

His throat dry and tight, he rasped, "The hospital."

"Why?"

"You were in an accident."

His niece squinted, as if trying to focus. "Accident?" she said in a puzzled voice.

"You don't remember?" *Please, God, erase all those details from her memory.* He'd forgotten everything between feeling the horse's tail twitch and waking up in the hospital. He wished he could wipe away the remaining fear. He only prayed that, unlike with his trauma, Chloe would never be haunted by the same terror.

She pursed her lips, and her eyes brimmed with questions. She obviously didn't recall the accident. *Thank God!*

He motioned toward Hope. "This nice lady stayed with you."

Chloe's nose wrinkled. "Nooo . . ." She hesitated. Then studied Hope again. Her drawn-out "Yes" expressed uncertainty.

"She waited with you until the ambulance came."

"That hurt my ears." Chloe's face scrunched up, as if in reaction to the loudness, and she cried out, "Ow!" Gingerly, she fingered the bandage on her head with one hand. Then she stared down at her other arm, teary-eyed. "I can't move it."

"Your arm is broken," Micah explained. "They put on a cast. And you have stitches in your head."

"They both hurt."

Her plaintive cry made Micah's heart ache for her even more. Chloe, who was always so active, would resent having her movements restricted. But more than her arm would be constrained by the news.

"I want *Mamm*."

"She can't come because—" Micah swallowed hard.

"But I need her. Call her, *Onkel* Micah. Call her now." She tossed her head wildly, glancing around the room.

"Where is she?" Her tone increased in shrillness with each plea.

As Chloe's panic mounted, so did Micah's. How did he phrase this? Explain it so she could understand? He closed his eyes. *Please, God, help me.*

A soft hand slid into his, and Micah's eyes flew open. Hope. Her gentle squeeze gave him courage.

"I'm so sorry, Chloe, but your *mamm* and *daed*, well, they were badly hurt in the crash."

Chloe only stared at him. She didn't understand his meaning. Chloe always preferred plain speaking. She wanted facts. No prettying them or softening them. Micah's eyes stung. Another gentle squeeze from Hope.

Clearing his throat, he tried again. "*Mamm* and *Daed* didn't make it."

Chloe lay stone-faced, uncomprehending.

He tried again. "They both went to be with Jesus."

A spark of fear flared in her eyes, and she screamed, "Noooo!" Tossing and turning from side to side, she repeated, "No, no, no, noooo!"

Jabin's eyes popped open, and he shrank back against the pillow. "*Onkel* Micah?"

Footsteps pounded down the hall, and a nurse burst into the room. "What's the matter?"

Chloe sobbed out, "I want my *mamm* and *daed*."

At almost the same time, Micah said, "I just told her—"

The nurse fixed her gaze on Chloe. "I'm so sorry, sweetie." She turned to Micah. "Do you need help?"

Yes, he needed help. Plenty of it. More than she or any human could give.

"I mean a sedative to calm her."

When Micah shook his head, she retreated and closed

the door behind her. He stood and untangled his hand from Hope's. He missed her comfort. Then he lowered himself onto the bed and cradled Chloe in his arms. She wept against his chest with great heaving breaths, soaking his shirt with tears.

"I . . . want . . . *Mamm*," she choked out between sobs.

He held her closer and swallowed back his own sorrow. "I know." He brushed her tangled hair from her forehead. It had come undone and would resemble a rat's nest in the morning. He had no idea how to pull it back into a bob. The lump in his throat grew larger. Chloe needed a mother, but all she had was him.

Micah almost missed the small, sleepy question coming from the other bed. "What's wrong with Chloe?"

Hope gestured toward Jabin. "I can hold Chloe if you want to tell him."

She took Micah's place, cradling his sobbing niece, and he headed toward Jabin's bed. The few feet between the beds seemed to have widened into a huge gap. Each step Micah took was one small slog toward causing another heartbreak.

He sat beside Jabin but couldn't chance holding or jarring him with his broken ribs and collapsed lung. His nephew struggled to sit, but Micah laid a restraining hand on Jabin's shoulder.

"Micah?" The word came out confused and breathy. Jabin winced. "What's wrong with me?"

"You were in an accident. Do you remember?"

A blank stare told him Jabin had no recollection, which was just as well.

"Your *mamm* and *daed* were in the accident." Maybe he could soften the blow a little, let his sensitive nephew down gently. "They were hurt so badly, Jesus took them to heaven."

"When will they come back?" Jabin asked groggily.

"Never." Chloe frowned at Micah. Evidently, she didn't approve of his explanation. Her tear-choked words rang out with finality. "They're dead."

Jabin's face crumpled. "No." The denial in his eyes matched the denial in Micah's heart.

Chapter Four

Hope couldn't leave now. Not when two sobbing children needed to be comforted. She kept her arms around Chloe and cuddled her close. The small girl buried her face against Hope's shoulder, and moisture soaked into the cape of Hope's dress. The cast clonked against Hope's side each time Chloe wriggled.

On the other bed, Micah set a hand on Jabin's head and spoke to him with soft, soothing sounds. Hope couldn't make out the words, but they seemed to settle the small boy. Jabin closed his eyes, but tears leaked out and trickled down the side of his face and onto the pillow. Hope's heart fluttered when Micah's large hands gently stroked the wetness from Jabin's pale cheeks.

Soon Jabin fell back to sleep, and Micah came over to hold Chloe, whose weeping had turned to sniffles. She whimpered when Hope handed her over, but soon she snuggled into Micah's arms. He rubbed her back until she quieted.

After a few minutes, he said, "I think she's sleeping," but he didn't sound sure.

Hope leaned over to peek at Chloe. The small girl's face had relaxed, and her long lashes made shadowy half-moons under her eyes. Combined with her deep, even breathing, it seemed she'd drifted off. Hope prayed those dreams would be healing ones, rather than nightmares.

She made the mistake of lifting her gaze to Micah's face. His relief and gratitude stirred an answering reaction. Quickly, she glanced away before she got drawn into their magnetic pull. "Chloe's, um, definitely asleep."

Micah lowered her onto the bed and tucked a pillow under her head. Then he smoothed the strands of hair from her forehead with a featherlight touch, and again, Hope marveled at the tenderness in those strong hands.

She had no idea how to deal with this intense pull of attraction. Swallowing hard, she focused her attention on Jabin's soft, whistling breaths. She'd never before experienced this breathlessness, this tumble of emotions. Not for any man.

"You didn't have to stay, but I'm so glad you did. *Danke*."

"I'm glad I could help." Her words came out too softly, too breathy, too filled with admiration. She hoped she hadn't given away her feelings. Could he read her wayward thoughts? Her burning cheeks matched the sparks Micah had kindled in her heart. Praying the dim lighting concealed her blush, Hope stood abruptly.

Admiration shone in his eyes. "I couldn't have done it without you."

If she hadn't been here, he would have coped. "I didn't do much."

"You did more than you'll ever know."

Desperate to leave before she was drawn deeper into his spell, Hope brushed past him and hurried to the door. "I need to go." She had chores to do and an eight o'clock meeting. *Focus on those. Forget this man and his appeal.*

"I'm so sorry you missed your sleep. I hope you'll be able to make up for it."

He was concerned about her despite his own lack of

sleep? And his heavy responsibilities? And his sorrow? What a kind, generous heart he had to think of others rather than himself.

"I–I'll be praying." Hope struggled to tear her gaze from his.

As she fumbled with the doorknob, it dawned on her that her half-apron was missing. Until now, she'd been so concerned about the children that she'd forgotten about her clothing. The ambulance staff had probably discarded the apron, soaked as it was with blood. Had Micah noticed and wondered why she'd come out partly dressed?

Hope bit her lip. Why was she worrying about a minor detail like that when those two precious little ones had lost their parents? Micah had more important things to worry about than her clothing. And why was she fretting about her appearance? Especially when she had no business thinking about Micah.

The door clicking shut behind Hope snapped Micah back to the dim, dreary hospital room. Most of the warmth and radiance departed with her. She'd been such a help and comfort.

It had been kind—more than kind—of her to stay all night, and to support all of them as they worked through some of their grief. She'd helped Chloe, and Micah had enjoyed her healing touch. He could still feel that soft hand in his. And he overflowed with gratitude that she'd stayed with him by the twins' bedsides long after they'd fallen back to sleep.

He appreciated all she'd done, but he'd been so caught up in caring for the twins, he'd neglected to find out more about her. His mind had been too fuzzy to concentrate. His thoughts too scattered.

Micah had one regret—not asking for her last name and address. She'd said she didn't know Anna and Ben, so she must not be part of their church district. If only he'd requested her contact information, he could at least thank her.

Right, Micah. That's all you want to do.

He shook his head. No time for anything other than that. He had the twins to care for, and funeral arrangements to make. Besides, after the burial, he'd return to New York so *Mamm* could help care for the twins. He needed to put Hope out of his mind, but he at least wanted to send her a thank-you note.

Each time he glanced at Chloe and Jabin, his eyes watered, yet the moisture did little to ease the scratchiness of his eyes. Despite his best efforts, his eyelids drooped. He jerked himself upright before he drifted off.

Squeezing the back of his neck and rolling his head to release the kinks, Micah prayed he'd be able to stay awake. If the twins woke again, he wanted to be there for them. It would soon be their usual waking time. Would they remember what he'd told them during the night? Or would they dismiss it as a dream? He hoped he wouldn't need to repeat the news. He wasn't sure he could say it one more time without breaking down. For their sakes, he needed to stay strong.

While she fed the horses and mucked out their stalls, Hope's mind kept straying to her meeting with Micah. Though his face had been tired and drawn, his eyes had softened when they rested on his niece and nephew. His love for them shone through. Despite being exhausted after traveling all night, he hadn't hesitated to stay awake for their benefit.

Her heart had gone out to him after Chloe had woken.

What a terrible thing to have to tell small children! Especially children you loved. As Micah struggled to explain, she'd reached for his hand without thinking and squeezed it to give him some support.

Her face burned at her boldness. At the time, all she'd thought of was supporting him when he was in pain. She hoped he hadn't thought . . .

Hope shook her head to dislodge the pictures of Micah drifting through her mind. She had no business thinking about him. Or any man.

Only Priscilla and the church leaders knew about *Daed*'s gambling problem. Hope could never admit her family's shameful secret to anyone else. Besides, she didn't want to burden a man she loved. What if *Daed* bankrupted her husband? She couldn't take that chance. Marriage was out of the question.

Speaking of *Daed*, she needed to finish with the horses and hurry inside to make breakfast. By the time she'd left the hospital, it had been almost six. Already past the usual hour for her chores. She'd barely managed a quick washup. As she'd dressed in fresh clothes, she remembered the apron. She took out another half-apron, but she'd have to sew a new apron to replace the one that—

Hope pulled her thoughts away from the tragic events of last night. She tried not to let those pictures seep into her mind again. But she couldn't forget the children. She murmured a prayer for the twins and their *onkel*. The *onkel* who kept crowding into her thoughts.

Don't dwell on him. Or the strange longing swirling deep inside. Hope concentrated on sliding the five straight pins into the back of her apron to secure it. With each one properly positioned, she was ready to face the day. Or as ready as she could be after last night.

Groggy from lack of sleep, Hope fought to stay awake

as she cooked bacon and eggs. She slid toast into the oven but forgot to take it out until the odor of charred bread filled the room.

Breakfast with *Daed* was a silent affair. He sniffed the acrid air but never said a word. Hope slumped into her chair, too tired to talk, and *Daed* sat with his head bent over his plate, avoiding her eyes. She hoped his hunched shoulders and reluctance to speak meant he was reflecting on his behavior. He'd need to confess to the bishop, but would that stop him from raiding the bank account again? What would she do if he took Priscilla's loan?

That worry stayed with her when she met Logan Russell, the therapist, in the barn office at eight. Hope decided against telling him about the missing money. No need to alarm him. He'd given up a prestigious career to come to work with her. Hope had no idea why; she just thanked the Lord that he had.

"I've lined up several students for sessions next week." Hope slid the paper toward him. "Here's your copy."

They'd advertised one free introductory session per child so prospective students and their parents could assess the stables and the program to be sure it would be a good fit.

Logan studied the list. "Good. Looks like you've noted the important information about each child's needs. That's extremely helpful."

Sometimes his smile made her uncomfortable. Hope wasn't sure why. His wide, toothy smile seemed genuine. Perhaps the gleam in his eyes made it appear overly friendly.

She returned a brief, cool nod to keep things business-like.

Evidently, Logan got the message. The fire in his eyes flickered and dimmed. He stood. "I'll do a quick check on the mares to decide which ones I think might be most suitable for each child."

"I thought we were planning to let the children select their own horses."

"Not for the free sessions. We want to be sure everything goes smoothly." Logan stood. "We can't risk losing any prospective students."

He'd hit on one of Hope's biggest fears. They had no students—yet. What if no one signed up following the free introductory sessions? She'd have to go back to waiting tables and find a way to repay Priscilla for any money the business had already spent. And she'd need to give up her dream.

Once she and Logan had made all the necessary arrangements for the various sessions, Hope rose and walked him out to his car. Then she hitched up the buggy and headed for Priscilla's.

When Priscilla greeted Hope at the door, Priscilla's *daed* hovered behind her. "I wondered if you were coming today," he said.

"I'm sorry I'm so late. I had a meeting with the therapist who'll be helping me with the business."

She should mention the accident last night, but she was too tired to discuss it. She'd tell Pris later. Much later. After she'd had some sleep.

But Priscilla picked up on her distress. "What's wrong? You're too upset to only be worried about money."

"I don't really want to talk about it." But when Priscilla shot her a stern you're-not-leaving-until-you-tell-me look, Hope gave in. Her voice husky, she sketched out the basic details of the accident.

"Oh, those poor children. I'll be praying for them. I heard there'd been an accident over near the intersection, but I never dreamed you'd been involved." Priscilla studied Hope's face. "What about you? You must be exhausted. Did you get any sleep?"

"Not yet, but I'll try to get some later."

"See that you do. I worry about you. You're under enough stress."

"I'll be fine."

Priscilla's *daed* looked at her with compassion in his eyes. "I'm sorry you had to go through all that. And we'll see about helping the children. Ben made all our harnesses."

Until recently, *Daed* had taken care of all the harness purchases. If Hope had gone to the shop instead, would she have known Ben? She swallowed the lump in her throat.

"The little ones often helped him in the shop, and so did his wife." Amos Ebersol rubbed the sides of his eyes. "They'll be missed. Do you know who'll be caring for the children?"

"I'm not sure. I expect their *onkel* will help, but I didn't ask."

"Ben's *daed* used to run the harness shop in town before they moved north. They live in New York State now, I believe."

"*Jah*, that's where Micah lives. Around the Fort Plain area." Hope had discovered that when she'd made the phone calls.

Amos nodded. "A lot of our Lancaster people have moved up there for the less-expensive farmland. He's not married?"

The question threw Hope off guard. "*Neh*." He was definitely clean-shaven.

"That's unusual. I believe he was only a few years younger than Ben." Priscilla's *daed* stroked his beard. "I hope there's nothing wrong with him. They said he was one hundred percent after his childhood accident, but sometimes . . ."

Hope had seen no indications Micah had any problems.

"I think he's fine." Her face heated, and she hoped they didn't realize she meant it for more than his mental capacity.

"Because he's not married, I expect he'll take the children to New York to his *mamm*," Amos said.

Hope tried not to wince. Why did the thought of Micah returning to New York bother her so much? She tried to clear her mind of the disappointment.

"Are you ready to go?" Amos asked with a quizzical look on his face. "Do you want to ride with me?"

"*Danke*, but I'd better take my own buggy. I might do some errands while we're in town." Though she probably shouldn't, she wanted to check on the twins. Their *onkel* was not part of the reason she'd been contemplating stopping by the hospital, was he?

After a hasty goodbye to Priscilla, Hope accompanied Priscilla's *daed* to the driveway, where his buggy waited in front of hers. One of his sons must have hitched up the horse while they talked.

Following Amos's lead, Hope wound down the country lanes and into town. He pulled to a stop in front of the bank and tied his horse to the long hitching post. Hope did the same.

Her breakfast sloshed around in her stomach as they made their way up the bank steps. All this money she'd owe Priscilla. What if she didn't get enough students to pay her friend back? Worse yet, what if *Daed* took it and gambled it away?

As Amos pulled open the glass front door, Hope asked, "Did Priscilla tell you why she was lending me this money?"

Amos nodded. "*Jah*, she did. I'm sorry it happened again." As one of the elders at their church, he'd been part of the group of men who'd suggested she take over the family finances.

He halted and pinned her with a serious look. "I hope

you'll take some advice. Why not open a new business account with this money, instead of keeping it in the farm account? And put the household money in an account under only your name?"

Of course. Why hadn't she thought of that? "That's a *gut* idea."

"I usually wouldn't recommend that to an unmarried daughter, but in this case . . ." His words trailed off as they approached one of the offices. "Try to spend the money in your joint account first. If there's anything left, that is. Leave only the bare minimum to keep it open."

If she did that, she'd not only protect their funds, she'd also prevent *Daed* from gambling again. Hope's spirits lightened. "*Danke,* I'll do that."

An hour later, Hope walked out of the bank with two new checkbooks and a bank balance that made her gasp. She had more than enough to keep the business running. Now all she had to do was make enough money to pay Priscilla back.

Micah scrubbed at his eyes with his fists. Sharp, indrawn breaths startled him. Chloe. Was she all right? She seemed to be breathing strangely. He jumped up and hurried to the bed.

Her chest rose and fell in an uneven rhythm, and she appeared to be gasping for air. Micah reached out to push the Call button for the nurse but stopped before he touched it. A tiny sob came from her lips, and she stuffed a fist against her mouth. Chloe was crying in her sleep. Or was she awake?

Either way, she was trying hard not to disturb anyone else. Micah couldn't let her weep alone. He lowered himself onto the bed.

"Chloe?" He whispered so he wouldn't disturb her if she were still sleeping. "I'm here." He set a hand on her back, and it vibrated as her shoulders heaved.

"Micah?" The word came out as a sob. "It's not true. I had a bad dream."

"I'm sorry." His words were almost as tear-clogged as hers.

"No, no, don't let it be real."

"I wish it wasn't."

"Why? Why? Why?" Each question grew louder and more anguished.

Micah glanced at the other bed. "Shh," he said. "Let's not wake Jabin." They should give him as much time in the dream world as possible before he had to face reality.

But Chloe didn't listen. Her next "why" rattled the glass vase on the windowsill. Jabin jumped and moaned. The door swung open, and a nurse hurried in.

At the sight of her, Chloe's next scream came out as a strangled gurgle. Her chest still heaved, but now she sucked back her sobs.

One thing about Chloe, she was easily distracted. She watched the nurse warily during the quick check of her vitals.

"Would you like breakfast?" the nurse asked.

Chloe's gaze darted to Micah, as if asking for permission. He nodded, and her eyes grew bleak. Had she been expecting him to say they were leaving?

That's what he would have wanted when he was in the hospital—to go home. But did Chloe realize what that would mean? The house would be empty. And everywhere they turned, it would be filled with reminders. Micah dreaded going there.

A cart rattled farther down the hall. "Let me check your brother." The nurse headed for Jabin's bed. A short while later, she jotted down the information. "Everything's looking good. The doctor will be in to see them around nine thirty."

Jabin hadn't stirred when she checked him. "We'll let him sleep. He can use the rest. We can feed him whenever he gets up."

Shortly after the nurse left, an aide entered carrying a tray. Micah helped Chloe to a sitting position. He had no way to fix her matted and knotted hair. With gentle fingers, he brushed it off her face and tried to smooth it behind her. But when Chloe bent over her breakfast tray, her hair fell like tangled vines on each side of her face, blocking her expression from view.

"Would you like breakfast?" the aide asked Micah.

He shook his head. "*Danke*, I mean, no, thank you." He didn't feel right taking the hospital's food. And those trays brought back bad memories. He'd bring some food with him if the twins needed to stay here long. Maybe he could make something for dinner, but that would mean going to the house, which he dreaded. He steeled himself to face it because he needed to care for his brother's animals and make funeral arrangements. But how could he desert the twins?

Chapter Five

Emerging from the cool, musty air inside the bank to sidewalks already baking in the morning heat sapped Hope's energy. She needed sleep, but her thoughts kept straying to Micah. He'd probably refused to leave the twins' bedsides even to eat. To be neighborly, she could stop by with breakfast sandwiches for all of them as an excuse.

As an excuse for what, Hope?

Did she need an excuse for being kind? And was kindness her only motive? Just because she'd enjoyed chatting with Micah—and he was easy on the eyes—didn't mean she was interested in him. Besides, she'd been the one who'd accompanied the children to the hospital. Shouldn't she at least check on them?

After wrestling with her conscience for a few minutes, she turned the buggy into the driveway of a fast-food restaurant and pulled into the drive-through. If he'd already eaten, she might look foolish. But she ordered one of the full breakfasts in case he hadn't. She also ordered small ones for the children, so it wouldn't appear she was bringing a meal to a man. And after being up all night, Micah could probably use a cup of coffee.

She slid from the driver's seat on the right over to the passenger side to pay the cashier and reach the bag.

Drive-throughs were set up for *Englisch* cars rather than Amish buggies. She set the cardboard carrier on the seat beside her and traveled the rest of the way to the hospital with the scent of bacon wafting through the air.

After she watered and tied up her horse, she headed into the ice-cold lobby. Shivering, she made her way to the elevator. Several times she almost turned back. Why was she doing this for a man she'd just met? Hope tried to tell herself she was stopping by because she was concerned about the children. She was, but she worried the food in her hands might reveal a different motive.

As soon as she entered the hospital room, Micah glanced over and smiled—or at least tried to smile. Despite his tired eyes and the stubble shadowing his chin, he appeared even more attractive in the daylight than he'd been last night. But he was obviously upset.

Before she could ask what was wrong, Micah sniffed the air. "Do I smell bacon?"

"You do." She held up the now-greasy bag and the children's boxes. "Have you eaten?"

He shook his head. "I didn't want to leave." He motioned with his chin to the bed near the door. "Jabin might be confused when he wakes up."

Hope crossed the room and handed Micah the bag. "He's been asleep all this time?"

"He woke when the doctor checked him but went right back to sleep."

"Then he probably needs his rest."

"That's what the nurse said." He reached for his wallet. "What's my bill?"

"Nothing." She patted her purse, filled with two brand-new checkbooks. "God gave me a windfall today. This is a small way of repaying Him."

Micah opened the bag and inhaled. "This smells so good." He pulled a twenty from his wallet. "I want to pay and tip you for the delivery."

"Don't be silly." She stepped back before he could put the money in her hand, although part of her wanted to feel his strong hand touching hers. "Please just consider it a gift from God."

He looked skeptical but bit into the sandwich and closed his eyes while he chewed the first bite. "Mmm." After he'd finished, he grinned. "Well, it's definitely a blessing."

Hope loved watching his eyes light up, but she forced herself to look elsewhere. Chloe sat up on the bed, her face damp and one hand clenched into a fist.

"Would you like some breakfast too?"

Her eyes dull, Chloe said in a flat voice, "I ate already."

"Of course." Hope should have thought of that. "Well, maybe you'll want a snack later." She pointed to the box beside Micah.

"Oh." Chloe's voice rose with excitement. "Does it have a toy in it?"

"It should." Hope picked up a box and set it on Chloe's rolling table. "Why don't you open it and see?"

Tears of frustration in her eyes, Chloe struggled to open it one-handed.

Rather than stepping in to help, Hope suggested, "You can use the fingers of your other hand too."

Chloe glared at her cast. "It's too heavy to lift. And it hurts."

Hope wanted to do it for the little girl, to make it easier, but Chloe needed to learn to do things herself. Micah watched them both, his eyes brimming with curiosity.

After whining a bit and getting no reaction, Chloe lifted

the cast and tore the plastic wrapper. Micah shot Hope a thankful smile as Chloe bent over her small toy.

Hope itched to comb and tame the straggly hair cascading over Chloe's shoulders.

"Would it be all right if I try to fix your hair?" she asked Chloe. "I don't have a brush, but I'll do my best."

Chloe pinched her lips into a tight line, as if to trap cries struggling to get out. Tears sparkled on her lashes like tiny beads.

Hope's heart went out to her. Probably her *mamm* had done her hair every day. Until now. It would be painful to have a stranger doing the usual routine in a hospital room.

When Chloe nodded, Hope sat on the edge of the bed and ran her fingers through Chloe's almost waist-length hair to gently remove as many tangles as she could. Several hairpins sprinkled onto the bed, and Hope unwound the elastic hair tie knotted at the end of a small snarl. As she smoothed down the hair, Chloe's chest heaved. Hope stopped what she was doing to wrap her arms around the small girl and pull her close.

"It's hard, isn't it?" Hope whispered.

Chloe nodded and leaned against her. Hope held her until she stilled, then she twisted strands tightly on either side of Chloe's forehead and drew all her hair back into a ponytail. After flipping it over on itself several times, she formed it into a bun and anchored it with pins.

"I don't suppose you have the netting?" Hope didn't see it on the bed or on the bedside table. She made the mistake of glancing over at Micah.

His moist eyes shone with more than gratitude. She had trouble tearing her gaze away.

"They probably took it off during the testing." His voice came out deep and throaty.

"*Jah*, they must have." She'd bring some netting when she stopped back.

Wait a minute! What am I doing? Why am I even considering returning?

After Hope finished, Micah said, "*Danke* for fixing Chloe's hair." As he studied his niece, his eyes grew bleak. "How will I ever do all that needs to be done? And they're discharging her today."

"Wunderbar." Hope was relieved the small girl's injuries weren't serious.

Micah's brow furrowed. He must not consider it as terrific as she did.

"What's the matter?" she asked.

Micah looked from Chloe to his nephew, asleep in the bed close to the door, and his frown deepened. "Chloe shouldn't be sitting in the hospital all day."

"I agree. I'd be happy to watch her," Hope volunteered. After all, what else did she have to do with her time? She could spend a few days helping him and the children. "If you'd trust me."

Trust her? *After she'd stayed all night at Chloe's bedside so his niece and nephew wouldn't wake up alone? After she'd so gently fixed Chloe's hair and still sat there holding her?* "Of course I trust you, but I couldn't impose on you like that. You've already done so much."

Chloe cuddled closer to Hope. Seeing their bond made Micah ache inside. His niece needed a mother figure, but he couldn't ask Hope to take over those duties.

"It's no problem," she told him. "As you said, she shouldn't be here all day." Hope laid her cheek against Chloe's hair, holding her the way Anna would—if she were still around.

Moisture blurred Micah's vision. "But—"

Hope waved a hand to stop him. "I'd love to have her. My dream right now is to work with children, but my business won't be opening until next week, so I don't have any pressing responsibilities."

Micah was about to ask her if she was a teacher when muffled sobs interrupted. Jabin had buried his face in the pillow. Micah rushed across the room. He wished he could scoop his nephew into his arms the way Hope was cradling Chloe, but he had to settle for stroking Jabin's forehead.

"Jabin needs you," Hope said softly. "I'll bring Chloe back at suppertime, along with a meal."

"I insist on buying this time."

"Nothing to pay for. It'll only be whatever I'm making *Daed.*"

She'd be cooking for her daed*? Did that mean she was unmarried?* His spirits rose. But he wouldn't be around here long enough to find out for sure.

Hope released Chloe, slid to the edge of the bed, and stood. When Hope turned and held out her arms, Chloe scooted right into them. His niece had certainly taken to this stranger. No, not a stranger any longer.

Hope pointed to Choe's hospital gown. "*Ach*, we can't take you out of here in that."

Another thing Micah should have thought about. Most likely they'd cut the clothes off both children to treat their broken bones and wounds.

"Should I go to the house and bring back clothes for both of them?" Hope asked him, setting Chloe on the bed.

"Would you?" As much as he disliked imposing on her, he had nothing for them to wear.

Micah gave her his brother's address. He choked on the familiar house number and street name. It had once been his home. After the rest of the family moved to New York,

Ben had lived there alone until bringing Anna there as his bride. Micah had visited them less than a month ago.

If he'd known that would be the last time he'd see them, he would have confessed his jealousy to God and to Ben, and asked for forgiveness. Growing up, Micah had resented his brother. Now it all seemed so foolish. So petty. He could never make things right. Why had he left all the important things unsaid?

Hope startled Micah from his regrets by hugging Chloe. His niece threw one arm around Hope's neck and clung to her.

"Don't go," Chloe begged.

"I'll be back soon. I'm just going to get you a dress. Then we can spend all day together."

But Chloe's terror-filled eyes followed Hope as she left the room. His niece didn't believe Hope's reassurances that she'd return. Who could blame her? She'd just discovered that people she loved and depended on could suddenly disappear from her life forever.

Micah had learned the same lesson.

Hope blinked as she emerged from the chilly lobby into the blazing sunlight. Upstairs in the hospital room, she'd been so overwhelmed by the gloom, she'd forgotten the day was bright and clear. And broiling.

Before she'd gone a mile, she had to dab at her damp forehead. When she reached Ben and Anna's house, she watered Biscuit. Then she mounted the back steps, but hesitated with one hand on the doorknob. It seemed wrong to walk into a stranger's house.

I'm not breaking in. I'm here for a purpose.

But that didn't alleviate her uneasiness. Only the reminder

that Chloe was waiting for her gave her the courage to open the door.

Inside the house, the air was slightly cooler. A breeze flowed through the open windows. The kitchen was neat and spotless. Hope entered the living room and mounted the stairs to the second floor. Each room she passed had been cleaned and straightened, readying the house for its owners to return. But they never would.

Her eyes welled with tears. How would the twins go on without their parents?

She found the children's rooms and collected clothing for each of them. With the clothes over her arms, she hurried downstairs. She quickly checked each room as she passed. They'd hold the viewing here, so she'd tidy anything out of place to make it easier for Micah. But other than picking up a few books scattered here and there to return to the bookshelves, Hope found little to *redd* up. Anna had been a meticulous housekeeper.

She'd opened the back door when it dawned on her that Chloe couldn't get her arm into the sleeve of the dress. By picking apart the seams on one side, Hope could help Chloe pin it shut. She found a pair of scissors in the kitchen drawer, opened the sleeve, and widened the armhole.

When she returned to the hospital, Chloe was waiting in the doorway. She threw one arm around Hope's legs and hugged hard. In her excitement, she clonked Hope's other leg with the cast. She might have a bruise there tomorrow, but it was a small price to pay for being greeted with such enthusiasm.

Holding up the dress, Hope smoothed down the little girl's hair. "Let's get on your clothes, so we can go to my farm." She led Chloe across the room, handed Micah all of Jabin's clothing, and then drew the curtain around the bed for privacy.

She laid Chloe's clothes on the bed and showed her the opening for the cast. "Do you need help putting it on?" After Chloe shook her head, Hope said, "I'll need to pin it after you're dressed."

She emerged from behind the curtain to find Micah had folded Jabin's clothes into a neat stack on the windowsill. She should have done that instead of draping them over her arm.

"I'm sorry. I could have done that."

"You've done enough. More than enough." Again, his smile spoke volumes.

An awkward silence descended, so Hope was grateful when Chloe pranced out from behind the curtain, one sleeve flapping loose. She was barefoot.

"Maybe I should have brought shoes," Hope said. Most women and children went barefoot when it was warm, but she had no idea about hospital rules.

"We never wear shoes, except for church Sundays. *Mamm* says . . ." Her face crumpled. She turned her back and dashed behind the curtain.

Hope caught Micah's eye. "Should I go after her?"

"Give her a little time."

She nodded. Micah seemed to have good instincts for dealing with the twins. Hope had been in her late teens when her *mamm* died, but sometimes she'd preferred being alone to grieve. Perhaps Chloe did too.

"How's Jabin?" she whispered to Micah.

"He drifts in and out." Micah kept his voice low. "Several times he's cried in his sleep. I worry about him a bit more than Chloe. She's always been more dramatic and bounces from one emotion to the next, so she'll express her feelings. Jabin hides everything inside."

The metal rings clattered on the curtain rod, and Chloe peeked out with red-rimmed eyes. Hope knelt and held out her arms. The little girl barreled into them so hard, she almost knocked Hope over. They both would have fallen if Micah hadn't reached out and supported her.

Hope almost keeled over from the warmth of his hands on her back. She steadied herself and forced herself to stay still, though she wanted to lean back against his hands. Her pulse thundered in her ears, and she prayed Micah couldn't hear it.

He seemed as reluctant to remove his hands as she was for him to release her. She had no idea how long they would have stayed there if Chloe hadn't grabbed Hope's hand and tugged her to her feet.

"Are you going to fix my dress now?" Chloe fluttered her sleeve in the air.

"That was clever," Micah said. "I wouldn't have thought about the cast."

"I unpicked it at the seams so it can easily be sewn back together once the cast is removed." Hope knelt in front of Chloe and rolled the dress sleeve above the cast. Then she slid out two of the pins holding the back of her apron together and inserted them to fix Chloe's loose fabric in place.

As soon as she was done, Chloe pulled Hope toward the door. "Are we going to your farm now?"

"We'll be back at suppertime." Hope was grateful to be facing away from Micah. Her heart rate was still galloping. She had no idea what he'd read in her expression if their eyes met, but she didn't want to chance it.

Chapter Six

Soon after Hope left with Chloe, a woman in Plain dress bustled into the room. "I'm Betty Troyer, the bishop's wife from the neighboring church district." The deep frown lines slashed across her forehead and her prim, tight mouth gave the impression that before she even got to know a person, she'd already condemned them.

Micah straightened up and searched his conscience for wrongdoing. "Pleased to meet you." Inside, he wasn't so sure he was, but he couldn't be rude. Fidgeting, he unsuccessfully tried to brush some of the wrinkles from his clothing so he'd look less disheveled.

Her sharp eyes took in every detail of his appearance from the bags under his eyes to the stubble on his chin. If only he'd had time to shave.

"My husband got a call from Hope Graber last night when she was trying to find relatives for the children." She waved toward the two beds, not seeming to notice one was empty. "You probably don't know Hope, but she's from our church district, and she went to a lot of trouble to locate you."

One more thing for Micah to feel guilty about. He bit back a sigh. "Actually, I have met Hope." He enjoyed watching the woman's eyebrows arch upward. "She stopped by this morning and offered to care for Chloe today. I greatly appreciated it because the doctor had just discharged her. Hope seems very nice."

He hid a smile as the bishop's wife, whose face scrunched up as if she'd sniffed a rotting fish, offered faint praise. "I suppose she is. It's surprising she turned out decent after that father of hers—" Betty Troyer broke off suddenly, perhaps aware she was gossiping to a stranger.

Micah wondered what sins Hope's father had committed. Were they as grave as Betty Troyer's face indicated? Or had he fallen asleep and snored during her husband's sermon?

When people were this critical, it was hard to tell if the person they were condemning had made a minor mistake or committed a heinous crime. Micah hoped her husband wasn't as judgmental. Her attitude made Micah grateful for the loving, accepting, and humble bishop in his own church district.

Betty waved toward Jabin. "I just stopped by to let you know their bishop is out of town for a family wedding, but he'll be back tomorrow. Some of the church women from their district offered to stop by to keep the children company while you prepare for"—compassion filled her eyes for a moment, making her look human and vulnerable, but she quickly shuttered it—"the funeral," she said briskly.

Micah had pushed that thought to the back of his mind. But her reminder shot through him with a swift, sharp pang. It was up to him to handle all that. "That's kind of them."

Betty sniffed. "They're only doing their duty."

Micah was determined to counteract her negativity. "I appreciate it very much, and thank you for coming."

"Yes, well, I should have been here earlier. If I had, Hope wouldn't have had to take the little girl."

Micah still felt bad about that, and Betty's barb added to his guilt. "It would have been *gut* to save Hope the trouble."

He'd been about to compliment Hope for all she'd done, but Betty inspected him with narrow, suspicious eyes, like a hawk waiting for a tiny misstep so she could swoop down and pin him with her claws.

Instead, he switched to complimenting Betty. "It was nice of you to take time from your busy day to stop by to let me know."

Betty stood up straighter, almost preening, but quickly drooped. She must have remembered God's warning about *hochmut* and curbed her pride. "Yes, well, it wasn't easy getting here, I can tell you that."

"I'm sure it wasn't." Nothing was easy for this woman, who seemed to find only negatives in life.

She continued as if she hadn't heard him. "Lucas—that's my son—threw a fit when I was walking out the door, and I couldn't leave Martha alone with him. She's my daughter, and she can usually deal with her brother, but she's not one hundred percent, so I don't like her to watch him when he's out of control."

"I'm sorry." Micah's irritation toward her lessened. It sounded as if she had major problems at home.

Her face reddened. "I don't want you to think Lucas is bad. He's autistic, and sometimes he doesn't know what he's doing."

"That must be difficult."

"It is." Betty appeared to be fighting back tears.

Micah reminded himself you never knew what others were going through. Often a brittle surface covered hidden trauma.

"Anyway, I just wanted you to know Sylvia Esh will stop by after lunch. And she'll be bringing her husband's cell phone so you can make calls. Oh, and the neighbor took care of the animals this morning, and he'll do it the next few days too, so you don't have to worry about them."

"*Danke*." Micah was expecting her to remind him they were doing their duty, or maybe she'd quote a Scripture verse about helping others in need. To his surprise, she did neither. Had his positive answers and interest in her life softened her a little?

"I'd better be going." Betty pivoted to face the door. Just before she strode out, she turned. "Sorry for your loss. Although we may not always understand God's purpose when tragedies happen, we must accept His will."

"*Danke*." Micah wasn't sure if he was thanking her for her spiritual reminder or for heading out the door.

As they'd descended in the elevator, Chloe clung tightly to Hope's hand. "What animals do you have on your farm?"

"Mostly horses. We used to have a big horse farm, but now we have only four horses." Five, if you counted Biscuit. "Would you like to help me groom them?"

Maybe she could do a little informal horse therapy today to help Chloe.

When they got to the farm, Chloe helped Hope rub down Biscuit. Like most Amish children, she was comfortable with horses and knew how to care for them. Maybe the familiar tasks would help to ease some of her grief. Learning to care for a horse was usually the first step in therapy, but Chloe already knew how to do that. Hope wanted to give the little girl one more tip.

"Could you get the currycomb?" Hope pointed to the plastic basket of grooming tools on a stool outside the stall.

"Sure." Chloe picked out the proper tool without prompting. She obviously knew how to use it. She let Biscuit sniff it before starting at the horse's neck with a circular motion.

The horse sometimes twitched, but he seemed to enjoy Chloe's attention, even leaning into the curry.

Chloe giggled. "I think she likes me."

"She definitely does. You must have the right touch." They shared a smile. "You know, Chloe, my horses are good listeners. And they can tell when people are sad or lonely or upset."

Chloe stopped for a moment and looked at Hope. Biscuit flicked her head to get Chloe's attention, but the little girl kept her gaze fixed on Hope.

"When I have a problem and no one to talk to, I lean my head against Biscuit's neck and tell her. She keeps my secrets. I always feel better after I talk to a horse."

Hope had grown up being told to be practical and not treat animals as pets. She'd hidden her bond with the horses, fearful she'd be mocked. Or worse yet, that her parents would forbid her to indulge in fantasies.

Biscuit wasn't one of the trained horses, but she was a gentle mare. She'd cooperate if Chloe wanted to confide in her.

"I need to check on some of the other horses. Could you keep grooming Biscuit?" At Chloe's nod, Hope pointed to the other tools. "You can use the stiff and soft brushes, but wait for me on the hoof pick."

She hoped Chloe would take advantage of her privacy to talk to the horse. After leaving the stall, Hope strode down the aisle but quickly returned, being sure to stay out of sight. Low murmuring came from the stall. Although she couldn't make out the words, it sounded like Chloe was confiding in Biscuit. Hope prayed it would help.

She waited until Chloe exited the stall to pick up the stiff brush. "Everything going all right?"

Damp-eyed, Chloe nodded and returned to the stall. If Chloe had been one of her students, Hope would have stayed in the stall with her to satisfy the insurance requirements. But the Amish way was not to hover. They gave their children freedom because they trusted God in all circumstances.

Logan had been horrified to find out that they let eight- or nine-year-olds drive pony carts. He'd be upset to think she'd allowed a seven-year-old to groom a horse without supervision. But Hope was sure Chloe's parents most likely had allowed her to do it at home. Although it might not fit proper *Englisch* protocol, especially the rules of the insurance company, Hope chose to follow her instincts. And she prayed for Chloe's safety and healing.

Jabin woke briefly when the nurse came in to check on him but soon went back to sleep. Micah coaxed him awake in time for lunch, but he remained bleary-eyed as Micah fed him the noon meal. Opening his mouth like a baby bird, Jabin ate whatever Micah placed in his mouth. If the food were changed to worms, Micah suspected his nephew might have eaten them with no reaction.

They'd just finished when Sylvia Esh arrived. A plump woman with friendly but tear-filled eyes, she dabbed at her cheeks with an embroidered handkerchief. "I'm so sorry about this tragedy," she said in a broken voice. "Ben and Anna will be greatly missed." She pursed her lips while examining Jabin, who had shut his eyes.

Micah suspected his nephew wasn't sleeping but had instead blocked them out. Jabin seemed to be dealing with his pain by avoiding reality.

"Poor little one," Sylvia exclaimed. "What a terrible thing for them to go through." Her gaze strayed to the empty bed. "Where's Chloe?"

"A helpful lady from another church district offered to

care for her after she was discharged this morning." Micah motioned to the chair by Jabin's bed. "Would you like a seat?"

Sylvia lowered herself onto the green plastic seat and opened her handbag. "I brought the phone. My husband said to tell you he has unlimited calling for his business. He didn't want you to worry about long-distance calls."

"*Danke*. I really appreciate it." Feeling uncomfortable, Micah took the phone she held out. Holding a cell phone made him feel guilty, and using someone else's made him nervous. What if he did something wrong or damaged the phone? He slid the phone into his pocket.

"I also wanted to give you this." She held out a slip of paper with a phone number printed on it. "Debbie's our usual driver, and she's free today. She'd be happy to take you wherever you need to go."

"*Danke*. I appreciate that." Micah took the paper and glanced at it before slipping it into his pocket with the phone. He looked up to find Sylvia studying him.

"You're not married?"

At the eagerness in her voice, Micah took a step back. "*Neh*. Not yet." He rubbed his hand over the stubble along his jaw. Had his unshaven chin confused her?

The corners of her mouth drooped at his answer. "I suppose 'not yet' means you're courting a girl back home."

What an odd thing to say. Usually, dating was a private matter. Besides, why would she be interested in a stranger's personal life? Yet, she looked as if she were waiting for an answer.

"I haven't had much time for that." Nor had he found a girl who interested him in his *g'may*. If someone like Hope had been one of the choices, he would have made time to court despite his busy schedule.

The almost predatory gleam in her eyes unnerved him.

And the way she continued to assess him made him ill at ease. Unlike Betty Troyer's judgmental glower, Sylvia's penetrating stare made it seem as if she were trying to see beyond his rumpled clothing, bloodshot eyes, and unsightly stubble.

Micah shuffled his feet, eager to get away from her scrutiny. "I should go. I need to get cleaned up, and I have phone calls to make." He forced a smile he hoped appeared pleasant. "I appreciate you staying with Jabin. I'll try not to be too long."

"Take as much time as you need." She waved a hand magnanimously. "I'm happy to stay until suppertime. Don't worry about Jabin. He knows me from church."

Micah hoped he wouldn't be gone that long. He and *Daed* could split up the phone calls. "I'm grateful for the phone and the babysitting," he said as he walked out the door with his duffel bag. Yet he left with an uneasy feeling that Sylvia had an underlying motive for staying with his nephew. He couldn't put his finger on it, but he intended to return as quickly as possible.

After Chloe finished grooming the horse and her low murmuring ceased, Hope entered the stall. "Are you ready to do Biscuit's hooves?" She held out the pick.

Although Chloe's eyes still reflected deep sadness, her pinched expression had smoothed out. "You were right. Biscuit is a good listener." She took the pick and waited patiently while Hope lifted Biscuit's hoof.

Once again, Chloe proved herself skillful not only with cleaning Biscuit's hooves but also with calming the horse when she grew restless.

"You're good with horses," Hope observed, and was rewarded with a faint smile.

"I help *Daed* with . . ." The hoof pick clattered to the ground, and Chloe's face crumpled. A small sob escaped from between pinched lips.

Hope set down Biscuit's foot and cradled Chloe in her arms. So many everyday chores and activities would bring back memories. Hope wished she had a way to absorb all that agony. Horses might help, but Chloe had to face each day by herself.

Her arms tight around Chloe, Hope waited for the storm to subside. Biscuit tossed her head and whinnied. Then she nudged Chloe with her nose. Perhaps she too was trying to comfort the crying child.

Chloe lifted her head to look at Biscuit. "You want to help me, don't you, Biscuit?" She stretched out a hand to stroke the horse's nose. "You remember what I told you?"

Biscuit tossed her head up and down as if to say *yes*.

"She answered me," Chloe squealed.

Hope hid a smile. "I told you she was a smart horse."

"She is." Chloe slipped from Hope's embrace to throw her arms around Biscuit's neck and bury her face against the horse's coat.

Hope gave Chloe some time with the horse before asking, "Are you ready to finish Biscuit's hooves?"

Chloe bent and retrieved the pick. Then she did the last two hooves while chattering to the horse. Once again, Hope marveled at how an animal could calm a child. She'd made the right decision in turning the farm into a therapy center.

Thank you, Lord, for giving me this opportunity. I'm so grateful You put this profession on my heart.

A deep peace about her future descended on her.

She wished she could help Chloe and Jabin. If only

they weren't returning to New York, Hope could offer her therapy services to Micah. For free, of course. She had no idea how long he'd be staying or if he'd even agree, but she could at least suggest it for whatever time he remained here.

Chapter Seven

News traveled fast in the community, and most people would show up for the viewing tomorrow night, but Micah had to decide who to invite to the funeral and burial. After a long discussion with *Daed*, they settled on which cousins they'd call and divided up the list. It would be nice if they could ask everyone, but with families so large, only one or two representatives from each set of cousins could come.

Hearing *Daed*'s husky voice on the phone, Micah choked back tears. He could only imagine how hard it was for his parents to lose their firstborn son.

Just before they ended their conversation, *Daed* said, "God gave up His beloved Son for us. I've read that story so many times, but I never understood the heart-wrenching depths of that sacrifice." He paused, and his voice shook. "Today I do."

After he hung up, Micah bowed his head and prayed God would comfort his parents. And Jabin and Chloe.

Micah had paced the sidewalk outside the hospital while talking to *Daed*, but now he needed to face some of the day's hardest tasks: visiting the funeral home and going to Ben and Anna's house. He dialed the number Sylvia had given him.

Debbie turned out to be a chatty, gray-haired woman in

a floral print dress so bright it hurt Micah's tired eyes. "I'm so sorry to hear of your loss. I have nothing else to do today, so I can wait for however long you need me to." She patted a novel on the seat beside her. "I have this to keep me company."

As they traveled to the funeral home, he learned most of her life history. Widowed early with three young children, she'd started driving during the day while they were in school. Now that her children were grown and lived in other states, she drove full-time, even taking families or groups to the shore in the summer or to Pinecraft in Florida for winter vacations.

"If I talk too much, just let me know, and I'll shut up," she said.

But Micah welcomed the distraction. He had no desire to think of what lay ahead. He made the arrangements with the funeral home to deliver the bodies the next day. Then he asked Debbie to take him to the house.

He should invite her in, but first he wanted to cross the threshold alone. Ben and Anna had never locked their doors, so the knob turned easily. Still, Micah hesitated. Going into the house would make it real. More real than it had been.

His hand shook a little as he pushed open the door and stepped inside. Everything remained the same as when he'd visited a few weeks ago. Except now, he'd never flop down on the sofa across from Ben, who loved to sit in the wooden rocker. Anna wouldn't smile as she entered the room with freshly baked cookies. And Micah'd never get to say *I'm sorry*.

Every place he looked brought memories flooding back. He'd been planning to make his calls from here, but he couldn't bear to sit on the sofa, staring at the empty chair.

The living room and dining room opened into each other,

which worked well for church services. By removing the living room chairs and shoving the dining room table against the wall, Anna and Ben could be placed side by side.

Soon, all was in readiness for tomorrow. Micah showered and shaved, then cleaned up after himself. He took one last look around. Heartsick, he stepped out on the porch and closed the door behind him.

"Where to now?" Debbie asked when he slid into the car.

Micah had to make the calls, but when he did, he wanted to be in nature. "Could we go to Central Park?" The Lancaster County park wasn't far from the hospital. Once he made his calls, he'd head back to be with Jabin.

"Sure thing." Debbie put the car in gear, drove down the driveway, and turned onto the country road that had meant childhood happiness to him.

After she pulled into the parking lot, she turned to him. "Do you know how long you'll be?"

Micah had no idea. Some relatives might want to talk and reminisce. "Maybe an hour?"

"In that case, I'll stretch out under the trees over there to read. You can come and get me when you're ready."

With it being summer, the pool was crowded with screaming children. Micah walked until he reached the waterfalls. The splashing water and green canopy of leaves overhead soothed his soul. Before making his calls, he prayed for God's peace. This had to be one of the hardest things he'd ever done. Last night, Hope had slipped her hand into his. How he wished he could have that comfort now.

Hope and Chloe cared for the rest of the horses, then went inside to make supper. *Daed* wasn't in the kitchen or the living room, which made her nervous. She hoped he wouldn't make a habit of taking afternoon naps or lying around. He needed to find something to occupy his time.

The house was so quiet, it seemed empty. If he'd gone with Art again . . . His gambling buddy might convince him he could earn back the money he'd lost. Again, she appreciated Amos's sage advice. Having most of the money in new accounts gave her a great sense of relief.

"*Daed?*" she called, praying for an answer.

"*Jah?*" he replied from the front porch. The rocker creaked loudly under his weight.

"I only wanted to let you know I'm starting supper."

"Good. I'm hungry." The chair resumed its groaning.

"So am I," said Chloe.

"What shall we make tonight?" Hope asked as she opened the refrigerator. "Does your *onkel* like Yumasetti?"

At Chloe's enthusiastic nod, Hope removed the ground beef from the refrigerator. Casseroles were easy to carry and made hearty, balanced meals. She pulled a chair over to the stove so Chloe could help cook the noodles and peas and brown the ground beef with onions.

When everything was ready, they cubed toast slices and mixed everything with sour cream and cream soup. Hope divided the ingredients into a larger dish for the hospital and a smaller glass pan for *Daed*. Then she let Chloe sprinkle cheese on top.

While the casseroles baked, they played Dutch Blitz, which got Chloe giggling because Hope agreed to play one-handed, so she didn't have an unfair advantage compared to Chloe's broken arm. Trying to hold and place cards in the center of the table proved difficult, and soon they both were laughing at the mishaps.

Hope removed the steaming casserole from the oven, covered it, and tucked it into a wicker carrier. "Ready to go back to the hospital?"

The question wiped all the joy from Chloe's face. For a short while, she'd forgotten and behaved like a normal, carefree child. Hope wished she had a way to bring back that smile.

Micah paid Debbie and thanked her for her patience, then hurried upstairs to the pediatric ward. As much as he disliked hospitals, he was eager to get back to the room to be sure Jabin was all right. Would he be awake? Crying?

None of Micah's guilt-fueled imaginings came true. When he entered the room, it appeared everything had frozen since he'd walked out the door earlier. Sylvia sat upright in the chair, her gaze fixed on Jabin, who lay sleeping.

"Oh, you're back already." Sylvia looked disappointed.

Micah handed over the cell phone. "*Danke* for letting me use it."

Sylvia waved it away. "No, no. You keep it for now. You may need it." She bustled around, gathering her purse. "Are you eating in the cafeteria here?"

"Not so far." And tonight, he couldn't wait for the meal Hope had offered to bring.

"Home-cooked meals are better for you than fast foods, don't you think?"

"Definitely. I don't normally eat fast foods." She must have seen the wrappers from breakfast in the trash can. Oh, and Jabin's meal remained uneaten on the windowsill, and the greasy scent still lingered in the air.

"You should keep up your strength, especially now," she said as she exited.

"*Danke* for staying with Jabin," he called after her.

He settled in the chair beside his nephew's bed, and Jabin opened his eyes.

"Micah?" he said in a weak voice. "You're back."

Glancing around, Jabin checked out the other bed and the chair. "Did the lady go?"

"Yes, she did." Now Micah felt guilty. Had Jabin been pretending to sleep while Sylvia was here?

"Where's Chloe?"

"She went with Hope to a farm."

His eyes half-closed, Jabin murmured, "She's nice."

If he was referring to Hope, Micah totally agreed. "Are you sleepy?"

Jabin rolled his head back and forth on the pillow, which Micah assumed meant *no.* "Are you doing all right?"

Another head roll.

"You're hurting?"

Turning tear-filled eyes toward Micah, Jabin said, "A little there." He lifted one hand and pointed to the opposite side of his chest. The one with the collapsed lung and broken ribs. "But a lot inside."

Micah was pretty sure Jabin didn't mean his physical pain. He reached out and laid a hand on Jabin's head. "I know. I do too."

"God can do anything, right?"

Jabin looked at Micah so trustingly, he guessed what was coming. But what could he say other than yes?

His nephew's eyes brightened. "Then if I ask for *Mamm* and *Daed* back, He could do it?"

"Of course, He could do it, but He probably won't." Micah prayed his response wouldn't damage Jabin's faith.

Wincing as if Micah had stabbed him, Jabin stared at him in disbelief. Then, a plaintive note in his voice, he asked, "Why not? I really, really need them."

"I know you do, buddy." Micah struggled to form words when his throat ached for this small boy who had to face such agony. "Sometimes God has different plans. He always has a reason for what He does, even if we can't see it."

"Why does He want my *mamm* and *daed*? Doesn't He know I need them?"

"I'm sure He knows, and He wants to comfort you. It isn't always easy to accept God's will." Especially when we're hurting and we'd rather rail against it or cry out in confusion and pain. Micah was struggling to trust God's providence, so how could he expect a seven-year-old to grasp it?

Jabin studied Micah for a long while before speaking. "What if God wants Chloe and you and my friend Thomas and Buttermilk and Daffodil and—?" He stopped when Micah held up a hand.

"I don't think He'll take everyone." At least, Micah hoped not. It had happened in the Bible to Job, who'd lost everything.

"You don't know, do you?"

Had Jabin picked up on Micah's uncertainty? "Only God knows that."

"If He took *Mamm* and *Daed* away, He might take other people too." Jabin tucked his head down toward his chest, like a turtle curling into its shell, muffling his words. "I don't think God loves me."

Micah stroked his head. "He loves you more than you'll ever know." Micah wished he had a way to convince Jabin of God's love. Right now, though, all he could do was be here for his nephew—and niece—and point the way to God by giving them as much human love as he could while they grieved.

* * *

Chloe squeezed Hope's hand tightly when they got in the elevator. The poor girl seemed terrified.

Hope bent down to Chloe's level. "We're just going to visit Jabin. I'm not taking you back here to stay."

The relief flickering in Chloe's eyes told Hope she'd addressed a pressing problem. She went to stand up, but Chloe gripped Hope's wrist so hard it hurt.

The little girl glanced around at the other people in the elevator, then lowered her usual loud voice to a stage-whisper. "I don't want the hospital to kill Jabin and Micah too."

"*Ach*, Chloe." Hope pulled her into a swift, one-armed embrace. "Hospitals make people better."

Chloe pulled back far enough to look directly into Hope's eyes. Then, as the elevator slid open on the pediatric ward, she announced, "This hospital killed my *mamm* and *daed*."

People waiting to head to other floors and those passing in the hallway all stopped and stared. Hope struggled to her feet and took Chloe's hand to lead her out of the elevator. "*Neh*, an accident killed your parents. They were too badly hurt to live."

She hoped her explanation would disperse the onlookers studying them warily. Instead, everyone gazed at Chloe with pity.

"I don't have a *mamm* or *daed*," she said to the staring, concerned crowd. "They died." She burst into tears.

Hope set down the wicker carrier and swept Chloe into her arms. She patted the little girl's back and murmured soothing words into her ear.

Micah poked his head from behind the room door. "I thought I recognized that cry." He hurried toward Hope and held out his arms.

Ach, he'd shaved and had on fresh clothes. If she'd thought him good-looking when he was unshaven and dressed in wrinkled clothing, cleaned up he was heart-stoppingly handsome. Except after seeing him, her heart went from stuttering to banging. Hope forced her gaze away as she transferred Chloe to him, but their hands brushed and increased her already rapid pulse. She bent and clutched the wicker carrier handle.

"Chloe," Micah said, "did you know there are sick children in all these rooms?" He waved a hand down the hall. "Every room here has children in it."

Chloe gulped back a sob and lifted her head to look where Micah had indicated. "Are they all going to die?"

"I hope not." Micah appeared taken aback.

Hope intervened. "Of course not." She kept her voice brisk and authoritative. "They came to the hospital to get better." They might not all make it, but she didn't want to dwell on the negative. "That's what Jabin's doing. He's getting well."

Micah's grateful glance did little to slow her racing heartbeat.

"Why don't we all go in the room," he said, "so we're not blocking the hallway?"

And causing a commotion with Chloe's statements. Hope followed them into the room and closed the door.

She set the basket on the wide windowsill. Jabin sniffed the air and closed his eyes. Teardrops trickled from under his lashes.

"Are you hungry, Jabin?" Hope asked.

A head bob that might pass as a nod was his only response. She went over to stand by the bed and took his hand. "Do you like Yumasetti?"

"*Jah.*" The word held a world of pain.

"Does your chest hurt?" she asked.

"N–no."

Still holding Chloe, Micah caught her eye and tapped one fist against his heart.

Hope nodded and turned back to Jabin. *Concentrate on*

the small boy, not the man. Or your thundering pulse. "You're sad?"

His chin went up and down twice before he tucked it toward his chest. He hunched his shoulders as if to protect himself from a blow. If only she could gather him into her arms. Even if she could, she had no way to shield him from sorrow.

Distraction had worked well with Chloe, who was now describing how they'd made the casserole.

"It smells delicious," Micah responded. "I'm sure you were a big help."

"I was," she said. "Wasn't I, Hope?"

"You certainly were." Hope bent closer to Jabin. "Did you know Chloe helped with the casserole?"

His eyes opened, and Hope used a finger to wipe away the tear tracks.

"She helps *Mamm.*" Jabin's eyes begged Hope to understand. "It smells like the kitchen."

"I'm sorry." She hadn't thought about the meal bringing back memories. She wished she'd brought a different casserole. After squeezing Jabin's hand, she rose and went to remove the casserole dish from the carrier.

A tap on the door stopped her. A woman stuck her head in.

"Sylvia?" Micah's eyebrows flicked upward, but then his face smoothed into a wary but welcoming smile.

"I was worried about you eating fast food, so my daughter Susie"—Sylvia opened the door wide and semi-pushed a girl about Hope's age into the room—"made a homemade supper for you."

The girl stood there awkwardly holding out a casserole dish.

"*Danke,*" Micah said, "but Hope is here and—"

Hope caught his eye and shook her head. She patted the

carrier to be sure the lid was fully closed, then slipped over to the door the women had just entered.

"She's welcome to join us," Sylvia said, but her slight grimace when she glanced in Hope's direction made it obvious that wasn't what she wished for at all.

"I should go." Hope edged closer to the door and turned to Micah. "Did you want me to take Chloe home for the night?"

"No need." Sylvia patted her daughter's shoulder. "Susie adores children, and we see Chloe at church. Susie would be delighted to care for Chloe."

Chloe howled and raced across the room. Flinging herself at Hope's legs, she hung on tightly. "I want to go with Hope."

His cheeks red, Micah shrugged and apologized to Sylvia. "I think Chloe has become attached to Hope. I'm sure she'd be happy to stay with you."

"*Nhh*." Chloe managed before Hope covered the small girl's mouth.

Both Sylvia and Susie had their gazes fixed on Micah, so Hope tapped Chloe's head and placed a finger to her lips. Chloe frowned but stopped protesting.

"For tonight, though," Micah continued, "I think it might be best for her to stay with Hope. If she's not a bother, that is," he added, with a questioning glance at Hope.

"Of course not. We have fun together, and Chloe's a good girl."

Micah's raised eyebrows questioned her last statement, but he followed it with a thankful smile.

"I'll be good. I promise." Chloe tucked her cast close to her stomach and cradled it with her other arm. Then she jumped up and down. "Please, please."

"*Jah*, you may go with Hope if you agree to do whatever

she tells you." Micah waited for Chloe's nod, then turned to Susie. "*Danke* for your offer."

Susie's cheeks flamed, and she stared at the floor. "You're welcome," she replied, her voice barely a squeak.

Running a finger around under his collar, Micah asked Hope, "Would you be willing to wait until Chloe has eaten?" The desperation in his eyes signaled he wanted protection from this matchmaking duo.

"I'd be happy to. Why don't I take Chloe to wash her hands?"

Hope didn't miss the downcast look on Sylvia's face as she took Chloe's hand and headed to the bathroom, but if she wasn't mistaken, Susie almost appeared relieved.

After Hope closed the door and turned on the water, she squatted in front of Chloe. "We're going to eat the casserole Susie brought, and I don't want you to tell anyone about our casserole."

Chloe thrust out her lower lip. "I want to eat ours."

"I know you do, but we need to be polite. We'll eat ours tomorrow."

"I get to go home with you tomorrow too?"

Hope shushed her gleeful cheers and directed her to wash her hands. When they emerged from the bathroom, Chloe was beaming.

"I can stay with Hope tomorrow too," she announced.

Hope wished she'd discussed keeping that quiet as well when Sylvia flashed her an irritated glance.

"Susie can help tomorrow."

"I don't want—" Chloe snapped her mouth shut when Hope tapped her on the shoulder.

"We'll have a lot of relatives, but if you wouldn't mind helping in the kitchen at the house, I'd be grateful," Micah said to Susie.

Both Sylvia and Susie smiled, but her *mamm* spoke for Susie. "We'd be delighted. Susie does a great job in the kitchen, as I'm sure you'll be able to tell from the casserole."

Sylvia motioned for Susie to join her as she cut the casserole. With her head low, Susie shuffled around, passing out the plates her *mamm* handed her, starting with Micah.

The tentative smile Susie bestowed on him started a flicker of jealousy in Hope's heart. Not that she had any right to think about Micah that way. She tried not to read anything into the smile Micah returned. Had it been polite? Kind? Appreciative?

Susie thrust a plate toward Hope. After murmuring her thanks, Hope studied Susie. She'd be attractive if she didn't hunch over. And she seemed sweet-natured. Had Micah noticed?

He kept his head bent over his plate, staring down at the food. Would it be wrong to hope her own casserole tasted better than Susie's?

Susie carried a plate toward the hospital bed, but when Jabin didn't respond to her whispering his name, she set it on the table beside him. He'd closed his eyes when the women had walked in the room and hadn't opened them since.

Interesting. Didn't he like them? Not that Hope blamed him. They were nice enough, but Sylvia had a plan, and Hope prayed Micah was savvy enough to avoid her clutches. She shook her head to dislodge those thoughts. She had no business longing to be part of Micah's future.

Chapter Eight

Micah accepted his plate from Susie with as polite a *danke* as he could manage. He'd been looking forward to sharing a meal with Hope. Now they'd be forced to make awkward conversation with Sylvia and Susie.

And how would he get rid of them after the meal when Sylvia had made her intention obvious? Susie was a nice-enough girl, he was sure, despite being so shy, but Micah had no interest in dating. At least he hadn't until he met Hope. But Sylvia would probably try to stay until Hope left.

He wished he hadn't asked her to help in the kitchen tomorrow. He could imagine the comments Sylvia would make. The only good thing was he'd be heading back to New York in a few days, so he could escape.

He'd be glad to put this all behind him—the viewing, the funeral, the designing mother—but it also meant leaving Hope for good.

He glanced up to find everyone had been served, and they were all staring at him. "I'm sorry. I—"

"We understand," Sylvia said with kindness. "You have a lot on your mind."

Micah bowed his head for the silent prayer, and they all followed his lead. All except Jabin, who'd retreated into his turtle shell again with closed eyes. Micah sighed inside. He'd also been hoping to keep his nephew awake and talking. But he thanked God for supportive church members, a hot meal, and Hope's kindness.

The conversation turned out to be as uncomfortable as he'd expected, with Susie ducking her head and remaining mute while her mother rattled on about her daughter's skills and good points, all of which guaranteed she'd make a fine wife. For someone else.

He might have been impressed by this catalog of virtues if he hadn't met Hope, who was staring at Susie with an odd expression, one he couldn't interpret. Several times, Hope tried redirecting the conversation, but Sylvia always jumped in to bring the subject back to Susie.

The dinner cart rattled in the hallway. Everyone had finished supper except Jabin, and Micah used that as an excuse to clear the room.

"*Danke fur koomen*. The meal was delicious, Susie. Much better than eating fast food."

Susie's neck, face, and ears blazed bright red. She mumbled, "You're welcome."

"The hospital staff will want to feed Jabin, so—"

Hope jumped to her feet. "We should all go. *Danke* for the meal."

Sylvia gathered her things with reluctance, seeming as if she were waiting for Hope to leave. Chloe skipped across the room and slid her hand into Hope's.

Micah pulled Sylvia's cell phone from his pocket and held it out. "Will you need this tonight?"

"No, no. My husband insists you keep it for the next few days."

"I'm grateful to him and you." When Sylvia's head tilted slightly to indicate her daughter, Micah added, "And to Susie too." He also wanted to thank Hope, but he sensed that might make for hard feelings. He'd wait to thank her privately.

As all the women started out the door, Micah called to Chloe, "I want to speak to you a minute."

She let go of Hope's hand and dragged her feet crossing the room. With no excuse to stay, Sylvia and Susie left, much to Micah's relief.

Are they gone? he mouthed to Hope, who was standing in the doorway, waiting for Chloe.

She peeked down the hall. "Almost to the elevator."

"Whew," he said. Then he directed his attention to Chloe. "Remember, be a good listener."

"I know." Chloe swept her good arm around in the air as if to wave off his concerns.

He turned to Hope. "I really appreciate you taking Chloe. I don't want to leave Jabin alone all night." He swallowed hard. "I know how lonely and scary hospital rooms can be at night when you're his age."

"*Jah*, I'd never want to think of him being by himself after all he's been through. But what about you?"

"I'll stretch out in the chair and prop up my feet." He wasn't sure if he'd be sleeping much tonight. He didn't like the thought of Jabin waking and thinking he was alone, but his nephew might be in the hospital for a week. He couldn't go without sleep for that long.

"Are you sure?" A cute little crease formed on Hope's forehead as she examined him. "You need sleep too. I could stay in the room overnight so you could get a full night's rest."

What a generous offer! He could never accept it, though. "I'll be all right." He pointed to the wicker carrier. "*Danke* for making a meal. I'm sorry we didn't get to eat it. It was kind of you to let Sylvia serve the meal she'd brought."

"I didn't want to hurt her feelings," Hope said.

Her thoughtfulness for others came out in everything she did. "I wish we hadn't hurt yours."

At the gentleness and caring in his tone, Hope's pulse fluttered. She glanced at Chloe to avoid letting Micah see her reaction. Chloe had her cast propped on the bed rail and was whispering to Jabin.

Luckily, a light tap sounded on the door, and a nurse entered, carrying a tray for Jabin. "Good to see he's awake." She pushed the rolling table over to the bed and set down the tray. "And how are you doing, young lady?" she asked Chloe.

Jabin squeezed his eyes shut and pinched his lips together as the nurse adjusted the bed.

"Does that hurt?" Chloe asked him.

He squinted one eye. "*Jah.*"

"My arm hurts too," she informed him.

"But you got a cast." He sounded jealous.

"It's not as fun as it looks."

Hope smiled at the two of them, but then Micah sat beside Jabin to pray with him and help him eat. His tenderness and gentleness touched her. What a wonderful father he'd be. The more she was around Micah, the more she found herself drawn to him. No matter how much she tried, she couldn't stop the feelings that flooded through her as he supported Jabin's left arm to help him lift the plastic fork to his lips.

"I know it's not easy to use this hand, but you're getting better every time," Micah assured the little boy.

Jabin missed his first stab at his mouth.

"It's all right. Let's try again." Micah moved up his hand to support Jabin's wrist. The bite went in, and Jabin chewed.

"At least my broken arm is on the left side," Chloe said.

Micah nodded in her direction. "You should thank God for that blessing."

Watching Jabin eat was distressing. But the little boy's sighs and disappointed looks when he spilled food or missed his mouth were offset by his *onkel*'s patience and encouragement. Because Micah was so engrossed in his task, Hope could stare at him without being noticed. Chloe hung over the bed rail, offering mostly unhelpful comments.

Perhaps for her own benefit, Hope should leave, but she waited until Jabin had finished his meal, then she stood. "*Daed* will be wondering where I am, so I'd better head off now."

"You're taking me?" Chloe screeched and raced over to join her.

"Of course I am." Hope bent to pick up the wicker carrier and set a hand on Chloe's shoulder, a difficult task when the little girl was bouncing up and down on her toes.

"Chloe," Micah said, "calm down or Hope might change her mind."

Her eyes wide, Chloe looked up at Hope. "You wouldn't, would you?"

"No," she assured her. Then she turned her attention to Micah. "I'd be happy to keep Chloe overnight for the next few days. And I can bring her to the hospital for visits." *And to the funeral*. Hope didn't want to remind any of them of that, so she didn't say it aloud.

"You really wouldn't mind?" Micah stopped assisting Jabin and studied her face.

This time, she made the mistake of meeting his gaze. Something more than gratitude flickered in his eyes for a second. That flare of interest spelled danger. Hope forced herself to look away. She wanted—no, needed—to keep this businesslike.

Micah must have sensed her attitude because he offered, "I'd be willing to pay you for your help."

Hope had only volunteered to be neighborly. And because she cared what happened to these motherless children. All right, so maybe it was also because the children's *onkel* intrigued her. She quickly squashed that thought. "I couldn't accept anything for taking care of Chloe."

"I insist." The firmness in Micah's voice made it clear he wouldn't accept her protests.

She'd save those for when he actually tried to hand her money. As much as extra income would be welcome right now, she'd never take it for helping someone in need.

Micah was surprised when she didn't argue. Paying her would ease some of his guilt for all the time she'd spent with him and the children. And it would help to keep her out of his mind in more personal ways.

"I'll bring Chloe back tomorrow," Hope said. "And just so you know, the house is spotless. I'm sure some of Anna's relatives will still come to clean, but—" She broke off at the panicked look in his eyes. "What?"

"Anna's relatives," he echoed faintly. "I forgot about inviting them. I don't know who to call." His brain seemed to be engulfed in a cloud, and all logical thought had disappeared. He couldn't even concentrate on normal tasks.

"Why don't you ask the woman who stopped by earlier—Sylvia?—to put you in touch with Anna's relatives?"

Micah held up the cell. "Because I have her phone."

Hope's cheeks turned a deep, rosy pink, making her even more attractive. "*Ach*, you must think I'm foolish."

He laughed, although the sound had a hollow echo that hurt his chest and his heart. "We're both suffering from lack of sleep. At least I know I'm not thinking straight."

"That's understandable." Hope's words and sympathetic look soothed like a caress.

Micah jerked his thoughts back from wandering in that direction. He needed to concentrate on funeral plans. "I know Anna's family. Most of them, that is."

He'd met them at the wedding, and some of them had dropped by when he'd visited. Right now, though, he could only conjure up vague glimpses of their faces. The names escaped him.

"Why not call one of them? Perhaps Anna's *mamm*?"

Carolyn. He remembered her name. That was a blessing. Did shock combined with lack of sleep make you so logy-headed?

"I should have done that immediately after you called last night." He'd been so focused on Ben and getting to the hospital to care for the twins, Anna's family had slipped his mind.

"You had a lot to do."

"That's no excuse." Brain fog should not have blocked out his duty to notify Anna's relatives. The only thing he could do now was to rectify his mistake.

"Are they local?" Hope kept bringing him back to the issue at hand.

Grateful for her prodding, Micah racked his memory. When he'd been here a few weeks ago, Anna had been missing her widowed *mamm* and two younger sisters, who'd moved to Smicksburg to live with her oldest brother.

"No, they live in Indiana County, a bit north of Pittsburgh." They'd need to get someone to care for the farm, gardens, and animals. They'd also have a four-hour trip by car. The sooner he called, the better. "I think all Anna's brothers live around Smicksburg too."

Hope helped him locate a phone number for Anna's

brother, who owned a meat market. He advertised online and had a phone number on his website. Taking a deep breath, Micah dialed and asked for Levi.

His voice wavered as he conveyed the news, and once again, Hope reached out and squeezed his hand. She let go after he hung up, disappointing him. If he'd been brave enough, he might have flipped over his hand to entwine his fingers with hers.

When he turned in her direction, she lowered her eyes and blushed.

"*Danke*," he said softly. "I can't tell you what that meant to me." Maybe he shouldn't have confessed. But her fleeting half smile before she ducked her head made him happy he had.

Hope had fought an inner battle between consoling Micah and protecting herself, but comforting him won out. His gratitude showed she'd made the right decision. At the time. Unfortunately, now she wished she could keep holding his hand.

"I–I'd better go. I'm sure Chloe's tired." And so was Hope. No doubt Micah was too.

"I'm not tired," Chloe protested, despite her yawns and sleepy eyes.

She let Hope guide her out the door. Before it closed behind them, Hope said, "Why don't I bring lunch tomorrow? Then you can decide when you want Chloe for—" She glanced at the little girl and couldn't bring herself to say *viewing*. How did a child this young deal with that?

Micah's face turned grim. "I've been trying to put that out of my mind, but I haven't succeeded. We can decide what to do."

"I'll stay with Jabin while you're gone tomorrow night."

"You've done so much already." Micah appeared overwhelmed, but a shutter descended over his features. "We can work out the payment at the end, unless you prefer that I pay you each day." He reached for his wallet, but Hope waved it away.

If it allowed him to accept the help he needed, she'd play along. Then, when it was time for him to settle his bill, she'd disappear. Why did the thought of never seeing him again make her so sad?

Chapter Nine

Micah stood in the doorway until Hope and Chloe disappeared into the elevator. Every time Hope walked away, a part of him went with her. He shook away the fanciful thought and went back into the room.

Jabin's eyes were drooping. By the time the nurse had removed the tray and lowered the bed, his nephew's breathing had slowed to sleeplike rhythms.

"If you're still awake," Micah whispered, "I want you to know I'll be right here all night long. You can wake me anytime you need me."

He dragged two chairs close to the bed, propped up his feet, clasped Jabin's hand, and fell asleep.

Whimpering woke Micah in the middle of the night. He opened his eyes to the nightmare of a hospital room. All his old fears flooded back, drowning him. Choking, struggling to breathe, he fought his way to the surface.

Slowly, the room came into focus. He wasn't trapped here alone. He wasn't a child any longer. Relief coursed through him, but his chest still ached from the rapid banging of his heart.

"Jabin, I'm right here."

His nephew gripped his hand so hard it hurt.

"It's all right. I won't leave you," Micah repeated over and over until Jabin fell back into a restless sleep.

Despite being overtired, Micah struggled to relax and drift off. He had so much to do, to figure out, to get through. How would he make it through the next few days while grieving for his brother and sister-in-law as well as trying to help the twins deal with their loss? Not to mention how they'd make it through the rest of their lives without their parents.

Micah woke early the next morning with a crick in his neck and dread in his stomach. He had a twinge in his back from sleeping in an uncomfortable position. And after holding his nephew's hand all night, Micah's arm muscles burned. But that was minor compared to what he had to face that day.

Micah grabbed a quick cup of coffee and a muffin in the snack shop and rushed back to the room, praying he'd make it before his nephew woke. He'd only eaten a few bites when Jabin moaned and rolled over. His face bleak, he only picked at his breakfast despite Micah's assistance and encouragement.

After the nurse came in to check on Jabin, he kept his eyes open, but their dullness worried Micah. Jabin barely responded to Micah's questions or attempts to start a conversation. Although his nephew's questions yesterday had been challenging, Micah preferred those to this silence.

A knock on the door provided a welcome interruption. Although his expression remained lackluster, Jabin at least turned toward the door.

"Eli," he said as a young Amish man entered, took off his straw hat, and rotated it nervously in his hands.

"Hey, Jabin." Eli's tense smile didn't reach his eyes, which were filled with compassion. "I'm so sorry about your *mamm* and *daed*."

For the first time that morning, Jabin managed a full sentence. "Micah says God won't bring them back."

Eli's brows rose, but he quickly lowered them. His face sober, he said, "I think he's right."

Jabin turned his head and burrowed it into the pillow, and his shoulders shook.

Taking a step toward the bed as if he wanted to comfort Jabin, the man hesitated as Micah stroked the back of Jabin's head.

"I'm Eli Chupp, the assistant manager at your brother's harness shop. I'm sorry to bother you, but Sylvia told me I could find you here."

Micah inclined his head in greeting. The harness shop had once belonged to *Daed,* and before that, to *Dawdi.* The shop where he'd been kicked by a horse. The shop he'd dreaded to enter every day they'd lived here. Just the thought of it gave him chills.

"I'm so sorry about Ben and Anna." Eli choked a bit, then cleared his throat. "They were a wonderful couple."

"*Danke.*" Micah's mind remained on the shop. One more thing he should have dealt with yesterday, after he called Carolyn. Anna's family would be arriving at the house in the early afternoon, and Micah needed to be there to greet them.

Eli shuffled his feet, and Micah turned his attention back to the room. If Eli wasn't careful, he might tear his hat.

"I hope it was all right," Eli said, "that I closed the shop and put a sign on the door that the business would be shut until Monday. Meanwhile, I've worked to get pressing orders filled and delivered. I've also taken over all Ben's duties until you decide what to do with the business."

"I appreciate that. I'll need to talk to *Daed* about the business."

With a nod, Eli headed for the door. "I'll do whatever

needs to be done while you're deciding. If you choose to sell, I'd be willing to buy it."

That might be the best solution. Micah had no desire to run the business, and *Daed* wouldn't move back to Pennsylvania now. "I'll let you know as soon as we've figured it out."

Hope had risen at dawn and tiptoed downstairs so she wouldn't wake Chloe. The little girl had wanted to sleep in Hope's room last night, so she'd curled up in the bed that had once belonged to Hope's older sister. The beds were close enough that Hope could reach out to hold Chloe's hand to comfort her several times during the night when she woke.

The first time, Chloe had been frightened by *Daed*'s snores, but Hope compared the noise to a train rumbling through the house, tooting its shrill whistle, which sent Chloe into gales of giggles.

"You have a train in your house?" she gasped after another belly laugh.

"Sounds like it, doesn't it?" Hope was glad the little girl could laugh. She'd be facing dismal days tomorrow and Saturday.

The next two times Chloe woke sobbing, Hope padded out of bed to hold her until she fell asleep.

Two nights with little or no sleep had taken a toll on Hope. Her low energy made every task seem difficult. She'd finished caring for the horses and mucking out the stalls when Chloe pattered into the barn. She'd dressed herself, and the sleeve was flapping. Strands of hair had pulled loose from the braid flopping down her back.

"Let's get you pinned up," Hope suggested, but they'd need to get the little girl a gray dress for the funeral. Maybe

Priscilla's younger sisters had a mourning dress. Their grandmother had passed more than a year ago.

After Hope had fixed Chloe's dress and hair, they made breakfast together. When Hope's *daed* entered the kitchen, Chloe giggled. She clapped a hand over her mouth, but stifling the sound only resulted in explosive snorts.

"What's so funny?" *Daed* asked.

Hope was torn between answering truthfully or changing the subject, but Chloe responded amid snickers, "We heard a train in the house last night."

With a puzzled look, *Daed* glanced from Chloe to Hope. "We're not near a station."

Hope set a hand on Chloe's shoulder, hoping to keep her quiet.

It didn't work. Pointing to his mouth, Chloe said, "The train came from there." When he still didn't seem to understand, Chloe said, "You have the best snores."

"I see." *Daed*'s face turned ruddy. He stayed silent while they served the meal and bowed for prayer. After they lifted their heads, though, he carried on a conversation as if nothing had happened earlier, and he was especially gentle with Chloe.

It reminded her of how he used to be when she was small, and Hope longed to have that *Daed* back. He even helped clear the table as Chloe and he chattered. Hope wished they could stay and spend the day with him, but she needed to get Chloe to the hospital.

"Sorry we have to leave, *Daed*."

He didn't even try to hide his disappointment. "I hope you'll bring Chloe back for another visit."

"I think she'll be sleeping here tonight and tomorrow," Hope told him.

"*Gut*. I'll look forward to it." He bent down to Chloe's level. "I'll do my best train imitation."

She giggled and threw her arms around his neck in a fierce hug.

When *Daed* stood, his eyes were shiny with tears. "I miss you being that age."

Hope did too. But she'd loved seeing this glimpse of her *daed*. If only Chloe could visit regularly. Maybe having a little one around would help. They'd miss her when she moved to New York.

Close to lunchtime, Hope and Chloe arrived at the hospital carrying the wicker basket and a gray outfit for Jabin. Micah's heart leaped when they appeared in the doorway. Chloe had on a gray dress, and her hair was neatly done in a bob.

"I didn't even think about their clothing," he said as Hope entered the room. "I can't thank you enough." One more thing he'd need to pay her for. "Where did you get the clothing?"

"They're hand-me-downs from my friend Priscilla. They don't want them back. Chloe's is a little loose, but Priscilla's sister is nine. I hemmed it up and took out the sleeve seam for the cast. I could take it in a bit, but I thought the larger size would make it easier for her to get it on and off."

Chloe bounced around the room. "Today we get to eat my casserole."

"It smells delicious," Micah told her, but his gaze remained fixed on Hope, who'd set the carrier on the windowsill and lifted out a glass dish.

Even Jabin perked up. Perhaps he was hungry enough to eat some of this meal after barely touching his breakfast. Ordinarily, Micah would have insisted on a clean plate, but with the viewing today, he let it go.

Hope and Chloe dished out the meal onto four plates, and after prayers, they all dug in. Micah wasn't sure if it was the company, his skimpy breakfast, or Hope's superior cooking skills, but this rewarmed Yumasetti casserole tasted ten times better than last night's.

For a while, everyone ate quietly. Micah sat beside Jabin and used his left hand to help his nephew lift forkfuls to his mouth, while he shoveled in his own meal with his right hand. They all laughed when one large, shaky left hand tried to help the smaller one but missed Jabin's mouth or dropped food.

"Well, Jabin, I can see how hard left-handed eating is. Maybe I need to switch to helping you with my right." As much as he disliked doing it, he had to turn his back on Hope. Maybe it was just as well, because whenever he faced her, his eating was as clumsy as Jabin's.

After they finished, Hope placed the plates back in the carrier and pulled out decks of Dutch Blitz cards. Micah longed to stay, but he needed to meet Carolyn at the house. They might already be there, cleaning.

"I thought it might keep them busy this afternoon." Hope cleaned Jabin's tray and set down the cards.

"I want the ones with the buggy on it," Jabin said.

Chloe thrust out her lip. "I do too."

"I like the green pump best. Or what about the yellow bucket?" Hope asked, but neither of them seemed interested in the other decks. "I guess we'll have to take turns."

Micah marveled at her patience as she got the twins to agree on who would get the cards first.

"I'd better get over to the house." He'd arranged for the funeral home to come at one thirty. That wouldn't give Carolyn much time to clean the living and dining room.

He took one last look at the three of them bent over the cards, haggling over how to make the rules fair to Jabin.

They all decided Hope should play left-handed. By the time Micah closed the door, Chloe was complaining her cast would slow her down. Jabin countered that his injuries slowed him down.

Knowing he was leaving them with Hope eased one of his worries, but another began as soon as he walked into his brother's house. Anna's mother, Carolyn, and her two daughters had arrived to clean along with Micah's three sisters, but so had Sylvia and Susie.

His sisters and Carolyn hurried over to hug him. Sylvia trailed behind them, shepherding her daughter in front of her.

"We came early this morning so your relatives didn't need to do much cleaning after their long trip," Sylvia announced. "Didn't we, Susie?"

After taking a surreptitious glance at Micah, Susie lowered her gaze and nodded.

"I'm so glad Susie is a good housekeeper," Sylvia said. "It made the job much easier for me. She's such a good, helpful daughter."

"*Jah*," Carolyn agreed. "It's wunderbar to have dependable daughters. And we appreciate all the cleaning you've done."

Sylvia appeared miffed that the praise had come from Carolyn rather than Micah.

"Thank you both," he said. Although he sensed he'd been supposed to praise Susie, he'd rather not give the wrong impression.

Micah wished he could escape up to his old bedroom and spend a little time alone before he had to face the viewing.

Please, Lord, give me the strength to—

"The hearse is here," Sylvia announced.

Susie tugged at her mother's arm. "Maybe we should go into the kitchen, *Mamm*."

Micah was amazed. It was the first full sentence he'd heard Susie speak. It must be hard to talk when your mother was so garrulous. He didn't have time to consider it more. He headed to the door.

Carolyn came up beside him, her eyes damp. "I found Anna's wedding dress."

Micah swallowed hard. That's what she'd be buried in. The dress she'd worn the day he'd been in Ben's wedding party, sat beside his brother at the meal . . .

Micah's throat closed, trapping waves of grief in his chest that pressed against his rib cage.

How jealous he'd been of Ben that day. Not because Micah wanted Anna as a wife, but because his brother had found love. And because, as usual, Ben's life seemed perfect. If only Micah had known what a brief time his brother would have on earth, would he have begrudged Ben his happiness?

Micah's sisters joined them, and his oldest sister put her arm around his youngest sister. "Elizabeth stayed up most of the night making Ben's white outfit. He is—was"—her voice broke—"about the same size as John, so she had a pattern."

Elizabeth waved away the praise. "I don't have as many little ones as you two."

First Hope, then Elizabeth and Carolyn. Without their help, he'd never have been prepared. And he supposed Susie and Sylvia should be on that list.

Now he had to get through the rest of today.

The lively game kept Jabin and Chloe occupied for several hours, with each demanding a turn with the buggy deck. Hope slowed her own reaction times to let the twins be first to place their number cards. And the rivalry was punctuated by lighthearted teasing and spontaneous laughter.

All the while they were playing, Hope's mind was on Micah, sending prayers and sympathy. She couldn't imagine how he'd fare.

When he finally arrived, his face somber, both children stopped their friendly argument and picked up his mood. For a few hours, they'd become immersed in their game and had forgotten the truth. Reality set in, and even the white Styrofoam boxes he carried didn't lift their spirits.

"One of the firehouses I passed was having a chicken barbecue," Micah said. "I know the twins like that. I hope you do too."

"It's one of my favorites." Hope loved the aroma of grilling meat wafting in the air, and biting into the crispy skin delighted her. "Thank you so much," she said as she accepted the box from him.

Micah glanced at Jabin's rolling table spread with the uncompleted game. "Did you want to finish up?"

Chloe swept all the cards into her hands while Jabin squawked and protested, "I was winning. I only had one more card left."

Micah held up a hand to stop them and set a box in front of Jabin.

His nephew inhaled deeply. "Yum." With one sniff, the fight was forgotten.

Micah cut the chicken and baked potato into manageable sections for Jabin. "The nice thing about this meal is that you can eat most of it with your fingers."

Then he opened his own box. "I thought if I ate now . . ." The lines around his mouth deepened.

"I understand," Hope told him. And she did. Despite all

the delicious food at *Mamm*'s viewing and funeral, she couldn't eat a bite. And she'd cared little for food during the dark days that followed. If only she had a way to be there for Micah.

When he finished his meal, he rose. "Chloe, let's get you cleaned up."

Chloe had barbecue sauce smeared around her mouth and all over her fingers

Hope jumped up. "I can do that." She led the little girl to the bathroom and gently wiped her face and hands. A few spots had landed on her dress, and Hope scrubbed at those.

Chloe's chin wobbled. "I don't want to go."

Hope knelt and enfolded the small girl in her arms. "I know." She wished she could erase Chloe's pain. The only thing Hope could do was pray.

Dear Lord, please comfort her and surround her with Your love.

Although losing their parents was devastating, the twins had Micah. He'd love and care for them. Nothing could replace their *mamm* and *daed*, but they'd be surrounded by a close, loving family.

Hope led Chloe out of the bathroom, and Micah took her hand.

"We'd better go." His complexion drained of color and strain lines bracketing his eyes and mouth, he took Chloe's hand and headed out the door.

Hope ached for them. As Jabin watched them go, his face scrunched up. She went over and took his hand, still sticky with barbecue sauce. She sat with him, murmuring soothing words, wishing she could sweep him into her arms for a tight hug to comfort him.

After a while, she said, "Maybe we should clean you

up before the nurse comes in to check you." She lifted his hand, tucked in hers. "We're stuck together with barbecue sauce."

A slight giggle came from his lips, but the sadness remained in his eyes.

"I'll get some wet paper towels from the bathroom."

Tears formed in his eyes as she gently wiped his hands and face with the damp towels, and Hope wondered if he was remembering his *mamm* cleaning him up after meals.

"Would you like to play some more Dutch Blitz?" she asked.

His lackluster *jah* seemed unenthusiastic. But she quickly cleaned up the table and discarded the empty boxes.

When she picked up the messy pile of cards Chloe had swept off the table, she said, "You can have the buggy cards all to yourself."

A little gleam of excitement flickered in his eyes, and Hope prayed the card game would provide a distraction. After they'd sorted the cards, she handed him the ones with the red buggy on them, and he grinned.

By the time he'd won the second game, he was crowing. Hope loved hearing him shout, "Blitz!" when he laid down his last card. He won five out of the six games. She only won her game because Jabin looked suspicious after the fourth round, and she didn't want him to suspect she'd been letting him win.

"Wait until Chloe hears how many games I won!" Jabin's proud grin stretched across his face. "She won't believe it, but you'll tell her, won't you?"

"Of course."

He basked in his wins for a few minutes, then his face crumpled. "I didn't get to say goodbye to *Mamm* and

Daed." He hunkered down in the bed and buried his head in the pillow.

Her heart heavy, Hope sat beside him and stroked the back of his head. How did children get over something like this? Then she sent up prayers for all three of them.

Chapter Ten

The past two days had drained Micah. Getting through the viewing and funeral. Holding Chloe's hand during the burial. Knowing he'd never see Ben and Anna again. Missing his *mamm* as he and *Daed* stood side by side. Agonizing for Chloe and Jabin, who would grow up without their parents.

Because they had an off-Sunday in the church district the next day, some of the relatives and church members visited Jabin in the hospital. Hope had attended her own church, but she came by to pick up Chloe that evening. His niece went with her, chattering about a train whistle. Micah was grateful for the light moments Hope provided for the twins.

Early Monday morning, Carolyn and her daughters departed for home. Micah breathed a sigh of relief that Sylvia and Susie, who'd insisted on staying all day Saturday after the funeral to clean up, and came again to visit the family all day Sunday, had not shown up as he bid them goodbye.

Through all the gloom, one shining light stood out and comforted Micah. Hope always seemed to arrive whenever he needed her. Unlike Sylvia, she never outstayed her welcome, and her help never felt intrusive. No amount of money would ever repay what she'd done for him and the twins. He wished he could let her know how much she meant to all three of them, but he was afraid he might reveal too much if he tried. He'd limit it to a thank-you note once he returned home.

Micah worried the twins had gotten too attached to Hope, and it would be as painful for them to leave as it would be for him. He'd be torn up inside when that day came.

Shortly after Carolyn left, the doctor announced they'd be discharging Jabin that morning. Although Micah was thrilled Jabin was well enough to go home, it meant they'd be departing much sooner than he'd expected.

Micah helped Jabin dress in the gray shirt Hope had brought. Jabin had gotten a roommate over the weekend, so the two boys chattered while Micah called Debbie. She was delighted not only to pick them up from the hospital but also offered to drive them to New York when they were ready to head back.

"I suppose if you're free and don't mind doing the drive, we should probably leave right after I pack up some things for the children." His spirits sank when she agreed she'd be happy to go today. He wasn't ready yet, but what excuse did he have to stay?

Hope woke tense and nervous on Monday morning. In a few hours, she and Logan would have their first student. If the session went well, they might convince his family to let him keep coming. Logan had planned everything ahead of time, so it should go smoothly, but this was the start of her business.

After a long prayer, which included petitions for Micah and the twins as well as for the new student, Hope headed downstairs to do the morning chores. To her surprise, *Daed* was sitting in the living room.

"Is the little girl here today?" he asked, his voice full of eagerness.

"Yes, she is. She was still sleeping when I left the room, but maybe you could listen for her while I go out to take care of the horses."

"Of course." His attempt at sounding nonchalant was spoiled by the excited twinkle in his eyes.

Hope smiled to herself as she fed the mares and mucked the stalls. Having Chloe around the past few days had been a joy for her *daed*. They were both going to miss her when she went to New York. And Hope pulled her thoughts away from the other person she'd miss more.

When she went into the house, *Daed*'s deep belly laugh overpowered Chloe's high-pitched giggles. How long had it been since *Daed* had laughed? Much too long. Not since *Mamm* had gotten sick.

Hope went into the kitchen to fix breakfast, and *Daed* and Chloe soon joined her, their faces bright and cheerful. While Chloe helped Hope make the oatmeal, *Daed* got out bowls and spoons and even poured glasses of juice. Her father helping in the kitchen was a first. Hope shot him a grateful glance.

After they sat at the table and prayed, she turned to her *daed*. "I have my first student coming for a session at eight. Would you be able to watch Chloe?"

With a huge grin on his face, *Daed* said, "I'd be delighted." He beamed at Chloe. "We'll have fun, won't we?"

She nodded, looking just as happy. Hope finished the meal with joy in her heart. If only *Daed* had something like this to do every day, it would help. He even stayed in the kitchen to dry the dishes. Then he and Chloe went into the living room together, and Hope met Logan in the barn to prepare.

By the time their first student arrived at a few minutes before eight, they were ready. Liam had never been around horses before, his grandmother informed them.

"In that case, it's best to begin by letting him get to know a horse," Hope told her. "We thought Molly might be a good mare for Liam."

"Once he's comfortable around the horse," Logan said, "if you choose to continue lessons, we'll teach him to groom, then to tack. Depending on how things progress, he may move on to riding." After giving a brief overview of the skills they'd be working on, Logan headed for a nearby stall, and Hope introduced Liam to the mare they'd chosen for him.

Liam shrank away as he watched Hope stroke and pat the horse. She explained what horses preferred and demonstrated where to touch Molly. Eventually, Liam approached, and with Hope's encouragement, he stayed an arm's length from Molly and tentatively put his fingers on her neck. His eyes widened, and he stepped back out of reach. Hope repeated her movements, and Liam studied her hands. The second time, he smoothed his hand along Molly's coat.

Gradually, he grew less tentative, and Hope was thrilled to see the wariness in his face relax. By the end of the lesson, he'd moved much closer to the horse, and the repetitive petting seemed to calm and soothe him.

When the time was up, Liam didn't want to leave. Logan encouraged him by showing him how to close and secure the stall door. Then he and Liam strolled along to meet the other horses, while Hope took his grandmother into the office.

"It seems as if Liam enjoyed his introductory class," Hope remarked as she offered his grandmother a chair.

Mrs. Snyder smiled. "I was very impressed with how you helped him to overcome his fears."

"He was very brave today. I think he'd gain a lot from working with the horses. Today we worked on sensory integration and following directions."

"I could see him get calmer as the lesson progressed. Liam seems very comfortable with you, and he seems to love being around the horses. Do you think it will be helpful to him in other ways?"

"Animal therapy helps autistic children, so I think working with horses will be good for him. I have a paper here that explains some of the benefits." Hope handed Liam's grandmother a copy of the information sheet she and Logan had created.

Mrs. Snyder perused the list. "I'm glad to see fine motor skills and speech development on here. Both of those will also help Liam. So, what are your rates?"

Hope gulped and told her. What if they'd set their prices too high?

After tapping her lip for a few moments, Mrs. Snyder said, "That's for a series of six sessions?" When Hope nodded, Liam's grandmother pulled out a calendar. "The thing is, I only have Liam two days a week once school starts. He'll be with me on Monday and Wednesday afternoons."

"What time were you thinking?" Hope held her breath as Liam's grandmother glanced out the window, seeming lost in thought. Would she sign him up for lessons?

"We could probably make it at four. Would that fit your schedule?"

Hope glanced at her calendar. They had a girl scheduled for next Monday afternoon, but Wednesday at four was open. "Would you like to start next Wednesday?" She hoped she didn't come across as overly eager, and then held her breath as she waited for an answer.

"I'm so glad you have openings." Mrs. Snyder reached into her purse and pulled out a checkbook. "Is a check all right?"

"That'll be fine." Wunderbar, actually. Fantastic. They were signing up a student!

Hope tamped down her excitement and thanked Mrs. Snyder calmly. She longed to run out and wave the check in front of Logan, but she reached into the lower drawer, pulled out the cashbox, and slipped the check under the bill tray.

Then she walked Liam's grandmother down to the stall where her grandson was waiting with Logan. When Mrs. Snyder took Liam's hand and walked toward the door, Logan lifted an eyebrow behind her back. Hope nodded, and Logan gave her a thumbs-up.

After Liam's grandmother drove away, Logan grabbed Hope's hands and twirled her around. "Great job!"

Although she appreciated his enthusiasm, she disliked him touching her. Holding hands with him was nothing like comforting Micah. She disentangled her hands and put distance between them, ignoring Logan's crestfallen expression.

Micah used the phone in the hospital room to call Debbie, and then he helped Jabin dress. After the driver arrived, an aide pushed Jabin down to the car in a wheelchair despite his protests. Micah settled him into the back seat before sliding into the front seat beside the chattering driver. The closer they got to the house, the more morose Jabin became. Once they arrived and went inside, he withdrew into himself.

An ache started deep in Micah's chest as Jabin circled from room to room, stopping to set his *daed*'s favorite rocking chair in motion, to run his hand over the kitchen chairs where his parents sat, to touch each glass jar his *mamm* had canned.

Rather than interrupting him, Micah went upstairs to pack the children's clothing. He rolled up a blanket from each of their beds. Perhaps having something familiar might ease some of their loneliness and grief. He carried everything out to Debbie's trunk, and when he returned, Jabin had disappeared.

Micah searched both floors before he found his nephew curled up on his parents' bed, nose buried in the pillows. Although Micah thought Jabin was sniffling into the covers, he was mistaken. His nephew was sniffing. Did the pillows still carry the scent of his *mamm* and *daed*?

If walking through the rooms and seeing the familiar objects tore Micah apart inside, how was this affecting Jabin? The house was exactly the same as the day he had left it, yet everything had changed. As much as Micah longed to hold his nephew, the way Jabin's body hunched in on itself revealed that he wasn't ready to accept physical comfort.

To give Jabin some privacy, Micah went downstairs to prepare sandwiches for the trip. He made extras so they could share with Debbie. When he returned, Jabin was in his own room, hugging a small teddy bear.

"Do you want to take your teddy along with you?" Micah set down a large cloth bag he'd found in the pantry. "Why don't you fill this bag with anything you and Chloe like to play with? Bring a few toys and books for the car and at the house."

A short while later, Jabin headed down the hall dragging Chloe's doll by one leg. The grocery bag bumped along behind him.

"Let me get that." Micah hurried over to take the bag filled with books, several jigsaw puzzles, crayons, and a coloring book. Then he rescued Chloe's doll. He wanted to pick up Jabin too, but when Micah knelt in front of his nephew and held out his arms, Jabin backed away.

Ignoring Micah, he sidled along the wall, stepped around Micah, and trudged downstairs with his head down. Rather than heading for the front door, he plodded to the back door and outside to the barn. Micah found him there moving from stall to stall, staring at the two cows, the family's other horse, and the pony.

Micah was relieved to see the stalls had been cleaned. The kindly neighbor who had been caring for the animals had offered to keep doing so until Micah returned from New York to sell the house. Micah was dreading that. He and *Daed* also needed to decide what to do about the business.

After Jabin reached the end of the row, Micah approached him. "We need to pick up Chloe." He tried to take Jabin's hand, but his nephew jerked away.

The pony whinnied and stuck his head over the low stall door. Micah held his breath as Jabin leaned close to rub the pony's nose.

Micah's inner alarm clanged loudly, and he struggled to stay rational. The pony was small, and the worst it could do was kick the wood slats. *It won't hurt Jabin. He's safe.* But Micah's nerves didn't calm until Jabin stepped back.

"I'm sorry," Micah said as he picked up Jabin. "We need to get to Hope's before she leaves for the hospital."

His nephew went rigid, and the silent protest made Micah hurt for the small boy who had lost so much. Micah wished they could stay longer because Jabin hadn't had the opportunity to say proper goodbyes. Perhaps after they picked up Chloe, he could bring them back here.

If only he'd thought to call Hope from the hospital room to warn her that Jabin had been discharged. He hadn't expected to take so long here at the house. It was already close to eleven. If Hope stuck to her usual schedule, she'd keep Chloe until noon, but if she decided to leave early, he had no way to contact her because he'd returned Sylvia's cell phone after the funeral.

Jabin stiffened even more when Micah carried him to the car. Micah mentally berated himself for not allowing enough time for Jabin to mourn. "I'm sorry, Jabin. I understand you aren't ready to leave yet, but we have to catch Hope. If you want more time, I'll bring you back here later."

Jabin only crossed his arms and didn't answer. Micah shut the car door and climbed in up front beside Debbie, who eyed Jabin in the rearview mirror.

"Poor kid," she said softly. "He's had so much to bear."

And, unfortunately, it was just beginning.

Keeping a safe distance from Logan, Hope headed into the office to discuss what they hoped to accomplish during Liam's next lessons, how they could have improved that day's session, and to make notes on the upcoming appointments. Then they spent a few hours making benefit lists for the children who would be coming for introductory lessons.

"These will help parents realize how we can help their children." Logan smiled at her. "I'm glad you came up with the idea."

Hope couldn't take credit for it. "I mainly wanted them for myself, to help me understand more about the goals of the therapy. I'm glad they'll be helpful for the parents."

She glanced at the clock. A little after eleven. "I need to

get going soon." She and Chloe had to make a meal and get to the hospital.

"Why don't we finish this one," Logan suggested, "so I can make copies for our files?" He glanced around the spartan office. "Would be nice to get a copier here."

So far, Hope had resisted getting office equipment that needed electricity, and Logan regularly complained about the inconvenience. She didn't have the funds for big expenses, but she also preferred not to make the business too worldly.

After they finished the final information sheet, Logan tucked it into his carrier bag along with his laptop and stood. Hope stayed seated with the desk between them, and Logan's disappointment was obvious.

She waited until his car pulled out before leaving the office. Then Hope headed toward the house with a bounce in her step. Their first student! They were on their way.

As she mounted the porch steps, an unfamiliar car pulled into the driveway. Another family interested in an introductory session? She paused and waited, but when the door opened, Micah emerged.

Hope hurried toward him. "What are you doing here?" She didn't mean to sound unwelcoming. Seeing him here was a surprise.

"The doctor discharged Jabin this morning, so Debbie is going to drive us back to New York."

New York? They were leaving? *He* was leaving? She hoped her dismay didn't show on her face. She'd enjoyed getting to know him and wanted to spend more time with him. She swallowed her own disappointment. "I–I'm glad Jabin is well enough to get out of the hospital."

"So am I."

Hope wasn't positive, but she thought he sounded discouraged. "Is everything all right?"

Micah glanced over his shoulder at the car. "Jabin's not doing well."

"Then why did they discharge him?"

A slight frown appeared on his brow. "I didn't mean physically. We just came from the house, and I don't think he had enough time there. He's sad, and I don't know how to help him."

Hope longed to reach out and comfort Micah. "Keep loving him and give him time."

"I plan to, but I wish I had a way to erase some of his pain."

If they weren't leaving for New York, she'd offer him free horse therapy. "Some children act out when they're grieving. Others hold it inside."

Chloe burst through the door, yelling, "Hope? Hope? Where are you? We'll be late!"

An ironic smile crossed Micah's face. "I suppose I don't have to worry too much about her dealing with her grief. She'll let it spill out. But that doesn't mean she won't be in pain."

"Oh, there you are." As Chloe rushed toward the barn, she spotted them and veered in their direction. "Micah, what are you doing here? Is Jabin all by himself in the hospital?" The questions flew out of her mouth without a break between them for an answer.

Before she could launch into another one, Micah held up a hand. "Jabin's in the car."

"He is? He's out of the hospital?" She dashed over and yanked open the car door. "Jabin, you're back."

Hope and Micah followed her. Jabin sat stone-faced and silent.

"What's the matter with you? Why aren't you looking at me? Are you mad at me?" Chloe demanded.

Micah set a hand on her shoulder. "He's not angry with you. He's sad because we went to the house. He wanted to stay longer." In a low voice only Hope could hear, he added, "He needed more time."

Hope hadn't realized how close she stood to him until he turned. They'd both moved nearer to the car door when they bent down to see Chloe and Jabin. Hope's insides fluttered as he looked at her. She squeezed her eyes shut a moment to get her runaway pulse under control.

"I'd like to get on the road, but I feel like I should take him back to the house for a while." Micah looked uncertain.

"That might help."

"But what if it only adds to his grief?"

"Why don't you ask him—?"

Chloe's scream interrupted her. "My doll," she screeched as she ran around to the other side of the car. "What is she doing here?" She yanked open the door and climbed onto the seat to snatch it up. Cradling the doll in her arms, she demanded, "Who put my doll in this car?"

"Your *onkel* did," Debbie said. "He wanted you to have something special for the trip. Wasn't that nice of him?" She beamed at Chloe. "Why don't you put on your seat belt, honey?"

"Why? I don't want to go anywhere. I want to stay here with Hope and Isaac."

Micah had rounded the car, and he leaned down to explain. "We're heading to New York to *Mammi* and *Dawdi*'s house. They can't wait to see you."

"I don't want to go far away without *Mamm* and *Daed*." Chloe wriggled away as Micah tried to secure her seat belt.

"Chloe, we need to go. You'll be spending time with your grandparents."

"I don't want to go."

Her screams brought *Daed* racing from the house. "What's the matter? Is Chloe all right?"

"No," Chloe yelled. "They're taking me away, and I don't want to go. Don't let them, Isaac."

Hope stopped her *daed* before he reached the car. "Chloe's *onkel* is taking them to his parents' house in New York. His *mamm* will be caring for them now."

"I see." *Daed*'s eyes grew bleak. He headed over and bent down to place a hand on Chloe's head. "I'll miss you, girlie."

Chloe clutched his arm. "Let me stay with you, Isaac."

Daed turned his head away to hide the moisture in his eyes. He pinched the bridge of his nose and then rubbed his fingers across his brow. From the time Hope was small, *Daed* had done that whenever he tried to avoid crying. Although Chloe had only been visiting for a few days, she and *Daed* had bonded. Watching her leave was hard for him.

When he'd gotten his emotions under control, he turned back around and set a hand on her shoulder. "I wish you could stay here, but you need to be with your grandparents now. They'll take care of you."

"I can stay here. You take good care of me."

Daed closed his eyes for a second. "We've loved having you. At a time like this, though, you should be with family." He swallowed hard. "You're good company, so you can help your *mammi* and *dawdi*. They're sad too, you know."

Chloe sobbed as *Daed* squeezed her shoulder and then gently shut the car door. He turned his back, and his shoulders heaved.

Micah approached and held out a hand. "I'm Micah Miller. *Danke* for all you've done for my niece."

"I'm sorry." Hope pushed the words past the huge lump in her throat. "I should have introduced you earlier. Micah, this is my *daed*, Isaac."

"Pleased to meet you." *Daed* shook his hand. "You have a lovely niece. It's been a joy to have her."

"I'm glad to hear that." Micah flashed Hope a rueful smile. "She can be quite lively sometimes."

"We could use a little of that here."

Hope pretended to be hurt. "Are you saying I'm boring?"

Micah quirked an eyebrow. "I didn't find you so." He turned to her *daed*. "You've raised a kind and generous daughter, Isaac. I can't thank you both enough for all you've done." He reached for his wallet. "I did want to pay Hope for her time."

Hope held up a hand and backed away. "Absolutely not. It was a pleasure."

When Micah pulled out some bills to hand to *Daed*, he refused to take them. "You heard Hope. She didn't help for pay. And we received many blessings in return."

Hope wanted to hug *Daed*, not only for supporting her but also for turning down the money. She appreciated his self-control.

When Micah got into the car, Hope stopped him. "Just a minute before you go," Hope said, and she hurried into the house. She returned carrying the Dutch Blitz cards and passed them through the window to Chloe. "It's a long trip, so you might want these to keep you occupied."

Chloe grabbed for them and accidentally snatched the small sheet of paper in Hope's hand.

"Wait, that's for your *onkel*." She pointed to the note. "Can you pass it up to him?"

Micah turned around, his eyebrows raised, and Hope wished she'd phrased things differently. "It's just our phone number. I was going to ask if you'd please call to let us know you arrived safely. I know *Daed* will want to hear." *And so will I*. She turned to hide her stinging eyes.

Then she went and stood beside *Daed*, and they both waved until Debbie turned out of the driveway.

As the car took off down the road, *Daed* sighed. "I'll miss that little girl. She brought sunshine to my days."

"Mine too," Hope agreed. "I'll miss all three of them." Especially Micah.

Chapter Eleven

Micah concentrated on the side mirror until they turned onto the road and Hope was no longer visible. If he had his way, he'd never be driving away from her. Why had he finally found a woman he'd like to date, only to have to leave her behind? She'd be the standard he'd use in the future when choosing a wife. But he had a feeling no one else would compare.

Chloe hadn't passed up the slip of paper with Hope's number on it. He didn't want to lose that. He turned toward the back seat and held out a hand. "Can you give me the phone number?"

She sniffled and clutched the paper and the box to her chest.

"Never mind," he said. "Just be careful with it." As much as he wanted to hold the note to be sure it stayed safe, if it comforted her, he'd let her keep it for now. He'd get it from her later.

Before they reached the crossroads, Micah turned to Jabin. "Do you want to go back to the house? I know you didn't get a chance to spend as much time there as you wanted."

Jabin stared straight ahead, his eyes dull. One brisk side-to-side bob of his head seemed to indicate no.

"You're sure?"

This time Jabin didn't respond. Micah wished he could find a way to connect. He hoped *Mamm* would be able to break down the wall Jabin had erected.

"You didn't ask me," Chloe burst out. "I want to go home. To stay."

"I'm sorry, Chloe, we can stop at the house if you'd like, but *Mammi* will be taking care of you now."

Crossing her arms and setting her jaw, Chloe declared, "I don't want to go to New York. I want to stay with Hope and Isaac." She continued to whine and fuss.

Micah massaged his forehead. One twin refusing to speak, the other never closing her mouth. Two opposite reactions to their sorrow, but it seemed as if they both agreed on one thing. Neither of them wanted to go to New York.

Micah could sympathize. In the space of a few days, they'd had to deal with so many tragedies and constantly changing circumstances from losing their parents to waking up in a hospital. Recovering from injuries to moving away from the only home they'd ever known. And now they were heading, against their will, to another state, one they'd visited infrequently.

Mamm and *Daed* usually came to Pennsylvania for visits rather than asking Ben and Anna to travel to New York, so his parents' home would be unfamiliar for both of them.

Even Micah was reluctant to head back to New York. Now that he'd met Hope, he didn't want to leave either, but he had no choice.

After Micah handed out the sandwiches, Chloe's grizzling stopped. At least temporarily. She soon started up again, this time with *when are we going to get there?*

"It'll be a long ride, Chloe," Debbie told her. "Why don't you play that card game Hope gave you?"

Surprisingly enough, Chloe settled back in the seat and opened the box. "I'll be the buggy. What do you want to be, Jabin?"

He kept his gaze fixed on the back of Debbie's seat while Chloe poked, prodded, and pleaded.

"Jabin won't play with me," she whined.

"Maybe you need to give him a little time," Micah said, although he suspected it might not help.

Every few minutes, Chloe would try again. Finally, she said, "Will you play if I let you have the cards with the buggy?"

Jabin blinked, as if surprised, but he didn't look at his sister or answer.

Chloe sighed. "Jabin doesn't like me anymore."

"That's not true," Micah assured her. "He just doesn't feel like playing."

"He won't even talk to me."

"Give him some time. There's a coloring book in the bag on the seat. Maybe you can do that for a while."

Rather than taking his suggestion, Chloe slumped back in the seat and closed her eyes. Micah hoped she'd take a nap, but when he peeked back at her, tears were leaking down her cheeks.

Micah wished they didn't have to wear seat belts. He wanted to scoop her into his arms and hug her. And to do the same for Jabin.

Hope usually left the phone in the office, but ever since she'd placed the ads, she'd carried it with her. As dinnertime arrived, Hope's concern increased. She hadn't heard from Micah yet. Shouldn't they have arrived by now? Pictures of the buggy accident came to mind and made her jumpy. She tried not to picture another car swerving out of control onto the wrong side of the road.

Please, Lord, keep them safe. And comfort them in their grief.

They'd almost finished their meal when the phone rang. Hope fingered it in her pocket, longing to answer it. No matter how large *Daed*'s business grew, they never answered the phone during meals. Back then, he'd only had an office phone, so it rang in the barn, not in the house. The answering machine took calls, and *Daed* returned them when it fit the family's schedule. Hope had tried to keep to the same rules even with her business cell phone.

"Go ahead and answer it," *Daed* told her. He sounded as eager as she was.

"Hello," she said in a cheery voice, praying the news on the other end would be good. Not like the last time she'd talked to Micah to give him devastating news.

"Hi. I was calling about your ad for a free introductory lesson."

"Oh." She hoped her disappointment didn't show.

Across the table from her, *Daed* raised eager eyebrows. Hope shook her head and mouthed, *A customer.*

His face fell.

The person on the other end described her daughter's shyness. "Laurel can't talk to people or look them in the eye. I worry about her self-confidence. One of my friends suggested animal therapy might help. She's twelve and is nuts about horses."

Hope managed a quick, "I see," before the woman plunged on.

"I thought about riding lessons, but I was afraid she'd shrink against the wall and refuse to participate. Do you think you could help her?"

"Hippotherapy can help children gain confidence."

"Hippos? You have hippos there? I'm sorry, but that's much too scary."

"Wait," Hope said before the woman clicked off. "*Hippo* means *horse*, so *hippotherapy* is therapy using horses."

"Oh." The woman sounded as if she weren't quite sure Hope was telling her the truth. "So, no hippos?"

"No, only gentle horses. Why don't you bring Laurel in for a free class? That way, you can see if it works for her."

"Well, I have to do something. I worry about her. What times do you have available tomorrow? We need to get started on this before school starts."

Hope knew the two appointments for tomorrow, one at nine and one at four. "Would you prefer morning or afternoon?" She hoped to end the conversation soon in case Micah tried to call.

The woman dithered until Hope said, "One o'clock would be best for our therapist."

"Fine, we'll come then."

By the time the woman finished reiterating Laurel's problems and hung up, Hope had to eat a cold supper. Afterward, she did the dishes and cleaned the kitchen, but Micah still hadn't called. She had his number, so she could call him, but debated whether or not she should bother him.

"No call yet?" *Daed* yelled from the living room.

Hope went to the doorway. "Not yet."

She'd barely said the words when the phone sounded again. She prayed it would be Micah, but this time her hello was more neutral in case it was a customer.

"I'm sorry to call so late. We got here around suppertime. I had trouble getting them to eat."

"They weren't hungry?"

"Actually, judging from the amount of food they ate,

they were quite hungry, but neither of them wanted to come to New York, so we've been dealing with some behavior problems."

"Poor kids. They've gone through a lot. It must be hard on them to be in a new state after losing their parents."

"*Jah*. I wish I could take some of their grief away. They're both also still in physical pain. Chloe's arm is itching under the cast, and the ride jostled Jabin's ribs."

"Well, I'll be praying for them and you. And your family, of course," she added hastily.

"*Danke*, we all need it, and I appreciate it."

Daed lifted an eyebrow, and she nodded.

"Tell Chloe and her brother I said good night," he called out.

"Did you hear my *daed*?" Hope asked.

Micah chuckled. "I did, and I'll repeat it. I'm sure it'll make them happy."

"Please give them a greeting from me."

"Will do. I guess I should let you go."

After a few awkward goodbyes, they both hung up. But Hope pressed the dead phone to her ear, wishing to hear Micah's voice one more time, regretting that she'd never talk to him or see him again.

Daed moped in his chair. "I guess they won't be back here."

"You're right." Hope's face most likely mirrored the disappointment in *Daed*'s.

Micah might come back to town to put the house and business up for sale, but she had no idea if or when he planned to do that. Even if he did, he probably wouldn't bring the twins. But if he came back, seeing him would only make saying another goodbye even harder. She needed something to keep her from dwelling on Micah.

* * *

After an hour of protests and fussing, Micah finally wrangled Chloe into bed. She stubbornly refused to lie down. Her back rigid, she ignored his suggestions to relax.

"I'm not sleeping here," she declared. "I want to sleep in Hope's room."

Micah patiently explained about the long trip from New York to Pennsylvania. "Remember how long it took us to get here?"

Scowling, Chloe insisted, "I don't care. I want to go back." She put her hands on her hips. The defiant posture wasn't spoiled by one arm in a cast. In fact, it made a poignant declaration. With her jaw set stubbornly, Chloe reminded him so much of Ben.

When Micah was younger, his brother often used that same you'd-better-agree-with-me-or-else tilt to his head to keep Micah in line. It almost always worked, but as an adult, Micah could resist. Although her resemblance to Ben made it much harder and brought tears to his eyes.

"We can't go back tonight. Debbie's already asleep in the den downstairs. If you go to sleep, we'll talk about it in the morning." Not that things would change tomorrow, but maybe after a good night's rest, Chloe would understand that this would be her new home. "You liked staying here when you came two summers ago. Pretend you're here for a visit."

"I'm not staying."

They'd reached a standoff. Micah wanted to insist she lie down, but what would it accomplish? It would only increase her rebellion. Sooner or later, she'd get sleepy. She couldn't sit up all night.

"Good night, then," he said as he stepped into the hallway and closed the door.

"No, it's not." Chloe's defiant voice followed him down the stairs. "And it never will be again." Her words ended in a sob.

Micah sank onto a chair at the kitchen table and buried his head in his hands. *Please, God, show me the best way to deal with Chloe.*

He couldn't keep letting her get away with defiance. But he didn't want to come down too hard on her on her first night here. Not when she'd just lost both her parents and left her home.

Mamm came into the kitchen. "Are you all right, *Sohn*?"

"*Neh*. I'm finding it hard to deal with Chloe. I know she's hurting, so I don't want to push too much."

After setting a kettle on the stove, *Mamm* sat in her usual place at the table. "That's smart. Ben always gave us problems. Chloe's just like him."

Micah had always assumed his older brother had been the model child. The one Micah could never live up to.

"Your *daed* and I spent many evenings on our knees praying for wisdom to deal with Ben. You were a much more obedient child."

What? He was better behaved than Ben? Micah struggled to believe it. All these years, he'd worried about not measuring up, about being like Ben. Instead, his parents might have preferred it the other way around.

Mamm plucked at her lower lip, a habit that meant she was deep in thought. Micah stayed silent, waiting for her advice. Instead, she pushed herself to her feet and poured some tea.

"Would you like a cup?" she asked.

Micah shook his head. He'd never understand how anyone could drink hot tea on a steamy summer night.

After she sat and sipped her tea, *Mamm* met Micah's eyes. "I think we need to be gentle and give her some time to come around. It's not easy having your whole world fall apart."

"I know." His *mamm*'s world had changed too. Still recovering from pneumonia, she hadn't been ready for her *sohn*'s death or being responsible for two young ones again. He'd try to do what he could to help, but after tomorrow, he'd be going back to work in the harness shop, leaving *Mamm* alone with the twins all day.

"I also worry about Jabin." His nephew hadn't spoken a word all through dinner.

"I do too." Deep lines creased *Mamm*'s face. "The quiet ones often have the hardest struggles."

They sat in silence, except for *Mamm*'s bouts of coughing, while she finished her tea. Even after she washed the cup and headed upstairs, Micah remained at the table. He needed to find a way to reach both Jabin and Chloe, as well as to relieve *Mamm*'s burdens. For both her physical and mental health.

Overhead, *Mamm* shuffled down the hall. She stopped, and a door clicked open. "Micah?" Her voice rang through the hallway. "Where's Chloe?"

"In bed."

"No, she's not." *Mamm*'s slow steps scuffed along to the end of the hallway. Following several loud knocks, another door opened. "She's not in the bathroom either."

Micah shot up the stairs to join her in searching. While *Mamm* went downstairs and knocked on Debbie's door, he headed into the twins' bedroom. Maybe she was hiding under the beds or in the closet. Jabin and Chloe had shared a room when they visited two summers ago while Ben and Anna used the upstairs guest room. Maybe Chloe wanted to be close to her parents. He checked the guest room. He even looked behind doors and furniture. No Chloe.

Panicked, he raced through the house, calling her name. No answer.

He headed back up to the twins' room and met *Daed* in the hallway.

Straightening his suspenders, *Daed* headed for the attic stairs. "I'll check up here." He turned to *Mamm.* "Chloe didn't come into our bedroom while I was in there. Can you look in Micah's room?"

Mamm nodded. "She didn't go down to the basement, because Micah and I were in the kitchen. And I think we'd have heard her if she came down the stairs, don't you, Micah?"

"Probably." Unless she was tiptoeing. "But I'll look in the living room and dining room next." Micah went into the twins' room.

Please, Chloe, jump out at me and giggle about tricking us. Be playing hide-and-seek.

Micah got on his hands and knees to peek under the bed, steeling himself for Chloe to scare him. She'd loved to do that when she was younger. Was she too old for those childish games?

Only an empty floor greeted him.

He crawled over to Jabin's bed and lifted the edge of the quilt. Nothing under there either. He eased his head back out from under the quilt.

"Micah?" Jabin croaked in a sleep-hoarse voice. "What are you doing?"

Had sleep loosened Jabin's tongue? If so, Micah would try to talk to him at night.

"I'm looking for Chloe."

"She went home." Jabin raised himself onto one elbow and winced. His ribs still gave him pain. He eased himself back down. "She wanted me to come with her, but I said no. I don't like being outside in the dark."

"Outside?" Micah tried to temper the shrillness in his voice. "You think she went out?"

Mamm and *Daed* hurried into the room, worried expressions on their faces.

"What's wrong, *Sohn*?" *Daed* asked.

"Jabin says Chloe left."

"You sure, Jabin?"

"*Jah*. She took her suitcase." Jabin motioned toward the closet where Micah had stowed the suitcases. He should have put the clothes in the drawers. He'd been lazy after their trip and planned to do it tomorrow instead.

Micah opened the closet door. Chloe's suitcase was gone.

Chapter Twelve

"She can't have gotten far. I'll run out and look for her," Micah said as he dashed down the stairs.

Daed followed him. "I'll hitch up the buggy."

"That would be good." Micah yanked open the front door. "I'll head south, but Chloe might not know which way to go. Why don't you head in the opposite direction?"

"I'll be praying," *Mamm* called down.

"Is Chloe in trouble?" Jabin asked before Micah slammed the door shut.

No, Micah wanted to tell him as he jogged down the gravel drive. *She's not in trouble. All we want is to find her safe and sound.* If anything happened to her—

He refused to give those thoughts a voice. Instead, he prayed and swiveled his head from side to side, searching the darkness for any signs of movement.

Behind him, the buggy clattered down the drive and turned north. A light swept the sides of the road. *Daed* had grabbed a flashlight. Micah wished he'd thought of that.

When he reached the crossroads, he stopped, uncertain which way Chloe might have turned. It was late, and he hated to disturb neighbors who needed to rise early tomorrow to milk and farm, but he couldn't explore all the backroads himself. The nearest house had four older teenage sons. Maybe they'd be willing to help.

Swallowing his pride, Micah knocked on their door. Soon the father and sons were hitching horses to wagons and vehicles. Two went east. The others headed down the side roads. They'd handed Micah an extra battery-powered light, and he continued south on the road they'd driven on coming from Pennsylvania.

He'd walked almost a mile when his light picked out a small bundle at the edge of the trees. Was it a pile of old clothes or a sleeping child?

Holding his light high, Micah headed toward it. The bundle shifted, seemed to curl and shrink. He pounded toward it. A small figure leaped up and raced for the woods, leaving a suitcase behind.

"Chloe!" he screamed. "Stop! It's Micah."

But the small girl darted into the trees. She could get hurt in there. Maybe he'd scared her by thundering toward her. Micah slowed and held the light beside his face.

"Chloe, look. It's me." He tried to keep his tone gentle. "You're not in trouble. We love you and just want to keep you safe."

He stayed still and silent until the frantic scrambling stopped. "Please come out of the woods. It's not safe in there."

No reply.

Micah tried again. "Chloe, *Mammi* is worried about you. She wants you to come back home."

"It's not home," Chloe spat out.

At least she was answering. If he kept her talking, he could locate her exact position. But he hoped he could coax her out. "I meant *Mammi* wants you to come to her house. I realize it's not your home."

Chloe had been especially close to *Mamm*, so he hoped his niece would respond to that plea.

"I want to go home!" Her words ended in a wail.

"I know you do. Will you come out so we can talk?"

"You'll only say no."

"I'll listen to what you have to say."

"Promise?"

"I promise." He wasn't promising to change his mind, but he'd listen with an open mind and heart.

Branches crackled underfoot, and then Chloe stepped out of the woods. Relief flooded through every cell in Micah's body, but he didn't move. He wanted her to come to him.

She scrubbed at her eyes with her fists. "It's a long walk."

"Yes, it is. It would take weeks to walk there." At a seven-year-old's pace. If she could even find her way.

"Weeks?"

Micah nodded. "That's why we hired a car. Do you remember how long it took us to drive here?"

"*Jah*." Her answer was hesitant.

"I bet you're tired from walking all this way." Micah squatted and opened his arms.

Chloe stared at him as if unsure she could trust him.

"Please, Chloe. I love you."

She approached one tentative step at a time. "Take me home, Micah." Then, with the last few steps, she flew toward him, almost knocking him off his feet.

Micah held her tight to his chest with one arm. With the other, he flashed his light over the trees, hoping one of the searchers would catch his signal. Then he went over and picked up her suitcase.

They hadn't walked far when a horse pulling a farm

wagon galloped toward them. The teen boy driving it pulled it to a halt.

"You found her." He beamed at Chloe. "We were worried about you."

Chloe hid her face against Micah's shoulder.

"I'm sorry. I didn't mean to scare her." The boy gestured to the seat beside him. "Hop on and I'll take you home."

Chloe lifted her head and stared at him with rapture. "You will?"

"He means to *Mammi*'s house," Micah informed her.

"Oh." There was no mistaking her disappointment.

"We'll sleep there tonight," Micah said, "because it's so late. And we'll talk in the morning."

She thrust out her lower lip. "I want to go now. I miss Hope."

So do I, Chloe. So do I.

After the twins had fallen asleep, *Daed* called Micah into the bedroom, where *Mamm* sat propped up with pillows, her face wan, her breathing rattily.

"*Sohn*," *Daed* said, "we're concerned about the twins. They seem unhappy about staying here."

Micah settled into a chair by *Mamm*'s bedside. "I'm sure they'll adjust, given some time. It's only their first day here, and they've been through so much."

"That's what's troubling me," *Mamm* said between coughs.

Daed paced over to the window and stared out at the darkness beyond. "This has been hard on all of us. I'm not sure your *mamm* is up to taking care of two little ones, especially if they might take off without warning."

"You don't have to baby me." *Mamm* followed a fond glance at *Daed* with a slight frown.

"The doctor is worried about you overdoing it," he said.

Micah had hoped *Mamm* would have improved more in the five days he'd been gone. Instead, she seemed weaker.

Daed faced Micah. "As much as we'd like to keep the children here with us, we've been wondering if they'd heal better in a familiar place."

"But *Mamm* can't travel all that way." She looked even more drained than she had been earlier. At the moment, she barely looked well enough to totter down to the kitchen to make another cup of tea.

"Exactly." *Daed* sent Micah a look indicating he'd been missing the point. "I need to keep the business running. Zeke filled in for you while you were gone, and I think he'd be willing to stay on as long as I need him."

Their neighbor's son, Zeke, had been underfoot as a lad, and now, as a sixteen-year-old, he made no secret of the fact that he was fascinated by harness making. Since graduating from eighth grade, he'd been angling to get hired. And Zeke had one qualification Micah didn't: he wasn't petrified of horses.

"So, what are you saying?" Micah was pretty sure he'd gotten *Daed*'s point, but he wanted to double-check.

"Your *mamm* and I both think you should take Chloe and Jabin back to Pennsylvania with you tomorrow and stay there."

"Stay there?"

"At least until the children have had time to adjust and *Mamm* is healthier. You could run Ben's business."

"I don't think . . ."

"*Sohn*, I know you're worried about having to deal with the horses, but Ben"—*Daed*'s voice cracked—"relied on his assistant, Eli, who can handle that part of the business. And both of the twins helped their parents, so it might be good for them to get back to a familiar routine."

"You don't think it would make them miss their parents more?"

"It might." *Mamm*'s voice wavered. "When my *mamm* died just before we married, I found chores brought both pain and relief. Doing something routine with your hands helps keep you busy and focused. But it often brings up memories of doing the jobs with someone you loved."

"Besides," *Daed* said, "both Ben and Anna would have chosen you for the twins' parent. Remember last Thanksgiving?" *Daed* pivoted and strode to the window. His shoulders shook.

Mamm picked up the story. "The twins followed you around all day, copying whatever you were doing. You were the only one who could get them to listen when they got too wild, and they both begged you to read them bedtime stories. Ben joked that you should have been their father instead of him."

Daed turned from the window. "I think he was a little jealous of you."

"Especially when Anna agreed that the twins behaved better for you than they did for her and Ben."

Ben, jealous of him? What were his parents thinking? Sure, the twins enjoyed having him around when he only visited several times a year, but now that he'd had to take care of them full-time even for a few days, that shiny new excitement had already worn off.

As of today, Jabin refused to speak to Micah most of the time, and Chloe had run away. Not a very good track record for a substitute parent. Ben and Anna had done a much better job.

"What will I do with them while I'm working?"

"Like your father said, they can work at the harness shop. I'm sure they have jobs they usually do."

"That's a lot of time for them to spend inside, and I don't know if I could keep an eye on both of them."

What if Chloe decided to run away again? Adrenaline still coursed through him from the terror of finding her missing. It would take a while for his pulse and nerves to return to normal.

Mamm looked thoughtful. "Wouldn't some of the ladies from church be willing to help?"

"I suppose." Sylvia and Susie popped into his mind. They'd jump at the chance to help out. A chance he had no intention of giving them.

Then *Mamm* brought up an important point. "Both Chloe and Jabin should be starting school next week, shouldn't they?"

"The first week of school is always half days, and we still have the rest of this week to get through." Micah dreaded the thought of Sylvia volunteering her daughter.

"I'm sure you could work out something with Eli," *Daed* said. "After all, he's been running the place, hasn't he?"

"*Jah*, and he offered to keep managing everything, but he's been handling both his job and Ben's."

Daed waved a hand like it was no big deal. "Ben wouldn't have hired Eli if he wasn't competent. I'm sure he could do it for another week or two."

"He probably would. He even suggested he might be willing to buy the business."

"It pains me to think of the business my *dawdi* started going to a stranger, but if Ben trusted him . . ." *Daed* stared off into the distance as his voice trailed off.

As much as Micah wished he could sell the business, he couldn't hurt *Daed* that way. "I don't have to sell the business if you don't want me to."

Daed shook his head. "God warns us against getting attached to worldly things." Almost under his breath, he muttered, "'Love not the world, neither the things that are in the world.'"

Pinning Micah with a look that pierced his soul, *Daed* said, "I gave that business to Ben and told him to do what he wanted. Now I'm turning it over to you. If you decide to sell, I'll trust your judgment."

With his fear of horses, Micah had never enjoyed being in the harness business, but he was *Daed*'s only son now. He had an obligation to be sure the business stayed running.

Mamm's eyes grew damp. "I was so looking forward to having the children here, especially after . . ."

"We could stay a few days if I can convince Chloe not to run away again," Micah suggested.

His mother shook her head. "That would be selfish of me. I think they need their home. They should be sleeping in their own beds, going to their own church, doing their usual chores, and having a regular schedule."

Daed went over, sat beside her, and took her hand. "We can visit when you're well."

"I'd like that," she said. "They'll have school to attend next week. That will keep them busy during the day. And having their friends around them should help."

Speaking of school, Hope had mentioned going to work with children this week, and he'd wondered if she were a teacher. Before his sister Elizabeth married, she'd taught school, and she always spent the week before school started fixing up her classroom. Had Hope taken off Monday to care for Chloe? He hoped he hadn't messed up her schedule. She'd be too kind to tell him if she had a conflict.

If she could be the twins' teacher, that would be special. Both of them liked her. For that matter, so did he. One advantage of taking the children back would be to see Hope.

Suddenly, he was eager to return to Pennsylvania.

* * *

Hope went to bed with Micah on her mind, dreamed of him all night long, and woke at dawn missing him.

At least she had three lessons to look forward to today, along with one on Tuesday and Liam on Wednesday. She'd need to fill the hours in between to avoid thoughts of Micah.

Hope's chores kept her hands busy, but her mind kept running and rerunning moments with him. From her first glimpse of Micah, with his tired eyes and stubbled chin, she'd been attracted by his outer appearance, but without his heart and compassion, he would have been an empty package. She liked his sunny smile, his deep laughter, his intense gaze. Even more appealing were his kindness, his gentleness, his caring.

Her heart still did little flips as she recalled his warm hand in hers.

"Hope?" a man's voice said.

She jumped, and the bucket of grooming tools in her hands clattered onto the cement aisle. Logan had come up behind her, but she'd been so lost in memories of Micah, she hadn't heard him.

"Are you all right?" He studied her with concern in his eyes. "I didn't mean to startle you."

"It's all right. I wasn't paying attention."

She knelt to gather the spilled tools, and Logan squatted in front of her. His hand brushed hers as he slid the hoof pick into the basket. She jerked back her hand, and he sighed.

What a difference a touch from Micah made. She hadn't moved away because Logan's touch sent sparks through her. Just the opposite, in fact. It left her cold inside.

To make up for hurting his feelings, Hope told Logan about last night's phone call.

"Why don't we meet in the office after our first lesson to discuss a plan?"

"Sounds good," she said. One more thing to take her mind off Micah.

The nine o'clock lesson went well, but once the girl's father heard the price, he said, "We'll think about it."

"Here's more information if you need it." Hope handed him the benefit list they'd prepared yesterday. Logan had set the copies on her desk this morning.

Once the father left, Logan came into the office. "We won't be able to work up a benefit sheet for Laurel's mother. As I've said a million times, a copier would come in handy."

Hope ignored his complaint and pulled out her notebook. If she'd hoped to stop thinking about Micah, it wasn't working. Even in the short spaces of time, like waiting for Logan to get out his laptop and turn it on, Micah was on her mind. And each time she glanced at Logan, her mind automatically compared him to Micah.

Hope supposed *Englisch* women might consider Logan handsome, but Micah had so much more than good looks. He had all the qualities she'd look for—if she were interested in courting. Which she most definitely was not. But why was she yearning for a connection and a relationship that could never be?

Chapter Thirteen

The minute Micah woke, he jumped out of bed and padded down the hall to check on the twins. To his relief, they were both still sleeping. After talking with his parents last night, Micah had stood outside Chloe's room and listened for deep, even breathing from both children. Then he'd gone to his room and prayed that God would keep Chloe safe.

This morning, he was praying a different prayer. *Dear God, please help me to become the best parent I can be.*

Thinking about taking sole responsibility for two young children weighed heavily on him. How would he teach them right from wrong? How would he discipline with love? How would he teach them to do their chores, especially Chloe? She needed a *mamm.*

Why did his thoughts immediately fly to Hope? He'd tried hard to make himself forget her, but now that they were headed back, his heart leaped at the possibility he might see her again. If she wasn't the twins' schoolteacher, he'd have to find another way to make contact. What excuse could he use? Maybe Chloe's desire to see Hope and Isaac would work. They also could return the Dutch Blitz cards.

Eager to get on the road, Micah wanted to wake both

children, but Chloe was probably exhausted after her long walk last night. He hoped a good night's sleep would make Jabin more talkative. Or perhaps knowing he was heading home might help.

Micah slipped downstairs and made a pot of coffee. He'd take a cup to *Mamm*. They'd all stayed up late last night, so she could use a wake-up mug this morning.

Debbie poked her head out of the room. "Is that coffee I smell?"

"It is. Come on out and have a cup or two."

She grinned. "I could use a pick-me-up this morning. I'll head back after that."

"There's been a change of plans."

She took a sip of coffee. "What do you mean?"

"*Mamm* and *Daed* think the twins should stay at their own house and attend school there, so I guess all three of us will be heading back to Lancaster this morning."

"All this way just to turn around and go back again? Almost seems like I shouldn't charge you for the trip." She held up a hand. "Wait, wait. I didn't say that. I have to pay for my gas and maintenance and—"

Micah interrupted her. "I'll be paying you. Don't worry. Anyone who put up with all that whining and fussing yesterday deserves every penny. I hope the twins will do less of it going home." He poured *Mamm*'s coffee. "We can leave right after breakfast, if that's all right with you."

"Fine by me." Debbie closed her eyes and took a sip. "*Mmm.*"

"I'll take this to *Mamm* and bring down the suitcases." Maybe it was good he hadn't unpacked the suitcases after all.

As he passed the twins' bedroom, Jabin was sitting up in bed, staring at the wall.

"Good morning," Micah called.

Jabin didn't even turn his head in Micah's direction. So much for his talkativeness last night. Maybe Jabin had been talking in his sleep.

Micah knocked and entered *Mamm*'s bedroom. She greeted him while she pulled the quilt over the pillows and smoothed out the wrinkles. "That smells delicious. After a sleepless night, it'll help me get started."

"Why are you making the bed when you should be in it?" Micah asked.

"Too much to do." She bent over from a spate of coughing.

After she caught her breath, Micah laid a hand on her shoulder and steered her to the chair near the bed. "First, you're going to sit down and relax while you drink your coffee."

"I don't have time. When did you plan to get on the road? I need to make snacks and sandwiches for your trip. And it's almost time to fix breakfast."

"Five minutes' rest won't delay our trip. Besides, Chloe is still asleep, so we can't go anywhere yet."

"The poor little girl." *Mamm* shook her head. "She's probably exhausted after last night."

"That's what I figured. I planned to let her sleep until *Daed* and I are done with the barn chores."

"Is Jabin awake? It might be good for him to help."

Micah grimaced. "He was sitting up in bed but unresponsive."

Mamm drained the last of the coffee. "I'll go and see if I can get him to talk."

He prayed she'd be more successful than he'd been. "I haven't told him about the trip back to Lancaster. That might perk him up a bit."

"I'll let him know." *Mamm* headed down the hall to the twins' room.

When Micah peeked into the room to grab the suitcases, *Mamm* sat beside Jabin, speaking softly. She took his hand, but he made no move to clasp hers. His hand lay limply between her workworn ones, and Micah's heart went out to both of them.

Heart heavy, he carried the suitcases downstairs, and Debbie tossed him the keys to load them in the trunk. Much of the day yesterday had been spent on the road, only to return to the exact same spot today. Micah hoped they were making the right move for the twins.

Hope was excited about working with Laurel because she expected to see some signs of improvement today. She and Logan finished the benefit sheet close to noontime, and she debated about inviting him into the house for the meal.

If he were anyone else, she'd have no hesitation about issuing an invitation. But part of her worried he might mistake it for more than simple kindness. Yet she couldn't leave him out here while she went inside.

"Would you like to have dinner with *Daed* and me?" At Logan's eager but puzzled look, she amended her question. "I mean, lunch." The *Englisch* didn't call their noon meal "dinner."

A huge smile broke across his face. "Thanks! That would be great. I didn't realize we had a one o'clock appointment today, so I didn't bring anything to eat."

His response added to Hope's fears he'd misinterpreted her intention. "I noticed you didn't have a lunch bag with you, and I couldn't let you go hungry. Not when we have two more students coming today." She hoped that was matter-of-fact enough to convey the message she wanted to send.

His downcast expression showed she'd been successful. Although she disliked hurting him, she needed to keep her expectations clear.

Perhaps she should discuss it with him rather than relying on him to pick up subtle messages, but she was reluctant to bring up the subject. Suppose she'd misunderstood his intentions, and he hadn't been flirting with her. Some *Englisch* men were much freer about showing interest in many different girls and even dating more than one woman, something Hope did not understand.

"It'll only be soup and sandwiches," she apologized.

"Sounds good to me." Evidently, Logan bounced back quickly from disappointments. "I'll finish these emails and go get washed up."

Hope went into the house to start the soup. She'd been planning to reheat chicken noodle soup, but she pulled a jar of spaghetti soup from the pantry. That would be a heartier meal. She'd put it on to warm while she made Lebanon bologna sandwiches.

Logan tapped on the door, and with an excited expression, *Daed* rushed into the kitchen to answer it. As soon as he spotted Logan, his eagerness changed to politeness. "Good morning."

"Logan's joining us for lunch," Hope told him.

"I see." *Daed* shot her a searching glance before opening the screen door.

"I really appreciate you feeding me today." Logan came into the kitchen and sat in the chair *Daed* indicated. "I didn't realize I'd be here at lunchtime."

Hope set a pile of sandwiches on the table and ladled out bowls of soup.

As soon as she sat at the table, Logan sniffed the soup. "What kind is this? It looks delicious." His brows rose when she said spaghetti. "Never heard of that. I can see there's spaghetti and meat in the tomato broth, so the name makes sense." He took three sandwich halves and passed the plate to *Daed*.

Logan dipped his spoon into his bowl as Hope and *Daed* bowed their heads for prayer. He slurped a mouthful but, evidently realizing his error, the spoon clattered into his bowl.

"Sorry," he said after they lifted their heads. "When I was little, my grandmother taught me to pray. I haven't done much since."

"Might be a good habit to take up again," *Daed* suggested.

Spots of color appeared on Logan's cheeks. "You may be right."

Conversation remained strained for a few minutes. Then Hope described the phone call from the previous evening.

Logan laughed so hard he almost spit out a mouthful of soup. "Hippos? She actually thought you had hippos?"

Hope shrugged. "It's an understandable mistake. I'd never heard the word 'hippotherapy' before I started learning about horse therapy."

"I suppose." Logan tempered his amusement. "When she arrives, should I offer to show her our hippos?"

"I wish I hadn't told you that," Hope said. "Now you'll probably scare poor Laurel so much, she'll refuse to enter the barn."

Logan sobered. "I'd never do that. I'd wait until Laurel was engrossed with the horses, then I'd ask her mom privately."

"And her mom would shriek and scare Laurel."

"Is she the shrieking type?"

Hope tapped her spoon against the side of her bowl, trying to decide how much to tell Logan. But he was a therapist, after all, and her partner. He should have some facts that might help them deal with a new student.

Finally, she said, "I do think she's rather emotional. Her mom talks so much, I had trouble getting her off the phone." Although maybe waiting for Micah's call had colored her view. "I do wonder, though, if Laurel ever gets a chance to talk."

"Hmm." Logan tapped his lip with a knuckle. "Perhaps the best therapy for Laurel is to give her time away from her mother."

Hope had thought the same thing last night. They had a bench where parents could sit to watch, but with her mom's eagle eye on her, Laurel might be too nervous to do anything.

"Why don't I take her mom into the kitchen to wait?" Logan asked.

They had a small kitchen area with two small tables and some chairs. Future plans included turning it into an employee break room. Once they had several volunteers, it would get some use.

"But then you won't be there to help, and you're the trained therapist."

"I wouldn't stay with her. I'd just explain that students do best when they can concentrate without any distractions, but we'll bring her out to see the end of the lesson. Fingers crossed we'll make some progress."

Hope glanced at the clock. "I should get the kitchen cleaned up. We only have twenty minutes until their lesson."

Logan pushed back his chair. "I'll get things ready in the barn. We'll use Nutmeg for Laurel."

Nutmeg, the quietest of the mares, had been a birthday party horse. She was used to standing still while crowds of children screamed and jumped around her. She barely flicked her head or tail when little ones poked or prodded her.

"Good choice." Hope rose and collected the dishes.

"Thanks for the delicious meal, Hope. Nice to see you again, Isaac." Logan headed for the door. One hand on the knob, he turned. "Isaac, you have a wonderful daughter."

"You know," *Daed* said, stroking his beard, "another man about my daughter's age told me that yesterday. An Amish man."

Hope wondered if *Daed* had included the remark about age to imply Logan was too old for her. He was in his early thirties. It also sounded as if *Daed* was trying to warn Logan off. She hoped her father understood she had no interest in the *Englischer*.

Getting Jabin to dress, eat breakfast, and get into the car drained Micah. Most of the time, he carried a rigid, silently protesting small boy from place to place. On the other hand, the minute Chloe heard the news, she bounded out of bed.

"*Danke, danke, danke*," she sang as she got ready. Before she left the room, she turned. "I love you, Micah." Then she raced downstairs. Throwing her arms around *Mamm*'s legs, she burst into tears. "I'm going to miss you."

Micah, descending the stairs with what felt like a wooden statue—Jabin—in his arms, shook his head. Would he ever get used to his niece's mercurial personality? At the moment, he was more concerned about her brother.

He set Jabin in his usual place on the bench. *Mamm* leaned over and plopped small amounts onto his plate while he sat with his hands in his lap. Micah was relieved when his nephew bowed his head for prayer.

"Time to eat, Jabin," *Daed* said after everyone else started.

A pained look on his face, Jabin lifted forkfuls to his mouth, barely looking at his plate or the others around him. He either fixed his gaze on the wooden tabletop or stared past Micah's shoulder at the wall.

"We're going home," Chloe trilled. "Aren't you happy, Jabin? We can play with Hope and Isaac again."

Micah disliked dashing her plans, but seeing Hope wasn't on their agenda. At least not yet, as much as he wished for it.

Near the end of Laurel's lesson, Logan slipped out to get her mother. He stopped the mom a short distance from the stall. Laurel had her back to her mother. A frown of criticism marred the mom's face. She looked ready to pounce on the slightest fault. Logan took her elbow and tapped a finger to his mouth, as if to remind her to be silent. Her frown deepened, but she didn't say a word.

Hope stood on the opposite side of the horse, holding Nutmeg's head steady, while Laurel put her arms around the horse's neck and buried her nose against Nutmeg's coat. "He smells so good," she declared.

Hope didn't bother to correct Laurel's misconception that the mare was a boy. She reinforced her spontaneous comment. "I think horses have the most comforting scent in the world."

Laurel lifted her head and, with a shy smile, said, "Yes, they do." Her words were so soft, she could barely be heard.

Her mom, a startled look on her face, stared. "She talked to you." Her voice rose in amazement.

The sound of her mother's voice produced a dramatic change in Laurel. The girl's hands dropped to her sides and curled into soft fists. She lowered her head, kept her gaze on the ground, and hunched her back.

"She's been talking most of the class. Laurel is very bright and eager to learn. She did a good job today with the currycomb. Nutmeg enjoyed the grooming."

Nutmeg turned toward Laurel and whinnied. "He's talking to me," Laurel mumbled, so softly only Hope could hear.

Hope smiled at her. "She's thanking you for taking such good care of her."

"You're welcome, Nutmeg." Laurel's voice, which had been quiet during the session, had become a whisper.

While Logan finished up the session and cleaned up, Hope took Laurel's mother to the office.

"Did Logan tell you he'd send you the benefit sheet?"

The woman nodded. "I gave him my email address. Can Laurel ride next week if we sign up for these classes?"

"Next week might be a bit too soon." When deep furrows appeared between the mom's eyes, Hope tried to explain. "The purpose of the therapy is to move gradually from getting acquainted with the horse to caring for it. Learning to groom a horse gives students a lot of self-confidence. They develop not only knowledge but skills to handle a huge animal."

Although the woman looked ready to interrupt, Hope plowed ahead without giving her a chance. "Laurel moved through several sessions' worth of lessons already today, so it's obvious she's a quick learner. If she keeps moving at this pace, it's possible she can progress to riding during a six-week series. If you're looking for Laurel to learn to ride, I'd suggest the six-month package. Once she understands the basics, she'll be on horseback in no time."

"Sign her up for that, then."

Hope handed Laurel's mom a copy of the pricing sheet, and she handed Hope cash for double the amount. "I want to get her a place on your calendar. I think she'll benefit from horseback riding."

From the mother's tone, it seemed she'd brag that her daughter was taking riding lessons. Even though Hope didn't agree with stretching the truth, it wasn't her place to judge. How Laurel's mom handled it was her business, but for right now, they'd just secured their second student, and for a full year. She couldn't wait to tell Logan.

When Hope and Logan waved goodbye to Laurel, her head still drooped, but she stood a little taller and prouder than when she'd arrived.

"I suspect Mom's not going to like the eventual changes in her daughter, once Laurel gains enough confidence to stand up for herself," Logan remarked.

Hope had been thinking the same thing. "Perhaps Laurel will use her new power wisely. She seems to be a smart girl."

"Yes, she's not only intelligent, she's also savvy."

As their car drove off, a large truck pulled in. Hope practically danced down the driveway. The sign had arrived. She hoped it would be in place before the next student arrived.

Two hours later, her lovely new wooden sign had been installed. Deciding where to place it for maximum visibility had taken time, but now it could be seen from both sides of the road. Graber's Horse Therapy: Hope for Children.

And she had hope for the future too.

Chapter Fourteen

As the miles ticked by, Micah grew more exuberant. As long as he kept his focus on Hope, his mood lightened. Just knowing he was moving closer and closer to her helped to mitigate the sadness of heading back to the house where he'd spent so much time with Ben and Anna. It distracted Micah from the weight of things left unsaid. Thoughts of Hope also took his mind off his two biggest concerns, both of whom were sitting in the back seat.

Moving back to Lancaster had energized Chloe, who'd been talking nonstop for the past four hours. She seemed to have adjusted to her brother's silence. To make up for his quietness, she chattered to everyone else. Debbie, who enjoyed conversation as much as Chloe, kept a steady stream of words flowing between them.

Like a rock in the midst of that river, Jabin sat, rigid and unresponsive. If Chloe asked him a question and received no answer, she pretended to answer herself, pitching her voice lower to capture his speech. She sounded so much like him, Micah turned around several times, believing Jabin had spoken. But he remained sullen and still.

Although everyone expressed grief in different ways, Micah worried about Jabin bottling up all his misery. He needed to find a way to reach his nephew and help him release his sorrow.

They made several stops to let Chloe run off some of her excess energy, but Jabin refused to get out of the car. Micah stretched his legs, and Debbie gossiped on the phone with friends. During their last pit stop, Chloe raced up to him, going so fast, she collided with his legs.

Glancing up at him with pleading eyes, she begged, "Can we stop to visit Hope and Isaac? I want to tell them we'll be staying home."

Micah checked the time. They'd make it to the Lancaster area around five. "It'll be close to suppertime when we get there, so I don't think it's a good idea to do that today."

Chloe threw back her head and wailed, "I need to tell them something."

As much as Micah wanted to say yes, giving in to her demands or tantrums would encourage bad behavior. In some ways, they'd rewarded her for running away, and he didn't want her to think she could control situations through her drama.

"We'll visit them, but not today." Although Micah would love to go today, he needed to restrain himself too and not barge in on them at an inconvenient time. "I have some things I need to ask Hope, so we'll make plans to go later this week."

He ushered a bawling Chloe back to the car. Jabin turned his head to look at her, his eyes filled with sympathy. The first emotion he'd shown in days. Maybe reaching him wouldn't be as difficult as Micah had feared.

"Oh my goodness," Debbie said. "I can't drive with all that racket. We'll never get to Lancaster at this rate." She turned to face the noise. "Sounds like you don't want to go home."

Chloe's sobs quieted to sniffles.

"That's much better." Debbie clicked her seat belt and started the engine. "Less than an hour to go."

"That's not long, is it?" Chloe asked through tears.

"Not if you find something interesting to do," Micah assured her. "That makes time pass quickly."

For him, Hope provided the necessary distraction that made the hour fly.

Chloe began her pestering as soon as she awoke the next morning. "When are we going to Hope's?" became a chant she repeated over and over.

"We'll see," Micah answered as he milked the cows. He'd notified the neighbor yesterday that he'd be around to do the farm chores from now on.

Micah wished he had a reason to show up at Hope's and transportation to get there. He couldn't keep hiring drivers. They could use Ben's old farm wagon temporarily, but they'd need a buggy.

Ben's buggy was gone, and so was his buggy horse.

Micah blocked the horrible nightmare from his mind.

Maybe he should go buggy shopping today. He was pretty sure he remembered how to get to the shop in Bird-in-Hand. With a steep gravel slope in front acting as a shelf for the rows of gray buggies lined up, the big red shop stood out in his mind. They'd passed it on the main road many times when he was young, and *Daed* often pulled in on hot summer days because the sign out front said "Water for Your Horse."

They'd go right by Hope's on the way. Well, not exactly right by, but close enough. A mile or so detour wasn't much. Not if it meant seeing her again.

Chloe continued to nag him as he carried the milk inside and started breakfast. To quiet her, he said, "We need to run some errands today. We could probably stop by Hope's for a short while."

"A short while?" Chloe whined. "I want it to be a long, long while."

So do I. "But we don't want to overstay our welcome."

Hands on hips, Chloe demanded, "What does that mean?"

"If you stay too long, people might not want you to come back another time."

"Huh. Hope would never think that." Chloe tossed her head, sending all the loose strands fluttering.

He'd let her sleep with her bob in last night, but now he had no idea how to fix it this morning. He'd try to figure that out after breakfast.

Micah stirred the oatmeal, which was bubbling up and trying to explode over the edge. He'd watched *Mamm* do this several times, and he'd followed the directions on the container for measuring, but he didn't remember her fighting a gushing volcano. He yelped as it overflowed onto the stove.

Lifting the pot in the air, he struggled to turn off the burner. Waterfalls of oatmeal cascaded onto the stove and floor.

"Why is oatmeal plopping on the floor?" Chloe wanted to know.

Micah had no idea. Except that he'd held the pot out in the air because he hadn't wanted the oatmeal to fall into the flames. He hadn't succeeded. A charred smell permeated the air. The blobs that had fallen before he rescued the pot had burned.

"That oatmeal smells stinky. I don't want to eat it."

Neither did Micah, but they had little choice. "We won't be having the badly burned bits. They're stuck to the stove."

Mamm had been right when she'd suggested having one

of the women from church come in to help. But the only two he knew well enough to ask were the last ones he wanted underfoot.

Maybe Hope would be willing to teach him a few things. He shook his head. It wouldn't be fair to ask her to do more than she already had.

Somehow, he carried a resisting Jabin to the table, opened a jar of applesauce from the pantry to put on the oatmeal, and served slightly singed oatmeal with warm milk straight from the cows. After breakfast, he ran a sinkful of soapy water and dumped in the pot and bowls. He'd let them soak and deal with the stove later.

Getting Jabin dressed and tackling Chloe's messy hair exhausted him. He ended up winding the loose ends around her bun, hoping they'd stay. Chloe complained bitterly that he was doing it all wrong.

"I know, Chloe, I know. I wish I'd paid more attention when your *mammi* was doing Elizabeth's and Mary's bobs." The only thing he remembered was his sisters placing their foreheads down on the kitchen table and *Mamm*'s fingers flashing back and forth, twisting, folding, and wrapping. But Micah had no idea how to make all those mysterious moves.

They'd only been up a few hours, and already Micah was exhausted. He now had a new appreciation for his *mamm*, who'd made raising five little ones seem easy.

Jabin had disappeared while he wrestled with Chloe's hair, and after a frantic search, they found him in the barn, petting the cow. He planted his feet when Micah told him it was time to go, so Micah left him there while he hooked up the farm wagon.

He was shaky enough about hitching up the horse without adding extra stress. He also didn't want the children to see him trembling. *Daed* always handled this at home, but

here, he was on his own. And if he got a buggy, he'd have
to do this twice today.

Mumbling a prayer, he steered clear of Daffy's back
legs. *Please, Lord, give me the courage.* Then, asking for
God's protection, he inched around the horse, keeping as
far away as he could to do what needed to be done, and
backed away.

Micah waited until his pulse and breathing returned to
normal—or as close to normal as possible. Then he waved
Chloe and Jabin toward the wagon. "Time to go."

Chloe rushed over, but Jabin ignored him. Chloe called
to Jabin, "Hurry, Jabin. We're going to Hope's house."

A mutinous expression on his face, Jabin dragged his
feet but eventually reached the wagon. Micah considered it
a victory that he didn't have to carry his nephew from the
barn. Jabin stiffened when Micah lifted him in, but he sat
where he was placed.

"I need to get something," Chloe announced as Micah
hopped into the wagon.

Micah debated between driving off and listening to her
fuss the whole time or giving her a few minutes to get what
she wanted. He decided waiting would be the easiest.

When she returned carrying Hope's Dutch Blitz cards,
he was glad he'd been patient. Returning the cards might
make a good excuse for visiting.

The ride to Hope's didn't take as long as he expected. He
stopped in surprise when they reached the driveway. A huge
sign announced horse therapy. Micah had never heard of
such a thing. And at an Amish farm?

Just seeing the word *horse* written on the sign was
enough to kick-start the old panic. He'd seen the large horse
barn and assumed they had a lot of horses, or that they
boarded them, but he hadn't dwelled on it. Now he was
forced to face reality. The woman who interested him had

built her life and business around horses. And he was deathly afraid of them.

The nine o'clock free lesson had ended, and they'd just signed up another student! Hope tried to act nonchalant when inside she was celebrating. This time she made sure to put the desk between them when she told Logan the news.

"Fantastic!" Logan rounded the desk, and irritation flashed in his eyes as she held the cashbox as a shield against his advances.

Tucking the bills into the correct slots in the cash tray allowed her to fend him off until she slid it into the drawer. She stayed bent over after the money had been stowed and opened the file drawer on the other side, which blocked Logan's access to her. "Last night I organized all our tip sheets." She waved a hand to the manila folders with neatly printed tabs she'd alphabetized.

Logan lowered his outstretched hands, evidently realizing her intent. "That was a good idea." He didn't sound enthusiastic.

Hope suspected his reaction had more to do with her avoiding him than his disinterest in her new filing system. She pointed out several tabs. "We don't have tip sheets for these yet."

"I won't have time to work on them today," he said stiffly, backing away from the desk. "I have plans."

She closed the file drawer and sat up. "There's no rush. So far, we don't have any students who need them, which means we can complete them when we have time." Tapping a finger on the calendar, she pointed out two new students who'd be coming for introductory lessons that week. "I signed them up yesterday evening."

"Good," he said in a clipped tone. "Or should I say *gut*?"

Was he mocking her *Deutsch* accent? "Either one would be fine. Wunderbar would work too." She smiled at him to show she remained unruffled.

"Sorry," he muttered.

Now that he'd moved a safe distance away, Hope stood. "I hope you enjoy your plans for the rest of the day."

His miserable expression made her wonder if he'd only said that to save face or to make her jealous. He obviously didn't understand she had no interest in *Englischers*. Maintaining the space between them, she walked him to his car. "I'll see you tomorrow for our first real lesson at four. Or, if you want to come early, we could work on some new benefit sheets."

"I may be busy, but we'll see." He slid into the driver's seat and turned on the engine.

The car jerked to a start and rolled down the driveway faster than usual, spitting gravel under its wheels. Logan had almost reached the street when a farm wagon pulled in. He slammed on his brakes and swerved to the right to avoid hitting it. When he turned onto the road, he'd slowed to a sedate pace.

She hoped avoiding his advances wasn't going to make their business relationship rocky. She'd been so focused on Logan, Hope hadn't paid attention to the wagon, but as it drew nearer, she was delighted to see Micah and the twins.

Chloe was waving frantically, and with a huge grin she couldn't control, Hope waved back almost as eagerly. She hurried over to the wagon when Micah pulled to a stop. "I thought you left for New York."

"We're back again." Micah signaled her with his eyes that he didn't want to talk in front of the twins.

"I have Dutch Blitz, so we can play together." Chloe waved the box in the air.

"Hope might have work to do," Micah warned her.

"Why don't you go into the house and ask my *daed*? I'm sure he'd love to play with you." Hope motioned to Jabin. "You too, Jabin."

He'd been sitting sullenly in the wagon, but after she smiled at him, he climbed down with a grimace and trudged toward the house.

"Is he still in pain?" Hope asked.

Micah rubbed at the wrinkles between his brows. "He might be, but he's not talking, so I can't say. I believe most of it is emotional, not physical."

Hope wanted to reach out to him, and to Chloe too. "If you'd be all right with it, I could do a little therapy with the twins to help them with their grief."

Micah hesitated. "I'm not sure about that. I never heard of this horse therapy stuff. Is it dangerous?"

If she wasn't mistaken, he was fighting to keep his voice from shaking. Something about doing therapy must scare him, but what? She wanted to reassure him. "No, there shouldn't be any danger, especially not for children like Chloe and Jabin, who've always been around horses. And our mares are extremely gentle and used to being around children."

Micah didn't look convinced.

His reaction confused Hope. She expected to have conversations like this with some of the *Englischers*, but the Amish all grew up around horses. By age three or four, most Amish children were feeding the horses and doing barn chores. She wished she could figure out what was troubling him.

Micah still hadn't responded, so she tried to convince him to let her help. "My heart goes out to Chloe and Jabin after—" Hope squeezed her eyes shut, trying to block out the terrible image. "I'm concerned about both of them.

Their circumstances are different than most, and horse therapy can help with grief."

"Could it possibly help Jabin? He's completely shut down and refusing to talk."

"Expressing their feelings is important for children after a tragedy. The ones who bottle up their feelings sometimes have a harder time adjusting. Often horses, as nonjudgmental listeners, give quieter children a safe place to begin expressing their emotions."

"How do you know so much about children's reactions?" The admiration in Micah's eyes sent shivers through her.

"I've been reading and taking classes, and Logan has been helping me. We've been creating tip sheets to explain the benefits for different needs. He and I can work up one on grief to show you." She wished they'd done that already. Micah seemed to need a lot of convincing.

"You know, Micah, a therapist recently told me about a widow who brought her two children for grief therapy. The mother spent an hour alone with a horse, and when she came out, tears were dripping down her cheeks, but being with the horse had transformed her. She hadn't been able to cry or express her feelings until she had that time by herself in the stall."

While she was talking about being alone with the horse, Micah's expression changed, and he stepped backward. A look of terror flared in his eyes. What had she said that upset him? Maybe she'd misread his reaction, and hearing about two fatherless children had brought back memories of the accident.

His voice a bit shaky, Micah asked, "You don't leave children alone with the horses?"

Not usually. Although she had allowed Chloe private time with Molly. "During lessons, Logan and I stay in the stall. If the child is on horseback, we have two volunteers who act as sidewalkers and stay beside the rider, and another one leads the horse. Logan and I both accompany them too."

When he hesitated, she said, "Unlike Chloe and Jabin, some of the *Englisch* students have never been around horses, so they need a lot of extra supervision. Amish children grow up caring for horses and are comfortable around them."

"Not always," he muttered. A worried frown creased his brow. "I'm willing to try anything to help Jabin, but I don't want him to get hurt."

"I promise he'll be safe. There's no way I'd take a chance of him getting hurt."

"I know you wouldn't." He held her gaze for a few long beats.

Beats that made her tingle. She broke his gaze. "I'd like to see if I could help, and I'd be extra-careful with Jabin and Chloe."

Although his eyes still looked wary, he said finally, "I trust you with them."

Despite his misgivings, he'd just given her a precious gift: his trust. Hope would do everything in her power to be worthy of it.

Chapter Fifteen

Micah hoped she couldn't tell his legs were trembling. He needed to get control of this fear. He couldn't pass it on to the twins. And as a role model, he should demonstrate his faith in God. He'd just told Hope he trusted her. And he did.

He also trusted the almighty and all-powerful God in all areas of his life. Except for this one. Why did he struggle to turn this terror over to the Lord?

"Micah?" Hope's soft voice brought him back to the present moment, and he met her gaze again. That was a mistake. He hoped his eyes didn't give away his feelings.

Taking the first step in faith that God would protect the twins, Micah said, "I'd like you to work with Chloe and Jabin. What do we need to do to get started?" He hoped he didn't sound too eager, but this would give him a reason to return, to see her again. "How much is it?" Cost didn't matter. He'd pay whatever she asked.

"I'm happy to do it for free."

Micah crossed his arms and shot her a stern look. "You have a business to run, and you need to make a profit."

"I have people who pay, but I don't charge my friend Priscilla. And I certainly wouldn't charge you."

He shook his head. "*Daed* and I do harness making, and

if we gave away harnesses to all our friends, we'd be out of business in weeks."

"I'm not giving away lessons to all my friends. Only certain ones."

"Look, I appreciate the offer, but you're just starting up, right?"

"How did you know?"

Micah waved to the sign near the end of the driveway. "That sign wasn't there the last time I was here, and in the hospital, you mentioned you planned to start working with children this week."

"Yes, I–I mean, we—started on Monday."

"You and your *daed*?"

"No, Logan and me. Logan's the therapist. I'm still taking classes."

"I see." He refused to examine the churning emotions at the thought of her working closely with that *Englischer*. "So, what are your usual fees? I insist on paying."

"We have an introductory offer this week for free lessons. Why don't you see if they help and then decide?"

Micah nodded. "All right. As long as you're not extending the offer only to us." He tilted his head to one side, as if trying to decide if she was being honest.

"You can read the newspapers and last week's *Die Botschaft* if you don't believe me."

"I'm sorry. I didn't mean to imply you weren't telling the truth."

Hope hadn't taken offense. "I understand. You don't want special privileges." Even if she'd be happy to give them to him.

"Exactly." He beamed at her. "Do we need to schedule an appointment?"

"That would be helpful. Let's go to my office to check the calendar."

As they walked into the barn, she asked him the question that had been on her mind ever since he'd pulled into the driveway. "How long will you be in town?"

"My family discussed it, and we decided it might be best for the twins to live here permanently."

Permanently? Hope swallowed back a joyous cheer. "All of you are moving down here, then?"

"No, only me and the twins."

"That's a lot of responsibility. It's not easy caring for children."

He laughed a bit unsteadily. "I've already discovered that."

When he told her about Chloe running away, Hope drew in a breath. "You must have been frantic."

"We all were." His expression revealed his relief after they found her.

Hope prayed horse therapy might help Chloe as well as Jabin.

"*Mamm* thought it might be best for the twins to start school with their friends to make their adjustment a little easier."

"That was wise."

"*Jah*, but I'm afraid I'm only adding to the chaos."

Hope tried not to laugh when he told her about the oatmeal. "How high was the flame?"

Micah shrugged. "I just turned it on and didn't check."

"Too high, probably. At least, that's what it sounds like. Next time, be sure the flame is low. It sounds like you got everything else right."

"*Danke*, I'll try that."

His face flushed a little, and she hoped she hadn't embarrassed him. "Everyone makes mistakes when they're learning to cook. I've had many a pot boil over. It happens even to experienced cooks."

"I appreciate you trying to make me feel better, but that wasn't the only thing I got wrong. I'm sure you noticed Chloe's hair."

She had. And she'd planned to get Chloe alone for a bit to fix it. "If you intend to do all these things yourself, it's a lot to learn. It might be good to get someone to come in and help with things like meals and caring for the children."

"That's what *Mamm* suggested, but the only people I know to ask are"—he laughed nervously—"Sylvia and Susie."

"Oh dear." Hope didn't want to be too critical in case he intended to ask them, but remembering the hospital room and Sylvia's intentions—

"You met them. I don't think they'd be, um, suitable."

She tried not to laugh at his horrified expression. "Well, Sylvia was a bit pushy."

"To say the least. I worried she might find a way to force me into courting Susie."

That was certainly obvious. Most parents didn't get involved in their children's dating or relationships, but Sylvia seemed desperate to pair up her daughter. Hope was glad Micah hadn't been taken in by the ruse.

"Not that Susie isn't a nice girl," he added. "And I'm sure she'll be a wonderful mother and homemaker, but . . ."

Hearing Micah compliment Susie twisted Hope's stomach. Sylvia had made him aware of her daughter's good points. Hope squinched her eyes at the possibility that Micah might make a hasty decision to give the twins a mother.

"Are you all right?" Micah asked.

Hope smoothed her face into a neutral expression. She had no claim on Micah, so she had no right to feel jealous of Susie. "If it would help, I'd be happy to watch the twins until they start school."

"I couldn't let you do that. You have a business to run."

"We've just opened, so most students won't be starting until next week. If I have lessons, the twins can stay in the house with *Daed*. He adores children, and he's already bonded with Chloe. They'd be good company for him, because he gets lonely."

Micah appeared about to refuse, so she said quickly, "It'd also make it easier for me to do some therapy with them and give you time to work. I assume you'll be taking over the harness shop?"

"I need to see what I can work out with Eli." Micah shuffled his feet. "He'd like to buy the business. I'd thought about selling it to him, especially when we planned to move the twins to New York. Now I'm not so sure."

"It's a big decision. You might want to give yourself time."

"*Jah. Daed*'s grandfather started the business, so it's been in the family a long while. My *daed* said he's open to selling, though."

Micah appeared reluctant to keep the harness shop, which seemed odd. From what she'd seen as she passed, the store always looked busy.

"It doesn't sound as if you want to run the business," Hope pointed out. "Is there something else you'd rather do?"

"It's not that I don't like harness making. I've worked hard to develop my skills over the years, and I enjoy the feel and smell of leather, the precision of the tools, but—" His eyes glassy, Micah stared off into the distance.

Hope longed to wipe the sadness from his face. Maybe she could talk him into horse therapy for himself. If it worked for the widow, it might help him get over his brother's death. She could at least offer.

"Micah?"

He jumped as if she'd startled him. "What? Oh, right. The lessons for the twins. What would work best for you?"

"They're already here. If you have time, I'd be happy to do it now."

"I was planning to get a buggy." Again, sorrowful and terrified expressions crossed his face.

Hope pressed a hand against her mouth as the accident came rushing back. Micah remained silent, no doubt reliving the same images. When she'd blocked them and could speak again, she offered, "Why don't you leave Chloe and Jabin here? I can use the time for the lessons. I imagine buggy shopping will be traumatic enough for you."

She had no idea how traumatic. At the thought of unhooking Daffy from the wagon and hitching her up to a buggy, the heavy weight pressing on Micah's chest barely allowed him to draw in shallow breaths.

"Are you all right?" Hope's gentle question penetrated his nervousness.

He needed to control his reactions. After a brief prayer, he managed a half smile. Before she caught on to the real reason for his distress, he changed the subject and tried to keep his words strong and firm. "I'll accept the free lessons only if you tell me how much I owe you for a series."

She opened a desk drawer and slid a pricing sheet across the desk. He waited until she let go before reaching for it. He didn't want to accidentally brush her fingers. He had enough trouble already with his heart rate and breathing.

He brought the sheet into focus. Wow! Lessons were expensive. But if you factored in the care and feeding of the horses, barn maintenance, equipment, insurance and licenses, taxes, mortgage, vet fees, and paying a therapist . . . Micah did some quick calculations. She'd need quite a few students to pay the bills to cover her costs.

It was none of his business, but doing all the management and bookkeeping at *Daed*'s harness shop had given him a lot of knowledge about running a business. "You don't have to answer if you don't want, but how many students will you need to turn a profit?"

"It depends on which packages they choose."

"I'm wondering if you'll get paid after you deduct all your overhead. I just did some rough figuring, and I'm concerned you'll need to work long hours to pay everyone else."

She laughed. "Now you sound like Logan."

"He must be sensible, then." Doing all the calculations had taken his mind off his fears, so he could concentrate more clearly on Hope.

"Do you think it'll be a problem?"

"I don't like the idea of you putting in ten- or twelve-hour days just to cover your bills. You might want to increase your fees." Micah almost chuckled to himself. He'd gone from being shocked at her rates to telling her she should raise them. "How do they compare to other horse therapy farms?"

"I didn't have time to do much checking. I went lower than Logan's previous employer, hoping it would make us competitive."

"You really should see. And figure out your total expenses to be sure you'll make money rather than just break even."

"I wish I had your understanding of the financial side of things. That's always been a struggle for me, ever since . . ." She stopped speaking, and her mouth twisted to one side.

"Since?" he prompted.

Hope shrugged and stared at the desktop.

It seemed as if she'd been about to say something important, then she'd clammed up. Micah had no right to pry, but maybe she needed help. He repeated his question again.

"Since, um, since I took over the bookkeeping for *Daed*," she finished hurriedly. "I had to learn on the job and never really liked it."

Something was upsetting her. She appeared so nervous, Micah wanted to reach out to comfort her. She'd once held his hand, but how would she react if he did the same? He clutched his suspenders to keep his hands still.

"I'd be happy to help, if you'd like. I've been doing accounting since I was sixteen, and I enjoy it. I could also figure out your overhead and pricing to keep the business profitable."

"That's kind of you." Hope looked as if she were eager to agree, but then her eyes grew shuttered. "But no, *danke*."

Why had she turned down an offer she obviously wanted to accept? Because she didn't want to spend time around him?

Hope clenched her hands in her lap. It would be such a relief to turn over that part of the business to Micah. He'd most likely do an excellent job if they'd kept their family business going for three generations. But the thought of letting someone, especially a man, gain access to her finances turned her stomach. After what *Daed* had done, she'd be wary about letting anyone else handle the business funds ever again.

When she met Micah's wounded eyes, she felt awful. She hadn't meant to hurt him, not after he'd been so kind about offering his assistance. "I'm sorry." How could she explain?

He turned and strode over to the small window so his back was to her. "No, I'm the one who's sorry. I shouldn't have interfered. I'd be hesitant to let a person I barely know look over my finances. Forgive me for being pushy."

"You weren't pushy," she said. "It was thoughtful."

"It's your business, and I'm sure you're doing a fine job. Why don't we go back to scheduling sessions? I'll sign them up for the six-week package. Is it all right if I bring the money when I pick them up?"

"Of course. Or you can wait until they take their first paid lessons." She couldn't believe how generous he was after she'd been unkind. "Also, I plan to give a discount for two children from the same family." She hadn't put that on their fee schedule, but she'd add it.

"That's all right." He faced her. "You don't need to do anything special for us."

"I intend to do it for everyone. With many Amish families being large, it might make a difference."

"That's true." Micah gestured toward her calendar. "They'll only have half days at school next week, so they could come in the afternoons. Once they begin full days, though, it'll have to be after school."

"What about Mondays at three thirty?" That way she'd see him again as soon as possible.

"That should be fine." Micah headed for the door. "I'll try not to take too long. I appreciate you giving them lessons today."

"I'm happy to do it."

Hope could hardly believe she'd have the twins for students. With the plan he'd selected, she'd see him every Monday for the next six weeks. Her insides fluttered with happiness.

Chapter Sixteen

Hope entered the house to find the twins playing Dutch Blitz with *Daed*. Although Chloe was grinning as she laid down a card, Jabin had a distressed look that didn't match his hand. He looked the closest to calling Blitz, but he placed his cards down listlessly. Hope prayed she could reach him with horse therapy.

To call it therapy, she should have Logan here, but she could do informal lessons. Sometimes just bringing children and animals together helped. Her horses usually sensed what she needed. So far, they'd shown they'd do the same for children.

"When you're done with that game," Hope said, "I'd like to take Chloe and Jabin out to the barn."

Daed's broad smile dimmed. Hope wanted to make it reappear. She'd promised Micah the children wouldn't be alone in the stalls with the horses. Maybe *Daed* would be willing to assist her. He was a seasoned trainer and loved working with horses.

"*Daed*, will you help us out in the barn?"

"Of course."

Hope had guessed right that Jabin would be the winner. She could hardly hear his "Blitz." After *Daed* and Chloe totaled up their cards to see who had the highest score, Hope beckoned to him. "Chloe, can you and Jabin clean up the cards?" Sorting the cards should take them a little while, giving her enough time to explain to *Daed* her purpose in the barn.

"I thought I'd start with Jabin, if you don't mind keeping Chloe occupied," she said to *Daed* after she'd told him about the therapy.

"I'd be happy to." He stood more erect than he had in a long time.

"*Gut*. Then we can have dinner before my turn with Chloe."

They returned to find the twins had placed the cards in their correct decks.

Chloe hopped off her chair. "Let's go," she said, motioning for the others to follow her. Then she skipped out to the barn, with everyone following her.

Daed called after her to slow down because he couldn't keep up. She obeyed and waited for him, giving Hope and Jabin time alone.

Jabin's head remained down as he shuffled out to the barn. Hope set a hand on his shoulder and gave it a light squeeze. He winced. Had she hurt him, or was that his reaction to being touched?

She dropped her hand to her side. "Did that bother your sore ribs?"

His shoulder blades went up in a semi-shrug. Maybe she should refrain from touching him. At least for now. They walked the rest of the distance to the barn in silence.

"Come into Daisy's stall with me," Hope said. Chloe would likely make a beeline for Molly. That way, several stalls would separate them. Hope set the horse's grooming tools on a stool right outside the stall.

"Will you help me currycomb Daisy?" she asked. "The tools are right there." She pointed to the basket behind him.

Slower than a pig mired in mud, Jabin inched his way over to the bucket and back.

"You know how to do this, right?"

Instead of answering, Jabin began working. His curry-combing was as lackluster as his walking.

She wanted to put her hand over his to direct him to move faster, but she curbed her impatience. Instead, she watched for times when he pressed a little harder.

"Look how Daisy leaned into that. You must be digging deep enough to get out the dirt and make her feel better."

Her encouragement gradually transformed his movements. Soon he was currycombing more energetically. When he stopped, Daisy nudged him with her nose.

"You have a horse at home, right?" Hope said as he switched to the stiff brush.

"*Jah.*"

A small victory. That was the first word he'd spoken around her today other than "Blitz."

"When you groom her, talk to her. Tell her how you're feeling, tell her what's upsetting you. Horses are good listeners."

Hope was pretty sure Jabin's slight head movement had been a nod. Maybe he'd take her advice.

"You can also tell secrets to Daisy. She's smart and can understand people's feelings. And I can't hear what you're saying."

Jabin's squinty side-eye made it clear he didn't believe her.

"You can whisper. I like to give people privacy, so I don't listen. But if you don't trust me, you can talk to Daisy in your thoughts. Horses can sense what you're feeling. Why don't you try it to see?"

He still looked skeptical, but this time about the horse's abilities. Moving closer to Daisy's head, he mumbled near her ear. Then he glanced over at Hope. She kept brushing Daisy's other side.

Satisfied she wasn't listening in, he leaned closer to Daisy, who turned her head and nuzzled him. A strange gurgling sound came from Jabin's mouth—a cross between a giggle and a sob. Hope stayed focused on her work and left the therapy up to Daisy.

After stopping at the bank for cash to pay Hope, Micah did his used buggy shopping as quickly as he could. He had no interest in any special features—unusual upholstery colors, fancy dashboards, cup holders, speedometers, dash lights, or propane heaters. Teens often favored those models. He preferred the least-expensive, four-seater one that was functional, safe, and sturdy.

The salesman, who answered his questions about the two buggies Micah was considering, pointed to the one with the battery mounted underneath rather than inside. "This one's a bit more expensive, but with the battery on the undercarriage, it would be much safer in an accident."

Micah winced at the word "accident." No amount of safety features could have saved Ben and Anna from that drunk driver. Micah struggled to wipe the picture from his mind.

"It also has LED lights."

When he'd helped his *daed* pick out a buggy, the only required safety features included battery-powered sidelights and an orange reflective triangle on the back. He could take the less-expensive model and have both of those. Only one thing stopped him: the twins.

Because he'd be carting them around, Micah wanted the

safest buggy he could find. They were all he had left of his brother. If anything happened to them . . .

He couldn't even finish the thought. They were his responsibility, and better than anyone, he knew the tragedies that could happen on the road.

"I'll take this one," he said, pointing to the more-expensive one. "Is there any way I could pay extra to have it delivered?"

"Two of the owner's sons should be able to get it out to your house later in the evening, after we close."

Micah exhaled a long, silent sigh. That would save him from hooking up another vehicle. He'd been around enough horses for one day. "They can leave it by the barn if I'm not there."

The ride back to Hope's went quickly, and her *daed* was exiting the barn as he drove in.

"Back so soon?" Isaac asked. "We were hoping the children could stay longer. Hope hasn't had time to give Chloe her lesson yet."

"I can wait. Where is she? In the barn?"

Micah had already turned in that direction before Isaac spoke.

"*Jah*, Chloe's in the barn. Hope and Jabin are in the kitchen fixing dinner. You're welcome to join us."

"Chloe's alone in the barn?" Dread washed over him. If something happened to her, he'd never forgive himself.

"She wanted to keep talking to Molly privately, so I left her there."

Oh, he'd panicked too soon. Hope said they had two adults in the stall during lessons. And if Chloe was talking to someone, she'd probably be in the office or kitchen, not with the horses. At least he hoped that was the case.

"I'll go check on her." Micah needed to assure himself she was all right.

"You do that. Then bring her in with you to eat."

"That's kind of you." Micah didn't want to impose on Hope. He'd just pay her and leave. Isaac had mentioned something about Chloe's lesson. If she hadn't had one yet, why was she hanging around the barn?

He prayed Molly was responsible. Although Micah's *daed* was dependable, he couldn't prevent Micah's childhood injuries. Micah would rather the twins not hang around in the barn before and after lessons. He'd speak to Hope about that.

Micah hurried into the barn, propelled by worry. Anything could happen. He jogged past the stalls toward the kitchen and office, staying close to the opposite wall, as far away from the horses as possible. As he passed the last stall, he screeched to a stop.

"Chloe," he screamed. "Get away from that horse. All the way to the other side of the stall."

She stared at him, her eyes wide, but kept her arms around the horse's neck.

"It's not safe to get so close." In his fear for her, his words came out more sharply than he'd intended.

"Molly won't hurt me."

Molly? Molly was a horse? He couldn't believe Hope and Isaac would leave a seven-year-old out here alone.

"Please, Chloe, step back. Come out of the stall." Trembling, he rushed over to grab her and yank her out of harm's way.

Chloe had looked at him as if he were crazy when he burst through the stall door. Maybe he was, but he'd never take a chance on her getting hurt. Wrapping his arms around her, he tried to drag her away.

She dug in her heels. "I'm not done talking to Molly."

The horse stamped, twisting her body and snorting.

"No!" Micah grabbed Chloe around the waist, lifted her

into the air, and rushed from the stall. After he'd slammed the door shut behind them and latched it, he set her on her feet. "You should never be in there with a horse by yourself." He could barely catch his breath.

Her chin quivered. "*Mamm* and *Daed* always let me."

Micah's gut twisted. He had no defense against that. He didn't want to remind her he was caring for her now. But he couldn't allow her to do something dangerous. "I don't want you to get hurt."

"I'm not going to." She crossed her arms and thrust out her lower lip.

"You have no idea how dangerous horses can be. One kick from their legs can send you back to the hospital. And you wouldn't get out in a few days." *If you even survived.*

In a smart-alecky voice, she said, "Only if you get too close when you're behind them." Then her tone changed to exasperation. "I'm not a baby. I know how to be careful around horses."

That might be, but it didn't mean he wanted to take any chances. Thank God she was all right this time. Micah wasn't so sure letting Chloe and Jabin take these therapy lessons was wise. As much as he wanted to help Hope get her business started, he couldn't put the twins' lives in danger.

Hope entered the barn to hear Micah scolding Chloe. She wasn't close enough to discern his words or Chloe's sharp answers, but the little girl had her arms folded and her chin jutting out.

All Hope could tell was that it had something to do with Chloe being in the stall with a horse. Feeling guilty, Hope rushed toward them. Micah had specifically asked if an adult would be with the twins, and she'd promised him two of them would be there. Unfortunately, *Daed* had left Chloe by herself.

"I'm so sorry," Hope said as she reached them. "When *Daed* told me Chloe was alone, I hurried out." She wasn't about to admit the other reason she'd dashed out here was to see Micah.

He turned toward her, his eyes filled with terror. Hope sucked in a breath. What had happened? Chloe appeared to be all right, if a bit defiant. A quick glance reassured Hope that Molly had suffered no injuries. Micah had no visible wounds, but he was trembling, and his chest was heaving.

"Are you all right?" she asked, alarmed by his pale skin.

"I am now." He inhaled a big gulp of air. "I found Chloe alone in Molly's stall."

Was that accusation in his tone, or had she only imagined it because she deserved it?

"And he pulled me out."

"Did something go wrong? Usually Molly's gentle. I've never known her to hurt anyone."

"She was stamping and snorting and—"

"Horses do that," Chloe snapped. "It doesn't mean she's going to hurt me."

"I'm sorry she scared you, Micah." Hope was puzzled by his over-the-top reaction to normal horse behavior. "I don't think Molly would hurt Chloe."

"Of course she wouldn't." Chloe stamped her foot and looked close to tears. "I was just talking to her."

"Horses are dangerous," Micah declared, his tone flat.

"I suppose they can be—"

"Can be? There's no 'can' about it. They are."

His emphatic tone and panicky expression made Hope wonder if he'd seen someone get hurt. "Did something happen to make you believe horses are dangerous?" she asked softly.

He stared at her. "How did you know?"

"I just guessed because you seem so upset." His fear was unusual for an Amish man who'd been around horses every day, starting from the time he was small.

Micah closed his eyes for a moment, then he gazed off into the distance. "When I was five, a horse kicked me. After two weeks in the hospital, I needed physical therapy to help me walk again. I still limp if I get overtired."

"Oh, Micah." No wonder he acted traumatized around horses.

"Every time I enter a barn or get near a horse, I feel that tail flicking across my forehead, knocking off my hat."

Micah's uneven breathing made Hope long to reach out to comfort him. Even Chloe stood still, her hands clenched into fists by her sides, staring at her *onkel*.

"Did it hurt you?" she asked.

"The tail? It stung, but I don't remember the horse's kick. The real pain came when I was alone in the dark hospital room. That still gives me nightmares."

No wonder he hadn't wanted to leave the twins alone in the hospital. It also explained why he'd been so grateful that she'd stayed until he arrived. Hope was so glad she had. She only wished she'd told him she planned to stay when she first called him, so he didn't have to endure the long ride there assuming the twins were alone.

Chloe moved closer and tucked her hand into Micah's. "The hospital made you scared?"

He nodded. "I was petrified."

"Me too," she said in a shaky voice.

Micah knelt in front of her and placed his hands on her shoulders. "I'm sorry. I tried to stay with you so you wouldn't be frightened." Then he opened his arms and drew Chloe close.

She buried her face against his chest, so her words came

out muffled. "I'm glad you were there. But I was scared about not having a *mamm* and a *daed*. I still am." Her shoulders shook. "That's what I was telling Molly."

Micah's eyes welled with tears, and Hope wanted to wrap them both in a hug. She remained silent as the two of them clung to each other. But she sent up prayers for their healing.

Chapter Seventeen

When Micah finally stood, holding Chloe tightly in his arms, he gazed over at Hope with blurry eyes. The sympathy on her face touched him, and her calmness quieted the anxiety racing through him. Once again, she reminded him of an angel.

"I apologize. I didn't mean to create a therapy session for you in the barn aisle." He lightened his tone, hoping it would come out as a joke.

To his relief, she smiled. "You're lucky this week's sessions are free."

He laughed. "That's good, because I only brought enough money for the twins." He tried not to let his concerns show, but after the scare he'd just had, he was undecided about letting them work with horses.

"Now that I know how hard it is for you to be around horses," Hope said, "I feel even worse about leaving Chloe out here alone and asking you to let them come for lessons."

"Everything turned out all right." Except that his heart was still hammering. Although he couldn't be sure if it was caused by fright or by being near Hope.

"You know, we do have lessons to help students get over their fear of horses. If you want, I'd be happy to help you."

Micah's whole body tightened. If he hadn't conquered this fear in more than two decades, he doubted a few children's lessons would help. "I don't think . . ."

"It might be worth a try."

How could he resist her pleading look? Even if it meant making a fool of himself. He couldn't look her in the eye as he mumbled, "All right."

Chloe glanced from one to the other. "You can do it, *Onkel* Micah. Horses aren't scary, are they, Hope?"

"Not for you or me," Hope answered, "but your *onkel* had a terrible accident. Learning to trust again after being badly hurt can be very difficult." As she well knew. That went for people, as well as horses.

Her head bowed, Chloe muttered something under her breath. The only word Micah caught was *God*. She didn't appear to be praying.

"What?" he asked.

She turned startled eyes to him, but then glanced at the floor. "Nothing."

Hope's troubled expression indicated she'd heard Chloe's words. He'd ask her later. Right now, he should pay and leave.

He'd had enough stress for one day, with burning breakfast, hitching up the wagon, buying a buggy, and rescuing Chloe from danger. It had been less than a week since the funeral, and only one full day of being a single parent. And he still had to deal with the harness business.

"Micah?" Hope leaned over and touched his arm.

Each of her fingertips set nerve endings zinging up his arm and through his body.

"Is everything all right?"

"Fine," he managed, when what he really wanted to say was "wunderbar." He longed to set his hand over hers, to feel the softness again. That desire warred with the one warning him to back away.

Realizing she'd touched him, Hope lowered her hand, although she wouldn't mind keeping it there on his strong, tanned arm. Did he look disappointed, or was that only her imagination?

"Why don't you both come in for dinner?" she suggested. "It'll give everyone a chance to calm down."

Micah shook his head. "We don't want to take advantage of you. You've done so much already."

"Don't be silly. We'd love to have you." *Great, Hope. Way to make your interest obvious.* "It really isn't much. Just soup and sandwiches."

"While we're here, I want to pay you."

Hope raised an eyebrow. "You're sure? I'll understand if you'd rather not." She could only imagine how terrifying it would be for him to deal with his fears.

Micah fidgeted. "I need to do something to help Jabin."

Chloe tugged at his hand. "What about me?"

"*Jah*, you too." He glanced at Hope. "Can't do one without the other, it seems."

Chloe frowned, and he added, "Not that I intended to try."

"Especially not with twins." Hope's understanding smile kindled a spark that might grow into a blaze if he didn't quench it.

She turned to lead the way to her office, and Chloe skipped beside her. "About Jabin," Hope said as she ushered them into the room, "he seemed to respond well to being with Daisy and spent a lot of time whispering to her."

Micah's jaw tightened. "Is Daisy a person or a horse?"

"A horse." Hope wanted to calm the fear flickering in his eyes. "Please don't worry. I was with him the whole time, holding on to Daisy. I promised Jabin I wouldn't listen, and I didn't try to hear."

"I talk to Molly too. She's a good listener."

At Micah's wince, Hope longed to reach out and touch his arm, but instead, she clutched the sides of her black work apron.

He reached into his wallet and counted out a stack of twenties. Then he held them out to her.

Hope shook her head. "I really don't feel right accepting this. I'm happy to work with the twins for free."

"Absolutely not. A business needs to make money, and you deserve to be paid." When she continued to hesitate, Micah laid the money on the desk. "I hope you don't make it this hard for all your customers to pay."

"Of course not." Hope followed her snappish response with a laugh. "I'm only making it hard for you."

A slight breeze coming through the window ruffled the money, and Micah said, "I'd suggest putting that away before any of it blows off the desk."

She didn't want to accept it. "I wish you wouldn't—"

"If you don't take it, I won't bring the twins for lessons."

That would mean not seeing him again. His threat made her want to snatch up the money, but she forced herself to pick it up slowly.

"Chloe and I will go outside while you put it away." Micah took Chloe's hand, headed out the door, and closed it behind him.

Hope, eager to be with him, pulled out the drawer, slid the money inside the cashbox, and hurried after them.

When she opened the door, she almost bumped into Micah. "*Ach*, I'm so sorry."

She wasn't sorry, though, that her hands brushed his arms as she slowed down and steadied herself. She might have managed to halt her feet, but she could do nothing to slow her galloping pulse.

"L–let's go in for dinner." She hoped Micah would attribute her sudden loss of breath to the surprise of almost running into him.

As they exited the barn, Micah hugged the wall opposite the horse's stalls. Hope moved so she was between him and the horses, and he rewarded her with a tight smile. He really was terrified. She prayed he'd agree to let her do some sessions with him. How could he handle ordinary duties like hooking up the buggy or feeding the animals?

Daed was waiting when Micah opened the screen door. "I thought you were never going to come. Jabin and I are hungry."

Jabin met her gaze for a second, but then lowered his head. Hope rejoiced. She considered even that brief look as progress.

Micah tried to leave, but *Daed* beckoned him inside and insisted he stay.

The phone rang twice, with parents wanting to enroll their students for a free lesson before the school year began. After she and Chloe put everything on the table, Hope turned off the ringer and set the phone on the countertop.

When they all bowed their heads to pray, Hope smiled. If only she could have family gathered around the table like this every day. But as quickly as her spirits soared, they nose-dived. A dream like this would never come true for her. Not ever.

* * *

Leaving the twins behind seemed unfair to Hope, who'd already watched them most of the morning, but after they'd finished eating, both Chloe and Jabin begged to stay, and even Isaac put in a plea for their company. Micah had to admit it would be easier to discuss the harness-making business with Eli this afternoon if the twins weren't along. And he worried about how returning to their parents' business would affect them.

"*Danke*," Micah told Hope and Isaac as Chloe took Hope's hand to drag her out to the barn.

"Jabin got a special lesson," Chloe said, "and I want mine."

"Just a minute." Hope slowed down Chloe's pulling. "Let's say goodbye to your *onkel* first."

"Goodbye," Chloe said, yanking on Hope's arm.

"I didn't get my turn." Hope faced Micah with a smile that brightened his whole day. Its sunshine thawed the icy sadness inside, and he wanted to bask in its warmth for as long as possible.

He might have, if Chloe hadn't practically jerked Hope off her feet.

"Chloe!" Micah stopped her. "Be careful you don't knock Hope over."

His niece stopped tugging and glowered. "Saying goodbye doesn't take that long."

Sometimes it did when you didn't want to say goodbye.

"I'm sure this won't be easy," Hope said. "I'll be praying."

Her caring touched Micah's soul.

"I can use the prayers." Micah lingered until Hope and Chloe disappeared into the barn. He'd rather stay here than face the harness shop, but he steeled himself to do his duty.

Being around Hope always brought a sense of calmness, one that stayed with him as he drove into town. He pulled into the parking lot and tied his horse to the hitching post.

He dreaded going inside, where he'd be around horses and his brother's memory. They'd spent many childhood hours there together in the family business, a place where, once again, Ben had proved to be a star. His brother moved smoothly between greeting customers, measuring horses, answering phones, and doing leatherwork, while Micah hid out at the tables in the back with the harnesses to avoid coming into contact with horses.

In addition to facing the responsibilities at the shop today, Micah had to face his brother's ghost. A ghost who did every job perfectly. A ghost who never made mistakes. A ghost who haunted Micah's dreams. A ghost with whom he needed to make peace.

If only he could ask Ben for forgiveness.

Before Micah went inside, he bowed his head and prayed for help and courage. Then, with God's strength, he stiffened his spine and strode across the asphalt toward the building that had been his workplace for many years. As he opened the familiar door, all the old memories washed over him. He closed his eyes to compose himself as images of *Daed* behind the counter and Ben talking to customers washed over him.

Rather than the bustling shop he recalled, the store was uncrowded. Eli stood behind the counter talking to a customer.

"Come in," Eli called. "Nice to see you, Micah. I'll be right there."

Micah waved to let Eli know to take his time. Strolling

around the shop looking at inventory and fighting back tears kept Micah busy until Eli had finished.

"It's good to see you," Eli said. "Someone mentioned you'd headed back to New York, so I wasn't expecting you to stop by for a while. Any thoughts on what you intend to do with the shop?"

"I'm not sure yet," Micah admitted. "My plans have changed, and I'll be staying in Lancaster with the twins."

Eli's face twitched a bit before settling into a welcoming expression, and Micah was pretty sure Eli was disappointed. He'd made it clear he'd like to buy the business.

"I'm still considering your offer," Micah told him. "I'm not sure yet what I'm going to do. If you're still willing to manage the business for now, I'd appreciate it."

With a quick bob of his head, Eli agreed. "Take whatever time you need. I know it isn't an easy decision."

If it weren't for the family ties to the business, Micah would have sold it right away, but he needed to respect *Daed*'s wishes and his heritage. "I'm glad you're willing to take care of things. Can you tell me how things worked here under . . . Ben?"

Eli lifted his glasses and rubbed his eyes. "Well, Ben enjoyed greeting the customers and handling the horses. He didn't do much of the crafting." As if worried he might sound critical, Eli added hastily, "I don't mean he wasn't skilled. He did a wonderful *gut* job when he sat down to work."

Micah had forgotten that about his brother. *Daed* often lectured Ben about concentrating and being patient. Ben had been good at making harnesses, but he'd been antsy, always hopping up to get something or talk to someone. Micah had been the one who did most of the tedious, detailed jobs. He'd always been ashamed of hiding out in the workroom while Ben measured horses and socialized. Was it possible *Daed* had valued Micah's skills as much as he had Ben's?

Pushing the thought aside as prideful, Micah concentrated on business questions. "I guess that meant you created the harnesses?" Micah looked at Eli for confirmation.

"Well, yes." Eli shuffled his feet. "You can measure horses all day, but if no one's making the products, the business won't go anywhere."

"That's true. So, you enjoy leatherwork, then?"

Eli shrugged. "Doesn't everyone?"

Micah wasn't sure his brother had. They'd both learned their father's trade from the time they were small. They had a family business to run, so they never had a chance to explore other career options. Perhaps Ben had been unhappy with his choice.

Hope came to mind as someone who'd chosen a profession she loved. Her face shone when she talked about horses or children.

With his interest in horses, Ben would have made a good partner for her. Hope needed a husband who would be an active partner in her business, someone who'd muck out horse stalls, assist with lessons, and groom horses. Unlike Micah, who avoided horses at all costs. Rather than an asset, he'd be a detriment. Mentally, he shook himself. No point in going there.

"What do you have in mind for the business?" Eli asked. "And what do you want me to be doing?"

The questions forced Micah's thoughts away from Hope. "You've been keeping things running since . . . since last week. How has it been going?"

"Well, we shut down last week, of course, so we're a little behind. I've contacted everyone, and we're working on the rush orders first. But so many people have been stopping by to offer condolences, I barely have time to sit down and work. Actually, this is the first time the shop's been quiet."

"You'd probably prefer to work on harnesses than handle the customers, I imagine." Given the choice, Micah certainly would.

"I never had a chance to wait on customers. As I said, Ben handled that, and Anna ran the cash register and did the accounting." He turned sorrowful eyes to the counter. "It seems so empty in here now."

A buggy pulled in, and Eli said, "Excuse me." He started toward the door but stopped. "Unless you'd rather take care of it?"

"No, no. You go ahead." The last thing Micah wanted to do was stand beside a horse. He strolled back to the workroom, where one older teen was working. The boy was so absorbed in his work, he didn't look up.

Micah definitely wanted no part of handling horses, but would Eli be all right with working out front? What if Micah sold the business? Would he miss harness making?

Eli joined him. "We have another order. Not sure how we're going to get it all done."

"I can come in to help tomorrow, and the twins start school next week, so I can do half days if it'll help you to catch up."

"That would be great. I was thinking we could hire someone to work the counter, if that's all right with you."

"Good idea," Micah said. "Maybe we could get someone who'd be willing to do the measuring too." That would save him from having to be around horses.

"A part-time bookkeeper would be nice too," Eli suggested.

"I'm happy to do accounting. I've done it for *Daed* for years."

"I'd really appreciate that." The relief on Eli's face was obvious. "I've struggled with that the past few days. You might have to straighten out the ledgers."

"I'll take a look when I come in tomorrow," Micah promised.

"That'd be great." Eli smiled.

Micah left with a lighter heart. He'd guaranteed he'd have no opportunity to be around horses—his greatest fear. Now, if only he could make peace with the past.

Chapter Eighteen

Emotionally exhausted from the day's events, and his mind whirling with thoughts of Hope and her gentle touch, the last thing Micah wanted after he'd picked up the twins was company. But when he pulled into the driveway of his brother's house, a buggy waited near the barn. After he got closer and saw the occupants of the buggy, his mood sank even lower.

Sylvia and Susie. He had no energy left to deal with Sylvia's plotting.

Maybe they only had a quick question he could answer without inviting them inside. He pulled beside their wagon and leaned out the window. They both appeared hot and sweaty, and Micah hoped they hadn't been waiting too long in the broiling late afternoon sun. Sylvia was driving the buggy, so he was closest to Susie. When their gazes met, her face flushed, and she gazed at the ground, waiting for her *mamm* to speak.

"We brought you some dinner." Sylvia gestured to the casserole dish Susie clutched in her hands.

"We already ate," Chloe announced.

Susie's face fell, and Sylvia's eyes flashed. She seemed at a loss for words.

Micah had hoped to let them down gently. "If we'd

known you were coming, we wouldn't have eaten such an early dinner." Chloe was seated beside him, so he gently squeezed her shoulder to signal her to keep quiet. He'd rather not tell Sylvia where they'd been.

Chloe seemed to get his message and leaned back in the seat with her mouth closed.

"I suppose you can put it in the refrigerator for tomorrow," Sylvia said finally. "Next time we'll let you know ahead of time."

That hadn't exactly been Micah's desired goal, but he reached for the casserole. "I appreciate it."

Susie's fingers bumped his in the exchange, and she jerked back, almost dropping the dish. Micah made a quick grab to save it. The contents sloshed up and over the side. The thick white sauce with bits of mushroom and overcooked celery reminded him of *Mamm*'s favorite last-minute casserole, one in which she mixed two cans of soup—cream of celery and cream of mushroom—to pour over the rice.

"Chicken-rice casserole?" he guessed.

Although Susie nodded, Sylvia added, "It's one of her specialties. One of many, of course." Before Micah could respond, she continued, "We also came to see if you and the children would like to go to the petting zoo tomorrow. Susie can pack a picnic lunch, and we can get ice cream next door."

"That sounds like fun," Micah said.

They both brightened, making him reluctant to dash their hopes.

"But I need to help out with back orders at the harness shop."

Susie ducked her head and whispered, "We could watch the children for you while you work."

Sylvia's lips pursed, and she frowned at Susie, evidently

displeased that her daughter had ventured a suggestion without getting *Mamm*'s approval. "And Susie can make dinner for you tomorrow evening." Her announcement brooked no disapproval.

Micah hated to reveal his plans, but he had to stop them from coming. "Hope Graber offered to watch the children tomorrow. *Danke* for your kindness, though."

Sylvia's furious eyes bored into him, and Susie's lips turned down. She appeared genuinely disappointed. Micah didn't want to impose on Hope next week too, so maybe God had presented him with this solution. Even so, he debated internally for a moment.

Did he really want to encourage Susie and possibly hurt her later when she discovered his disinterest? Still, he really didn't want to take advantage of Hope's kindness. "I could use someone to watch the twins next week after their half days of school," he said tentatively, half-hoping they'd have other plans.

Susie sucked in a breath, her face alight with joy. With her cheeks flushed and eyes sparkling, she appeared rather attractive.

Sylvia's gloating smile showed she'd gained a big advantage in her courting scheme. Yet she still had to push for more. "Don't worry about meals next week. Susie would be delighted to make supper every night."

Micah had been afraid Sylvia might volunteer to do that. "You don't have to." His protest, made more because he didn't want to give them the false impression that he was interested in Susie, came off more like concern for over-working Susie.

Waving a hand, Sylvia insisted, "Susie would love doing it. She has only the two of us to feed, so having a whole family"—her embarrassed laugh made it clear she'd used those words on purpose—"to cook for would be, um, good practice for the future."

Micah would prefer she not practice on him, but he had no way to phrase that politely.

Evidently mistaking his silence for assent, Sylvia beamed. "Now that we have that settled, we had one other idea to discuss with you. Because the church funds may not be able to cover all the hospital bills, Susie came up with a wonderful idea for a fund-raiser."

Oh no. When Micah had paid his percentage of the bill, he hadn't thought to ask about the state of their hospital aid. If it had been depleted by other large bills, he could add more to the fund. He should also help with a fund-raiser. "I'd be happy to help," he told Sylvia, "but it's been a long day, and I was hoping to get the children in bed early. Can we talk about it another time?"

Though irritation flickered in her eyes, Sylvia forced a smile. "Of course. Susie and I can meet you after work tomorrow." She heaved a loud sigh. "I'm sure this has been a wearying time for all of you. I've struggled every day since my husband passed." Whipping out a handkerchief embroidered with flowers, she dabbed at her eyes. "It's a shame the poor little ones have to face the same grief."

"I'm sorry." Now Micah sympathized with her, which added to his guilt for trying to get rid of them. "I didn't realize you'd lost your husband recently."

"It's been ten years," Susie said.

Sylvia sniffled. "But it feels like yesterday."

"I understand." No matter how many years went by, you'd still miss someone you'd loved.

Squeezing in six new students between Chloe's and Jabin's lessons proved to be a major challenge. Hope hadn't anticipated more calls yesterday evening after she watched the twins. She and Logan also needed time to plan for the lessons, so Chloe and Jabin spent much of Friday with *Daed*. Not that he seemed to mind.

Most of the parents who signed up their children for lessons handed her money because they were used to the many Amish businesses in town that took only cash, so by the end of the afternoon, the money box was bulging, and they also had some checks under the cash tray.

She'd need to make a deposit, but the banks were closed now, and they had students scheduled most of Saturday. Once pupils were back in school next week, she'd make a trip to the bank. They had two more free lessons tonight, but Hope locked the office and barn doors after Logan left. Then, with a skip in her step, she crossed the lawn to make supper.

She reached the back porch in time to hear Chloe sigh. "I'm hungry."

Daed sighed. "It's almost six, and Hope hasn't started dinner yet. I wonder what's taking her so long. Micah isn't here yet either."

"He's going to be late," Chloe said. "He's working with Susie on a fund-raiser."

Susie again? Some of the joy leaked out of Hope's day, and she paused with her hand on the screen door handle.

Susie's *mamm* sure managed to find flimsy excuses to throw her daughter and Micah together. Not that Hope was jealous, of course. It just seemed as if Susie wasn't the right match. Actually, Hope couldn't think of anyone who'd be a good choice, except . . . no, she had no interest in or time for marriage.

"What's the fund-raiser for?" *Daed* totaled the points in his hand.

Chloe's gloating smile revealed she'd won, but then she sobered. "Me and Jabin."

Although *Daed* kept his pencil moving on the paper, he looked up. "He needs money to take care of you?"

"No." Chloe shook her head." "It's to pay our hospital bills."

Hope had assumed the church would help to take care of the bills. But Micah also had funeral expenses, as well as hospital expenses for both children. Maybe they didn't have enough money to pay their share of the hospital bills. She'd be happy to contribute. With the full cashbox, she should have enough to pay the bills and donate something. She could also volunteer time and offer services and baked goods.

"*Ach*," *Daed* said, "I didn't realize." He tapped his pencil tip on the paper. "I'd like to help."

And how did he plan to do that with no income? If they were doing a Stop and Shop, maybe he'd offer to watch a table. Although that wasn't a good idea because he'd be handling money.

Daed leaned back in his chair. "I have an idea."

His tone gave Hope chills. That plan had better not include gambling. She'd pretty much cleaned out the bank account they'd shared for home expenses, so he'd have little money to "borrow." Art would most likely sneer at such a tiny amount for gambling.

With his back to the door, *Daed* had no idea she'd been standing at the screen door. She yanked at the door so it squeaked loudly as it opened, and he jumped. He swiveled to face her. Was that guilt she'd surprised in his eyes?

"You startled me, Hope." He turned back around and began scooping the cards into a jumbled pile, his movements jerky.

"Sorry," Hope said, but she prayed she'd scared the idea

out of him. She pushed her worries to the back of her mind. "I thought I'd start supper early because Logan and I have a few evening lessons scheduled. Want to help me, Chloe?"

The little girl hopped up from her chair. "Are we eating with you?"

"Seems so." Hope headed to the sink to wash her hands. "How long do you think Micah will be?"

"A long, long time." Chloe's sigh came from deep within her chest. "Sylvia likes to talk and talk." Then Chloe hung her head and mumbled, "Sorry."

Hope hid a smile. Chloe had been disrespectful, but Hope longed to agree. Sylvia not only dominated conversations, she also dominated people. "Do you think Micah will eat here?"

Chloe frowned. "Sylvia might make him eat Susie's casserole."

Hope turned away so Chloe couldn't see her grimace. No doubt Sylvia would insist on him eating with her and Susie. *Why does it bother me so much? It's not like I have any interest in a relationship.*

Liar, her conscience taunted.

Chloe continued chattering, but Hope didn't pay any attention until Chloe said, "Sylvia wanted us to eat Susie's casserole last night, but I told her we already ate with you."

Hmm. I wonder how that went over. Hope could picture Sylvia's annoyance at having her plans dashed.

"Sylvia looked mad." Chloe mimicked Sylvia's glower. "She likes people to do what she says, doesn't she?"

Hope shouldn't encourage Chloe to criticize, but when Chloe stared up at her with a question in her eyes, Hope felt compelled to answer truthfully. "*Jah*, I believe she does."

Before she could add that they shouldn't judge people, Chloe's frown deepened. "I do too. I'm like Sylvia, aren't I?"

Hope had never made that comparison, but Chloe and

Sylvia did have some similarities. Chloe's openness and honesty, though, would balance her faults. Unfortunately, Sylvia didn't seem able to admit she was mistaken.

With Chloe staring at her expectantly, Hope struggled for an answer. "We all want our own way most of the time. That's why God sent Jesus—to take away our sin and teach us by His example."

Chloe crossed her arms and pinched her mouth shut, reminding Hope of the comment Chloe had mumbled in the barn. She didn't trust God. Hope could understand how a child who'd just lost both parents could be angry at God. She sent a petition up to heaven that they could heal Chloe's pain and bring her back to the faith.

She also needed to remember to discuss this with Micah when Chloe wasn't around to hear. Horse therapy might help Chloe release some of her pain, but they also needed to find a way to help her heal spiritually.

Hope put an arm around Chloe's shoulders. "It might not feel like it right now, but God loves you."

Chloe shrugged off Hope's embrace and moved farther away. The little girl muttered something, but Hope only caught one word. *Lie.*

Lord, please help me to find a way to reach Chloe with Your love.

Before Hope could come up with a response for Chloe, a loud banging at the front door interrupted them.

Daed pushed back his chair. "I'll go see who it is." After the front door clicked open, Hope could barely hear a low murmuring of voices before the door banged shut.

"Who was that?" she asked when *Daed* returned to the kitchen.

"Art. I told him we had company."

Hope was so surprised, she almost dropped her glass

canning jar of chicken breasts. "You did?" Setting the jar on the counter, she turned to face him.

His eyes shifted from side to side. "I'd rather spend time with"—he gestured toward the twins—"all of you."

Something in his voice didn't quite ring true, but maybe it was only disappointment about not spending time with Art. Or maybe he was struggling with temptation.

At least he'd chosen to send Art away. She needed to stop judging and count her blessings. "That wasn't easy, but I'm so glad you did."

He didn't meet her eyes as he sat at the table. He may not have intended it, but he copied Jabin's downcast eyes and bowed head.

Huffing from behind her drew Hope's attention. Chloe was struggling to open the jar lid. Hope rushed over to grab the jar before it crashed to the floor.

"Let me get that," she said, taking the jar from Chloe. "Sometimes when I can, the lids stick extra tightly." She twisted the metal ring from the canning jar and pried the lid, which made a satisfying pop.

Chloe looked disappointed, so Hope pushed two soup cans toward her. "Why don't you open these?" She handed Chloe the can opener.

Running her finger under the words on the label, Chloe read, "'Cream of celery soup.'" She turned the other can so the name faced her. "This is mushroom soup, isn't it? Is it for chicken-rice casserole?"

When Hope nodded, Chloe groaned.

"You don't like it?" Hope had cooked the rice that morning during breakfast so she could pull together a quick supper, and it was too late to change the menu.

"It's not that," Chloe answered. "This is the same casserole Susie gave us last night."

Oh great! She'd be feeding Micah the same meal he'd probably be eating all weekend. Unless he was already eating it with Susie right now, which would be even worse.

Micah was working in the back room of the harness shop when the bell on the door jangled. Eli got up to answer it, and Micah breathed a sigh of relief. So far, Eli had handled all the customers that day, and Micah greatly appreciated it. He loved being back here, inhaling the aroma of leather and holding the familiar metal tools.

After a time of sorrow and guilt, remembering being here with *Daed* and Ben, Micah fell into his natural rhythm and drifted into daydreams of Hope as his hands cut and carved and punched. Keeping his mind on her kept him from drowning in grief.

"Hey, Micah, someone's here for you."

With his thoughts still on Hope, Micah jumped up and hurried out, only to be slapped back to reality. Sylvia and Susie stood there waiting. His stomach plunged. He'd forgotten all about them. Swallowing his frustration, he tried to greet them in a friendly, but businesslike, manner.

Sylvia's broad smile dimmed. "We came to talk about the fund-raiser."

Had he arranged for them to meet him here, or was this Sylvia's way of ambushing him so he couldn't escape? He'd been so drained last night when they'd talked, he couldn't remember the conversation.

"Fund-raiser?" Eli asked. "For Ben and Anna?"

Now it was Sylvia's turn to be frustrated. "*Jah,*" she said in a tone intended to shut down Eli's participation, but he ignored the frostiness of her answer.

"When will it be?" Eli asked. "The harness shop will

definitely contribute—" He stopped and glanced at Micah for approval.

"Of course," Micah agreed.

"And we can each donate some labor time if you're having a silent auction," Eli offered.

"I'd been thinking of a Stop and Shop," Sylvia said, angling her body away from Eli to exclude him from the conversation. "We haven't decided yet, because we planned to talk to *Micah*."

At her heavy emphasis on Micah's name, Eli stepped back. "Sorry. I guess I got ahead of myself here."

"No, you didn't." Micah moved back so Eli remained a part of the circle. "This should be a group effort."

Neither woman responded. Sylvia pursed her lips, and Susie shrank farther into herself, her back hunched over and her head bowed. For her sake, Micah regretted adding another man to the circle, because it seemed to intensify her shyness. He'd done it for his own protection. He wished he could reassure Susie that she had nothing to fear.

Eli glanced from one to the other. "If you're sure?"

Sylvia opened her mouth, but Micah cut her off. "Of course we are."

"Actually," Sylvia said, "we planned to invite Micah to supper at our house to talk about it."

"I see." Eli started to turn away.

"We made extra food." Susie's quiet voice stopped him. "We have plenty." When Sylvia glared at her, crimson splashed across her cheeks. "We do," she insisted.

"I intended to give Micah the leftovers so he had food for the weekend." Sylvia's exasperation came through in her tone.

"Don't worry about me," Micah said. "We have plenty to eat, especially with the wonderful *gut* casserole you brought last night."

"Maybe I shouldn't," Eli said. "My brother Laban is here in the back."

"He could come too." Susie seemed determined to include Eli.

Micah appreciated it, but Sylvia's face was livid. She wouldn't be impolite and disinvite Eli, but Micah worried Susie might get in trouble.

"I don't want to put anyone out." Eli looked from Susie's welcoming expression to Micah's pleading eyes to Sylvia's barely controlled fury.

Though she stared at the floor and spoke in a barely audible voice, Susie settled it. "You wouldn't," she said firmly.

Sylvia turned and headed for the door. "Supper will be ready soon."

"We'd better hustle, then," Eli said.

Micah turned to him. "Why don't you tell me what I can do to help close things down for the night?" Then he stopped. "Wait, I need to go home to milk the cows."

Sylvia halted with her hand on the push bar. "Please hurry. We'll keep it warm for you."

When the door closed behind them, Eli sent Micah a searching glance. "Do you think I should go? Sylvia didn't seem too keen on having me."

"But Susie did."

"You think so?" Eli smiled. "She's always seemed like such a nice girl, but very shy. I was surprised she spoke up to her *mamm*."

Micah had been too. So had Sylvia—and she'd been upset. He hoped she wouldn't lecture Susie the whole way home. Maybe, just maybe, with Eli along, Micah could steer Sylvia's and Susie's attention to a different bachelor. Eli would be much better bait for Susie. And Micah would prefer to be the worm that wriggled free of Sylvia's hook.

Chapter Nineteen

By the time Hope and Logan finished the two early evening lessons, Micah still hadn't arrived. *Daed* and the twins were sitting in the living room, reading.

"I'm a little concerned about Micah." *Daed* waved toward the couch. "These two should be getting into bed soon. And so should we."

Hope worried about Micah too, but not for the same reason as *Daed*. She kept imagining Sylvia convincing Micah to court Susie. Despite telling herself she had no business caring, the very thought of it made her nauseous.

Pushing away the troubling thoughts, she said, "I do need to get up early. We got several more calls this evening, so we'll have some back-to-back lessons tomorrow."

Logan had wanted to schedule some of them for Sunday. Although it was an off-Sunday for Hope, she refused to work on the Lord's Day. Logan had complained about packing so many lessons into one day and left irritated.

"I'm glad the business is going well," *Daed* said.

It definitely was. "We've signed up quite a few of the children who came for free introductory lessons. One of the boys who's coming tomorrow will actually be riding rather than grooming, so Logan called his two teenage nieces to be sidewalkers."

Neither of them sounded particularly thrilled to get up early on their last Saturday before school started, but Logan had promised to pay them well for their time. Hope had no idea how much he planned to pay them, but she did have a full cashbox, so it shouldn't be a problem.

Logan had suggested they advertise for volunteers rather than hiring help. Some of the Amish teens in her district might be willing to assist her; they were all comfortable around horses, and most had many younger siblings, so they were used to dealing with children. And they also got up early every day of the week.

Chloe yawned, and Jabin's eyes drooped closed. Maybe Hope should send them up to bed. She wouldn't mind going to sleep herself, but who would answer the door when Micah arrived? She couldn't trust *Daed* to stay awake, and once he fell asleep, nothing woke him. Besides, she'd much rather be the one to greet him. The possibility of seeing him made her sleepiness vanish.

"Come on, you two," Hope said to the twins. "You can sleep here tonight."

"We can?" Chloe jumped off the couch and headed for the stairs, while Jabin trailed behind sleepily.

Hope put them in the same room so they wouldn't be lonely or scared if they woke in a strange place. Jabin fell fast asleep soon after he said his prayers and crawled into bed.

She turned to Chloe. "Ready to say your prayers and go to bed?"

Chloe sat on the bed and crossed her arms. "No."

Although Hope suspected the answer related to prayer, she asked, "You're not tired?"

The only response to that was a huge yawn. As she'd guessed, Chloe was not being stubborn about going to sleep. Hope sat on the edge of the bed and held out her arms. Chloe snuggled into them.

"I heard you in the barn earlier," Hope said, "but then you said your prayers at mealtime."

"No, I didn't. I bowed my head and closed my eyes, but I didn't say anything."

"You're mad at God?"

"Yes." Tears slipped down Chloe's cheeks. "I prayed for *Mamm* and *Daed* to come back, and God didn't listen. I'm never praying to Him again."

"Oh, Chloe." Hope held the little girl closer and struggled to respond. Telling her God cared about her or had a purpose wouldn't help. Not at this point. That could come later. Right now, she needed to reach Chloe where she was.

"Everyone says God is love," Chloe burst out, "but He's not. If He loved me, why would He take away my *mamm* and *daed*?"

Logan had given Hope some books to read on autism, anger management, and grief therapy. And one of the stages grieving children often went through was anger. Maybe it would help Chloe to know she wasn't alone.

Hope leaned her chin on the top of Chloe's head. "Many people get angry after someone they love dies. Sometimes people get upset with the person for leaving them. Other people get mad at themselves. And sometimes we blame God."

"They do?" Chloe lifted teary eyes and examined Hope's face. "I'm scared God will punish me for being angry."

"I'm sure God understands you're hurting. Sometimes we say or do things when we're in pain, but we don't mean them, or we change our minds later." *Please, God, let this be one of those situations.*

"I do mean it." Chloe set her chin. "And I won't change my mind."

"We don't always like God's will. Even Jesus didn't want to do God's will."

"Really?" Chloe sat up straighter. "But He was always good."

"*Jah*, but He didn't want to die and prayed He wouldn't have to. In the end, He agreed to do whatever God wanted."

"Oh." Chloe slumped down.

"And Peter turned away from Jesus. Peter pretended he didn't even know Jesus."

"I know that story."

"I figured you would. Later, Peter ended up starting the church and being a missionary. And what about Jonah? He didn't want to do God's will, so he ran away."

"I did that too."

"I know." Hope cringed. Micah had mentioned that, but she'd forgotten. That probably wasn't the best example. "But you were lucky Micah found you."

"It was scary out there at night." Chloe nibbled at her lower lip. "But it wasn't as scary as being inside a big fish." She leaned her head against Hope's shoulder.

Hope hugged her and prayed that God would heal Chloe's pain. She also hoped she'd reassured Chloe that others had turned against God but returned to their faith. Chloe might be angry at God now, but Hope wanted the little girl to realize God understood and would be there when she was ready to go to Him for comfort.

Perhaps horse therapy might lessen some of the anger. Hope prayed that would be the case. She also needed to discuss this with Micah. Maybe they could work on this together. He should at least know the stages of grief so he could be prepared to cope with them for himself as well as the twins.

A slight breeze drifted through the window, and the air hung heavy with rain. Hope tucked Chloe under a light

sheet, but long minutes passed before Chloe closed her
eyes. Finally, her breathing slowed, and Hope eased off
the bed.

"Don't go," Chloe murmured.

Hope sank onto the bed to wait. She sang a few hymns,
hoping it would put Chloe to sleep. This time when she
stood, Chloe didn't stir, so Hope headed downstairs.

A buggy clattered up the gravel drive as Hope reached
the lower landing. The living room was empty, so *Daed*
must have gone to bed. That meant she'd be alone with
Micah. Not a good idea.

She'd need to keep their talk brief. She'd save the talk
about Chloe's faith for another time. All her nerves zinging,
she hurried to the door to meet Micah.

After insisting he needed to pick up the twins, Micah
had finally broken free of Sylvia's grasp. He still wasn't
sure why she'd used the excuse of a fund-raiser to get him
to come to dinner. They'd barely talked about it.

Eli brought it up several times and seemed as confused
as Micah when the conversation went nowhere. Susie ventured to add a comment or two to Eli's fund-raising ideas
until her *mamm* quelled her with a look.

After that, they ate in silence, except when all three
men—Eli, Laban, and Micah—complimented the food and
agreed to second helpings. That mollified Sylvia a bit,
and she listed many of her daughter's other good points.

Eli agreed enthusiastically, and Micah only seconded
those comments. It kept him out of the limelight but irritated Sylvia. Laban mainly kept his head down and ate.

Micah replayed the meal as he pulled into Hope's driveway. Tension had been pulling at his stomach ever since
Sylvia showed up at the harness shop, but it eased a little

as he climbed out of the buggy. Seeing Hope always soothed him, except concern over his lateness wouldn't let him totally relax. She needed her sleep with the early hours she kept to take care of the horses and the business.

Hope was the only one in the kitchen when he tapped on the back door. Micah's pulse rate jumped. He didn't often have a chance to be with her when the twins weren't around. But where were the twins? The kitchen opened into the living room, and the couch and chairs appeared empty. Chloe and Jabin weren't alone in the barn, were they? He glanced over his shoulder, but the barn door was latched from the outside.

"I'm sorry I was so late," Micah said when she answered the door. "I got stuck at dinner."

"Chloe said you needed to plan a fund-raiser."

"We didn't make much progress on that. Sylvia had other things in mind."

"I bet I can guess what they were." She tried to keep sarcasm from her tone, but she wasn't successful.

"I'm sure you can." Micah ran a nervous finger around under his collar. "I thought I'd never escape."

Hope shot him a sympathetic smile. "I can only imagine."

"I didn't mean to keep you up so late. I'll take the twins and let you get to bed. Where are they?"

"I hope you don't mind, but they both looked so tired, I put them to bed. Jabin fell asleep right away. Chloe took a little longer, but she drifted off right before you arrived."

In bed? But that meant they'd stay the night, and he'd have to pick them up tomorrow.

One part of him rejoiced that he'd see her again tomorrow, but the other wished he hadn't imposed on her again. No matter how awkward Sylvia made it, he should have left. "I feel terrible I wasn't here to pick them up."

Hope waved a hand. "It's no problem. We enjoy having

them. I haven't seen *Daed* this happy in years, but . . ." A troubled look crossed her face.

Ach, what had they done? "I'm sorry if they caused problems." Micah's guilt over his lateness increased tenfold.

"I'm concerned about Chloe."

Of course. He could have guessed she'd be the troublemaker. "What did she do?"

"It's more what she refused to do. She wouldn't say her prayers." Hope's voice trembled. "She says she doesn't believe in God anymore."

Micah sucked in a breath. "Is that what she said in the barn too?" He'd only heard the word "God," but Hope had appeared worried then too.

"*Jah*, she's angry at God." Hope nibbled at her lower lip. "Questioning God and loss of faith sometimes are reactions to death."

One more burden to bear. Micah felt his heavy load increase. "How can I help her see the truth?"

He didn't realize he'd spoken aloud until Hope answered. "Chloe needs to come to her own understanding of God. I'm not sure you can do anything to make her change her mind. Well, except pray. I'll be praying too."

Micah's *danke* could never express all the gratitude in his heart. "I'm grateful for your prayers." Right now, he could show his appreciation by leaving so she could get to sleep. "I'd better go. I know you're tired. What time should I pick them up tomorrow?"

"Our first student will come at eight, but *Daed* can watch the twins until you get here."

"I'll get here before that." If he got here early enough, he might get to spend some time with Hope.

Her smile warmed him inside and out. "You're welcome to have breakfast with us."

"You've already done too much for us. I appreciate it, and I'd like to do something in return."

"I've told you before. *Daed* and I both enjoy spending time with Chloe and Jabin. We don't want anything at all. Being able to spend time with them is payment enough."

But Micah couldn't accept all she'd done for him and the twins without reciprocating. Yet how could he ever repay her? It wasn't like he could bring her meals or treats, or offer to help with the horses. He shivered just thinking about being around them in the barn.

What could he give her in exchange? Harnesses? With her horses' equipment being used constantly, she might need upkeep or new equipment. "Could I repair or replace any of your harnesses?"

Hope tapped a finger on her lip for a second and looked thoughtful. "The harness for the pony cart needs some repairs. I'll have *Daed* show it to you next time you're around, and you can tell us whether it should be repaired or replaced."

"Most are worth repairing if it's done right. If it can be fixed, I'd do my best for you." Maybe he should have stopped before he added "for you." But part of him wanted to let her know his true feelings. Maybe this could be a first step as he worked up the courage to ask her out.

So far, he hadn't seen another man around, but that didn't mean she wasn't dating someone. If she lived in his church district, he'd know for sure. He should find out first, but he wasn't sure how. Sylvia might know who he could ask, but—

"That would be helpful," Hope said, startling him.

For a second, he thought she'd read his mind. Then he snapped back to the original conversation about harnesses, glad she didn't know what he'd been wondering. "Happy to do it." He only wished he could do so much more.

* * *

After Micah left, Hope fell into bed exhausted and drifted into dreams of him.

A shrill scream shattered the night stillness.

Hope woke, frightened and disoriented. She couldn't place the sound.

Another screech dissolved into sobs. The twins. Hope jumped from her bed and hurried down the hall to find Jabin sobbing hysterically and thrashing on the bed, punching the air with his fists.

"No, no, no!!" he cried. Although his eyes were open, he didn't seem to see her. Not a nightmare then, but a night terror.

"Jabin," she whispered, "it's all right."

Her words only agitated him more. He kicked and yelled and flailed his arms. Hope longed to wrap her arms around him, but with the way he was hitting out, she couldn't get a grasp on him.

Chloe cried out and crouched against the wall beside her bed. "What's wrong with Jabin?"

Hope went over and gave her a quick hug. "He's having a bad dream."

"Make him stop. He's scaring me."

"He's asleep and doesn't know what he's doing."

"No, he's not sleeping." Chloe pointed at her brother. "Look, his eyes are open."

"*Jah*, but he isn't awake." Hope went back to Jabin's bed and waved a hand in front of his face. "See, he doesn't even know I'm here."

She'd heard it wasn't good to wake children during night terrors, but would talking to him help? Using a soft voice, Hope repeated, "You're safe, Jabin. Everything's all right."

That felt like a lie. Would anything be all right if you'd lost both of your parents?

At times, it seemed her soothing words calmed him; then his keening began again. After what seemed like forever, but probably was only five or ten minutes, Jabin closed his mouth, collapsed back onto the pillow, and curled into a ball, whimpering. Hope sat beside him on the bed and rubbed his back, which seemed to help.

Chloe snuggled back under the sheet and closed her eyes. Hope sang a few more hymns until they were both still and breathing easily. By the time she crawled back into bed, it was only two hours until dawn. Outside, a rainstorm sent water sluicing over the windowpanes. The sound lulled her to sleep, a sleep filled with dreams of Micah.

The rain ended just before dawn, leaving the ground damp and spongy. Micah finished the farm chores quickly so he could head to Hope's. Last night he'd had an idea of a small way he could help today. With much prayer and trembling, he managed to hitch up his new—or rather used—buggy, which had been delivered while he was away last night.

Because the sun had not yet risen, Micah turned on the buggy's battery-powered lights as the horse plodded through the shadowy grayness. He turned into the driveway as Hope led two horses out of the barn. He shuddered just imagining changing places with her and being sandwiched between a horse on each side. Hope reached the paddock gate, opened it, and—

Chloe emerged from the barn leading a horse. Micah clutched Daffy's reins and sucked in a breath. He couldn't believe Hope would let Chloe handle a horse alone.

Forcing himself to continue up the gravel drive, Micah

prayed for his niece's safety. He resisted the temptation to jump out and stop her, mainly because he feared his approach might spook the horse. Worse than being around horses himself was seeing children near them. Especially children he loved and wanted to protect.

Micah was still trying to calm his racing heart when Jabin exited the barn with another horse. Not Jabin too! Why had Hope let the twins take charge of horses? He clenched his teeth and sent up more prayers that both children would make it to the field safely.

Once again, he reconsidered letting them come for therapy. Maybe he should cancel it. Hope's new business needed money, but was it worth putting the twins at risk?

When Hope turned and waved at him, the thumping in Micah's chest ramped up. She turned to Chloe, took the lead rope, and released the horse into the paddock. Wrapping an arm around Chloe's shoulders, Hope looked at Jabin, who trudged toward them, head low and shoulders hunched.

Micah's gaze bounced back and forth between Hope and Jabin. He held his breath until his nephew transferred the lead rope to Hope. She said something to him, and he straightened, looking almost pleased and proud.

After Hope let Jabin's horse into the pasture and closed the gate, Micah released the air trapped in his lungs, but his chest remained tight.

The picture of Hope with one arm around each twin stirred something deep inside Micah. She'd make a wonderful *mamm*. Both of the twins adored her, and they needed a mother figure in their lives, but would it be fair for him to ask Hope, or anyone, to date when they'd need to take on a ready-made family?

* * *

Hope steered the twins in Micah's direction. "You're early." She meant it as an observation, not a criticism, but she was unsure it came out right.

"I decided to come and offer my services in mucking out the stalls." He'd brought his work boots and gloves.

"You didn't get enough doing your own barn?" She kept a teasing note in her voice, but she was touched he'd been willing to help.

"Guess not," he said.

"Well, I already promised Chloe and Jabin they could each clean a stall. I'm afraid they might be disappointed to lose out on a favorite chore."

Chloe's face twisted. "I hate scooping up manure. You can take my place, Micah."

Hope laughed. "That's very generous of you to share, Chloe."

Jabin kicked at a clod of dirt on the ground. "You can take my turn," he mumbled.

"I do consider cleaning stalls as part of the therapy," Hope said as they headed toward the barn, "but for today, we could give them a break and let them stay with *Daed* while we work."

Chloe cheered and jumped up and down. "Please say yes, Micah."

"All right." Micah smiled as the twins raced toward the house.

In a few seconds, the back door banged behind them, and she and Micah were alone. "I–I guess we should get started, so I can get breakfast ready."

"Why don't you go ahead and cook? I can take care of all the stalls."

"You don't need to do my chores." If she allowed him to do her work, she'd feel guilty.

"After you've taken care of the twins, it's the least I can do."

Hope wished she could get him to believe she didn't need to be repaid. But if he was anything like her, he probably disliked accepting favors. "Fine. Let's each do two." Maybe then he'd consider them even.

"You go ahead into the house. I can handle everything out here." He set his free hand on her shoulder and gently turned her toward the house.

Hope's shoulder throbbed where his fingers touched. Heat radiated through her. She couldn't break free even if she wanted to—which she didn't.

She wanted to lean back against him, but she fought the urge. Luckily, Micah let go, but she remained frozen in place, her nerve endings zinging.

Behind her, the barn door opened. She turned, but Micah had already gone inside. Hope wanted to follow him. Instead, she went into the house to fix breakfast. She pulled out her mother's recipe for coffee cake.

You don't need to compete with Susie. But even that warning didn't stop Hope from making the tastiest family recipes. Why was she trying to prove her homemaking abilities to Micah when she had no interest in him?

Chapter Twenty

By the time Micah finished in the barn and returned to the house for the twins, Hope was taking a coffee cake and an egg casserole out of the oven. The tantalizing aroma of cinnamon made his mouth water. Micah had switched out of his boots and left them outside, and he'd washed at the outdoor pump, but some of the barn odor still clung to him. Quite a contrast to the delicious scents coming from the kitchen.

He called through the door, "Chloe and Jabin, time to go."

"No." Chloe stomped over to the table, carrying the coffee cake pan. "I want to eat this. I helped make it."

"I understood the twins were staying here today," Hope said. "They didn't really get an actual therapy lesson yesterday because Logan wasn't here. Plus, I made enough breakfast to feed all of you. It's the least I can do after you mucked out the stalls."

While Hope was talking, Jabin and Chloe slid onto chairs at the table. If Micah took them home, they'd have to eat one of his attempts at breakfast. With a sigh, he went inside and joined them. Not that it was a hardship to spend more time with Hope or eat a delicious breakfast. But how could he ever pay her back when she outgave him every time?

After they ate and her father had left the room, Hope turned to Micah. "I have an idea for helping you reduce your fear of horses, if you'd like to try. I'd need Jabin's and Chloe's assistance."

Jabin remained stone-faced, the way he'd been all through breakfast, but he didn't refuse.

Chloe raced to the door. "What do we need to do? Are we going outside with the horses now?"

Dread pooled in Micah's stomach. He tried to hide his anxiety.

Hope must have sensed it, though, because she reassured him, "You won't need to get close to the horses. It's a gradual exposure technique." Her gentle tone, combined with her sweet smile, made it hard to resist.

She removed some carrots from the refrigerator and herded the twins to the door. Then she checked to be sure Micah was following them. He trailed them to the paddock.

He'd spent years avoiding horses. When the family went somewhere in the buggy, *Daed* always hitched up the horse. Since Micah had been here, he'd had to do it twice, and even though Daffy was old and docile, both times had left him shaky afterward. Micah's steps slowed. Did he want to expose his fears to Hope?

Before they reached the gate, Hope knelt to talk to the twins, who both nodded. Then she handed them each some treats. By the time Micah neared the spot, the twins were already scampering off.

Hope stood and beckoned to him. "We're going to stand some distance away, so you'll feel safer. But Chloe and Jabin are going to interact with the horses while you watch."

A loud "No!" exploded from his lips. He would have raced after the twins if Hope hadn't stepped in his path.

Her voice soft and soothing, she set a hand on his chest to stop him. "I know it frightens you to see children around horses, but they'll have a fence between them and the horses. And believe me, all my horses are docile."

Split-rail logs provided little protection against biting, kicking horses. Torn between the soft hand holding him in place and Chloe and Jabin's safety, Micah opted for saving the twins.

But Hope anticipated his dash and sidestepped in front of him. "They'll be fine," she assured him. "I would never put a child in danger."

Although he longed to believe her, his brain flashed out fear signals urging him to race to their rescue. Only the compassion in her eyes held him still.

Touching Micah's chest had been a mistake. The heat searing Hope's palm set her whole body tingling. His heart thumped out a frantic rhythm. How much was fear and how much was from their physical contact?

Concentrate, Hope.

Reluctantly, she lowered her hand but blocked him from chasing after the twins. Taking a breath to steady herself, she motioned for him to follow her. "We're going to stand where we are to watch. In therapy, we gradually move closer and closer to the horse, but for today we'll stay here."

Micah stood rigid as she moved to stand beside him. Hope wished she could ease some of his terror.

"I've asked the twins to do three things. For the first one, they'll keep their distance from the horses."

Chloe and Jabin stopped pretty far back from the fence, as she'd instructed. Molly pricked up her ears and looked in their direction. The other horses lifted their heads.

"Do you see Molly's ears?" Hope wanted Micah to learn

to read horses' movements and expressions. "They're up because she's curious. When horses pin their ears back, they're dangerous. That's when they'll lunge, bite, or kick."

At the word "kick," Micah recoiled. If only she could comfort him. He must be reliving his pain. She clutched at her work apron to stop herself from reaching out.

Chloe and Jabin held the treats behind their backs while they approached the fence. At Micah's sharp, indrawn breath, Hope's stomach clenched. She'd bonded so closely with him, she experienced his terror.

"Look at Molly's tail. Swishes send different messages. Right now, she's relaxed and interested. If she were upset, her tail would be twitching in annoyance." Hope had pointed out the tail because he'd said he'd been swatted by the horse's tail.

Micah crossed his arms as if protecting himself from a blow. "If I'd known that, maybe I would have stopped bothering the horse."

Interesting. That was the first time he'd admitted he'd been part of the problem. A five-year-old wasn't to blame. But if Micah took responsibility for his childhood actions, he might take back some of his power relating to horses.

The horses meandered in the children's direction, but when the twins obeyed Hope's third directive and pressed up against the fence with their arms extended, offering treats, thundering hooves shook the ground.

Molly led the charge, and the others galloped behind.

Beside her, Micah sucked in a breath and rose onto the balls of his feet, as if preparing to run. Hope grabbed his hand to hold him back. She wanted him to experience his dread while he was far enough away to observe but not participate.

His white-knuckled grip cut off her circulation. His pulse pounded terror signals into her hand.

Hope longed to calm him, to comfort him. "They only want the treats." She kept her words firm, sure, and certain. "I promise, none of the horses will hurt Chloe or Jabin."

His voice husky, Micah countered, "But we're too far away to help if they do."

"I trust my horses. I'm hoping you'll see you can too," she replied. "Don't worry, they'll slow before they reach the fence."

"What if they don't?"

"They will. Otherwise, they'd crash into the rails." Even as she spoke, the horses slowed and nudged one another out of the way to reach the treats. Hope had told the twins to hold their arms far enough apart so each horse could have a carrot. The twins followed her instructions, and soon all four horses were nibbling.

As they got closer to the end of the carrots, Chloe and Jabin let go, and Micah exhaled. But immediately, he emitted a strangled noise and froze when the twins climbed on the bottom fence rail and leaned in to pet the horses.

Hope squeezed his hand. The twins getting that close to the horses hadn't been part of her plan for this morning, and she hadn't intended to add to Micah's distress.

"I'm sorry," she told him. "I didn't mean for them to climb up there. Do you want to call them over?"

"*Jah*," he said, keeping his gaze locked on the twins, "but I won't. I think I understand what you're trying to do."

She and Logan had worked out similar steps to help children, but Micah had completed several exposure steps at once. A warm glow filled her at his courage. "You're brave for standing here and watching."

Micah waved off her praise with a stiff flick of his hand. "I have a long way to go."

"But you've made a good start," she said as Chloe and

Jabin both jumped down from the fence and ran toward them.

After the twins were far from the horses, Micah's grasp on her hand eased a bit, and his face relaxed into a genuine smile as he met her eyes. "Thanks to you."

Happiness filled Hope, and her lips curved up to match his. And then she was lost in the gratitude flooding his brown eyes, the sweet pressure of his fingers, the appreciative curve of his lips. So near hers.

Logan's warning not to get too involved flashed through her mind. But how could she prevent herself from celebrating each victory? From cheering about the results? Would she go through this gut-wrenching sympathy and ultimate rejoicing with each child she helped? Or were her emotions connected to deeper feelings Micah stirred in her?

Hope had called him brave, but she had no idea of the chills running through him when the horses thundered toward Chloe and Jabin. Even now, with the twins far from the horses, Micah's muscles remained so tense they hurt, and adrenaline coursed through his body, but he clung to the one lifeline still keeping him steady—Hope's soft hand.

A car zoomed into the driveway, and Hope let go of his hand. "I guess we both need to get to work, but I hope you'll let the twins stay here. *Daed* will miss their company if they go."

Micah hesitated. Once again, she was giving, and he had no way to return the favor. If he left the twins here, though, he'd have another excuse to see Hope. And that was tempting. His brow furrowed as he tried to recall his conversation with Sylvia. He'd asked them to watch the twins in the afternoon next week, but had she said something about taking care of them today? Or had she said Saturday? That whole conversation, along with last night's, had become one huge blur.

Evidently interpreting his silence as fear for the twins' safety, Hope said, "They really will be fine here. They'll spend most of the day with *Daed*. Even if they do go near the animals, they both know to keep their distance when circling a horse. If you'd done that . . ." Hope winced.

"I don't remember if I was warned to stay away. Knowing *Daed*, he'd probably told me many times. But I was curious. I climbed on things, broke things, and tried new things. At least until the horse kicked me."

"You were probably cute." She gave him a special smile, then turned to wave at the *Englischer* who'd parked his car on the other side of the barn.

The man strode toward them. "Are you ready?" he called. "Why are the horses still in the pasture? We need to prepare for the first student." He glanced at Hope, standing so close to Micah, and his eyes narrowed.

Had this man spotted their hands intertwined? For Hope's sake, he prayed not.

She took several steps back. "I'll bring the horses in now, Logan. I was helping Micah get over some of his concerns about the twins taking lessons."

True, that had been part of it. But for Micah, it had been so much more. Or maybe the connection had only been on his part.

A frown creased Logan's brow as he studied Micah. Then he turned to Hope. "I'm the therapist."

Her nervous laugh made Micah worry. Did Logan bully her? He almost stepped between them to send Logan a warning.

But Hope lifted her chin and responded tartly. "If we need a therapist, I'll be sure to let you know. Micah's a friend, so this was more like advice rather than an actual session."

A friend? That was a good start, but Micah wanted to be more, so much more. He suspected, though, that he should leave now, before Logan got even more upset. "Thanks for the helpful advice," he told Hope. "About the twins . . ."

"You are going to leave them here, aren't you? They should have their free lessons with Logan."

Logan's brows lowered. Not quite a frown, but almost. "When are you planning to fit in those lessons? We have a pretty full schedule already." Unwelcoming vibrations flowed from him.

Micah worried about causing extra stress for Hope. "I can take them to work with me. I don't want to put you to any trouble," he told her.

"It's no trouble at all," Hope insisted. Then she turned to Logan. "Micah planned to sign up the twins for grief therapy."

Logan's frosty glower melted into a lukewarm "Nice to meet you." And when Hope mentioned Micah had already paid for six weeks in cash, Logan managed a semi-enthusiastic welcome and reached out to shake Micah's hand.

Logan clamped Micah's hand extra hard in a you'd-better-keep-away-from-her handshake. His look warned Micah off as well.

Micah had wondered if Hope had a boyfriend. From the actions of this *Englischer*, he seemed to have some claim on her. Maybe Micah should keep his distance.

Before Micah even drove off, Logan began snapping out orders. He wasn't usually this bossy or short-tempered. Was he nervous about the long list of lessons they had scheduled today? Logan glowered at Micah's departing buggy. Was he blaming Micah for causing their late start, or did something more underlie Logan's irritation?

"We have to get the horses inside before Xavier shows up. And we need all hands on deck."

Another car pulled into the driveway and drove around the barn to park next to Logan's. Not stopping to find out who it was, Hope hurried two horses from the field.

Chloe skipped over. "Can I help?"

Hope handed over Molly's lead and whistled for Daisy. Jabin stood nearby, his hands thrust in his pockets, his head drooping. He'd perked up a little when he'd fed carrots to the horses. Maybe she could interest him in helping now.

"Jabin? Could you take Daisy to her stall?"

He scuffed his toe in the dirt by his feet and didn't answer. But then he plodded toward her and took Daisy.

"Chloe," Hope called, "be sure to latch the stall door." She assumed Jabin also would hear and obey.

"I know." Chloe's impatient answer floated from the barn.

Hope had just put one of the horses into the stall when a teen girl dressed in cut-off jeans and a tank top bopped into the barn.

"Hi! Where's Uncle Logan?"

"In the office, I guess." Hope pointed to the last room on the right. This must be one of Logan's nieces. "I'm Hope. And you are?"

"Oh, sorry." The girl giggled. "I'm Angelique, his niece. I'll be right back to help. I promised Uncle Logan I'd let him know as soon as I got here."

"Nice to meet you, Angelique," Hope said to the girl's disappearing back. She led the other horse into the stall and then checked the latches to be sure all the doors were secured.

"Why don't you go inside and spend time with my *daed* while we have our first classes?" Hope suggested to the twins. "We'll bring you out for lessons later. Maybe after the noon meal."

Chloe smiled. "I'm going to beat Isaac at Uno today. He promised we could play that instead of Dutch Blitz." Her brother trailed behind as she left the barn.

With the twins taken care of, Hope went in search of Logan. She found him in the office with Angelique.

"So, Violet said she had to finish texting her boyfriend before she left. She refuses to text and drive after her fender bender."

Logan pushed the lower desk drawer shut. "She'd better hurry. Xavier will be here in five minutes. Or sooner. Can you go out and watch for him?"

"Sure." Angelique headed for the office door.

As she exited, Logan turned to Hope. "That cashbox is stuffed full. The money in there needs to be deposited."

"I planned to do it on Monday morning. With all the lessons we have scheduled for today and tomorrow, I don't have time to hitch up the buggy and drive into town."

"I don't really like the idea of having that much money sitting here all weekend." Logan swiveled the desk chair around and rose. "We can figure out a deposit schedule later. Right now, we'd better go and greet Xavier."

Hope could manage the deposit schedule on her own. She tried not to resent Logan's bossiness. He'd been grumpy since he'd arrived. Usually, he was cheerful and upbeat. She wished he'd go back to his normal personality. She hoped the students would help to transform his grouchiness.

When they got outside, Logan scanned the yard. "Violet was supposed to be here ten minutes ago. It's not like her to be late." He pulled out his phone and punched a button.

The constant ringing carried to where Hope stood. No answer.

"Where is she?" Logan fumed. "We can't do this lesson without her. Xavier's mom is pulling into the driveway now."

"I have an idea," Hope said. "Can you greet them? I'll be right back."

"Where are you going? We need you here. We're already one person short."

Hope ran to the house and yanked open the back door. "*Daed?*" she yelled. "Where are you?"

He limped into the kitchen, his forehead crinkled in confusion. "What's wrong?"

"One of our sidewalkers hasn't shown up yet. We need someone to walk beside the horse while this little boy rides. Would you do it? Please?"

Daed would be perfect. He knew more about horses than she and Logan put together, and he loved children. He had a good heart. She prayed he'd agree.

Chapter Twenty-One

Daed glanced into the distance with a thoughtful expression. "When do you need me?"

"Right now. Xavier's already here."

He turned startled eyes to her. "Now? The twins and I just started playing Uno. Can you two play by yourselves?" he asked them.

"It won't be much fun without you, Isaac," Chloe grumbled. "Jabin never talks to me."

"I won't be gone long," *Daed* told her.

"I'd better get out there to greet Xavier, but can you meet us in the barn?" Hope asked, hoping he'd hurry.

Logan had Xavier outside by the horse and was squatting down, talking to the boy. He must have already escorted his mom back to the kitchen to wait. Angelique stood nearby.

Hope hurried over. "My *daed* will be right out to help. He's great with horses and kids."

Relief flared in Logan's eyes. "I'm sorry about Violet. I'll read her the riot act once I get ahold of her, but right now we need to get this lesson started."

The back door slammed, and *Daed* headed toward them. "What do you need me to do?" he asked when he joined them.

Logan briefly explained *Daed*'s responsibility as a

sidewalker while Angelique listened, and Hope introduced herself to Xavier.

"Remember to walk at the rider's leg," Logan repeated as he assisted Xavier into the saddle and adjusted the stirrups. With Hope on the opposite side for support, Logan demonstrated the holding techniques. "I think your arm over his thigh will work well for Xavier, but you can also use the ankle hold. For other riders, you may need to support the students under their arms or on their backs. Any questions?"

When *Daed* and Angelique shook their heads, Logan assigned his niece to the side where he was standing. "Could you go around and take Hope's place on that side?" he said to *Daed*. "She'll be leading the horse."

Hope's heart soared as they prepared to set out. Their very first lesson on horseback. She was almost as excited as Xavier.

Logan instructed Xavier in a kind, but firm, voice, and the little boy's face screwed up in concentration. When he obeyed the instructions, and the horse moved forward, Xavier's eyes opened wide, and his expression mingled fear and exhilaration.

By the time they returned to the barn and Logan helped Xavier dismount, the small boy's face was glowing.

His mom emerged from the kitchen, her eyes shining. "I was watching the lesson through the window. You did great!" She knelt and hugged Xavier.

"We like the students to take care of the horse after each lesson, as much as they can," Logan told her.

"Oh." She stepped back. "I'm sorry. I didn't mean to interrupt his lesson. I'm just so proud of him."

Hope smiled at her. "You should be. He did a wonderful job." Her heart sang when she turned to Xavier, who was beaming.

According to his mom's phone call, he'd retreated into his shell after being teased at his private school open house because he couldn't do the things the other children were doing. She wanted him to gain self-confidence. If today was any indication, he was well on his way. Hope prayed he'd carry that newfound confidence with him to school.

When Xavier was finished, Hope went to the kitchen to get his mother, who bubbled over with praise. "I didn't expect him to get so much out of one lesson. It's like you're working miracles here."

Hope repeated one of the points she'd learned in her classes. "When children can care for and influence an animal, especially one that's so much larger, their sense of control over their world grows."

"Well, whatever you're doing, it seems to be working. I'd like to reserve Xavier's spot for ten o'clock on Saturdays, if you have an opening then."

They hadn't booked any Saturday morning appointments for next week yet, so the time was definitely available. "That will work for us, starting next weekend."

"Great!" Xavier's mother glanced at her phone. "Oops! We'd better run. Xavier has another appointment." She dug around in her huge, oversized leather purse and pulled out a suede wallet. She thrust a few twenties into Hope's hand. "Will you take that for a deposit, and I'll pay the rest next Saturday?"

"Do you want a receipt?"

Ms. Lopez shook her head. "We can take care of all that next week. I'll come early."

"If you're sure . . ."

Hurrying out of the kitchen, Ms. Lopez motioned for Xavier to follow her over to the car. Hope and Logan accompanied her and waved goodbye to them, then she started toward the office. She didn't have much time before the next student started, and they needed to get things ready.

Daed stood in the aisle when she entered the barn. "Xavier made a good start, but I finished with Daisy. Did you need me to help with anything more?"

"No," Logan said, "but we really appreciate you helping us, sir." He shook *Daed*'s hand. "I'll get Molly ready for the next student."

After Logan strode off, Hope turned to *Daed*. "None of the other students will be riding today, because they're all beginners and new to horses." She and Logan might need to use the technique she'd used on Micah for those students.

Thinking of Micah sent her mind skittering to holding hands, being close enough to . . .

Hope jerked her thoughts back to her job. She couldn't afford to let her thoughts wander.

Daed's gaze fixed on the money in her hand, and she quickly stuffed it into her pocket. She'd put it in the cash-box later. No point in exposing him to temptation.

"Thanks so much for helping out this morning," she said.

"I enjoyed it. It's been a long while since I helped a child ride." His mouth drooped. "You were the last. I'd hoped your brothers . . ."

One of *Daed*'s greatest regrets was that all her brothers had moved to Indiana, so he rarely got to see his grand-children.

"I know," Hope said softly.

"And until you marry . . ." He left that hanging between them, as he had many times before.

Hope longed to tell him not to count on that. But if she did, she'd have to tell him why. She couldn't point a finger of blame at him or hurt him that way. So she used her other excuse. "I won't have time for courting with the business just starting."

"Maybe you could find a man who would help with the business, like your *mamm* used to." His voice husky, he said, "Working with someone you love is a real blessing."

Hope had seen her parents working as a team, and she'd love to have that kind of a partnership with her husband, where they helped and supported each other. The only problem was that even if she could marry, she was attracted to a man who was petrified of horses.

Thinking of Micah reminded her. "I have to prepare for the next lesson, but Micah offered to check the harness for the pony cart. Could you ask him to look at it when he comes back for the twins?"

With a quick nod, *Daed* scooted down the aisle, as if eager to get away. Hope debated about ducking into the office with the money, but she'd taken long enough. She couldn't be late for the lesson. Making a good impression was important. She'd take care of the cash later. Hope hurried outside after *Daed* to find the next student already waiting.

Logan frowned in her direction. "This is Hope, the owner I was telling you about. She also works personally with the students."

"I'm Jasper Groveton. Pleased to meet you." A rotund man with a few tufts of white hair near his ears held out his hand. After she shook it, he pushed a tiny boy forward. "Shake hands with the lady, Kelvin."

Hope took the small boy's hand in hers, but he appeared so fragile, she was almost afraid she'd crush it.

Logan invited Kelvin into the barn to select a horse, while Hope stayed behind to talk to the man. "We talked on the phone last night, and I explained Kelvin is a foster child. Not only was he neglected and malnourished but he's also dealt with some major trauma and abuse, so I wanted him to have some therapy to heal."

"I'm so sorry."

Jasper nodded. "Poor kid's led an awful life, and he might be afraid of the horses at first. He's from the inner city, so all this is new to him. But I think it'll be helpful in the long run."

It sounded as if Jasper had already made up his mind to continue with a series of lessons. "Yes, children often develop close bonds with a horse, which helps them heal emotionally and learn to connect with people too," she said.

"That's what he needs."

"We'll see that he gets it. I should get back there to help, but you're welcome to wait in the kitchen if you'd like. I'll show you where it is." She led Jasper down the center aisle and into the kitchen. "We'll get you after the lesson."

Kelvin still stood in the aisle by Molly's stall. Logan knelt beside him, murmuring soothing words. "Horses are big, so they can look kind of scary. Once you get to know them, though, you'll find our horses are gentle and friendly."

Somehow, Hope would have to do the same with Micah, walking him through his terror. She wished he were here to see Kelvin's gradual progress toward the stall. Logan got the little boy to take one step at a time, feeling the fear each time, then facing it.

Once Kelvin entered the stall, he inched toward the horse, with Logan's encouragement. After patting and reassuring Molly, Hope went around to the other side to hold Molly's head, so she wouldn't startle Kelvin with any sudden movement.

"See how Miss Hope touched Molly? Molly didn't hurt her, and she won't hurt you."

His teeth chattering, Kelvin took the next baby step closer. The nearer he got, the tenser his face grew.

Logan continued to encourage Kelvin until he touched his fingers to Molly's coat. He yanked his hand back. "*Eww.*"

"You don't like how she feels?" Logan asked.

Kelvin took a few steps back. "It ain't that. She's warm, and—*eww*—her side wiggled."

"She's just breathing. Like you." Logan pointed to the rapid rise and fall of Kelvin's chest. "And you're warm too. It means you're both alive."

Kelvin didn't look convinced. "I guess."

"Check your skin," Logan suggested. "Are you warmer or cooler than Molly?"

"Dunno." But Kelvin did rub his arm.

"Would you like to touch Molly again to see?"

"Don't wanna go touching some animal."

"What about if I pet Molly to see if I can tell the difference?"

Crossing his arms, Kelvin assumed a nonchalant expression. "Have at it."

Despite Kelvin's pretend bravado, he was trembling. Hope wished she could put her arms around him to give him a hug. The poor kid. So young, so jaded, and so unsure of himself in this situation.

Logan stepped over to Molly and ran his hand down her neck. Molly snorted. Hope gave her a little leeway to toss her head but regretted it when Kelvin's eyes rounded and he backed toward the door.

"I'm outta here."

"Molly won't hurt you," Hope told him. "She makes noises sometimes just like you sneeze or talk. Horses talk too."

His back against the wood, Kelvin's eyes narrowed. "What'd she say, then?"

Hope smiled at him. "Maybe she was letting us know she'd rather be touched by you instead of Logan."

"Yeah, right." Kelvin snorted.

Molly turned her head in Kelvin's direction, and Hope laughed. "Molly must think you're trying to communicate with her."

"I doubt it," he muttered, but his lips curled into the tiniest half smile.

"You know," Logan said, "you two could have a contest to see who could snort the loudest."

"You crazy?"

"Just an idea." Logan shrugged, but despite his nonchalant attitude, his gaze remained intent and focused.

Kelvin studied the horse, now more curious than frightened. Hope wondered if their comments had encouraged him to see what he had in common with the horse. Often, that made such a huge animal feel more approachable.

Molly stomped her back hoof and twitched her tail.

Kelvin cringed but then put on a you-don't-scare-me expression. "Why's she doing that?"

"Probably swatting at a fly," Hope told him. "You have hands to do that, but all of Molly's limbs are on the floor. She needs some way to get rid of pesky bugs."

"Wish I had me a tail to use on some pests."

"Sounds like something you could talk to Molly about," Hope suggested. "She's a good listener."

Kelvin stared at her with a skeptical look.

"I'm serious," Hope said. "Most of the students who come here like to talk to the horses."

"It's not as weird as it sounds," Logan added. "Horses won't tell anyone's secrets."

"Duh. They can't talk."

"Great point." Logan waved toward Molly. "Want to try it?"

"Nah." Kelvin scuffed his toe in the straw in front of him. "Not right now."

Did that mean he'd be willing to do it at a later date? Had they made a breakthrough?

With Hope and Logan's encouragement, Kelvin eventually took a few tentative steps toward Molly, stretched his arm way out, and placed two fingers on the horse. For today, that was a major accomplishment.

His eyes shining, Logan met Hope's gaze, and they shared secret, triumphant smiles until the appreciative gleam in Logan's eyes flared into a look that made Hope uncomfortable. She quickly lowered her lashes.

She had to be careful Logan didn't interpret her friendliness and excitement over a student's success as something more. She needed to make her intentions clear. Even if she'd ever consider courting, she was with the church, so she could never date an *Englischer*. Besides, she'd only been dreaming about one man. A dream she quickly squashed.

Micah headed to the harness shop, his nerves still zinging. The intense fear still lingered, but his inner alarm mingled with exhilaration. He'd stayed in place during Hope's experiment—a personal victory. She'd never know the internal battle he'd waged. Every fiber of his being urged him to grab the twins and yank them to safety. If he hadn't been reluctant to let go of her hand . . .

How hard had he squeezed her fingers? His grip might have crushed her bones, but it had kept him grounded. And that soft palm against his had set his pulse hammering from more than fear.

He'd only just arrived at work, and already he was wishing the day were over so he could see Hope again. She held a magnetic pull for him, making it hard to stay away. If only the hours would move swiftly now, but slow once he reached her farm. After today, he'd only see her on Mondays, when the twins had their lessons. Waiting a whole week seemed unbearable.

Micah's spirits plunged even more as he pulled into the parking lot. Each time he came here or went to the house, the weight of guilt and loss overwhelmed him. He clung tightly to the memory of Hope's calming presence the same way he'd grasped her hand. Holding fast to that tiny ray of sunshine amid the darkness, he headed for the entrance.

One hand on the door, he stopped short, arrested by two faces staring at him through the glass. The delicious breakfast he'd shared with Hope now curdled in his stomach.

Sylvia and Susie. What were they doing here? The casserole dish in Susie's hands provided a clue.

Though he wished he could turn and flee, Micah pushed open the door and forced a smile. "You're here early."

Eli hadn't switched the sign on the glass from "Closed" to "Open." And some of the blinds hadn't been raised.

"Well, when we didn't find you at the house . . ."

The accusation in Sylvia's tone increased Micah's guilt. She'd also left her sentence dangling, as if hoping to discover his whereabouts.

When he didn't give her that satisfaction, she gestured toward Susie. "My daughter made you an egg casserole, although it's probably lukewarm by now."

"You don't have to feed me." Micah winced inside at how ungracious that sounded. "I mean, I'm grateful for your kindness, but I don't want to be a burden."

"It's not a burden." Susie's response was, as usual, barely audible.

"*Danke* for thinking of me," Micah added, "but I've already eaten breakfast."

Sylvia glowered, but before she could speak, Eli interrupted. "Even if you're stuffed, Micah, I don't know how you could resist that delicious smell. It's been making my mouth water the whole while they've been waiting for you."

With a soft *ach*, Susie turned toward Eli. "I'm so sorry. We should have offered you some."

"We only have one plate," Sylvia pointed out.

"That's perfect, then," Micah said. "You can feed Eli."

Eli waved away the offer. "I didn't mean to take Micah's breakfast, I only meant I didn't know how he could turn down something that smelled so good." He stammered the last few words, his face as red as Susie's cheeks.

"I'm so full right now," Micah said, "I couldn't eat a bite, even though it's tempting. No point in letting such wonderful *gut* cooking go to waste."

Sylvia's forehead, which had creased into deep craters, smoothed into shallower crevices. At least he'd mollified her a little, but she still wasn't pleased that Susie's meal, once again, had not hit her intended target.

Eli's enthusiasm made up for Micah's refusal, though, at least for Susie—if the way she ducked her head to hide her rosy cheeks and shy smile provided any clues.

Hiding his own smile, Micah thanked them both again and escaped to the worktables in the back room, saying over his shoulder, "I really need to get to work, but thank you both for thinking of me."

As soon as they were out of sight, he expelled a long, slow breath and let his muscles relax. His jaw ached from holding in the stress. Sylvia and Susie were kind and giving, so why did spending time around them make him tense up? Maybe because Sylvia's underlying motives never stayed hidden. They oozed into her every look and action, leaving him wary about his words or glances. If he offered an innocent compliment about Susie's cooking, Sylvia's self-satisfied smile skewered him as though he'd nibbled her bait and a cage door would spring shut behind him, trapping him.

Honesty would be the simplest solution, but Micah wasn't ready to share his growing feelings for Hope with anyone before he had a chance to find out if she was available and interested in him. Coming up with a plan to do that eluded him.

They'd only met recently, and although they'd shared some intense and emotional events, he didn't want to scare her away by pressuring her too soon. And before he could even broach that subject, he needed to find out if she was committed to anyone. Surely she wouldn't be involved with that *Englischer* who helped her with the business, would she?

That worry consumed the first hour of the morning as Micah concentrated on getting the next order completed. After concluding Hope wouldn't allow herself to be snared by an *Englischer*, Micah let himself imagine what might happen if she were free.

The hours passed quickly in daydreams as he anticipated holding her hand for reasons other than comfort. Eli broke into Micah's musings several times to ask questions or remind Micah to eat lunch.

"You really get absorbed in your work, don't you?" Eli said.

Micah struggled to come up with an honest answer. "Actually, I drift off. I'm usually thinking about other things." He prayed Eli wouldn't ask what had occupied his attention today.

"I see." Eli smiled. "I do the same. Once you've mastered the work, your hands move from task to task automatically." He opened his lunch cooler and unwrapped a sandwich. "I hope your thoughts were happy ones."

His clear-eyed gaze made Micah squirm. Had Eli used the word "hope" on purpose because he'd guessed who'd been on Micah's mind?

Chapter Twenty-Two

After his lesson was over, Kelvin walked beside Jasper with a swagger in his step. "I wasn't afraid of no horse."

"I'm sure you weren't." Jasper winked at Hope and Logan over his shoulder. "You're as brave as they come, my man."

They exited the barn, and Kelvin hurried to the car, slouched in the back seat, and shoved earbuds in his ears, but Jasper stayed behind to talk.

Logan recapped the lesson, and Jasper smiled. "Sounds like it went well, then. I'll call you early next week to set up a time for lessons. We have six foster kids, so coordinating schedules can be a bear."

"We'll look forward to it," Hope said.

She'd enjoy working with Kelvin. He'd donned a hardened shell on the outside to cover his insecurities. So different from Micah, who opened up and shared his vulnerabilities. It took strength of character to do that.

Perhaps someday Kelvin would be strong enough to reveal his hurts and his needs. Kelvin had more trauma to hide from the world, but Micah could serve as an example.

A longing took root in Hope's heart. A longing to work with a partner who shared her vision and her faith. A partner who loved God and horses. A partner who—

Hope broke off abruptly. With a business to run and *Daed*'s gambling, she had to curb these longings. But a little shoot of possibility took hold. *Daed* had sent Art away to spend time with the twins, Maybe they'd help to change him.

"You ready for the next student?" Logan asked, jerking her back to the barn and their work.

Hope pushed her daydreams about a future with Micah aside, or at least tried to, and concentrated on the next two lessons. Neither of those students seemed inclined to continue lessons.

Logan brushed it off. "Some people will accept anything free, even if they have no intention of signing up."

Hope couldn't imagine doing anything like that. Micah had done the opposite—paid for the lessons even before the twins had their free lesson.

"That reminds me," she said. "Micah paid for six weeks of lessons. I worked with Chloe and Jabin a little yesterday, but I promised him we'd give the children their free lesson today whenever we can fit them in."

Logan's face darkened. "The Micah who was here this morning?" The sarcastic edge to his words seemed intended to cut.

"Yes. I've scheduled the twins for Monday afternoons."

"If they've already paid, why do they need a free lesson?"

Hope tilted her head to one side and just stared at him.

Lowering his gaze, he muttered, "All right, but it's going to make things awfully tight."

"We'll manage," she said, trying to offer encouragement before he stalked off.

"Let's get ready for the next lesson," he said stiffly.

Hope prayed working together the rest of the long day wouldn't be uncomfortable.

Once the next student arrived, though, Logan resumed

his professional manner, and they worked cooperatively until noontime. One of the mothers from Hope's church was bringing her daughter with Down syndrome at one.

"If we cut our dinner—I mean, lunch—hour short, we can fit in one of the twins before Esther arrives," Hope suggested.

"I'll run into town quick to grab some fast food and be back by twelve thirty."

"To save time, you could eat with us again. It's nothing fancy. Just the usual soup and sandwiches."

"Sounds good to me."

After Hope slipped the twenties from her pocket into the cashbox, she slid the receipt book and pen into her pocket. The afternoon promised to be even busier than the morning, especially if they squeezed in a lesson for Jabin.

When she came out, Logan was washing up at the outdoor pump, and she took her turn. Then he followed her inside. "*Daed*," she called, "Logan's joining us for dinner."

"Good, good," he answered. He jumped to his feet. "That reminds me. I forgot to get the harness from the barn to give to Micah."

At Micah's name, Logan's jaw clenched.

"I'll go do that now, so I don't forget," *Daed* said.

"But we're in the middle of the game," Chloe protested.

"I won't be long. You can wait for me, or the two of you can go on without me." *Daed* hurried to the door. "Be right back."

By the time he returned, Hope had warmed the soup, and Chloe had coaxed Jabin into making sandwiches with her. Logan offered to help, but Hope insisted he sit at the table. She didn't want him to spoil her daydreams of working in the kitchen with Micah.

His face red, *Daed* huffed and puffed through the kitchen. "I'll just run upstairs to wash up."

That was odd. He usually used the outdoor pump. Had the exertion been too much for him? Maybe he was embarrassed to let Logan see how winded he was. Perhaps carrying the harness and assisting with the morning's lesson had drained him. After all, he usually spent most of the day sitting on the couch. He'd also been watching the twins the past few days. She needed to keep a closer eye on him. She didn't want to overtax him.

When *Daed* returned, they sat down for their meal. This time Logan kept his hands in his lap until they all lifted their heads following the prayer.

They discussed the lessons, and *Daed* surprised them both by offering some good suggestions. It might be nice to have his help with the business. He'd enjoyed being a sidewalker today, and he'd been doing a wonderful *gut* job with Chloe and Jabin.

They'd be going back to school next week. No doubt he'd miss their company. Maybe he'd be interested in working part-time.

Chloe begged to be the first student after they ate, so *Daed* volunteered to wash the dishes. Hope stared at him.

"What?" he demanded. "You don't trust me to clean a few plates?"

"It's not that, it's just—" Hope closed her mouth before she blurted out hurtful words.

She'd been doing everything—household chores and barn duties and handling finances—since *Mamm* died. *Daed* hadn't once offered to help. Hope tamped down her negative thoughts. Maybe being around the twins had brought back some of his true personality. Years ago, *Daed* had always helped friends and family. Was it possible—?

Daed still stood there, staring at her.

Hope smiled. "*Danke*, that would be great."

She and Logan headed to the barn, with Chloe chattering

the whole way. Between Hope's joy at the changes in her *daed* and her memories of Micah's hand gripping hers, she barely listened until Chloe mentioned taking the pony cart to a friend's house.

"Micah's going to let you do that?"

Chloe pinched her lips together. "He'd better." Her mutinous expression didn't bode well for Micah. "All my friends drive theirs."

Jah, children driving pony carts often trotted past their farm. With Micah being so traumatized by his childhood encounter with a horse, Hope was amazed Chloe had no fear of riding or driving after her parents' accident.

Maybe she didn't connect the open cart with the buggy. And she'd been dazed and lying on the ground, so she might not have seen the twisted wreckage.

A scene that still haunted Hope's nightmares.

"Maybe once Micah fixes the harness, you can practice on my pony cart here at the farm."

Chloe screeched to a standstill. "Practice?" She planted her hands on her hips. "I already know how to do it. *Mamm*"— her chin quivered, and her words were shaky—"taught me how to hitch the pony to the cart and how to drive it."

Hope had better warn Micah. With Chloe's determination, she'd be liable to hitch up the pony and take off without permission.

To impress Chloe with the seriousness of her message, Hope squatted in front of the little girl and looked her square in the eye. "I don't ever want you to use that cart without Micah's permission. Do you understand?"

Chloe took a few steps back at Hope's vehemence. "It's *my* pony cart."

"I'm sure your *mamm* wouldn't have let you take off without asking." Hope disliked using that to pressure Chloe, but she didn't want to risk her getting hurt.

"*Mamm*'s not here," she said in a broken voice.

"I know, but *Onkel* Micah is." Hope opened her arms, and Chloe rushed into them and buried her face against Hope's shoulder.

After letting Chloe cry for a few minutes, Logan set a hand on her shoulder. "You know, horses can help you too."

Hope had forgotten all about Chloe's session. Chloe lifted her head and stared at him with teardrops glistening on her lashes. Then she nodded.

Logan took her hand and then held out his other to assist Hope to her feet. She smiled to let him know she appreciated the gesture, but she rose on her own. Better not to encourage him. And for some reason, she had no desire to touch anyone else's hand after she'd held Micah's.

As the afternoon dragged on, Micah checked the clock. He intended to slip out before Sylvia and Susie waylaid him for dinner. An hour before closing time, he stood and put away his tools.

"I hope you don't mind if I leave early to pick up the children. I'll come in tomorrow to finish this."

Eli laughed. "You don't have to ask my permission. You're the boss."

Micah blinked. For a short while, he'd forgotten about Ben. Now it all came flooding back. But until now, this hadn't been Micah's shop. It had been *Dawdi*'s, *Daed*'s, and Ben's. Never his. Even now, he felt like an imposter.

"Listen, Eli, it's been years since I worked here. You know this shop much better than I do. I'm counting on you to run things."

Eli started to protest, but Micah plowed on. "Later, when I'm more settled, we can talk about the ownership of the business. For now, I want you to give yourself a pay raise.

You take whatever salary Ben was getting, and pay me yours."

"I can't do that."

"You can and you will." He walked away before Eli could argue.

"What should I tell Sylvia and Susie if they show up?"

That I'm avoiding them? So Eli had picked up on their campaign after such a short time? "Say, um, that I needed to pick up the twins."

"And that you're sorry you missed them, of course," Eli added.

Micah made a noncommittal grunt. He hadn't planned to encourage them, but he couldn't be impolite. "If they brought food for me, be sure to thank them, but you're welcome to it. Please let them know I already have dinner for tonight."

If he had to, he'd take Chloe and Jabin out for dinner at their favorite buffet restaurant, the way he used to when he came to visit. They could all use a little boost. Maybe he could even convince Hope and Isaac to come along. That might be one way to repay Hope.

She'd fed him and the twins more than enough times. Surely she wouldn't object to one simple meal from him. That possibility set Micah dreaming of Hope's angelic face across the table.

Hope barely had time to breathe all afternoon as they went from one student to the next, and she'd stuffed two checks in her pocket and handed out the receipts as she and Logan welcomed the next students.

One of the parents promised to call about setting up lessons after discussing it with her husband; another wanted to think about it. A third one's eyes opened wide when Hope quoted their prices, and she scurried away.

Hope exhaled a long breath when they finished with their final student before supper. They'd have an hour break before their two evening sessions.

Maritza's mother chatted as she led her autistic daughter toward Hope's office. She didn't bat an eye at the cost. "Are hundreds all right?" she asked.

"Certainly." Hope took the hundreds and bent over to open the lower desk drawer. "Let me get you some change." She flipped the latch on the cashbox. "I have an opening for Maritza at noon on Saturdays, if that'll work for you."

"She's with her dad then, but I'm sure he can manage to get her here."

"That's—" The cashbox was empty. Hope stared into the opening as if expecting the missing money to materialize. "I, um, I'm sorry. I don't have change after all. My partner must have taken the bank deposit." Logan hadn't mentioned taking the cash to the bank, but he had been concerned about it. Why hadn't he left some cash for change?

Flustered, Hope returned the money. "Why don't you wait to pay on Saturday, when Maritza comes for her session?"

"If you're sure?" After Hope's quiet yes, Maritza's mother slid the bills back into her wallet and took her daughter's hand. "She'll see you Saturday, and I'll be sure my ex brings the correct change."

"I'm looking forward to it," Hope said weakly, her attention still fixed on the cleaned-out cashbox. She barely registered their leaving.

All of the carbon copies of the receipts remained in a neat stack in the drawer beside the cashbox. Before she made the deposit, Hope had planned to reconcile the cash with the statements and then file the carbon copies in the proper file folder.

Why would Logan make a deposit but leave the receipts? She'd explained her procedure. Normally, he was a stickler for following rules. She'd have to make it clear that she didn't want him handling the money.

She added up the receipts, subtracted the checks, which remained under the cash tray, and jotted down the total cash missing—$4820. Some loose change rattled around in the bottom of the metal box. Even the rolls of coins she kept for change had disappeared. Hope paper-clipped the stack of receipts together and set it on her desk. Then she strode from the office to find Logan. She wanted to be sure the cash he'd taken matched the receipts. He didn't have access to the business account, but she'd authorized him to make deposits. Should she change that?

Logan was cleaning Buttercup's saddle. "That went well, didn't it?" He smiled over at her. "You OK? They seemed enthusiastic. Did they decide not to sign up?"

"It's not that. Could you come into the office when you're done?"

"Sure. But why so serious? Did something bad happen?"

"Let's talk about it in there." Hope pointed to the office.

"I'm finished here." Logan put away the sponge he'd been using and followed her.

She rounded the desk and sat down, one hand on the receipts. "I'd been planning to reconcile these tomorrow." She slid the stack across the desk.

Logan picked them up, removed the paper clip, and thumbed through them. "Looks like the cash receipts from this week." He glanced at her, his brow crinkled.

"I know I agreed to let you make deposits, but I'd prefer

to make them myself. I did explain about my plan to reconcile the receipts first, didn't I?"

"You did. And as for deposits, you own the business. I'm fine with whatever you decide as long as I have access to the account books so I can keep an eye on how everything's going."

And to be sure she didn't cheat him out of his profit. Hope's jaw clenched. "When I went to get change for Maritza's mother—" Hope reached into the drawer and pulled out the cashbox. After unlatching the box, she flipped open the lid to reveal the empty money tray. "We need to keep change in here at all times."

The puzzled frown on Logan's face deepened. "Definitely. But where's the money? You didn't have time to make a deposit." The hesitancy in his voice indicated he was baffled.

"No, I didn't." Hope took the total she'd jotted down, subtracted the amount of change from it, and handed him the paper. "That's how much is missing from the box, plus"—she reached for the ledger, opened it to the section labeled "Cash on Hand," and pointed to the most recent entry—"this amount."

"I don't understand. Are you saying someone stole all that money?" His eyes narrowed. "Wait a minute. You're not accusing me?"

"No, no." Hope shook her head to back up the denial. She didn't want him to think she questioned his integrity. "I thought maybe . . . I hoped you'd taken it to deposit it." She buried her head in her hands. "I guess not."

All this had been to avoid thinking about the real culprit. The one who'd sprang to mind the minute she'd spotted the empty box. She'd shoved that idea aside immediately, hoping and praying Logan had the money.

Logan pulled out his phone. "We'd better report this to

the police. One of the parents must have gotten into the box during our lessons. We need to get locks on the door, the desk drawer, and lock up that cashbox."

Hope held up a hand to stop him. "Wait a minute. Maybe you'd better sit down." She motioned toward the chair. "This might take a while." She regretted her long-ago decision to keep *Daed*'s problems to herself.

"Whatever you have to say can wait. We should get the cops out here first."

"Not until I explain something."

Uncertainty flashed in his eyes, but Logan dragged one of the chairs closer to the desk and plopped into it. "OK, shoot."

"I probably should have told you this earlier, but"—Hope fiddled with the paper clip to avoid Logan's eyes—"my father has a gambling problem. He took money from the bank account before the business opened, and I borrowed from a friend to replace it."

"What?" Fire in his eyes, Logan shot to his feet. His chair slid backward, scraping across the floor. "And you didn't think that was important enough to tell me?"

"I–I didn't want to worry you."

"You didn't want to worry me?" His voice rose, charging the air around them with angry vibes. "You didn't think I had the right to know my investment was in danger?"

Hope hung her head. "I'm so sorry."

"Sorry won't bring back the money. And a third of what's missing belongs to me."

"I know." Hope blinked back tears. "I'll repay every penny."

"How? When you've just admitted all the money you put into this business is borrowed? You told me you'd saved—" After one glance at her face, he abruptly stopped his tirade.

"I didn't mean to lie to you." She tried to keep her voice steady but had little control over the wavering.

"I know." He pulled back his chair into place and sat. Then he reached across the desk and tilted her chin until he could look her in the eye. "We can figure it out together."

Hope jerked back from his touch. Not because it tingled the way Micah's touch had, but because it made her feel icky. She caught her lower lip between her teeth at his emphasis on the word "together." Somehow it sounded less like business partners and more like a dating couple.

When they first met, she'd made it clear their relationship would be strictly professional. Today, he'd crossed that boundary by touching her. And by his implications. Right now, though, she had to set that aside to deal with a more pressing problem.

"I have no proof *Daed* did it, but I need to check with him first." Part of her hoped he was to blame. Even though it meant more debt and heartache. But another part of her wished it were a stranger.

"That makes sense. Did you want me to wait here while you check?"

Hope stood. Might as well get it over with. "I'll be back shortly."

Logan flicked his chin upward to show his support. "So sorry." His words sounded genuine.

"*Danke*," she whispered as she picked up the cashbox.

Crossing the lawn and entering the house, she steeled herself for the truth.

Chapter Twenty-Three

"*Daed*," Hope called as she opened the screen door.

"*Jah?*" he answered from the living room.

Hope crossed the kitchen and peeked into the living room, but she kept her hand with the cashbox concealed.

"Do you know anything about this?" she asked, then pulled the box from behind her.

All hope she'd had of his innocence fled. His flaming cheeks and cagey expression revealed his guilt.

"Why would I—?" His bravado faltered as she glared at him.

"Don't lie and make it worse."

He held up his palms in surrender. "I planned to replace it."

"Oh, I'm sure you did. Except you lost again, didn't you?"

Daed squirmed.

Hope held up a hand. "Never mind. I already know the answer. I don't want to hear any excuses."

"I don't know for sure it's lost. Art's at the track now."

The whininess of his tone grated on Hope, and she closed her eyes to gain control. She bit her lip, unsure whether to burst into tears or explode in rage. "I thought you sent Art away when he stopped by."

"I, well, I did. But he came back again today. He promised it was a sure thing, with great odds."

A sure thing? Like all the other sure things he'd ended up losing? A vise of pain tightened around her upper skull. Hope squeezed her eyes shut and rubbed her forehead. She couldn't afford to have a headache. Not now. Not when they had more students scheduled.

Daed babbled on as if trying to excuse his behavior. "The bank account's so low, I couldn't take money from there."

Hope had purposely left that statement out so the new balance would discourage him.

"When I saw you putting those twenties in your pocket, I figured you'd have more in the office. I wanted to replace some of the other money I'd lost, so I borrowed—"

Hope snapped, "Taking anything without the owner's permission is not borrowing, *Daed*. It's stealing."

"I wasn't stealing." He lowered his head and mumbled, "I guess I was."

"I need to get out there before Logan calls the police."

"The police?" Alarm flashed in *Daed*'s eyes. "Will I be arrested?"

"I can't speak for Logan. A third of the money was his." Hope turned and left the room.

She doubted Logan would report it as a theft. And, despite the dwindling loan from Priscilla, Hope intended to replace the money—or at least Logan's part of it.

Guilt nagged at her for not reassuring *Daed* of that, but she hoped that stewing a while might help him recognize he'd committed a crime. What if he'd taken money from someone else? That chilled her. He really could end up in jail.

Hope had been raised to forgive "seventy times seven."

No matter what anyone had done, if they confessed, she needed to forgive. She'd slipped out before *Daed* could apologize, mainly because she wasn't quite ready to extend forgiveness. That might take some wrestling with her conscience, and with God.

On Saturday morning, after doing the barn chores, Micah headed back into the house with Chloe and Jabin. They cleaned up and changed out of their work clothes, and then Micah attempted breakfast.

As smoke filled the kitchen, he remembered Hope's suggestion to keep the flame low. He'd just lifted the pan of eggs and adjusted the heat when someone knocked at the front door.

Chloe sprang up from the table. "I'll get it."

Micah waved a hand in the air, hoping to dissipate the acrid gray clouds rising from the frying pan. He froze in place at the sound of Sylvia's strident tones. *Ach!* Much too early in the day to deal with her.

Jabin's head sank low into his turtle pose. He probably wished, like Micah did, he could crawl into a hard, protective shell to hide.

What were they doing here again? Micah eavesdropped on the conversation, hoping to get a clue so he could head off any of their plans.

"Phew." Sylvia cruised into the kitchen with Chloe and Susie trailing behind. "What's burning?"

Micah stood, clutching the pan, struggling not to appear as foolish as he felt.

"Let me have that." Sylvia strode over, snatched the pan from his hand, and snapped off the burner. "Good thing we brought breakfast with us. I can't bear to think of these poor children eating this. Or going hungry."

Micah's mouth flopped open, but he snapped it shut before he retorted.

Please, God, give me patience, he begged.

Sylvia motioned for Susie to enter the kitchen. "You can set those on the table, so these children can eat a good meal." Sylvia carried the smoking pan to the back porch. "That'll help clear the smell," she said after she returned.

With an apologetic glance at Micah, Susie lowered the containers onto the table and peeled back the foil to reveal scrambled eggs and scrapple.

Sylvia opened the refrigerator. "*Gut*, you have applesauce in here." She plopped the jar on the table and waved at Chloe, directing her to sit. "Let's eat."

Micah clenched his teeth. The two of them were inviting themselves to a meal without asking him?

He forced himself to take a deep breath and relax. They'd been kind enough to bring breakfast. Despite Sylvia's tendency to overpower those around her, he should be grateful. Inside, his spirit rebelled, but he slid into his usual seat. He could fight her commands, or he could show humility, which was what God expected.

At her mother's urging, Susie, her face red, sat directly across from Micah. Following the prayer, Sylvia orchestrated the meal, directing people to take more food and correcting the children's table manners. Chloe, who usually chattered all during the meal, ate in silence, and Jabin only lifted his head to take quick swallows of milk.

Micah had to admit this breakfast tasted better than his attempts, although the tension at the table contrasted with their pleasant meals at Hope's. Still, he needed to be polite. "*Danke* for the food."

Susie tittered. "You're welcome."

Her mother beamed. "I wanted you all to have a hearty breakfast before our trip to the petting zoo."

What? Micah struggled to recall the conversation. "I thought we canceled it yesterday."

Chloe groaned.

Did that mean she wanted to go? Or was she upset that they weren't going?

"We didn't want to disappoint the children, so we decided we'd go today instead." Sylvia stared at him as if daring him to disagree.

Micah cleared his throat. "I'm sorry, but the shop is way behind on orders after being closed for the funeral. I planned to take Chloe and Jabin with me to work." He'd been dreading that. This would be the first time they'd return to the shop since their parents . . . He swallowed hard.

"We could take the twins while you work," Susie volunteered.

"That's very kind of you." Micah turned grateful eyes in her direction and wished he hadn't. Sylvia and Susie might misinterpret his meaning.

Chloe bounced on her chair. "I love going to the petting zoo. Can I get mint chocolate chip ice cream?"

Susie smiled at her. "Of course. What flavor would you like, Jabin?"

His head still low, Jabin stayed silent.

"He likes vanilla with sprinkles," Chloe said, and a fleeting smile crossed Jabin's face.

Micah tucked that information in the back of his mind. Maybe he'd use it to get more smiles another day.

Susie insisted on doing the breakfast dishes, and she and her *mamm* soon set off with Chloe and Jabin. Micah waited until they'd gone before attempting to hitch up the horse. He didn't want them to see his struggles.

At work, Micah had trouble concentrating. His thoughts kept straying to the twins and their outing, but daydreams of Hope overshadowed his concerns about Sylvia's campaign.

After enduring another supper at Sylvia's that evening, Micah was grateful to head home, although he dreaded facing them again the next day at church.

As he'd feared, Sylvia staked out Susie's claim with a few well-chosen hints. Micah had no way to combat her comments. While they were true, the way she said them implied a much greater connection between him and Susie. He supposed it didn't matter, as he had no interest in beginning a relationship with any of the single girls in the *g'may*, but he sighed with relief when he and the children headed home after the church meal.

Although Micah appreciated Susie caring for the twins this coming week, he dreaded going to Sylvia's every day. At least tomorrow, he had an excuse to get away.

That excuse—taking the twins to their lessons at Hope's— filled him with anticipation. The past two days without seeing her had been long and dreary.

That excitement stayed with him as he helped the twins pack their school supplies the next morning, and Micah hummed a tune as they set off.

Jabin hung back as Micah walked them across the parking lot, but Chloe skipped ahead.

"What's your teacher's name?" he asked.

"Mim," Chloe replied over her shoulder.

Micah shook hands with the teacher, who introduced herself as Miriam.

"I'm so glad to have Chloe and Jabin back." Her eyes clouded. "I'm so sorry for their loss. Ben was your brother?"

A lump in his throat, Micah nodded.

"Chloe seems livelier than usual," she remarked, "but I expected to cope with some behavioral changes. What about Jabin?"

Micah glanced at his nephew, who still trailed far behind. "He's barely been speaking."

"I'll keep that in mind and give them both some time to adjust."

"I appreciate it. Also, I wanted to let you know that Susie Esh will be picking them up at noon this week."

The speculation in Mim's eyes made it clear she'd heard Sylvia's rumors. Micah wanted to deny them, but if he did, might it bring more predatory *mamms* to his doorstep? He said a hasty goodbye and hurried off to work.

The whole day, he kept one eye on the clock, but rather than sweeping around, the minute hand seemed to stick and jiggle at each second.

"You're eager to leave?" Eli teased. "You spend more time glancing at that clock than you do at that harness."

"Sorry," Micah muttered. "I'm worried about the twins' first day of school and getting them to an appointment on time."

"I see." Eli drawled out the words and raised his eyebrows.

Did he suspect Micah's real motives for clock watching?

Micah bent his head to concentrate on the leather in front of him. "I'll pay more attention to the work."

Eli laughed. "I'm not worried about that. You're so good at this, you could do it with your eyes shut."

"I doubt that." Micah determined not to glance at the time until after lunch. And he kept that promise for twenty long minutes.

Eli appeared relieved when Micah put away his tools later that afternoon and took off. Even the stomach-churning trip to Sylvia's didn't dampen Micah's joy at seeing Hope again.

When Sylvia opened the door, she stared at him. "You're early. We weren't expecting you until suppertime."

"I forgot to tell you, the twins have an appointment today."

"But you'll be back for dinner? Or we can bring it to you."

"That won't be necessary, but thank you." Micah didn't plan to impose on Hope, so he'd take the children out for a meal.

As soon as Sylvia called the twins, Chloe raced for the door.

"Don't forget your safety vest," Susie called after her, holding up the bright yellow vests the scholars wore when they walked along the road to the schoolhouse.

Chloe hurried back and jammed her arms into the armholes.

"I didn't mean you needed to wear it," Susie protested softly, but Chloe had already taken off for the door. Susie smiled at Jabin, who took his vest from her and clutched it to his chest.

Chloe danced around beside Micah. "Are we going to Hope's now?"

"Hope Graber?" Sylvia's brows drew together, and disdain dripped from her words. "I thought you said you had an appointment."

"We do." Although reluctant to tell her, Micah added, "They'll be getting horse therapy lessons."

"What foolishness. They're around horses all the time." Her mouth pursed. "I can't believe an Amish woman would do something that worldly. All these children need to heal are prayer and proper discipline."

Micah's curt nod cut off any further criticism of Hope. Had she run into trouble with other members of the community for her job choice?

"Hurry up," Chloe urged Jabin. "We're going to Hope's."

Was that a quiver of a smile? It disappeared before Micah could tell for sure, but Jabin did move faster.

As eager to leave as Chloe, Micah put an arm around Jabin's shoulders to usher him from the house. The gray cloud that always descended on him when he interacted with Sylvia disappeared, and sunshine shone in Micah's heart and soul. He couldn't wait to see Hope.

All weekend long, *Daed* had moped around the house as he waited to hear back from Art. If the news had been good, no doubt Art would have stopped by to celebrate. The fact that he hadn't meant he was avoiding *Daed*, which in turn indicated he'd lost the money.

Heartsick, Hope went out to the barn on Monday to meet Logan for a noon planning meeting. He'd agreed not to press charges against her *daed*, and she assured him she'd take his share from the loan Priscilla had given her, but it had added a major layer of tension to their business relationship.

"I deposited all the checks this morning," Hope told him when he entered the office, hoping it would help ease things between them.

"Good." His testy, one-word answer showed he hadn't forgiven her or her *daed*.

Hope sighed to herself. "Thanks for installing all the locks." She hadn't been happy that he'd chosen to do it on Sunday, but she'd refrained from criticizing him. She and *Daed* hadn't been doing anything special on their off-Sunday, but it bothered her to see anyone working on the Lord's Day.

Logan thawed a little, but his response was still tart. "You're welcome."

Sliding a paper across the desk, she said, "Here's a list of the students who'll be coming after school today."

Logan scanned the page, then tapped a stubby finger on the first two names on the list. "Are these the twins who got lessons on Thursday and Friday?"

Hope disliked his irritated tone. "Well, actually, they didn't have real lessons on Thursday, but yes, they were here both days."

"And their dad got special attention?"

"Uncle," Hope corrected. "I only wanted to help him get comfortable with the idea of the children being around horses."

"Um-hmm." Logan shot her a sideways, I-don't-believe-it glance. "So he paid for both of them?"

"Yes, he did. You can check the books if you don't believe me."

"No need to get so defensive."

Hope nibbled on her lip to keep from defending herself.

Logan leaned back in the chair and studied the paper. "OK, here's what I think we should do with each of these."

While Hope took notes and pulled out information sheets for each parent who hadn't already received one, Logan discussed their strategies. Hope chimed in with additional suggestions, and he smiled at her.

"You have good natural instincts. You'll do well at this once you've completed your training."

"That's a relief, because I'm planning to do it for the rest of my life."

"You mean until retirement?" Logan teased.

Hope relaxed a little now that they were back on friendly

footing. "Have you ever seen an Amish man or woman retired or just sitting around?"

"No, I guess not," Logan admitted as he stood. "I'm happy to know you intend to continue the business, but just so you're aware, I plan to retire at sixty-five. Or much earlier, if I can manage it."

"I see," Hope said. "I'm sorry to hear you intend to be lazy."

Logan laughed. "Yeah, right. I have a few errands to run, but I'll be back before the lesson at three thirty."

A lesson Hope eagerly awaited. She'd see Micah again. After seeing him almost every day since she'd met him, she'd missed him the past two days—despite all the chaos.

Micah pulled into Hope's driveway a little after three. In his eagerness to see her, he'd hurried Daffy along. Now he wished he'd driven more slowly. He didn't want her to read too much into his early arrival. Or did he?

Hope must have heard the buggy clattering up the driveway because she stepped out of the barn and waved. And the sunshine in Micah's heart turned into a brilliant glow.

While he tied up the horse, Chloe hopped out and ran to Hope. "I can go first, right?"

Hope glanced in Micah's direction, one eyebrow raised, as if to check with him. Judging from Jabin's slowness, his nephew didn't appear eager to challenge Chloe for first place.

"That's fine with me." Micah ushered Jabin along. "And I suspect it'll be all right with Jabin."

"*Gut!*" Chloe squealed.

"You know what?" Hope seemed to be studying Micah,

but then she lowered her gaze. "Because you're all here early, what if we let your *onkel* go first?"

Micah's step faltered. *What?*

"Like we did the last time?" Chloe asked, and Hope nodded.

He'd endured that, but just barely. He'd rather not repeat the experience.

"I was thinking we could try inside the barn this time." Hope looked up at him with a smile.

No! The twins would be too close to the horses and in a confined space. But how could he say no to that encouraging expression? That sweet smile?

Hope led the way to the barn, but this time Jabin wasn't the only one dawdling.

Chapter Twenty-Four

When Micah reached the barn door, Hope stood waiting. She positioned herself on Micah's left to walk between him and the horse stalls. Had she done that on purpose? If so, he appreciated her thoughtfulness.

Not that it helped much. He tried to tamp down the rising panic as both twins drifted closer to the left.

"Chloe? Jabin?" Hope called after them. "Come here a minute."

Micah exhaled a pent-up breath he hadn't realized he'd been holding. *Please keep them away from the horses.*

Chloe scampered back to Hope, while Jabin took his time. Hope knelt to talk to them, and Micah took that opportunity to edge even closer to the barn wall on his right.

A horse snorted and stamped in its stall, and Micah's heartbeat thundered into a rapid crescendo.

Hope looked up at him. "Are you all right with this?"

He'd been so busy trying to calm himself, he hadn't even heard her plan. He had to trust her. His lips refused to move, so he nodded.

"Great." She brushed off her hands and stood.

Her eyes, shining with sympathy, made him long to prove himself, to appear strong and in control. He fought an internal battle to uncurl his fingers one by one, but he couldn't unwind the spring-coiled tension in his chest waiting to explode.

"We'll let Jabin go first," Hope announced.

Go first for what? If only he'd listened to her instructions to the twins, he'd be better prepared.

Chloe jumped up and down beside Hope, begging for a turn.

"Jabin's going to start," Hope told her.

"I'm hot," Chloe whined. "And I don't want to wait."

Hope's lips curved upward. "It won't hurt you to take the second turn. It's good to learn patience. If you're hot, why don't you take off your vest? You can put it in the office for now."

Although he was too nervous to fully appreciate it, Micah admired Hope's ability to keep Chloe busy. Keeping an eye on his niece distracted him, so it took a few seconds before Micah realized Jabin had headed toward a stall on his own.

He choked back a command to stay away, and Hope rewarded him with an encouraging smile. A smile that twisted his already coiled-up insides. A smile that made him want to conquer his inner demons. A smile that made him wish he could take her in his arms and forget he was in a horse barn.

The blood raging through Micah's body lessened a little as Hope took a few steps away but increased as Jabin called Molly over to pet her.

"I'll be right back," Hope said, and she headed toward him.

Micah missed her comforting presence. He tensed as she opened the stall and ushered Jabin inside.

Chloe came zinging back and grabbed his hand. "How come Jabin gets to be first?"

Micah's throat was too dry to answer. Hope and Jabin stood as far from the horse as possible, but they were still within kicking distance if the horse turned. Micah longed to beg them both to come out of the stall. Just when he couldn't stand it any longer and opened his mouth to call to Jabin, Hope backed out of the stall with his nephew.

She came over and, with Chloe still clinging to one of his hands, she squeezed his other. "How are you doing?"

"Pretty shaky," Micah admitted.

"Do you want Chloe to try it?"

No! At least Jabin stood still and calm. Chloe, on the other hand . . .

Before he could shake his head, Chloe darted into the open stall. "I can do it too." She didn't stand as far away as Jabin had, and Micah sucked in a breath.

Please, God, keep her safe.

He gripped Hope's hand hard.

"Chloe, remember what we said. Back to the wall."

"I'm not scared of Molly." Chloe took another step forward.

Hope's voice cracked like a whip in the cavernous barn. "Chloe!"

A pout on her face, Chloe backed up.

"I think that's enough for one day," Hope said. "Come out of the stall and latch it. Logan should be here soon."

"What's this about Logan?" a man's voice echoed through the barn.

Hope immediately dropped Micah's hand and turned toward Logan. "You're here already."

"I'm often early. What's so surprising about that?" His eyes narrowed at her closeness to Micah. "Unless . . ."

Micah squirmed. Had Logan seen them holding hands?

"Unless what?" Hope challenged Logan. He wouldn't finish that thought. At least not around the students.

She guessed right. Logan lifted his chin and his nostrils flared, but he didn't respond.

Hope turned to Micah. He'd put on a brave face, but she sensed the effort it took. She suspected he'd rather not walk down the aisle to the kitchen, and she wished she could keep holding his hand. "Why don't you wait in the house with *Daed* during the twins' lessons?"

He exhaled a sigh. "*Danke*. I'll do that."

Logan waited until Micah exited before joining her. "What was that about?"

"We have students right now," Hope reminded him.

"We'd better talk later."

With a brisk nod, Hope rounded up the twins. "Because Jabin got to go first before, why don't we let Chloe take her lesson now?" She checked with Jabin, who shrugged. "You can go inside with Micah."

He nodded and took off at his usual ambling pace. Then she and Logan began Chloe's session. The whole time, Hope's stomach churned.

Logan exhibited his usual patience with both children during their lessons, but his instructions to her remained snippy, even after the lessons ended. They stood together to say goodbye to Micah and the twins, but as soon as Hope headed for the house, Logan flicked a thumb over his shoulder in the direction of the office.

"We need to talk."

Hope followed him down the barn aisle, her draggy steps no match for his brisk stride.

The minute the door closed behind them, Logan snarled, "You don't have time to get involved with that widower and his kids."

"He's not a widower. He's their *onkel* . . ." Hadn't she told him that earlier?

"Whatever he is."

Hope narrowed her eyes. "What business is it of yours?"

Logan stood and paced across the room, his back to her. "What are you learning in those therapy courses of yours? Don't they teach you not to get attached to clients?"

Clients? Hope hated that word. These weren't clients, they were children. Children she cared about. Children she longed to help. Children she'd bonded with more closely than she should. Children whose *onkel* she'd fallen for. Hard.

All along, she tried to guard against getting involved, and yet . . .

"You're right," she whispered. But how did you go back and undo falling for someone? "Maybe I should turn their sessions over to you." No matter how much it hurt.

Logan pivoted to face her. "That won't solve the problem." Anger simmered under his words. "You're too softhearted for your own good."

At least he hadn't figured out the truth. A truth Hope could barely admit to herself. She cared about the twins as if they were her own, and from time to time, she wished she could be their mother. A picture of holding hands with Micah flashed before her eyes. They were heading to church together, each one holding the hand of a twin. The joy that tingled through her made her so light, she could float away.

"You're doing it again." Logan's sharp words snapped her back to the office and to reality.

Could he read the longing in her expression? Hope lowered her eyes and pretended to study the balance sheets on the desk in front of her. But her mind remained on Micah, and the deep desire burning inside splashed heat up her neck and onto her cheeks. She lowered her elbows to the table and pressed her palms against her cheeks, hoping to hide them from his scrutiny.

His eagle eyes searched every inch of her face, exposing the truth. "This man, the twins' uncle . . ." Logan's dismissive tone, and the fact that he avoided saying Micah's name, made her wonder if he was jealous.

He had no need to be. Hope had made it clear in her early talks with Logan that she had no intention of letting a romance derail her business plans. Love and marriage were not for her. Until she got all her debts paid off and the business was making a profit, she couldn't entertain that thought. And even then, with a *daed* like hers, she'd never put a husband or children at financial risk. Especially not someone she cared about so deeply.

Logan stepped close to the desk, splayed his hands on the wood, and hunched over her like a wildcat ready to spring. "Are you even listening to me? Your eyes went all dreamy."

Hope shrank back from his intensity. "I–I'm sorry." She had no idea if she was apologizing to him, to Micah, or to herself. Or maybe to all three.

Logan straightened up. "I am too." Yet his gaze bored into her. He flipped his palms up and into the air, as if dismissing the subject. "Look, in addition to professionalism, my main concern is financial. I gave up a high-paying job to come here, and I'm counting on this as my livelihood, my future."

What did her interest in Micah have to do with finances? No matter how attracted she was to him, she'd never act on it. "What do you mean?" Hope asked.

"Look, I put up with your father's pilfering." He stopped and stared at the closed door. "That wasn't locked when we came in, was it?"

Hope shriveled under his glare. She'd forgotten to do that earlier. "I'm sorry. I won't forget again."

"See that you don't."

She bristled. This was her business, and Logan had no right to order her around like this. As quickly as her temper rose, she calmed it. God wanted her to be humble, and she should be an example of His peace.

Keeping her tone measured, she said, "I don't understand why you think my friendship with Micah is connected to the business income. He's paying for the lessons."

"That's not what I'm talking about."

"Then maybe you'd better explain, because I don't get it."

Once again, Logan turned his back to her. "It seems to me you're mighty interested in him. Next thing you know, you'll be closing down the business to get married."

"I made that clear when we first set up the business." Her voice rose. "I have no intention of marrying anyone. Not ever."

Micah stopped dead outside the office. He hadn't meant to eavesdrop, but he couldn't help overhearing Hope. The finality of her words chilled him.

All his dreams of a possible future with her had just crashed, smashing into tiny pieces on the floor. At least he hadn't asked her about courting. He only hoped his interest in her hadn't been too obvious.

Inside the office, Logan growled a response, too low for Micah to hear. Should he knock or come back later? If Chloe didn't need her safety vest, he'd be tempted to leave it there and go. But she and Jabin would be riding their scooters to school tomorrow, so he had no choice. He waited for a break in the conversation and tapped at the door.

"Come in," Logan called.

Hope stared at him with a sickish look on her face. Had she realized his interest in her? Her faint "Micah?" twisted his insides.

"I, um, Chloe needs her safety vest. She left it in here."

"I don't see it anywhere." Logan's less-than-friendly

answer and suspicious glare indicated he suspected Micah had a different motive for returning to the office.

"Sorry." Micah shot him an apologetic glance that did nothing to erase Logan's frown, and Micah wished he hadn't barged in on their private conversation.

"It's all right," Hope assured him. "I did tell Chloe to bring it in here, but I don't see it."

The tiny room held no furniture besides the desk and two chairs. "Knowing Chloe, she probably tossed it somewhere. Under the desk, maybe?"

"Let me look," Hope offered.

Her eyes met Micah's, but conscious of Logan's glower trained on the two of them, Micah let his gaze skitter away. Besides, Hope had made it clear she wasn't interested in a relationship. At least not one that led to marriage. He had to be careful to hide his true feelings.

She ducked under the desk. "It's right near your left foot, Logan. Could you get it?"

Without saying a word, Logan swooped down, picked up the safety vest, and held it out on one finger.

Micah was as reluctant to take it as Logan was to hand it to him, but Micah forced himself to be polite. "Thank you."

"I'm glad we found it." At Hope's kind smile, Micah's heart thudded.

As much as he longed to stay and bask in that warmth, he needed to leave. Yet he struggled to walk away.

Logan crossed his arms, a signal for Micah to get out of the room *now*. It almost seemed as if Logan had sensed Micah's attraction to Hope and was declaring her off-limits. Too absurd. Hope wouldn't be attracted to an *Englischer*, would she?

He shook his head. No, she'd said she wouldn't marry *anyone*. That would include Logan. At least, he hoped it did.

Loud throat-clearing startled Micah from his thoughts.

He'd been standing there staring at Hope. Logan's narrowed eyes flashed a warning.

Micah put on a cheerful expression to cover his disappointment and, throwing his shoulders back, he turned to leave.

"Have a good week," Hope called after him.

Micah wished her one as well, but after the news he'd just heard, having a good week seemed impossible.

Hope stared after Micah as he left the office. If she'd been closer to the door, she'd have watched him walk down the barn aisle and . . .

Logan made a choking noise. She'd completely forgotten he was there. Micah distracted her from everything going on around her. Hope had no desire to return to a pointless conversation—or argument—with Logan.

"I should probably make sure they haven't forgotten anything else." And see if she could smooth things over with Micah after Logan's annoyance. Actually, the smartest move would be to keep her distance.

"Of course you should." The sarcasm in Logan's voice sliced through the air, stabbing at her lame excuse.

Pretending to ignore his cutting remark, Hope headed for the door. Their next student didn't arrive until early evening. "Can you lock up if you go out for a meal?" Not waiting for a response, she hurried after Micah.

"That's exactly what I meant," Logan called after her. "You're letting emotion cloud good judgment and business sense."

He was probably right, but where Micah was concerned, Hope didn't care. By the time she exited the barn, Micah was emerging from the house, a reluctant Chloe in tow.

"Micah?" Hope called.

He stopped and waited for her to reach the porch, but he avoided looking directly at her. She hoped he hadn't still been in the barn earlier when Logan accused her of being interested in Micah. How much of the conversation had he overheard?

Hope mounted the porch steps. "I want to apologize for Logan's attitude."

Micah didn't look directly at her, but he waved a hand in the air, as if to brush it off. "I'm sure he has his reasons."

His refusal to meet her eyes hurt. Was it his way of letting her know he wasn't interested? He must have heard her declaration against marriage. At least she hoped he had. Then he wouldn't think she was chasing him right now. Even if she was.

Micah shuffled his feet, making her aware she was blocking the steps.

"Sorry." Hope shifted so he could pass, but he didn't move.

"*Neh*, I'm the one who's sorry. I didn't mean to interrupt your business."

Surely, even if he'd only heard the last thing she'd shouted, he'd know the conversation had turned personal. Perhaps he was only being polite.

"That's all right. Actually," she confided, "I was grateful to end the conversation."

Micah looked at her as if assessing the truth of her words. An odd expression crossed his face, but she couldn't quite place it. Chagrin, maybe? But why would he feel embarrassed or humiliated? She must have misread his reaction.

She wanted to ease his discomfort. After all, he'd only wanted to find the vest, not be privy to gossip. She tried to laugh it off, but her attempt ended up sounding more like a cross between a snicker and a sob. "Logan's always searching for hidden meanings. Sometimes he's wrong." *But this time, he's absolutely right.*

Not that she'd admit it. But she definitely was attracted to Micah, and she'd fallen hard—for him and the twins.

Chapter Twenty-Five

As Chloe found one excuse after another to delay leaving on Friday morning, Micah struggled not to snap at her. Although nobody enforced his starting time at work, he wanted to be there during business hours, and he disliked being late.

After her fourth trip upstairs for an item she'd forgotten, Micah blew out a long, exasperated sigh. "We need to leave now."

"You don't have to wait for me," Chloe said. "Jabin and I can get to school by ourselves."

Micah had given in and let them take scooters to school, but he liked to keep an eye on them for at least part of the way. "Please make it quick."

Ignoring his foot tapping in a you'd-better-hurry-or-else rhythm, Chloe dragged her feet coming down the stairs. When she saw him still standing by the back door, disappointment clouded her features.

"I thought you were leaving."

Micah placed his hands on his hips. "Have you been trying to get rid of me?"

Chloe dipped her head and mumbled, "*Jah*." Then she

straightened and tilted up her chin. "I want to take the pony cart to school."

"Absolutely not." Micah's chest tightened at the thought of her and Jabin in a tippy cart directly behind the pony's back legs. "It's much too dangerous."

His niece glared. "I knew you'd say that."

"And you're too young." Even as Micah said it, his excuse sounded weak.

"My friend Maria's eight, and she drives hers."

"Not to school. Besides, you're only seven." Micah seized on that.

Tears shimmered in Chloe's eyes. "But I already know how to do it. *Mamm* taught me."

Micah knelt and hugged her. "I'm sorry." As much as it pained him to see her grief, he couldn't give in on a safety issue. "Let's talk about it next year, when you're eight." Not that he'd necessarily agree then, but maybe it would put off the argument.

"That's too long." Her eyes still damp, she mounted her scooter when Micah handed it to her, but the conflict was far from over.

If she already knew how to hitch up the cart, what if she sneaked out to the barn one day and took off?

All day long, he worried about Chloe defying his rules. He had to find a way to protect her.

Hope walked her Friday afternoon student to the exit, opened the door, and stopped.

"Micah?" She hadn't been expecting him.

"I don't want to interrupt your work," he said, "but when you have a minute, I'd like to ask a favor."

"I'll be right back." She walked Kelvin and his foster dad to their car, but her mind stayed on Micah.

"That your boyfriend?" Kelvin's loud question rang out.

Surely Micah had heard. Hope's face burned. "No," she whispered, but her flushed face and flustered motions must have revealed her feelings.

"Coulda fooled me," Kelvin muttered before Jasper shushed him.

She hoped Micah hadn't also guessed the truth.

After seeing Kelvin off, she rushed back toward Micah, but Logan loomed in the doorway to the barn, and she slowed her pace.

When she reached Micah, he followed her gaze to where Logan stood, hands on hips, staring at them. "I know you're busy, so I won't keep you long," Micah said. "Just one quick question. Would you be willing to board our pony here?"

Conscious of Logan's stare, Hope didn't meet Micah's eyes. "Of course, but why?"

"Chloe wants to drive the pony cart."

"Yes, she told me that." Micah's surprised look made Hope feel guilty. She should have mentioned it to him.

"I told her no, but I'm pretty sure that won't stop her."

Hope smiled. "Knowing Chloe, you're probably right. Logan might know someone with a horse trailer who could pick up the pony."

Micah shot a wary glance in Logan's direction. "I don't know if—"

Hope didn't wait for him to finish. She hurried to Logan and asked, then beckoned Micah over to make the arrangements.

"My brother has a trailer," Logan admitted grudgingly.

Micah looked as if he wanted to refuse, so Hope took over. "Could he get the pony tonight or early tomorrow morning?"

Blowing out a martyred sigh, Logan pulled out his cell and called. "What time tomorrow?"

Hope nudged Micah, who seemed reluctant to answer.

Micah responded, "The harness shop opens at nine, so I leave for work at eight thirty. Any time before that's fine. And I'll gladly pay for his time and gas."

Trying to smooth over the awkwardness after Logan hung up the phone, Hope turned to him. "Why don't you have your brother come here in the morning, and *Daed* can ride with him to show him the way?"

That would give her father something to do. He really missed Chloe and Jabin, and he'd been moping around ever since the twins started school.

Micah turned to leave. "I need to pick up Chloe and Jabin right now, but thanks for arranging everything." Micah's impartial glance from her to Logan cut her deeply. Not even a brief smile. Not that she'd been expecting him to show her any special attention. But she couldn't help wishing.

At least she'd see him tomorrow. She followed the buggy's slow progress down the driveway. Maybe having the pony here meant he'd stop by more often.

"How often does he visit when I'm not around?" Logan's annoyed tone grated on her.

Not often enough. "I don't think that's your business." She kept her response tart to prevent any more questions.

"I'm warning you . . ."

Hope spun and faced him. "My life and friendships have nothing to do with the business."

"That's not true. We've already talked about that."

Hope fixed him with a calm and steady stare until he stalked off.

Micah had washed the last breakfast bowl and handed it to Chloe to dry when a loud engine growled in the driveway.

Chloe nearly dropped the dish, and Micah grabbed for it. "Finish drying so Jabin can put it away."

"What is that?" Jabin backed up and covered his ears as the trailer rattled to a stop near the back door.

"Don't worry. It's only a horse trailer." Micah set a hand on Jabin's shoulder.

Without being asked, Chloe did Jabin's job of putting the bowl in the cupboard. Micah sent her a thank-you smile. The truck engine died, and Micah took the twins' hands to keep them close when they went outside.

A man who looked like Logan jumped from the truck cab. Micah forced a friendly smile. He shouldn't judge anyone before getting to know them. The passenger door creaked open, and Isaac emerged.

Chloe screamed a welcome and raced toward him.

Isaac held up a hand. "Don't knock me over," he said, but he accompanied his warning with a smile. He eased himself to the ground and held open his arms for a hug. "I miss your long visits. I wish you'd come and spend more time."

"We want to." Chloe flung her arms around his neck. "Don't we, Jabin?"

Jabin approached slowly, a ghost of a smile on his lips. To Micah's surprise, he nodded and stepped into Isaac's hug. Chloe threw one arm around her brother and pulled him close.

"Did you come to play with us?" Chloe asked Isaac.

He shook his head. "We're here to pick up your pony and take it to our farm."

Chloe whipped her head around to glare at Micah.

Before she could say anything, Isaac groaned and stretched. "Can you help me stand, Chloe?"

With a sideways glance, Micah sent a silent thank-you to Isaac for defusing the situation. Isaac nodded and then struggled to his feet despite Chloe's enthusiastic tugging, which seemed more likely to yank him off balance.

"*Danke.*" Isaac patted her on the head. After he helped

Logan's brother load the pony, he headed over to Micah. "Hope said you had to work today. Could I take Chloe and Jabin back to the house with me? I really enjoy their company."

Micah hesitated. "I planned to take them to work with me."

"Please?" Chloe begged.

Although Jabin remained silent, his eyes pleaded with Micah to let them go. Even Isaac waited for his answer with an imploring expression. How could Micah say no, especially if it meant he'd get to see Hope later?

At his nod, Chloe grabbed Jabin's hand and scrambled into the truck, then reached down a hand to help Isaac, who beamed at her. After they took off, Micah headed off to work, humming a hymn.

When he strode into the shop, Eli glanced up. "You're cheerful." Then his face fell. "Are you going to Sus—I mean Sylvia's—for lunch today?"

Micah shook his head. If he had been, he wouldn't be this joyful. "No, I just solved a problem this morning." Having the pony moved to Hope's meant Chloe would be safe, but his happiness stemmed from more than problem-solving.

Eli's features relaxed into a smile. His interest in Susie was apparent and might be the perfect solution for a different problem.

"Listen, if Susie does stop by, maybe you could take my place."

"You don't mind?" Eli searched Micah's face.

"Not at all." Micah had no desire to court Susie. None at all.

Once Micah reassured Eli of that, humming and whistling filled the workroom until noontime. Both of them spent the rest of the morning with songs in their hearts and on their lips.

Micah slipped out a little early to avoid running into Sylvia, and Eli gave him a grateful smile as he finished closing out the register. He appeared as eager to take Micah's place as Micah was to give it up. Only one person interested him, and he was heading to see her now. Only she had no interest in him. Or anyone.

Hope greeted the twins when they arrived with *Daed* and turned the pony into the pasture. "Would you like to feed him some carrots?"

At Chloe's enthusiastic "yes," her father went into the house and returned with two carrots.

"Stay on this side of the fence," Hope warned.

She and Logan had one student after another lined up, so she wouldn't be able to keep an eye on the twins. "You'll watch them?" she asked *Daed*.

"Of course. I invited them as company." He laid a hand on Jabin's shoulder. "Do you two want to come inside and play a board game?"

The pony had already nibbled Jabin's carrot, so he turned willingly, but Chloe was still holding out her carrot.

"I want to stay with Chips for a while." Chloe waved her carrot, and the pony trotted toward her. "He might be scared in a new place."

A car pulled into the driveway, and Hope went to greet her student. Logan waited for them near the barn. In Hope's last glimpse of Chloe before they ushered Graham inside, the little girl had her hand through the split-rail fence. Although Hope couldn't hear what Chloe was saying, she was talking earnestly to the pony.

Hope smiled at the picture of the two of them together.

It must be hard for Chloe to be separated from her beloved pony. If it had been a student out here, Hope would have been obligated to stay and keep her company. But Chloe was here as a friend, and Amish parents didn't coddle their children. Logan might feel differently, but he'd already walked into the barn with Graham.

During their third lesson of the morning, a strange banging and clanking came from the closed-off end of the barn where they kept their buggy and farm wagon. Did *Daed* plan to take the twins somewhere? But when he didn't come inside for Biscuit, she decided he'd changed his mind.

As she and Logan finished the lesson and were walking Priscilla and her younger brother Asher out to their buggy, Micah drove in. Beside Hope, Logan stiffened. He still spoke kindly to Asher, but he kept an eye on Micah's approach.

As he pulled to the end of the driveway, Micah screamed, "*Chloe!*" He jerked his horse to a stop and slammed on the buggy brake. Without even stopping to tie up Daffy, he dashed toward the pasture fence.

Chloe, a gleeful expression on her face, was driving a pony cart around the track. Ignoring his shouts, she urged the pony into a gallop.

Behind him the back door of the house slammed. "*Nooo!*" Isaac shouted as he scuttled toward the fence. "Chloe, that harness isn't—"

Snap! The harness let loose on one side. The flapping leather spooked Chips. She bucked and bolted.

Micah froze. His childhood nightmare unspooled before his eyes. Only this time it was happening to Chloe.

With a loud screech, Chloe dropped the reins and gripped

the metal rail of the pony cart. Eyes wide and panicked, she hung on as the cart tipped onto one wheel. Then it rocked back down.

Logan and Hope raced from the barn, followed by a woman and a young boy. They'd never make it in time.

Only Micah was near enough to help.

Save Chloe! Save Chloe! That thought drowned out his terror.

The pony tore around the circular enclosure. As Chips made the turn and headed toward him, Micah hoisted himself up onto the split rails and vaulted the fence. *Please, Lord, keep Chloe safe.*

He'd have only one chance to grab the flying reins.

Hooves thundered toward him. The pounding crescendoed like his heartbeat. Sickness enveloped him. He couldn't breathe. He couldn't swallow. He couldn't do this.

Stay back! Jump out of the way! Save yourself! His brain warred with his heart. *Save Chloe!* He couldn't let anything happen to her.

God, please help me.

"Grab Chloe," a man's voice yelled close to his ear. Logan dropped to the ground beside Micah. "I'll get the pony."

A whoosh of air rushed past Micah, pinning him to the fence as Chips passed. He had only a split second. The thud of hooves paralyzed him. The reins whipped wildly through the air. Instinctively, he ducked to avoid getting smacked in the face.

And almost missed Chloe.

"Micccahh!" she screamed as she went past.

He dove for her.

She tightened her grasp on the metal sidebar as the cart tipped. "I'm falling," she shrieked.

He wrapped his arms around her and yanked. "Let go," he ordered as Chips dragged the two of them along.

Chloe released the bar, and her weight catapulted him backward. He slammed to the ground and lay stunned.

Chloe landed on top of him, so he cushioned her fall. Micah ached all over from the impact. Even his teeth hurt from the jarring. But Chloe was safe.

Thank you, God! Thank you, thank you, thank you.

Gingerly, he sat up, hugging her close. She clawed at him, digging the fingernails of one hand into his skin and clonking him with her cast. She'd buried her face against his shoulder. Her chest rose and fell as she gasped for air. Too winded to speak, Micah patted her back.

Logan still hadn't caught the pony. The cart had over-turned, slowing Chips a little. Logan positioned himself near the fence and waited until the pony rounded the track again. This time Logan caught the reins and lifted up. Micah had been taught to do that for runaway horses, but he doubted he'd have remembered. He was grateful that Logan had the presence of mind to execute the right moves.

Finally, Chips stood shuddering, covered in sweat, his flanks heaving.

"Easy, boy." Talking soothingly to the pony, Logan undid the harness. "You're all right," he repeated over and over.

The words washed over Micah like a litany. He stood, with Chloe still clinging to him. Hope rushed through the gate and wrapped her arms around both of them. The comfort of her embrace and her "Thank God, you're safe" should have calmed his hammering heart. Instead, his pulse jumped into an unsteady rhythm.

She stared up at him with admiration shining in her eyes. "I can't believe you went in there with a runaway pony. That was so brave."

Though he swelled with pride at her compliment, Micah tried to dismiss it. "So did Logan." He flicked his chin toward the track, where Logan was walking the pony to cool it down.

"But Logan has no fear of horses. You do, but you didn't let it stop you. You saved Chloe."

"Is she all right?" Isaac's voice, tight with terror, penetrated the fog surrounding Micah.

Her face scarlet, Hope stepped back at her *Daed*'s approach and let her hands fall to her sides. Micah missed her warmth and closeness. Chloe still clung to him with her uninjured arm and kept her face hidden. Her breathing remained swift and uneven, much like Micah's heartbeat.

"I'm so sorry." Isaac set a hand on Chloe's head and blubbered. "If she's hurt, I'll never forgive myself."

Chloe lifted her head and met his eyes. "I'm all right," she wheezed out and wriggled away from Micah. He set her gently on the ground.

"This is my fault. All my fault." Isaac wrung his hands.

Chloe rushed over and flung her arms around his legs. "No, it isn't." She hung her head. "I sneaked out when you went upstairs to get something."

"I thought you had a lesson or went out to help Hope. I should have kept a better eye on you."

"It's over now," Micah said, "and everything's fine." Except maybe for his heart.

Chapter Twenty-Six

Hope's cheeks still burned from being so forward with Micah. She'd been so glad he and Chloe hadn't been hurt, she'd gotten carried away in her relief. And she'd made a fool of herself in front of everyone—*Daed*, Priscilla, and most of all Logan. Now he'd never believe her denials.

Logan led the pony past them without meeting her eyes. "I'll rub him down."

"Thanks." Hope wanted to assure him that her hug had only been for Chloe, but she couldn't lie. And she couldn't explain in front of everyone.

As he passed Priscilla, Logan said, "I'm sorry about this." He squatted in front of Asher. "Maybe we can reschedule your lesson."

"I'll check with Hope." Priscilla thanked him and strode over to Hope. "I didn't want to interrupt your conversation, but I'll take Asher and go now."

"He hasn't had his lesson." Hope owed her best friend an apology. Of all the people who deserved a lesson, Priscilla should be first on the list. Without her, Hope wouldn't have this business.

Asher stood beside his older sister, flicking the brim of his hat.

Priscilla leaned closer to Hope and whispered, "Asher

does that when he's upset, so we'd better leave." Then she took Asher's other hand and led him to their buggy.

Hope wished she could ask Priscilla to stay, but she and Logan had another student arriving soon. "I'll talk to you tomorrow at church," Hope called after her, and Priscilla waved her acknowledgment.

After Logan disappeared into the barn and Priscilla's buggy rolled down the driveway, *Daed* clenched his hands together. "Chloe's accident was my fault." He stared at the ground. "I was supposed to ask Micah to fix that harness."

The harness. Hope had almost forgotten about her request.

"Then it's my fault," Micah said. "You told me you needed a harness fixed. I should have asked which one and taken it to my shop."

"No, that wasn't your responsibility." Hope hastened to reassure him. He deserved no blame.

But where had Chloe found the harness? If it had been with the rest of the tack, she and Logan would have seen Chloe dragging it out of the barn.

Hope turned to *Daed*, who squirmed.

"I'm sorry, Hope." He lowered his head and mumbled, "When I said I'd get the harness for Micah, I, umm, did something else."

Something like steal from the cashbox. "But the harness was gone from the tack room."

"I didn't want you to know I lied about why I went out to the barn, so I leaned the harness on the other side of the old shed." He pointed to a ramshackle shed on the far side of the backyard.

How had Chloe found the harness? Hope squeezed her eyes shut as *Daed* continued his confession.

"I was going to give it to Micah that day, but once you found out about—"

Hope's eyes flew open. Was *Daed* blaming her?

He held up a hand. "That was no excuse for forgetting to give it to Micah. Like I said, this is all my fault."

A heaviness weighed down Hope's spirits. Not only had *Daed*'s gambling cost them money, it had almost injured a small girl. A small girl she cared about. A small girl she wanted to protect. A small girl who'd just lost her parents.

Rather than lash out at *Daed*, Hope prayed for patience and control. "When the harness was gone from the tack room, I assumed Micah had it." She could barely get out the words.

Daed looked from one to the other. "I'm so sorry." Then he met Hope's gaze again. "For everything." Tears formed in *Daed*'s eyes. This time he seemed genuinely remorseful. Maybe realizing he'd almost hurt Chloe had made an impression.

Micah stared at the two of them, confusion written on his face. Hope lowered her lashes. She couldn't look him in the eye. How could she explain about *Daed*'s gambling? Or her reasons for hiding their family's shameful secret? Maybe concealing it all these years had been a mistake. But she hadn't realized anyone might get hurt.

Daed looked Micah in the eye. "I'm to blame for putting Chloe in danger. Will you forgive me?"

"Of course." Micah squeezed Chloe's shoulder. "She's fine, and it's all over, except . . ." He glanced down at Chloe.

She hung her head and scuffed one foot in the dirt. "I'm sorry."

"I think we all learned an important lesson today," Hope said.

Chloe brightened. "I did. I learned God answers prayers." She looked up at them, her eyes shining. "I prayed and prayed out there that God would help me. And He did."

Hope smiled down at her. "I'm so glad, Chloe." Then she met Micah's joy-filled eyes and couldn't look away.

Micah rejoiced that Chloe had been willing to pray. He hoped it would be a big step on her way back to believing in God.

Hope's enthusiastic response had touched him, and the mesmerizing blue of her eyes drew him in. Micah was lost, drowning in their depths.

If Logan hadn't arrived to break the spell, Micah had no idea how long he and Hope would have locked eyes.

"So what happened?" Logan demanded. "The leather on that harness was so badly worn, it snapped under pressure."

"I'm sorry," *Daed* said. "I wish I'd given it to Micah instead of . . ."

Micah couldn't let Isaac take all the blame. "Hope mentioned it to me, and I should have asked about it."

Logan's stare skimmed from *Daed* to Micah, and he crossed his arms. "Is everyone trying to sabotage this business?"

Hope jumped in. "No one is sabotaging anything."

She surprised and impressed Micah with her willingness to correct Logan. Had she been standing up to him that day in the office too? How often did he confront her? Micah longed to protect her.

To his surprise, Logan appeared contrite. He mumbled something that might have even been "Sorry." Then he said, "We need to check all the equipment immediately. We can't chance having another accident."

Micah stepped forward. "I can do that. I'll make any needed repairs."

Logan looked at him askance, and once again Hope

hurried to Micah's defense. "Micah owns Miller's Harness Shop in town."

"Really?" Logan seemed skeptical. "That's where I go for all my repairs and new purchases. Very reliable and top-quality products. How come I've never seen you there?"

"I just moved here from New York to take over my brother's—"

Logan cut him off. "I'm sorry, man. I should have made the connection." A slight flush slid across Logan's high cheekbones. "I—we appreciate you looking at the tack."

"No problem."

"By the way," Logan continued, "you did an awesome job out there earlier."

"Thanks, so did you." If Logan hadn't come along when he did, Micah might have dragged on the pony's reins and maybe ended up tipping Chloe out of the cart. She could have been badly hurt.

"It's my job." Logan brushed off the praise. "Speaking of jobs, we have a student coming in"—he glanced at his watch—"about five minutes."

"Looks like she's already here." Hope nodded toward the driveway, where a car had just turned in.

"I'll let you get back to work," Micah said. "Chloe, let's go. Where's Jabin?"

At his question, Hope pointed to the porch, where Jabin stood with his hands clenched together and his eyes squinched.

She beckoned to him. "Are you all right?" she asked as soon as she was near.

"Chloe made me scared," he admitted.

Micah put an arm around his nephew's shoulder. "She frightened all of us."

"I'm sorry," Chloe said. "I just wanted to have fun."

"I thought you were going to die." Jabin pressed a knuckle against his lips and looked ready to cry. "And Micah too. Then I'd be all alone."

"I didn't mean to scare you." Chloe went over and took her brother's hand.

Micah knelt and embraced them both. "I'm so grateful to God to have both of you." When he glanced up and met Hope's teary eyes, he wished his hug could include one more.

Hope's heart overflowed with longing as Micah cuddled the twins. If only she had the right to join them. Warmth flooded her as she pictured the earlier scene when she'd rushed over and—

"Are you ready for our student?" Logan's sharp question interrupted her musing.

She pulled her attention from Micah and placed it on Maritza, who was trailing behind her father. And she did her best to keep it there as they taught Maritza and, later, explained their planned program to her father.

Usually, Hope loved this work, but today, she couldn't wait for their one o'clock meal break. The morning's scare with Chloe had drained all her energy, and her memory of hugging Micah brought both exhilaration and chagrin.

"You're thinking about him again, aren't you?" Logan asked as they waved goodbye to Maritza's disappearing car.

Hope didn't answer. She'd rather not get into another disagreement with Logan.

"He's an OK guy," Logan admitted. "He jumped right in and rescued Chloe. That took a lot of guts."

"Especially with his fear of horses."

Logan's brows rose. "You've mentioned that before. He didn't appear frightened. He dove right in there."

"Probably because he put Chloe's safety above his terror."

"Touché."

"Huh?" Hope stared at him, unsure what he meant.

"I know you didn't intend it as a criticism of me, but your jab hit its mark."

Hope frowned as she went back over her words, trying to figure out how she'd hurt Logan. "All I said was, Micah overcame his fears."

"By thinking about someone else's welfare." Logan rubbed his forehead. "As I'm sure you've noticed, most of my decisions are for my own benefit."

"I didn't mean that. Besides, you didn't hesitate to help," Hope pointed out.

"I suppose not, but that's not what I'm talking about." He turned his back to her and strode to the window. His words, when they came, were tight and strained. "When I saw you in that tight little group, hugging the two of them, I realized I'd never be a part of what you have. I don't share your lifestyle or your faith."

"The Amish aren't the only ones with a strong faith in God. Many *Englischers* believe in Him too."

Logan waved a hand in the air. "That wasn't my point. I'll think about all that God stuff later."

"You never know when it might be too late. Look at Jabin and Chloe's parents. They never expected to—"

"I know." Logan's harsh tone silenced her. "I meant I'd think about God and faith later today. Right now, I want to finish what I started to say, not get sidetracked."

Hope longed to say talking about God was never a detour. God was the main focus of everything, but she stayed quiet and waited for Logan's explanation. And prayed God would touch his heart.

"When I saw that group hug, I was on the outside looking in, wishing I were a part of it, yet knowing I never would be."

"I'm sorry you felt excluded."

"Hope . . ." Logan's warning held a note of impatience.

She started to apologize but pressed a hand over her mouth before a "sorry" could escape.

"Seeing the three of you together made me realize how good you are for one another. And Micah's right for you in many ways that I'd never be."

Too bad Micah didn't see that. Or did he? Today, when they'd looked into each other's eyes, she'd wondered.

"It's obvious he cares about you. And that you return those feelings."

Hope bit back a gasp. If Logan had recognized that, what had Micah seen? She was grateful Logan had his back to her so he couldn't read her reaction.

"As much as I wish things could be different, I won't block your happiness."

She'd been right about Logan's jealousy, but he hadn't been standing in the way of anything. As much as she wished it could be different, she and Micah had no relationship.

Micah waited until Hope and Logan took the little girl and her father back to a stall before heading for the tack room. Isaac had offered to watch the twins while Micah checked the equipment.

"I'll be a good girl," Chloe promised, "and listen to Isaac."

"*Danke* for trusting me," Isaac said when Micah gave

his permission. "I know I don't deserve it. Not after what I've done."

"We've all forgiven you. Now you need to forgive yourself."

Isaac's eyes grew moist. "You have no idea what I've done."

"Whatever it is," Micah said, "you can confess it to God and ask for His forgiveness." It seemed odd to be counseling an elder, but Isaac seemed to need to hear that truth. No doubt he already knew to extend forgiveness to others. It wasn't Micah's place to lecture Hope's *daed*.

But it reminded Micah he also needed to forgive. He'd been carrying a grudge against Logan because he spent so much time with Hope. Micah needed to let that go. Besides, Hope wouldn't get into a relationship with an *Englischer*. She'd made it clear she had no interest in marriage.

But unless he'd misinterpreted it, the look in her eyes today had told him differently.

As Micah walked quietly into the barn, Hope's gentle encouragement floated to him. "Here, Maritza, you can do it."

He resisted the urge to move farther up the aisle to peek into the stall where she was working. Instead, he examined every buckle and buckle tongue, every breeching and breast collar strap, every terret. He studied the stitching, examined the leather to be sure it wasn't dry or oily, checked for thin or weak metal. Most of Hope's tack was in good repair, but he did find a few things that could be replaced, just to be on the safe side.

All the while, he enjoyed Hope's musical voice instructing Maritza. He could have done the work much faster, but he was reluctant to leave. He excused his delay by telling himself he had to get Hope's permission to make the repairs. He supposed he could ask Isaac. Although her father never seemed to participate in the lessons, he probably handled the financial affairs.

As Micah headed out of the barn, one of the horses whinnied and stamped in her stall right near him. He edged against the opposite wall, and his old dread came back to haunt him, but Micah focused on the morning's rescue. If he could save Chloe, he could handle these fears. With God's help, of course.

Chapter Twenty-Seven

When Micah went to collect the twins, he found them in the kitchen with Isaac, making sandwiches.

"You'll all stay for dinner, won't you?" Isaac asked. "After all, Chloe and Jabin have been doing most of the work."

Micah couldn't refuse the invitation. Besides, he'd been trying to stall long enough to see Hope. Now he'd get to eat with her. "Can I do anything to help?"

Isaac shook his head. "We have everything almost ready. Why don't you wash up and have a seat?"

After doing what Isaac suggested, Micah sat at the kitchen table while Chloe slathered mayonnaise and mustard on homemade bread, Jabin layered on ham and cheese, and Isaac supervised.

Now might be a good time to ask Isaac about the tack. "I found several items that could use some reinforcement. Did you want me to take them to the shop? I can give you an estimate first."

"You'll have to ask Hope. It's her business."

"Oh, I thought maybe you helped out with the finances."

Isaac's face paled, and the knife he'd been holding clattered to the counter.

Micah hopped up from the table. Had he cut himself? "Are you all right?"

"F–fine," Isaac assured him, but he appeared far from fine. After a few seconds, he regained his composure and picked up the knife. "Hope's been in charge of the finances and the horse business since she turned eighteen."

Eighteen? That was rather odd. Fathers normally handled the money for their daughters.

Isaac must have read the question in Micah's eyes, because he said, "I, um, well, I wasn't very trustworthy with money." He looked as if he planned to say more, but the back door creaked open.

Hope entered but stopped in the doorway. "Micah? I wasn't expecting you to still be here."

She didn't want them here? So much for waiting for her to finish the lesson. "I only came inside to get Chloe and Jabin. We'll be leaving."

"No, no." Hope hadn't meant that the way it sounded. "You're welcome to stay."

"That's good, because I invited them to eat with us." *Daed*'s voice wavered.

Had something happened to upset her father? Maybe the incident with Chloe had shaken up *Daed* more than he'd admit.

And since when did he make a meal? Was it his way of apologizing for the accident?

Micah shifted and glanced toward the door, as if unsure whether to go or stay. "I did tell your *daed* I found a few things that should be reinforced or repaired. Nothing dangerous. Not like—"

He glanced at Chloe, who was carrying the serving plate of sandwiches to the table.

Hope's chest clenched. Although *Daed*'s gambling and forgetfulness were partly to blame for that accident, she bore some responsibility too. She should have followed up to be sure Micah had gotten the harness.

"Anyway," Micah continued, his attention still on Chloe, "I asked your *daed* about the repairs, and he said you're in charge of those decisions." He looked up at her as if for confirmation.

"*Jah*, that's true." Hope couldn't answer the other question in his eyes, not without sharing *Daed*'s secret. And she would never betray her father.

She did need to take care of the tack, though. "If everyone doesn't mind waiting a short while to eat, maybe Micah and I could go out to the barn, and he can show me what needs to be fixed."

Chloe's lips set into a mutinous line, and she appeared ready to protest.

But when *Daed* muttered, "Of course. We don't want anyone getting hurt," her irritated expression cleared, and she nodded.

Micah headed for the door. "None of these things are urgent, but they could be problems later."

Walking to the barn with Micah proved to be torture. He stayed so close, their hands brushed several times.

Hope could have—should have—put some distance between them, but she liked the tingling thrill that ran through her whenever they accidentally touched. She imagined him clasping her hand in his large, warm one, and she could barely breathe.

What would he do if she reached for his hand? He hadn't pulled away when she'd hugged him. But they'd both been so overcome with emotion, it had seemed natural. Maybe he'd been too stunned to rebuff her.

She shook her head and pushed away her fantasies. If

she were free to date, Micah would be her first choice, but she needed to keep her mind on the business, especially with *Daed*'s recent—

"Hope?" Micah called her name twice. "Is something wrong?"

"What?"

He opened the door to the tack room. "You were frowning, so I thought maybe . . ." He faced her. "Look, if money's a problem, I can do the repairs, and you can pay me later, whenever you can afford it."

Money? Money was a problem, but not in the way he meant. And right now, an even larger problem was that she'd been going all gooey inside, while he'd been thinking businesslike thoughts.

Hope forced herself to concentrate on the tack. "Why don't you show me what repairs we should take care of? And don't worry about the bill. I have enough to pay for whatever needs to be done."

"If you're sure?"

"It'll be fine." At least she hoped it would. With *Daed*, she never knew.

Micah studied Hope. Something was bothering her, but she'd been adamant it wasn't finances. Had he upset her by walking so near?

Though he'd warned himself to move away, he hadn't been able to resist the temptation. And each time his hand grazed Hope's, he fought the urge to entwine his fingers with hers.

She'd taken his hand several times in the past, and the memory of her gentle touch set his blood racing. His body still held the imprint of her hug this morning. But each time, she'd only meant to comfort. If she had any idea of what her kindness had stirred in him, would she keep her distance?

Yet her eyes told a different story. Or had he only imagined what he'd dreamed of seeing? Right here, right now, the softness of her gaze invited him to . . .

To what?

Micah cleared his throat and broke the spell. His voice husky, he said, "This, um, buckle tongue—"

He lost his train of thought as she leaned nearer, and her shoulder rubbed his biceps. If she tilted her head the slightest bit, her *kapp* would graze his chin. He resisted the urge to tip his head in her direction, but his mind conjured up fantasies of touching his lips to the glossy brown hair peeking out from the front of her prayer covering.

"Micah?" Hope looked up, and he changed his mind. He'd much rather press his lips to hers.

He shook himself. He'd been doing leatherwork for more than a decade, but the names of every part or piece had fled. He struggled to untangle his tongue and his thoughts.

Hope said his name again softly, each syllable an invitation. Although his conscience warned him not to, Micah leaned over and kissed her lightly on the forehead. Then he stepped back. "I'm sorry. I shouldn't have done that."

She lowered her head so he couldn't see her eyes and whispered, "I didn't mind."

Had he heard her correctly?

Micah reached out and, with a tender finger, tilted up her chin so he could read the truth in her eyes. The tenderness, the longing, the joy shining in them reflected his own desire.

"But you said—I'm sorry, I didn't mean to eavesdrop—but you told Logan you had no intention of marrying."

Her eyes grew troubled. Then they filled with tears.

She jerked herself out of his arms and fled from the barn. Over her shoulder, she called, "Take whatever tack needs repairs and I'll pay whatever it costs."

Micah stood there, stunned. What had he said or done to cause that reaction? Had it been Logan's name?

Shoulders slumped, he loaded what he could into the buggy. He'd send Eli by with the farm wagon to pick up the broken harness.

Before he finished, Chloe burst out of the door with a paper plate wrapped in foil, and his spirits plunged. Could she have made it any clearer? She didn't even want him to come into the house to eat.

He swallowed the lump blocking his throat. "Did you two eat?"

When she nodded, he said, "Be sure to thank Isaac and"—he tried to manage a neutral tone, but his voice came out raspy—"Hope. Also, please tell Jabin we're leaving."

"But I want to play a board game with Isaac. I didn't get to . . ."

Her protest died off at Micah's stern frown. Evidently remembering why she'd missed playing the game, she snapped her mouth shut and ran back to the house.

Micah had made a terrible mistake today, and he couldn't get out of here fast enough.

Hope dragged through the rest of the day. Around the students, she concentrated on their needs and managed to remain cheerful. But as soon as they left, she plunged into gloom. She worried she'd hurt Micah by her rejection.

She prayed he didn't think she'd run because she didn't care for him. Or because he'd kissed her.

Hope brushed her fingers over the spot where his lips had landed with such a gentle touch, like a butterfly alighting.

"Are you ready for Lucas?" Logan's barbed question sliced her romantic fantasies to shreds.

"Of course," she answered. Right now, though, she could barely remember Lucas, let alone the lesson they'd planned for him.

When their day ended, she fixed *Daed* his supper but only picked at the tiny amount she put on her plate. As was their custom, she ate what she took, despite every bite tasting like gritty, uncooked cornmeal. Then, pleading exhaustion, she rushed upstairs to bed as soon as she'd finished the dishes.

Daed trudged up after her, and on the landing, he stopped her. "I'm so sorry. Will you forgive me, *dochder*?"

Hope had no idea whether he was apologizing for Chloe's accident or so much more. Her rote "*Jah*, I forgive you" did little to ease his guilt-ridden expression. But tonight, Hope ached too much inside to dig further.

"Let's pray about it," she suggested. Her prayers would be pleas for forgiveness. She needed to release her anger and resentment. And to let go of bitterness.

From time to time as she moved into her early twenties, *Daed* had dropped hints about her getting older and not having a husband. Over time, they'd both grown used to her being single, and *Daed* had stopped asking.

She'd been glad, because she couldn't explain he was the reason she'd discouraged any interest from men at church. That had never been a hardship. She'd never met anyone who made her heart sing. Until now.

And now *Daed* stood in the way of her happiness. But

she could never tell him. She could only pour out her sorrow to God and release her pain.

The next morning at church, as the married women greeted one another with a holy kiss, Hope blinked back tears. It reminded her of the kiss she'd almost shared with Micah. A kiss she'd longed for with all her heart. A kiss she'd never experience.

She closed her eyes and pressed her fingers to her forehead, still sensing the imprint of his lips. Why hadn't she let him kiss her first before she fled?

Priscilla drew Hope aside. "What's wrong?"

Hope drew in a shuddery breath. Then she glanced around at the chattering women. If she explained here, someone was sure to overhear, and before the service started, she'd be the subject of everyone's gossip.

Sensing her need for privacy, Priscilla took Hope's arm and steered her toward the stairs. "My cousin Hannah won't mind if we talk in her bedroom."

After they'd settled on Hannah's bed with its bright patchwork quilt, Priscilla put an arm around Hope's shoulders. "Tell me."

Hope spilled out all her interactions with Micah, except for the butterfly kiss skimming her forehead. That secret remained hidden in her heart. "I'm sure and certain he's interested in me." The kiss and the look in his eyes had been proof. "But I ran away."

"Why?" Priscilla's gentleness soothed Hope's aching heart.

Although she couldn't be honest with Micah, she could tell Priscilla the truth. "My *daed*."

Priscilla hugged her. "*Ach*, Hope, your *daed* has laid many burdens on you. But this should not be one of them."

"I can't tell Micah the truth. And I can't marry anyone. What if we married and *Daed* stole money from him?"

"Why not tell Micah? Let him decide." Priscilla grabbed both of Hope's hands and gave them a comforting squeeze. "Besides, how would he get money from your accounts? *Daed* said you opened new ones."

Hope bit her lip. Should she tell Priscilla that *Daed* had stolen the cash?

"What is it?" her friend demanded. "We tell each other all our secrets."

Bowing her head to hide her tear-filled eyes, Hope recounted *Daed*'s theft.

Priscilla sucked in a sharp breath. "*Ach*, Hope, I'm so sorry. You can change the dates for when you pay me back."

"*Neh*, I'll still repay you on time. But don't you see? I can't trust *Daed*. How can I risk the man I love getting hurt?"

"You love him?"

"I–I don't know. We're only getting to know each other."

But Hope's conscience gave a different answer.

She'd fallen for Micah in the hospital room when he laid his hand tenderly on Chloe's head. When he stayed awake all night to comfort the twins. When his face shadowed with stubble and his eyes darkened with grief, he smiled and thanked her profusely for the breakfast sandwich. When . . .

A better question would be: When hadn't she been attracted to him?

An even more important question would be: Did she love him?

She had only one answer to that.

Jah, with all her heart.

Chapter Twenty-Eight

Last Monday, Micah had rushed out the door to pick up the twins at school, so they'd be early for their lessons with Hope. Back then, the clock seemed to have molasses poured into its gears. Today, every time he checked, the hands raced around the clockface, and the hours zipped past.

Each tick of the clock resembled a death knell. *Bong, bong, bong*. Another hour closer to facing Hope. What would he say to her? How would she react?

They'd been too busy today for Eli to pick up Hope's harness, so Micah took the farm wagon to get Chloe and Jabin after school.

Their teacher beckoned him over. Not another problem with Chloe, he hoped.

But Mim beamed at him. "Last week I had to scold Chloe several times for refusing to pray. Today, she folded her hands and bowed her head voluntarily. Later, when we were on the playground, she told me about the runaway pony cart and how God answered her prayer."

"I'm glad," Micah said. He had noticed a change in Chloe's behavior over the weekend, but he needed to make sure she understood that believing in God wasn't dependent on Him answering prayers the way she wanted.

"Many people have been praying for her, for all three of you." Mim's eyes held sympathy. "I know it can't be easy, so if there's anything I can do to help, please ask."

Micah took an involuntary step back. Not another Susie situation. "*Danke*."

Mim continued, "We have many parents who can help watch the children, and I understand Sylvia has been organizing meals."

"*Jah*, she has." If "organizing" meant delivering every meal and dragging her daughter along. But Micah relaxed a bit once he realized Mim hadn't been volunteering to take on Susie's role. "And if I need help, I'll let you know."

Micah called to Chloe and Jabin. "Toss your scooters in the wagon. We need to hurry to get to your lessons on time."

"I'm so sorry," Mim said. "I didn't realize I was holding you up."

"It's no problem. We don't have far to go." They should still make it before three thirty, and he should thank Mim for delaying him. This way, the twins could go straight in for their lesson without leaving extra time for an awkward conversation.

When they pulled into the driveway, Hope and Logan were waiting outside the barn. As soon as Micah stopped the wagon, Chloe hopped out and dashed over. Evidently, her near accident hadn't scared her away from horses.

Micah finished tying up the horse, and Jabin stuck with him. Had Chloe's experience frightened him?

They arrived in time to hear Chloe announce that she would let Jabin have the first turn. Micah met Hope's eyes, and both of them raised their brows. Maybe he'd been wrong about her fear.

"Are you sure?" Hope asked.

"Very sure." Chloe hopped from one foot to the other. "I'll go visit Isaac."

"Wait a minute." Hope knelt in front of Chloe. "It can be scary when a horse or pony bolts, but it's important to get back on. Or, in this case, spend some time around horses."

Perhaps that had been Micah's mistake. He'd spent most of his life avoiding horses. A near impossibility for an Amish man. *Daed* had aided him in that, but maybe trying to protect him had been the wrong approach.

Hope had tried to get him used to seeing the children getting close to horses, but so far, he hadn't experienced it himself other than when he'd rescued Chloe. If things had been different between Hope and him, he might have asked her to try.

He tuned back into the conversation as Chloe declared, "I'm not afraid of horses."

Hope's dazzling smile charmed Micah as much as it did Chloe. "I didn't say you were. I only wondered why you wanted Jabin to go first."

Chloe glanced at the ground and circled one toe in the dirt. "When the pony started going fast, I got really afraid. I prayed and prayed."

"Praying is a good thing to do when you're in trouble. It's also good to pray at other times too."

"I know," Chloe said in a small voice. "But I promised God if He kept me from getting hurt, I'd try hard to be good." She met Hope's gaze and burst out, "But it's really, really hard."

Pinching her lips together but not quite hiding her smile, Hope enfolded Chloe in her arms. "I can imagine it would be."

As his niece clung to Hope, Micah's heart expanded in his chest so much that his ribs hurt. Chloe needed a mother figure like Hope in her life. Someone who understood her and steered her in the right direction.

Then it dawned on him. He'd only been thinking about dating Hope, not about the future. At least, not for her. Any woman he courted would need to take on two lively twins. Hope was wonderful with children, but that didn't mean she wanted an instant family. Maybe that was why her eyes seemed to indicate interest, but she fled anyway.

Logan shifted uncomfortably and tapped his finger on his watch face. "Three thirty. We should get started." His brisk command changed to a softer tone as he addressed Jabin. "I guess you're first, young man."

After Hope hugged her again and stood, Chloe sidled up next to Micah and slid her hand into his. She stared wistfully after her brother. "Have a good lesson, Jabin," she called before the barn door shut.

This new, improved version of Chloe might take some getting used to. As much as he liked the change, he wondered how long it would last.

Isaac came out on the porch, and Chloe rocketed toward him, almost throwing him off balance as she launched herself into his outstretched arms for a hug.

"You remind me of Hope when she was your age," he told her as Micah reached the porch.

"Really?" Micah asked. *Chloe and Hope? I don't see any similarities, but maybe that's why she understands Chloe so well.*

Isaac stared down at the porch. "Hope was lively and full of energy. Life—and the things I've done—have weighed her down. She had to take on a lot of responsibility."

"She still seems happy," Micah observed.

"Yes, she's made the best of things. And her strong faith in God helps too." Isaac set a hand on Chloe's head. "And one of my mistakes nearly killed this little one."

"Anyone could have forgotten to get a harness repaired, and it's not your fault Chloe sneaked out."

"You don't understand. That harness never should have been taken out of the barn. I hid it by the shed to cover up my wrongdoing."

Micah had overheard a cryptic conversation between Isaac and Hope after the accident, but it made no more sense now than it did then. What had Isaac done that was so bad?

"And I've hurt my own daughter. I don't want to do the same to Chloe."

What did he mean? Micah wanted to reach down and grab Chloe. Maybe he shouldn't have allowed the children to visit Isaac.

Isaac shook his head. "I've prayed about this and prayed about it."

Chloe piped up, "God answered my prayers."

"I wish He'd answer mine," Isaac muttered, but too low for Chloe to hear. Micah barely picked up the words.

"I promised Him I'd be good, and I have. All day Sunday and all day today."

Isaac smiled down at her. "I have too. I've actually been good for quite a few days in a row. You know, Chloe, that might be the best way to look at it. One day at a time." He gazed off into the distance, then back down at her. "Maybe you're God's answer to my prayers."

She stared up at him, her eyes shining. "I am?"

He nodded. "I think so. I'd been looking at how over-whelming it is, but all I need to do is think about all the days I haven't done wrong. It makes me feel stronger, a little more able to say no the next time."

Chloe smiled at him. "Can we play Uno?"

"Sure. Why don't you run in and set up the game? I want to say a few things to your *onkel*. Then I'll be right in."

When the screen door slammed behind her, Isaac turned to Micah. "I know you're probably wondering what I'm rambling on about." He pursed his lips for a few seconds. "I have a gambling problem. I stole money from my daughter."

Micah tried not to show his surprise. *Poor Hope*. "Does she know?"

Isaac nodded. "I took all the cash from her box her first week in business."

When Micah paid her, there'd been a thick stack of bills in there. "She had quite a bit of money."

"Several thousand dollars," Isaac admitted. "My friend Art told me about the horses. I always won. I'm a good judge of horseflesh. But he bet on something else and lost it all. Maybe if he hadn't gotten me into other things, I'd still be winning, and no one would know."

He sighed heavily. "That's not true. God knows. And I knew it was wrong, but I couldn't stop myself. I kept trying to win the money back but got deeper and deeper into debt."

"Are you coming, Isaac?" Chloe called.

"Shortly," he answered, then he returned to his story. "I would have kept spiraling even deeper, if it hadn't been for Hope. After she discovered my secret, I confessed to the church leaders, and they put her in charge of our finances."

Micah's eyes widened. When she was eighteen? That's what he'd said the other day.

"So, I'm a millstone around my daughter's neck. I worry she'll never marry because of me."

"I don't think—"

Isaac cut him off. "You're probably wondering why I'm telling you this."

Micah nodded.

"I was young once, and you've been looking at Hope the same way I looked at my Martha, God rest her soul."

Micah's face heated. Had it been that obvious? If so, maybe that was why Hope had run.

"I've also seen how my daughter stares at you when you're not looking. So, I thought you should know the truth. I hope it won't scare you off."

No, Isaac's story hadn't scared him off. Hope running from him had done that.

Hope and Logan encouraged Jabin to talk to Daisy as he groomed her. His strokes slow and methodical, he spoke in such a soft voice, they couldn't hear. Daisy tossed her head and nickered.

"You do understand," Jabin said loudly.

Hope, who stood on the far side of the horse, smiled at Logan, and he winked at her. Before, she would have worried he was flirting.

But after Saturday's conversation, they seemed to have come to an understanding. Logan may not like her interest in Micah, but he realized he had to adjust. She hadn't explained she could never have a relationship with Micah. She'd kept that to herself.

Jabin had finished currycombing Daisy's neck when he leaned his head against the horse and burst into tears. Hope wanted to take him into her arms and comfort him, but she stayed in position and prayed.

After his sobbing had turned into hiccupping gasps, Logan said gently, "Do you want to talk about it?"

At first, Jabin didn't respond. He swiped at his eyes with his fists and continued to gulp in air.

"Daisy will listen," Hope whispered.

Jabin lifted his head until he could look her directly in the eye. "Will you listen too?"

"Only if you want me to."

His voice quavered. "I do."

"Then I will. I promise."

Between sniffles, he currycombed the horse in short bursts and spoke in the same rhythm. "I thought Chloe was going to die. The pony cart got smashed like our buggy."

"You remember that?"

Jabin nodded. "*Mamm* screamed, and"—he ducked his head, and tears dripped down his nose—"*Daed* turned hard, but . . .

It went against protocol, and Logan would probably lecture her later, but Hope couldn't let Jabin cry alone. She lifted her chin. "I'm coming around to be with him."

Logan's eyes flashed a warning, but then he nodded. "He's more than a student to you, isn't he?" He looked from her to Jabin with compassion in his eyes.

"Yes, he is." When Hope reached Jabin's side, she knelt and wrapped her arms around him.

Once again, he wept. This time, on her shoulder as she held him close. Then, in broken sentences, he recounted everything he remembered. Sights, sounds, sensations. In a torrent of words, he poured out his confusion, his terror, his grief.

When he finished, he sagged against Hope, limp and spent. She cuddled him close, wishing she could ease his pain.

"I don't want anything to happen to you and Micah and Chloe and Isaac." He squeezed his eyes shut. "You're my family now."

Hope longed to agree. Instead, she squeezed him tighter.

Jabin put his lips beside her ear and whispered, "I love you."

"I love you too," she responded.

"If we're going to stay on schedule," Logan murmured, "we should get Chloe soon."

"Are you ready to go?" Hope asked Jabin. After he nodded, she stood and took his hand.

Before they left the stall, Jabin glanced over his shoulder at Daisy. "We lost Bella too."

"Bella?" Hope squeezed his hand.

"Our horse. She looked just like Daisy."

Ach, could she have made a worse choice for a therapy animal? "I'm so sorry, Jabin. I didn't know. We'll choose a different horse next time."

"*Neh*, I like Daisy. And when I asked her if she'd pretend to be Bella, she answered me and said yes."

Daisy had tossed her head and whinnied. Horses did have an uncanny ability to sense people's needs. Perhaps Daisy knew exactly what this little boy needed. It might also have been divine intervention. God had orchestrated the perfect circumstances for Jabin's healing.

When they reached the barn door, Hope faced Logan. "I'd like to take him in there alone and talk to Micah. I'm sure he won't mind if we start Chloe's lesson a little late."

"Fine," Logan agreed. Although his answer was short, it contained no criticism. "Hope," he said as she started to walk away, "what you did in there might be unconventional, but you have good instincts. And your gamble paid off."

Hope winced at the word "gamble." Had Logan used it intentionally?

"I'm sorry," he said. "I should have used a different expression. I only meant you made the right choice, given the situation."

As soon as Micah spotted Jabin's tearstained face, he leaped up from the couch. "Is everything all right?"

"The session went well. I think it helped." She needed

to explain to allay his concerns. And she wanted him to understand Jabin's fears.

"*Daed*, could you watch the twins a minute? I have something I wanted to discuss with Micah."

Her father's eyes lit up, and he looked from one to the other with a hint of a smile. *Sorry, Daed, but this talk isn't what you're supposing.* And it never would be.

Micah followed Hope through the kitchen. "You're sure Jabin's all right?" He kept his voice low so his nephew wouldn't hear.

"Positive, but I want you to know what happened in his session."

Behind them, Chloe offered to let her brother pick his favorite deck and start the card game. Micah raised his eyebrows. Two concessions on the same day? Chloe really was trying hard.

"*Danke*," Jabin said. "I want this deck. I'm putting down this card."

"Jabin," Chloe said with a touch of exasperation, "sometimes when I'm being nice, you can say, 'Chloe, you can go first.' You don't always have to take the first turn."

Hope covered her mouth, probably to hide her grin, and Micah bit back a snicker. They both waited until they got outside the door to give in to their laughter.

"You know, your *daed* told me you were a lot like Chloe when you were younger."

"He's probably right. Why was my *daed* talking about me?"

Micah preferred not to tell her. He changed the subject. "You said you wanted to tell me about Jabin."

Hands on her hips, Hope said, "You didn't answer my question."

"We can talk about that later." Much later. When he had enough courage to hear her honest answer.

"You're right. I don't want to cut into Chloe's time." Hope launched into a description of Jabin's session.

Micah's stomach churned as she explained that Chloe had passed out after the accident, but Jabin had been awake the whole time. He'd assumed both children wouldn't remember the trauma.

No wonder Jabin had gone silent and retreated into himself.

"I wish I'd known," Micah said. *Poor Jabin.* He squeezed his eyes shut. *All that pain.*

"Don't blame yourself." Hope's soft hands reached for both of his.

His eyes flew open to meet her compassion-filled ones.

No words could express the depths of his gratitude, but he had to at least try. "*Danke* for all your help. You've done so much for the three of us."

"I was happy to do it." When he squeezed her hands, her cheeks pinkened. She slipped her fingers from his and took a step back. "I'm sorry."

"Never be sorry about comforting someone." He wanted to reach for her hands again but resisted the urge. Here, in plain view of passersby and possibly Logan, wasn't the time or place.

Micah searched for signs that their closeness affected her as much as it did him, but with her eyes downcast, he couldn't tell. Isaac had piqued Micah's curiosity. Had Hope's father been right about his daughter's feelings? Micah longed to find out.

"Hope? I—"

Logan appeared from the barn. "Is Chloe coming?"

he called.

"I'll get her." Hope turned to Micah. "I'm afraid she'll have a short lesson, with Jabin getting extra time and me talking to you."

Micah stepped back so he could open the screen door for her. "I'm sorry I disrupted your schedule."

"You're never a disruption." Her teasing smile left him wondering.

Chapter Twenty-Nine

Had she made a mistake being so forward with Micah? She could never seem to get it right when she was with him.

Hope pushed aside her concerns to concentrate on Chloe.

"You said I should get back on a horse if I fall off." Chloe headed to the pony stall. "So I need to practice on a pony cart."

"Not today." Hope's nerves couldn't take that stress today after everything else that had happened. Besides, she had an excuse. "The cart hasn't been repaired yet."

Logan convinced Chloe to work with Molly, and once she started grooming, Chloe talked nonstop to the horse. She told Molly about her fear in the out-of-control cart and her desperate prayers.

Hope's eyes filled with tears as Chloe described Micah's rescue. Her own heart had stutter-stopped when Micah dove for that pony cart. He could have been badly hurt, but he hadn't hesitated. Not even his dread of horses had held him back.

And he hadn't even tried to break his own fall. He'd clung to Chloe and cushioned her descent with his body. Luckily, he hadn't broken anything. He'd winced and limped afterward but never complained about any injuries.

A real-life hero.

"Hope?" Logan waved to get her attention. "We're supposed to be concentrating on Chloe, not daydreaming."

Heat crept up Hope's neck and onto her cheeks. From Logan's furrowed brow, he must suspect exactly where her thoughts had wandered.

Shutting the door on her longings, Hope stayed present with Chloe, but as she left the barn afterward, all her desires came flooding back. Before she met Micah, she needed to get these feelings under control.

"I'll see you after dinner—or should I say 'supper'?" Logan said as he got into his car.

"You don't need to come back. I forgot to tell you, our seven o'clock lesson canceled. Roger is sick."

Logan frowned at the nearby wagon, where *Daed* and Micah were loading the broken harness. Jabin tried to help lift it but only seemed to be getting in the way, while Chloe danced nearby.

"I'll see you tomorrow afternoon, then," he said before driving off.

She waved a brief goodbye and started toward the wagon, but someone pounded hard at the front door.

"I'll get it," Hope called.

Whoever it was hadn't driven into the driveway. It had to be one of their neighbors from the other side. They must have made their way across the fields.

With the way they were banging, it had to be an emergency. Hope raced through the back door and into the living room to yank open the front door.

A man stood on the porch, a beefy fist ready to batter the door again.

"Art?" Hope stared at him in shock.

He looked equally as disturbed to encounter her. "I, um, wanted to speak to your *daed*."

"I don't think . . ." They'd all been through enough

trauma and tragedy the past few days. The last thing *Daed* needed was to talk to his gambling partner.

"It's not what you think." Art glanced around, as if expecting someone to pounce on him.

Were creditors chasing him? That might explain his frantic pounding on the front door.

"Could I come in?" He checked over his shoulder again.

Reluctantly, Hope opened the door wider and stepped aside so he could enter. He yanked the door from her grasp and slammed it shut behind him.

"What's the matter?"

"Nothing to worry about." Art turned to her with a charming smile. "I have something to tell your *daed*."

"He's busy outside helping someone." At least she hoped he still was.

"But–but—"

"I'd be happy to give my father a message."

"It's not exactly a message." Art reached in his pocket and pulled out a huge stack of thousand-dollar bills. "I, um, lied to him about not winning." A flush splashed across Art's cheeks, and he thrust the money into her hands.

"I can't take this." Hope tried to give it back, but Art stuffed his hands into his pockets.

"Part of it is yours."

"Mine?" What was he talking about?

"Your dad told me he'd taken the money from your cashbox, so I guess the win's actually yours."

He was returning the missing money? *Hallelujah!* But she wanted nothing to do with the rest of the winnings.

She thumbed through the stack and found several smaller bills at the bottom.

As she counted out the exact amount taken from the cashbox, *Daed* called through the screen door, "Is everything all right?"

Hope was too stunned to answer. Everything was all right, but it was also all wrong. She didn't want *Daed* coming in here. "It's fine."

But she hadn't answered fast enough. *Daed* clomped through the kitchen and stopped in the entrance to the living room.

He faltered. "What's going on here?" His face paled at the wad of money in Hope's hands.

Art hung his head and shuffled his feet, but he didn't answer. Hope wasn't about to make this easy for him. He needed to own up to his deceit. The silence stretched for several long seconds before Art swallowed and cleared his throat.

"I fibbed to you about the horses. You won. But I . . ." He lowered his gaze to the floor. "I had big debts to pay off, so I said you lost."

"You lied?" *Daed* stared at his friend as if unsure he'd heard right. Then his gaze went to the money in Hope's hands. "But how—?"

"How did I manage to pay it back?" Art grinned. "I won big last night, so I wanted to, um, clear up all my debts, including to you. It feels good to have a clear conscience."

A clear conscience? When he's using gambling money to pay back what he'd stolen? Hope shook her head. What right did she have to judge him when she had her own flaws and sins?

Hope tucked some of the bills into her pocket and handed the rest back to Art.

His brows drew together into a frown. "What's this?"

"I took my business money back, but I won't accept a penny of gambling winnings."

"I–I don't understand." Art looked toward *Daed*, a question in his eyes.

Desire flared in *Daed*'s eyes as Art extended the money in her father's direction.

Please don't take it. Please, Daed.

Her father took a step forward, his arm outstretched.

"You won this fair and square," Art said, waggling the money.

Daed squeezed his eyes shut, and his face screwed up, etching pain into every line. "My gambling almost cost a little girl's life." He dropped his hand to his side. "Hope's right. We can't accept it."

"I don't feel right taking this." But Art pocketed the money.

"Maybe you can donate it to charity," Hope suggested, "because it bothers your conscience."

Art patted his pocket. "I might just do that."

From his expression, Hope suspected the money would end up as Art's next bet. "If you'd like, I know a good cause for that money, and the man's right outside. Why don't you come with me, and we can turn it over to him right now?"

Art's sour face revealed his reluctance to part with the money, but when *Daed* chimed in to say he'd like to contribute the money, Art followed Hope to the back door.

"This is for a good cause, Art," *Daed* said. "You remember that bad buggy accident a few weeks ago?"

After Art's strained nod, *Daed* continued, "These two Amish children lost both their parents, and their district's been planning a fund-raiser to help pay their hospital bills and the funeral costs."

When Hope opened the back door, Micah was boosting Chloe onto the wagon seat.

"Wait," Hope called. "We have something for you."

Micah helped Jabin into place. Then he headed toward her.

"Art has a donation toward the fund-raiser," she said. "Art, this is Micah."

A sickish look crossed Art's face, but he reached into his pocket and held out some bills. The stack looked a lot smaller than what she remembered, and Hope suspected Art had kept some for himself. That was between him and God.

Micah's dazed expression matched Hope's surprise when she'd first seen the money. "*Danke*, I mean, thank you." He held out a hand to shake Art's.

Daed elbowed Art. "Did you give him all of it? Looks like there's still more in your pocket."

His jaw tense, Art pulled out another stack of thousand dollar bills.

"I don't know how to thank you." Micah stared at Art for a few seconds. Then his gaze flicked to *Daed* and finally to Hope.

She enjoyed seeing him so astonished. Maybe it would be enough money that he wouldn't have to do the fund-raiser with Susie.

After waving goodbye to Micah, Hope led a deflated Art to the front door. "I hope you'll stay away from my *daed*. Gambling has cost our family a lot."

She had no idea *Daed* had followed them into the house until he spoke. "Art is my friend."

Hope's heart sank. She'd wanted to discourage Art from returning. Maybe it would keep *Daed* from temptation.

Daed nudged her aside. "I'll make my own decisions."

Her shoulders slumped, Hope stepped back. She had no say in this. All she could do was pray.

"Art, we've been friends for a long time. And you introduced me to gambling. Many times, I wished you hadn't, but that thrill of winning had too great a pull."

Swallowing hard, Hope clenched her fists at her sides. Would he ever overcome its appeal?

"Like I said earlier, we almost lost a precious child a few days ago because of my obsession. God spared her, and that woke me up to the damage I've been doing. When I think of all the people I've hurt—my daughter, my wife, my customers, and little Chloe—I . . ." He choked up.

Art's face had squinched up at the mention of God. But as her *daed* listed those he'd affected, a deep sorrow filled Art's eyes.

Maybe God would touch both of them. Hope prayed so.

"We've been friends a long time, Art, and I don't want that to change. But from now on, we can't talk about gambling."

"Sure," Art mumbled, but he didn't quite sound convinced. He fumbled for the doorknob and let himself out onto the porch. "See ya."

Daed called after him, "I'll be praying for strength for both of us to resist temptation."

He got no response from Art, but Hope sent up a prayer of thanksgiving.

Micah had just readjusted the broken harness in the wagon when Hope emerged from the house, rubbing her eyes. Was she crying?

After all she'd done for him, Micah couldn't drive away if she was hurting. Who'd been at the door? Had she gotten bad news?

"Stay here," he said to the twins and slipped from the wagon. "Hope," he called as she headed into the barn. "Is anything wrong?"

She waited for him in the entrance. "No, things are going

right. And I pray they'll stay that way. I have to put some money in the office."

Micah followed her through the barn. The horses snuffling or banging in their stalls now seemed mild compared to Chips's wildness on Friday.

"*Daed* turned down an invitation to go with Art."

"So that was Art, his gambling buddy?"

Hope stopped with one hand on the office doorknob. Color drained from her face. "How do you know that?"

"Your *daed* told me."

Her mouth rounded into an *O*. "He did?"

"I hope Art gave you enough money to replace what your *daed* gave him."

She stared at him, her eyes wide. "*Daed* discussed that with you too?" When Micah nodded, Hope shook her head and opened the office door. "What else did he tell you?"

"That he believes he's a millstone around your neck. And that he suspects you haven't married because of him. And also because of all your responsibilities." Micah followed her into the room.

She spun to face him. "He said that?"

"How else would I know it?"

"I don't know," she mumbled as she unlocked the lower desk drawer and pulled out the cashbox.

Micah rejoiced as she counted out several thousands and some smaller bills. He hoped she'd gotten the full amount. If not, he'd give her some of the fund-raising money to replace it.

"*Ach*, I took an extra ten by mistake." After placing it on the desk, Hope took out a small slip of paper with a number written on it and laid it on top of the money. "I'll reconcile this later and make a bank deposit first thing tomorrow morning."

Once the drawer was locked, she held out the ten. "You can add that to your fund."

"You're not missing any?"

"No, I got every last dollar. This isn't mine."

Micah reached for the bill, purposely brushing her fingers as he took it. Hope sucked in a breath, and he stilled. Had she felt the same jolt when they touched?

"Hope?" he asked, moving his fingers to cover hers.

Her breathless "Yes?" gave him hope. Hope gave him hope. Never taking his gaze from hers, he pocketed the bill, then reached for her hands to draw her close.

"Would you let me court you?"

A bleak look entered her eyes. "But *Daed* . . ."

"We can face that together."

Still, she hesitated. "You're sure?"

"I'm positive." He lifted a finger to stroke the soft skin of her cheek, and she trembled. Blood thundered in his ears. He slid his finger to her full, generous lips, and they parted.

Hope had always been the one to take the initiative, but this time it was his turn. He swept her into his arms and cuddled her close. Then he bent his head and pressed his lips to her warm, inviting ones. He wanted to stay in this heavenly place forever. Just the two of them.

"Micah?" Chloe screeched.

Small feet pounded down the aisle toward the office. He'd forgotten all about the twins waiting in the wagon. Entwining his fingers with Hope's, he stepped a respectable distance away from her before Chloe and Jabin burst into the office.

"What's taking you so long?" she demanded.

Micah's lips curved into a smile, and he winked at Hope,

who stifled a laugh. "We had some important business to take care of." But that reminded him of one of his concerns.

As Chloe hopped from one foot to the other, Jabin inspected their hands, his head tilted to one side.

"Hope?" Micah dreaded asking the question. She had so much responsibility already. What if she didn't want more?

She looked at him expectantly, but the words stuck in his throat. "I'm afraid I'm a package deal."

"That's the best part," she said, letting go of his hand to open her arms to Chloe and Jabin.

They ran to her, and she hugged both of them. Then, with a sly sideways glance, she said, "There's room for three."

His heart overflowing, Micah wrapped his arms around all of them. "I'm afraid we might not get much time alone together."

"Actually," she said, "I know a great babysitter."

Micah laughed. "That's good, because I'm looking forward to spending a lot of time with you." Her loving smile melted him. "How soon is that babysitter available?"

"Let's find out."

Then, with Chloe and Jabin between them, all holding hands, they headed to the house to check.

Epilogue

A huge smile on his face, Micah hurried into the harness shop with the twins. He had some important business to transact. This shouldn't take long. As soon as he finished, Hope was expecting him and the twins for supper.

Eli glanced up from checking out a customer at the counter. His eyebrows rose. "I thought you'd taken today off." He handed the man some change and his purchases.

"I did." Micah had had a wonderful day alone with Hope before he picked up the twins at school and Hope taught her late-afternoon lessons. "I have something I want to discuss with you."

After a quick glance at the clock, Eli nodded. "We'll be closing in fifteen minutes."

Micah didn't want to wait. He was eager to get to Hope's. "You don't have any customers right now, and I promise this won't take long. We can stop if anyone comes in." He set a sheaf of papers on the counter.

"What's this?" Eli moved over to look at the papers.

Micah turned them to face him. "Read it and see."

Eli skimmed the page, and his face paled. "*Neh.*" He shook his head. "This is impossible. You can't mean it."

"Keep reading," Micah said.

As he turned each page, Eli shook his head. When he

reached the end, he looked up with tears in his eyes. "You can't do this."

"I can and I will. I talked to *Daed* the other night, and he agreed. I'm so glad I found all the papers we need in Ben's desk drawer."

Eli stared at him dumbfounded. "I can't accept these terms. What are you going to do?"

"I have other plans." At least, he prayed he did. Perhaps he should have made sure of that before he'd given Eli the building and the business.

"You should at least get a percentage of the sales for the first few years in addition to this small down payment and the low mortgage payments."

"That's up to you," Micah said, "but I'm fine with only what's in the agreement." He'd tried to make everything affordable. Although, he had to admit, if he were in Eli's place, he would have insisted on paying more, so he understood Eli's reluctance. "Or you can pay extra on the mortgage, so you get it paid off faster."

"I can't agree to—"

A loud jingling cut off Eli's arguing, and Micah turned. Chloe had hung several more leather strips of harness bells on the doorknob. When Micah saw who'd entered, he groaned inwardly. He'd hoped to escape without seeing them.

Sylvia strode through the door with Susie trailing behind, as usual. Directing her attention to Micah, Sylvia announced, "We've come to get you for supper."

Chloe burst out, "We can't come. We're going to Hope's. Besides, we don't want—"

Micah shot her a look intended to silence her, but knowing his niece, it wouldn't be effective. "Chloe," he commanded, "come here, please."

As the door slammed behind Susie, setting up another

loud jangling, Chloe marched across the room, a mutinous expression on her face.

Micah squatted and hoped the clamor of the bells would cover his whisper. "It's not nice to say things that will hurt people's feelings."

Puffing up like a chicken ruffling its feathers, Chloe retorted, "But it's true."

"It may be true, but is it kind?" he whispered.

She crossed her arms. "Why do I have to be kind when she isn't?" Rather than modulating her tone, Chloe spoke loudly enough to be heard across the room.

Micah cringed. "Enough," he said. "We don't base our actions on what others do. We do what Jesus expects. Would Jesus be unkind?"

Chloe thrust out her lower lip and shuffled her feet. After a moment, she hung her head. "I guess not. Hope would be nice too, wouldn't she?"

"Of course. And if she hurt someone's feelings, she'd apologize." Micah was thrilled that Chloe wanted to emulate Hope.

Her face squinched up, Chloe asked, "Do I have to?"

Micah nodded and stood. "I'm sorry," he told Sylvia.

Chloe flicked Micah a begging glance, as if hoping to get out of her apology, but he returned her plea with a you-have-no-choice look.

Instead of using her usual boisterous voice, Chloe stared at her feet and mumbled, "I'm sorry" to Sylvia.

"*Jah, vell.* They say children speak their minds." She sniffed, but it almost sounded like a sniffle. "I taught my children to be seen but not heard."

That was quite evident from Susie's silence and her mouselike squeaks when she answered questions. But the jab at his parenting reminded Micah he'd never measure up to Ben. What would his brother have done?

Micah had to stop asking this. Ben was no longer here. His brother had left a void that might never be filled, and Micah needed to make his own decisions, not set up imaginary competitions with his brother.

Chloe searched Micah's face nervously, as if waiting for him to impose a gag rule like Sylvia's on her.

Would he want to turn Chloe into another Susie? A different face floated into Micah's mind. Hope. If he had to choose, he'd prefer a woman who spoke her mind. One who wasn't afraid to be herself. One brave enough to open a business the community viewed as unconventional. Isaac had said Chloe reminded him of Hope. If Chloe could grow up to be as special as Hope, he never wanted to stifle her personality.

He tried to telegraph that to his niece. She must have gotten the message because she beamed.

Her lips pursed, Sylvia studied them both. Although her posture and facial expression radiated judgment, Micah detected a longing in her eyes. Did she wish for a bond like the one he and Chloe shared?

Despite her bossiness, Micah sympathized with Sylvia. How hard it must be to go through life bullying people to get your way, only to have them avoid you. Most likely, Sylvia would never experience genuine friendship or love.

She brushed her hands together briskly, as if to chase off sentimental thoughts. Then she focused on Micah. "We made a meal with all your favorite foods. I'm sure you can cancel your plans." Although she hadn't lost her determination, her voice held a little less sternness.

"*Danke* for the invitation," Micah said, "but I won't cancel on my special friend."

Sylvia's eyes practically popped out of her head. "Sp–special"—she choked on the first word—"friend?" She fanned herself with one hand. "You're courting?"

At Micah's nod, a sick look crossed her face. "But–but what about Susie?"

All color had drained from Susie's face, and she stared at Micah with wild, desperate eyes. She seemed to be pleading with him, but he didn't understand her message. Did she want him to fake an interest to save her from her mother? As much as he wanted to help her, he already had a woman he loved with all his heart.

"What about Susie?" Eli asked. "Is something wrong?"

"I–I thought . . ." Sylvia pressed a hand against her chest. She swooned, as if about to faint.

Eli grabbed a chair from behind the counter and rushed around. He caught Sylvia and lowered her into the chair. "Would you like some water?"

She waved him away, but Susie gasped out a breathless "*danke*" as she hurried to her mother's side.

"*Mamm*, are you all right?" Then as if suddenly realizing she was standing close to Eli, she sucked in a breath, and their eyes met.

Hope's eyes had mesmerized Micah the same way. Eli had rescued Micah the last time Sylvia had shown up. Now Micah could return the favor. Striding over, he took Sylvia's elbow, careful not to disturb Eli and Susie, who barely registered his presence.

"Why don't you come with me, Sylvia, and let Susie do her own courting?" He steered her toward the door, earning him a grateful glance from Eli.

"But–but–but . . ."

She'd used that word quite a bit already today, and Micah suspected she might end up repeating it a lot more. Without giving her time to finish her thought, he ushered her out the door and to her buggy.

"In fact, why don't you head home and get supper ready? You might be having company for dinner after all."

"But Susie—" she said faintly.

"I'm pretty sure Susie will find her own way home."

A dazed Sylvia followed Micah's directions and headed off.

Hope paced the kitchen floor. Supper had been ready for ten minutes, but Micah still hadn't arrived. Had he forgotten, or had something else come up? Should they start eating? She and Logan had one more student after dinner, so she didn't have much time.

What if something terrible had happened? Visions of the buggy accident came to mind. It had been around this time of day when—

"*Dochder*, you'll wear out the floor from all that pacing. What's the matter?"

"I'm worried about Micah. He's usually early, and he knows I need to get back to work. What if they—?"

Daed interrupted her. "Pray about it."

Of course. She should have been praying for their safety. She'd just bowed her head when buggy wheels crunched on the gravel outside. Hope's plea turned to gratitude, and she rushed out to meet Micah and the twins.

"Sorry we're late," he said.

"Where were you? I was so worried about you." Hope wished she could throw her arms around him. Restraining herself was difficult, especially when she met the heat in Micah's gaze.

He entwined his fingers with hers. "I had to rescue someone."

Hope sucked in a breath. She'd been afraid of that. "Who was it?"

"Susie."

"She was hurt?"

Micah chuckled. "*Neh.*"

A frisson of envy snaked through Hope's heart. He'd spent time with Susie instead of her?

Micah stopped walking, while the twins dashed ahead. "Hope, look at me."

She didn't want to meet his eyes. But he stood waiting, patient and steady. She lifted her gaze to meet his.

He reached out and cupped her face with his hands. "You don't have anything to be jealous about. You're the woman I love."

Hope hung her head. "How did you know?"

"I guessed because I've spent my whole life being jealous of my brother. I always saw myself as inferior to Ben. I could never measure up. Today, I realized it's time to release those negative feelings. And my guilt."

That must be so freeing. Hope had spent the past few years feeling ashamed and concealing *Daed*'s gambling. But wasn't hiding wrongdoing rather than confessing it also a sin? She posed the question to Micah.

He looked thoughtful. "But you didn't do anything wrong. It's up to your *daed* to confess."

"You don't understand." Maybe after he knew the truth about her, he'd change his mind about courting. "I didn't keep it a secret only for *Daed*'s sake. I did it for myself. Out of pride. I wanted people to believe we were a perfect family, a godly family." It was the first time she'd ever admitted the truth, and she kept her head down.

"I guess we both learned a lesson about *hochmut.*"

Startled, she looked up. "But you weren't being prideful."

"Why do you think I resented Ben? Because I couldn't do what he could do. I wanted to be as good as he was or better. What is that if not pride?"

Hope had never thought about it that way, but jealousy was believing you deserved what someone else had. Micah was right. That was *hochmut*, for sure and certain. Humility wished for the best for others. Hope had to admit she wasn't there yet. Not when it came to Micah. "So, I should be glad you helped Susie?"

He laughed. "*Jah*, you should. Once you hear what I actually did, you will be." Then he told her about Eli and Susie.

By the time he got to the part about escorting Sylvia from the store to leave the two lovebirds alone, Hope was laughing so hard, she could barely breathe. She was happy for Susie, and she also was relieved to discover Susie wasn't still a rival.

As Micah started toward the house, Hope stopped him. "Wait a minute. Why were you at the store? Today was your day off. Did you sneak in to work after you left here?"

"I'll explain after supper and your evening lesson. When we're alone, just the two of us."

From the look of suppressed excitement on his face, he was hiding something. Or was it because he couldn't wait to spend time together?

Neither could she.

They rushed through dinner so Hope could finish before her student arrived. Once again, *Daed* offered to do the dishes and asked the twins to dry.

After the lesson, Hope hurried back to the house to find all four of them playing a board game.

Micah jumped to his feet. "We should put the twins to bed."

Now that the two of them were courting, Chloe and Jabin often spent weekends at her house. They begged to come, and she loved having them. She valued the precious gift of helping Micah tuck them into bed.

"It's still early," *Daed* said. "We haven't finished our

game. Why don't you two go on out? I'm happy to put them
to bed."

As much as Hope enjoyed the bedtime routine, she
couldn't wait to spend the evening with Micah.

"Be good for Isaac," he warned.

Chloe huffed out a loud sigh. "We always are, aren't we,
Isaac?"

"*Jah*, they're two little angels."

"Hmm . . ." was Micah's only reply. Then he said his
goodbyes, smiled down at Hope, and hurried for the door.

Her spirits soared. He seemed as eager to be alone with
her as she was to be with him. The minute they were out of
sight of the living room, he took her hand.

Once they reached the porch, Micah turned to her.
"Could we go out to the barn?"

The barn? Hope had been dreaming of taking a romantic buggy ride under the stars. As they headed outside, she
pointed to the brilliant pinpoints of light just becoming
visible overhead. "It's a beautiful night."

"*Jah*, it is." His jaw set, Micah snapped out the clipped
answer without even looking up.

What was wrong? Before supper, he'd seemed excited,
and he'd said she was the woman he loved. Now he seemed
tense and anxious. Had he changed his mind? Did he plan
to break up with her?

When they got to the door, Micah hesitated.

"You sure you want to do this?"

He swallowed hard, then nodded. He opened the door
and strode inside. He didn't exactly walk in the center of
the aisle, but he didn't sidle against the opposite wall. That
was a major improvement.

He stopped near Nutmeg's stall. "Which horse is the
gentlest? Isn't this the one?"

"*Jah*, he's the one who did children's parties."

"All right. I want to touch her."

"What?" Hope was positive she'd misheard him.

Over the past few months, they'd gotten Micah accustomed to the twins being around horses. He cringed a little when Jabin or Chloe went into a stall, but he admitted he didn't fight the urge to yell for them to come back. Micah had even approached a stall once or twice, with plenty of encouragement and verbal pushes. But he'd never, ever gone inside.

At her skeptical look, Micah insisted, "I'm serious, Hope. I'm determined to get over this fear." He had to do this. Had to prove it to himself. And to Hope.

He took a deep breath and, keeping his hand as steady as possible, opened the stall door. Hope moved beside him and reached for his hand. He wanted to hold it for support, but he shook his head.

"*Danke*, but I'm going to do this alone." And pray he survived.

"Do you want me to hold Nutmeg's head?" she asked.

Having Hope there to focus on might help. "All right."

She brushed past him, but he hardly noticed because he was so busy controlling the panic choking him. He flattened his back against the stall wall so hard, the wood pressed into his shirt. He could feel each plank, each indentation. He closed his eyes and concentrated on counting those rather than focusing on the horse less than two feet away.

Nutmeg snorted, and Micah's eyes flew open. Hope patted Nutmeg and repeated, "It's all right. You're safe."

Was she saying that to the horse? Or to him? Maybe she was trying to soothe both of them.

Dear God, help me to do this.

Praying each step of the way, Micah inched across the floor, nearer and nearer. Blood thundered in his ears. His heart battered his ribs. He clutched his suspenders to stop his hands from trembling.

Rather than looking at the horse, he focused on Hope's face. Her brows drawn together and tense lines around her smile revealed her anxiety, but her eyes offered encouragement.

Step by step, he edged closer. The smell of warm horseflesh filled his nostrils and choked Micah. Overpowered him.

The distance between him and the horse lessened. Micah stopped breathing. His chest ached from lack of air and sore ribs.

He'd almost reached Nutmeg's side when she twitched her tail. The whoosh of wind. The flicking hair.

Micah froze. Childhood nightmares engulfed him. Wave after wave of dread washed over him, drowning him. He couldn't move forward. He'd never be able to do this.

"It's all right. You're safe," Hope repeated. This time her litany wasn't for the horse. It was for him.

Whispering a prayer for strength, he fixed his attention on her. Lifted one foot. Took a step. Then another. Stretched out a hand. His fingertips brushed the horse's coat.

Nutmeg snorted. Her flanks heaved. A shiver slid up Micah's spine, but he held his ground. He hadn't come all this way to give up. This moment would determine his future.

He kept his hand in place. Forced himself to step right up to the horse. Then to slide his hand along her neck. For the first time in thirty years, he'd voluntarily touched a horse.

Hope's proud smile warmed him, but he had his own

inner validation. He'd done something he'd never dreamed he'd do. And he'd done it for love.

With God's help and Hope's support, he'd conquered a lifetime of terror. Not that he wasn't still afraid, but now that he'd done it once, he could do it again, lessening his fear each time. And he'd proved himself worthy. Worthy of the request he'd ask of Hope tonight.

Hand in hand, they exited the stall. Hope was thrilled for Micah's progress, but watching him had drained her. She'd faced each frightening step as if she were inside his body. Her heart had echoed the pounding of his. She froze when he did. Her arm crept out quarter-inch by quarter-inch with his. He ran tentative fingers along Nutmeg's coat. In her imagination, her hand followed.

She'd melded with his body and emotions, experiencing his foreboding, his bravery, and ultimately, his exhilaration. Yet, she still didn't understand his motivation.

"Why did you do it when it scares you so much?" she asked.

"I'll tell you later. Right now, let's get out of here."

Despite Hope's love of horses, tonight she agreed totally with that sentiment.

Micah insisted on latching the stall door, so she stood back and let him. Her heart brimmed with love for this man who'd confronted his inner demons and emerged victorious.

He already had every ounce of love she had to give, but when he'd approached Nutmeg, her heart had expanded enough to encompass the whole world. He'd moved beyond fearless to become her hero.

As Micah shut the barn door behind them, his loud

exhale seemed to release all his pent-up tension. His grip on her hand eased into gentleness. Hope breathed out her own anxiety and relaxed enough to enjoy the star-studded sky.

Spending time in the barn had been taxing. She'd love to spend time appreciating the beauty of the night, but Micah strode across the lawn to the house.

Ordinarily, she'd ask for what she wanted, but after what Micah had just been through, she'd let him take the lead. Whatever he needed to recover, she'd be willing to cooperate. With a regretful glance at the constellations, she kept up with his rapid pace.

"Maybe we could sit on the porch swing and look at the stars?" he suggested.

Had he read her mind the way she'd read his?

The way Hope smiled at him made the past hour of terror worthwhile. He'd proved his courage once tonight, but he still had another, even more nerve-racking thing to do. He only prayed he'd make it through the next half hour.

They circled the house to the front porch and settled on the swing. Micah sat close enough that their shoulders brushed, and he set the swing into slow motion.

Hope gazed up and sighed. "It's so beautiful."

Micah agreed, but he'd focused on a different beauty. The woman he loved sitting beside him. Until he told her what he'd done today, he'd find it impossible to enjoy the heavens.

They swayed back and forth in companionable silence for a while. Hope's face, lit by moonlight, reflected her delight.

His heart overflowed with gratitude that she'd agreed to court. How had he been so blessed?

Hope glanced over at him with love in her eyes, and his throat went dry. How would he ever manage the words he needed to say?

"Micah, you were incredible in the barn tonight. I'm awed by your bravery." She studied his face. "Are you all right? You've been so quiet."

He swallowed hard. He'd plunge in and pray for the best outcome. If Hope was the right woman for him, she'd understand. If not, his decision might lead to a breakup.

A soft squeeze from her hand gave him courage. "Hope, I sold the harness shop to Eli today."

Eyes wide, she stared at him. "You did? But why? It's been in your family for a long time."

"Eli plans to keep the name and the traditions, so our family's legacy will remain. But I wanted to move on, to invest my money elsewhere."

"You're going to open a new business?"

He shook his head. He wished she'd guessed so he didn't have to ask. "I want to invest in an established business. If you'll let me."

Let him? "You want to be part of the horse therapy business?" Hope could hardly believe it. "But what about your fear of horses?" She couldn't bear to think about him enduring daily torture.

"If you're willing to be patient with me, I'd like to overcome my fears so I can work with the horses."

So that was what he'd been doing tonight? Proving himself? Demonstrating to her that he could confront his terror? That touched her heart. He'd given up his shop to be with her, to support her business. Could he have given any greater demonstration of his love, his caring?

Micah was on the edge of his seat, still waiting for her answer. When she didn't reply, he said, "I won't be much help at first, but I can do the accounting, if you'd like."

Hope didn't answer because she was so dumbfounded. He'd hit on her sore spot—finances. She'd vowed never to let anyone else handle the books, not after what had happened with *Daed*. But this was Micah asking, not *Daed*.

"Micah, I'll be honest. It scares me to let someone else— anyone else—take over the finances after *Daed*'s problems. It's not that I don't trust you, it's just really difficult."

He held up a hand. "I understand. I can do other things. Muck out stalls, mend harnesses, run errands."

"No, I mean *yes* to the accounting. I–I'd like to trust you with that."

He studied her face. "You would? Seriously?"

"Yes, I'm quite serious."

"And you're all right with me being part of your business?"

Hope wanted to shout for joy, but she managed to contain herself. "Yes, I'd like that." Being around Micah all day, every day, would be pure joy.

Hope's yes gave Micah the courage to continue.

He took both her hands in his and cleared his throat. "I'd like it if we could make it more than a business partnership. I want to spend my life with you, working with you, sharing our lives and our dreams." He took a deep breath. "Hope, will you marry me?"

"Oh, Micah," she breathed. The love-light shining in her eyes revealed her answer.

He didn't need the words, but when she opened her mouth to speak, he waited for her confirmation.

"I'd love to marry you, but I can't."

Micah's heart plunged to the depths. She'd told Logan she'd never marry. He should have listened. But why had she agreed to court him? Courting implied you were considering marriage.

"Marrying you is a package deal."

In his excitement to marry Hope, he'd forgotten he was asking her to take on an instant family. Hadn't she said earlier that she didn't consider the twins a drawback? Maybe not to dating, but perhaps to marriage?

"I don't want to be selfish," Hope continued. "The twins have had enough upheaval in their lives. I won't marry you unless they both agree."

Wait. She hadn't turned him down. "But if they do?" he asked.

"Let's ask them."

Micah hopped up from the swing, setting it jiggling. He steadied it so Hope could slip off, then took her hand. He prayed Chloe and Jabin hadn't gone to bed already. And that they'd give their enthusiastic consent. Both of them liked her. This shouldn't be a problem, should it?

When they walked in holding hands, Chloe noticed them first and set down her piece.

"Hey, no fair," Jabin protested. "You were only supposed to move two spaces."

Chloe didn't respond, and he swiveled his head to see what had caught her attention. Seeing Hope and Micah's entwined hands, he frowned. Hope's *daed* raised his eyebrows and sent them a warning look.

Reluctantly, Micah let go of Hope's hand.

Two frowns and one smile. That didn't bode well for his chances.

* * *

Hope missed the strength and support flowing through Micah's fingers. This might be the hardest thing she'd ever done. If *Daed* felt this unsure of himself when he played the ponies or the slots, she had no idea how he carried on.

She'd be too frightened to gamble. Yet here she was, gambling on her future.

"Chloe and Jabin, could you come here a minute? Your *onkel* Micah asked me a question, but I can't answer him until I find out what you like."

"Chocolate chip ice cream." Chloe hopped out of her chair.

Hope hid a smile. If they agreed to the marriage, she'd definitely treat the twins to ice cream cones to celebrate. Would it be fair to bribe them?

"Are we supposed to pick ice cream?" Jabin sounded uncertain.

"That wasn't going to be my question."

Chloe's face fell, and her skip slowed to a trudge. If she was in a bad mood, she might nix the whole idea. Hope wished she'd waited to deny the ice cream.

Her stomach in knots and her future hanging in the balance, she knelt on the floor so she could look both of them in the eye.

"Your *onkel* asked me to marry him," Hope said. "Is that all right with you?"

Chloe bounced up and down. "*Jah!* I prayed you'd marry Hope." Chloe flew across the room to hug Micah.

"It would mean we'd all live in the same house," Hope explained.

"Good!" Chloe beamed. "Can we stay here so I can be with Isaac and you and the horses?"

Hope looked at Micah, and he nodded. "It would make the most sense for your business."

Jabin turned his back, and his shoulders heaved. Chloe rushed from Micah's side and circled her brother. "What's the matter, Jabin?"

"I miss *Mamm* and *Daed*." He choked out a sob.

Maybe this was too much change for Jabin all at once. Or maybe he'd never accept her. She should have made it clear she didn't expect to take his *mamm*'s place, especially not right away. Maybe over time they'd become a family.

Hope wished she hadn't set this condition for responding to Micah's proposal. Still, she could never marry him if Jabin didn't approve.

"But don't you like Hope and Isaac?" Chloe pressed.

Jabin's answer was inaudible.

"You should be happy they're getting married."

Scrubbing at his eyes with his fists, Jabin shook his head.

Exasperated, Chloe put her hands on her hips and appeared ready to blast him when *Daed* called to him.

Jabin went to him, and *Daed* pulled Jabin onto his lap and cuddled him close. "It's hard getting used to new things, isn't it?"

Jabin nodded. The two of them whispered quietly for a short while. From time to time, Jabin's head bobbed up and down vigorously. Other times, he shook his head.

"You're sure?" *Daed* asked finally.

"*Jah*."

Daed hugged him. "Let's tell Hope your answer." One hand on Jabin's shoulder, *Daed* hobbled toward her. Jabin kept pace with *Daed*, slow and steady, supporting him until they both stood in front of her.

"Jabin," *Daed* prompted, "is it all right with you if your *onkel* marries Hope?"

The small boy studied Hope with tears in his eyes. Then he nodded.

Daed beamed. "Like Chloe, I've been praying too," he admitted. Then he gazed down fondly at Jabin. "I've always wanted a grandson who lived nearby."

"And a granddaughter?" Chloe asked.

He smiled. "Definitely."

Chloe danced toward them, dragging Micah by the hand. She tried to throw her arms around everyone, drawing them all into a group hug.

Hope met Micah's gaze. "The idea seems to be popular."

Is that a yes? Micah mouthed, staring at her with anxious eyes.

"Definitely," she answered, echoing her *daed*.

The love shining in Micah's eyes told her she'd made the perfect choice.

Daed untangled himself from the group hug first. "I think we should all celebrate with ice cream. Why don't the twins and I go hitch up the buggy?" He winked at them. "You two take your time."

When the house was quiet, Micah said, "You have no idea how I panicked. What if one of the twins had said no?"

"I was terrified they might." Waiting for Jabin's answer had been the longest five minutes of her life. "I'm so glad they agreed."

"I am too." Micah took her into his arms for their own private hug. Then his lips descended, and Hope lost track of time.

When Micah finally stepped back to take her hand, he said, "Good thing we didn't already buy the ice cream."

"It would have melted by now," Hope murmured. Not only because of how long they'd taken, but also because of the heat between them.

As she and Micah went outside to join the rest of their soon-to-be family, Hope whispered a prayer of thanksgiving. She'd never expected to marry, and certainly not to someone as wonderful as Micah. She might never gamble, but he'd just made her the luckiest woman in the world.

Please turn the page for an exciting sneak peek of Rachel J. Good's

HIS PRETEND AMISH BRIDE,

coming soon wherever print and eBooks are sold!

As she did every day, Priscilla Ebersol finished mopping the kitchen floor, but today she hurried through her Saturday morning chores, because she and Matthew planned to have a picnic at the lake. The crunch of buggy wheels in the driveway stopped her. Matthew hadn't come this early, had he? She was still wearing her black work apron and a kerchief rather than her prayer *kapp*. She'd have to run up and change her dress too.

She peeked out the window. *Not Matthew. The bishop.* Why had Bishop Troyer come calling?

Priscilla hurried to the door to greet him. "*Gude mariye*, Laban. I'm afraid *Mamm* and *Daed* aren't here. They left for Centerville Bulk Foods a short while ago."

The bishop stood on the doorstep a moment. "I would have preferred to have them here, of course. But this can't wait. I'm sure you know why I'm here."

Actually, she didn't. But she couldn't leave him standing on the doorstep. "Please come in." Priscilla opened the door wider so he could enter.

Brushing past her, he headed into the living room and plopped down in the rocker. When she entered the room he asked, "Are any of your brothers or sisters around?"

"The girls went with Aunt Mae to clean *Dawdi*'s house

this morning. Zeke is organizing the basement, and Asher is helping."

"Perhaps you could ask Zeke to keep Asher downstairs until I'm gone. That would be best, don't you think?"

"Of course." Asher's behavior could be unpredictable. They didn't always know what would set him off. Noises, smells, and touches often did, but sometimes it seemed random.

Priscilla knocked on the basement door. Zeke had hooked it to prevent Asher from wandering off. Her brother clomped up the stairs and unlatched the door. "*Jah?*"

"Bishop Troyer's here. Could you keep Asher in the basement until Laban leaves?"

"That won't be a problem. Emma knocked two puzzle boxes off the shelf before she left. Both have one thousand pieces, and Asher is sorting them into the correct boxes. Good thing one is fall colors, and the other is of a green field with purple flowers."

"That's a perfect job for him." Asher loved painstaking, repetitive work.

"I know." Zeke grinned. "I'm getting a lot done while he's doing a job that would make me nuts." Then he raised an eyebrow. "What does the bishop want?"

"I have no idea, but I'd better not keep him waiting." While Zeke rehooked the basement door, Priscilla scurried back to the living room and sat across from the bishop.

Laban stared at her, his gaze sober and sad, as if she'd done something sinful. She tried to think of anything that might merit that look. Nothing came to mind. Yet a heavy ball of guilt formed on her insides, and she lowered her eyes.

"It always pains me," the bishop said, "when I have to speak with members about their . . . um, failings. Especially in a case where, up until now, you've been such a wonderful role model for the children entrusted to your care."

Children? Had she done something wrong at school? Priscilla loved working as an assistant at the special needs school under Ada Rupp. Ada was mentoring Priscilla, so she could take over as head teacher next year. Had she made a major mistake? If so, why hadn't Ada mentioned it?

"I've already spoken to Matthew about this, and he's expressed remorse."

Matthew? Now Priscilla was thoroughly confused. She couldn't imagine Matthew doing something that would require a visit from the bishop. And what did it have to do with her?

"My greatest concern," Laban said, "is the influence your behavior will have on the children. When you took the teaching job, you agreed to be an example they could follow. It grieves me to know that's in question."

With each word the bishop spoke, Priscilla struggled to figure out what he meant. Her thoughts were as jumbled as the puzzle pieces Asher was sorting. What had she done that the bishop considered grave enough to come here to discipline her?

His shaggy brows pinched together, Bishop Troyer leaned so far forward, the tips of the rocker touched the floor. His glasses magnified his piercing gaze, which penetrated deep into her soul. Priscilla shrank back, intimidated.

Swallowing hard, as if it hurt him to speak, the bishop said, "After Deacon Raber caught you and Matthew in a, umm, compromising position last night, Matthew at least had the grace to face the disapproval and apologize. But you fled. Of course, that would be one's natural reaction, but you need to confess. And I'll also expect you to apologize to Leroy."

Priscilla pinched her lips shut to hold back the words that longed to burst from her lips. *But . . . but . . . I wasn't out with Matthew last night.*

She couldn't contradict the bishop. Yet this had to be a mistake.

If it was true . . . Priscilla's chest constricted until she ached to breathe. Matthew wouldn't have been with someone else. She had to talk to him, straighten out this mix-up.

With nervous fingers, she pleated the fabric of her apron, her throat too tight to speak. She'd been taught never to talk back to her elders, and she certainly couldn't accuse the deacon of making an error. Keeping her head bowed, she listened quietly to the bishop's lecture on staying away from all appearances of evil.

"I still need to discuss this with the school board," he concluded. "I'm not sure we can keep you on as a teacher."

But I didn't do anything wrong, she wanted to say. Instead, she clamped her mouth shut to trap the words.

The bishop rose. "If you haven't already confessed to your parents, I expect you to do so. Matthew has pledged it won't ever happen again. He'll kneel and confess before the church. I trust you'll do the same."

Confess in front of the church? What did the bishop think she and Matthew had done? Her thoughts whirling, Priscilla pushed on the arms of the chair to stand and let the bishop out, but he laid a hand on her shoulder to keep her in place.

"You don't need to see me out. Stay there and continue your confession to God." He strode from the room.

Priscilla sat, stunned and confused. The vague sound of the front door shutting after the bishop echoed down the hall. The sharp sound reverberated inside her head, as one mental door after another slammed shut, cutting off rational thought. Matthew. Teaching. Confession. None of the bishop's words made sense.

What did he think she'd done? And what had he meant about Matthew?

* * *

Gabriel Kauffman opened the doors of his milking barn to turn his camels out to pasture. He stood in the center of the rural road, watching for cars and buggies as the camels clomped across the street to one of his fields.

A buggy horse flew around a curve in the road, heading straight toward him and the last two baby camels.

"Stop," Gabriel shouted, waving his arms and jumping up and down to attract attention.

The man holding the reins was leaning forward, urging his horse to gallop at breakneck speed. He hadn't seen Gabe.

Gabe yelled louder, gesturing wildly.

The driver glanced up, and his mouth opened in a wide *O*. He drew back on the reins. Dragged the horse to the right.

Gabe threw himself in front of the last camel baby. He'd take the impact. Try to save his littlest one.

At the last second, the buggy swerved. Almost tipped onto two wheels. With one final wrench on the reins, the man whipped into the store driveway. Gravel sprayed from the wheels, pelting Gabe.

Behind him, the tiny camel let out high-pitched squeaks. Poor little thing must have been hit by flying gravel. Heart pounding, Gabe whirled to check on her as the buggy tore several hundred yards up his driveway. Then it came to an abrupt and shuddering halt.

Gabe herded the baby into the field and closed the gate behind her. Arms crossed, he turned. He expected *Englisch* cars to speed on these back roads, but most buggies plodded along. This one had acted like a late-night, buggy-racing teen.

The man circled in the driveway and headed toward

Gabe at a sedate pace. With a sheepish look on his face, the driver pulled up next to Gabe.

"I'm so sorry. I didn't mean to scare you. I was in a hurry and didn't expect to find anyone on the road."

"I see." Gabe wasn't quite sure why any Amish man would travel at that pace. It had to be hard on the horse. And it had been equally hard on Gabe. His pulse still drummed in his temples, and his chest ached from the rapid staccato of his heart.

The man glanced toward his field, rubbed his eyes, and looked again. "Camels? I thought that's what I saw. I've never seen camels here before."

"That's because I just bought the farm. I needed more farmland for my animals, so I moved to the Lancaster area."

"Why camels? Why not cows or goats?" The man shook his head. "I'd love to stay and ask more questions, but I'm in a hurry."

"You surely were." Gabe hoped his words didn't sound overly critical.

"I apologize again." Thrusting out his hand, the man said, "Welcome to the neighborhood. I'm Matthew King."

"Pleased to meet you, Matthew. I'm Gabriel Kauffman." He shook hands. "I won't keep you, but stop back any time."

"I'll do that." Matthew settled his straw hat more securely on his head and flicked the reins.

Gabe waited until Matthew had galloped out of sight before walking along the shoulder of the road to the building that housed his store.

His eight-year-old nephew, Timothy, gave him a gap-toothed smile. "I don't need help."

Gabe ruffled Timothy's hair as he passed. "I know. I'm

headed into the office. I trust you to handle the business out here."

So far, few local people were aware he'd opened the store, but many of his out-of-state regulars headed here on weekends. They all swore by the benefits of camel's milk and were willing to pay the high prices.

Gabe sank into his wooden desk chair and took several deep breaths. He was still a bit shaky after the near accident. Pulling out the account books, he forced himself to record yesterday's sales. Concentrating on a mundane task should help. But visions of another accident haunted him.

He'd thought moving here would erase the past. Instead, another out-of-control buggy flashed through his mind. Gabe buried his head in his hands. Would he ever be free of that nightmare?

When Matthew's horse galloped into the driveway a short while after Bishop Troyer had left, Priscilla hurried to the door and flung it open. Now she'd find out what the bishop meant.

Matthew tied his horse and hurried up the sidewalk to the house, glancing over his shoulder several times. His face and shoulders were set into such tense lines, Priscilla's stomach roiled. The worries she'd tried to push from her mind flooded over her.

"Are you all right?" she asked.

"It's been a rough morning. First the bishop confronted me. Then I nearly collided with a camel."

Surely she'd misheard him. "A camel?"

"*Jah*, some man just bought that large farm for sale in Bird-in-Hand. He's raising camels."

"A camel farm?" Priscilla practically shrieked. "Are you

serious?" She tried to calm herself, but if Matthew was right, this might be the answer to her prayers.

"Do you know if he'll be selling camel milk?"

Matthew stared at her like she was crazy. "Who'd want that?"

"Lots of people." Not wanting to face his skeptical look, she kept her real answer to herself. But she wanted to buy some.

"Look, we can talk about that later." He waved a hand dismissively. "I need to explain something before the bishop gets here."

"You're too late. He's already been and gone." And Priscilla wanted an explanation for the bishop's lecture. She hoped Matthew could clear up her niggling doubts.

"Laban said he had some errands to run. I thought I'd beat him here." Matthew's face drained of color. "Wh–what did you tell him?"

His pallor and shaky voice set off alarm bells in Priscilla's mind. Something was wrong. Very, very wrong.

"What could I tell him?" she asked. "I had no idea what he was talking about. I just listened to his lecture about sin."

Matthew blew out a long, slow breath. "Oh, good. That was perfect." Fear flashed across his face. "You didn't deny it was you?"

"I didn't deny or confirm anything. But I want to know what's going on."

A dull red crept up Matthew's face, and he lowered his head. "Pris, I'm really sorry. I owe you an apology. I, um, did something terrible."

The small windmill blades churning in Priscilla's stomach whirled faster, scraping and scratching her insides. She longed to flee. She didn't want to hear words that might tear her world apart.

"I don't want you to think I didn't love you. I did."

Did? That meant he loved her in the past, but no longer?

"I don't know how to explain this, but I–I, well, I met Mara Bontrager in the apple orchard one day. She came out to give me some instructions from her *daed*. She stayed to talk to me. I, um, thought she was . . ." His voice trailed off.

Priscilla didn't want to hear any more. She could sense where this was going. His boss's daughter, a pretty, petite blonde, was a bit of a flirt. But would she flirt with a man who was courting someone else? Evidently, she had.

"It started out innocently," Matthew insisted. "She'd come and sit with me while I ate lunch." He hung his head. "Soon, we started sharing lunches she'd fixed. I didn't mean for it to progress."

And all this time, he'd still been courting her? Priscilla balled her hands into fists.

"One day, she asked if I'd meet her in the orchard after dark." He swallowed hard. "I know I shouldn't have gone. But I did."

Those whirling blades were scraping Priscilla's insides raw. She wanted to hold up a hand, beg Matthew to stop. It took all her willpower to choke back a cry of anguish.

"We met again last night, and . . ."

Priscila averted her gaze from his scrunched-up face, the guilt in his eyes. *Don't finish. Please don't say any more.*

"We got a little carried away." Matthew extended his hands, as if begging for forgiveness. "I'm sorry, so sorry. I didn't mean to hurt you."

But he had. How could she deal with this betrayal? Did she still want to court him?

"When Leroy saw us, we'd been kissing—"

Kissing? She and Matthew had never kissed. Not yet.

And Matthew and Mara had done more than kiss. At least according to the bishop. Priscilla squeezed her eyes shut, wishing she could block out the image of Mara in Matthew's arms. Her insides felt as if he'd twisted her heart in his bare hands, squeezing out all the joy and love, leaving her drained and depleted.

Priscilla couldn't meet his eyes, so she concentrated on Matthew's shirtfront, his Adam's apple bobbing up and down. All she wanted was for him to finish and go.

When he spoke again, his voice was thick and uncertain. "We, um, did a little more than kiss. That's when Leroy Raber spied us."

Priscilla willed herself to sit still. She forced her hands into a serene position in her lap. Her insides might be in shreds, but she'd keep her outer composure.

"I, um, shielded Mara until she could turn and run. Leroy assumed it was you."

An understandable mistake. She and Mara were about the same size, and Leroy would expect Priscilla and Matthew to be together.

"You didn't correct him?" Her words came out shakier and more desperate than she'd intended.

Matthew pursed his lips and stared at the floor. "You know how strict her *daed* is. I didn't want her to get in trouble."

But what about my reputation? We're the ones who are courting. We've even been talking about marriage.

"Anyway," Matthew continued, "I came over to ask you a favor. Would you be willing to—"

Forgive you? It wouldn't be easy, but she'd get down on her knees tonight and pray for the right attitude, for God to give her His heart, His love, His mercy, His forgiveness. And for Him to heal her hurts.

Matthew hesitated. "I know this is a lot to ask, but could you let everyone think it was you in the orchard?"

She'd been expecting him to apologize. Instead, she sat

there stunned. "You're asking me to lie?" Not only lie, but to cover up his wrongdoing? With another woman?

"Not lie exactly," Matthew said. "Just not contradict Leroy."

He expected her to stay silent as gossips repeated the falsehood? What if some parents objected to her teaching their children? Or the school board decided she wasn't a fit teacher? Allowing people to believe an untruth was lying by omission, so he was asking her to lie for him.

"You have such a good reputation, I'm sure the rumors will die down quickly." Matthew held out imploring hands. "If people knew the truth, Mara's reputation would be ruined."

"I see." Priscilla said stiffly. But she didn't. Not at all.

Matthew was willing to smear her reputation to save Mara's. And he expected Priscilla to protect a cheater. Mara wasn't the only one to blame. Matthew had willingly participated in the betrayal.

She squeezed her eyes shut to ease their stinging. And prayed no tears would fall.

"I'm sorry." Matthew reached out and touched her arm.

His fingers burned her flesh. Her eyes flew open, and she jerked her arm away. Did he think they could go back to their old relationship?

"Will you forgive me?"

"It's what God wants us to do." Priscilla managed to push the words past her tear-clogged throat. But her heart protested. She'd wrestle with this later, when she was alone in her room.

Matthew heaved a loud sigh. "I knew you'd understand." He rose. "Oh, Bishop Troyer recommended we stay away from each other for a while to reduce the temptation."

The only temptation Priscilla was fighting was throwing one of the couch pillows at him. "I don't think the bishop was referring to me." She hoped the sarcastic edge to her voice would stab his conscience.

His flushed face revealed her barb had reached its target. "I suggested we could break up."

So you'll be free to court Mara? A worm of bitterness wriggled through her heart.

When she didn't answer, he shuffled his feet. "I thought maybe you could tell everyone you broke up with me."

Matthew was offering to let her save face after he'd destroyed her hopes, dreams, and reputation? She pivoted, her back to him. "Consider it done." Then she forced herself to walk from the room slowly and demurely.

Matthew followed her into the hallway. Until the front door closed behind him, Priscilla maintained her façade of politeness. Then she leaned her forehead against the door, and her calmness cracked into a million pieces.

Connect with Us

Visit us online at
KensingtonBooks.com
to read more from your favorite authors, see books
by series, view reading group guides, and more.

Join us on social media

for sneak peeks, chances to win books and prize packs,
and to share your thoughts with other readers.

facebook.com/kensingtonpublishing
twitter.com/kensingtonbooks

Tell us what you think!

To share your thoughts, submit a review,
or sign up for our eNewsletters, please visit:
KensingtonBooks.com/TellUs.

Books by Bestselling Author
Fern Michaels

___The Jury	0-8217-7878-1	$6.99US/$9.99CAN
___Sweet Revenge	0-8217-7879-X	$6.99US/$9.99CAN
___Lethal Justice	0-8217-7880-3	$6.99US/$9.99CAN
___Free Fall	0-8217-7881-1	$6.99US/$9.99CAN
___Fool Me Once	0-8217-8071-9	$7.99US/$10.99CAN
___Vegas Rich	0-8217-8112-X	$7.99US/$10.99CAN
___Hide and Seek	1-4201-0184-6	$6.99US/$9.99CAN
___Hokus Pokus	1-4201-0185-4	$6.99US/$9.99CAN
___Fast Track	1-4201-0186-2	$6.99US/$9.99CAN
___Collateral Damage	1-4201-0187-0	$6.99US/$9.99CAN
___Final Justice	1-4201-0188-9	$6.99US/$9.99CAN
___Up Close and Personal	0-8217-7956-7	$7.99US/$9.99CAN
___Under the Radar	1-4201-0683-X	$6.99US/$9.99CAN
___Razor Sharp	1-4201-0684-8	$7.99US/$10.99CAN
___Yesterday	1-4201-1494-8	$5.99US/$6.99CAN
___Vanishing Act	1-4201-0685-6	$7.99US/$10.99CAN
___Sara's Song	1-4201-1493-X	$5.99US/$6.99CAN
___Deadly Deals	1-4201-0686-4	$7.99US/$10.99CAN
___Game Over	1-4201-0687-2	$7.99US/$10.99CAN
___Sins of Omission	1-4201-1153-1	$7.99US/$10.99CAN
___Sins of the Flesh	1-4201-1154-X	$7.99US/$10.99CAN
___Cross Roads	1-4201-1192-2	$7.99US/$10.99CAN